Troubles in Paradise

Troubles in Paradise

A Novel

Elin Hilderbrand

Little, Brown and Company

New York   Boston   London

Copyright © 2020 by Elin Hilderbrand

Hachette Book Group supports the right to free expression and the value of copyright. The purpose of copyright is to encourage writers and artists to produce the creative works that enrich our culture.

The scanning, uploading, and distribution of this book without permission is a theft of the author's intellectual property. If you would like permission to use material from the book (other than for review purposes), please contact permissions@hbgusa.com. Thank you for your support of the author's rights.

Little, Brown and Company
Hachette Book Group
1290 Avenue of the Americas, New York, NY 10104
littlebrown.com

First Edition: October 2020

Little, Brown and Company is a division of Hachette Book Group, Inc. The Little, Brown name and logo are trademarks of Hachette Book Group, Inc.

The publisher is not responsible for websites (or their content) that are not owned by the publisher.

The Hachette Speakers Bureau provides a wide range of authors for speaking events. To find out more, go to hachettespeakersbureau.com or call (866) 376-6591.

ISBN 978-0-316-43558-1 (hardcover) / 978-0-316-54174-9 (large print) / 978-0-316-59312-0 (Canadian) / 978-0-316-70647-6 (signed) / 978-0-316-70645-2 (Barnes & Noble signed) / 978-0-316-70646-9 (Barnes & Noble signed Black Friday)
LCCN 2020938382

10 9 8 7 6 5 4 3 2 1

LSC-C

Printed in the United States of America

For TGF

AUTHOR'S NOTE

The Paradise series has come to an end. (And oh, how I hope all of you who are about to read this book are not only now realizing that it is the third one in a trilogy. If so, first go and read book 1, *Winter in Paradise,* and book 2, *What Happens in Paradise,* and then this one will make more sense!) I will dearly miss Irene, Huck, and the gang, and I hope you will too.

As many of you may realize, the hurricane described in this novel is fictional, though it is based on the all-too-real events of the fall of 2017, when Hurricane Irma and then Hurricane Maria—both category 5 storms—hit the Virgin Islands. This is a case where real life is far stranger than fiction. I could never have ended this series with not one but two life-threatening storms rolling through the islands; no one would have believed it. As with the other books, the St. John portrayed in these pages is one that lives only in my imagination. The hurricanes hit a few months before I started writing this series, and, having nothing to draw on but my memories, I created an island that is half before-the-storms St. John and half after-the-storms St. John. The most important thing to know now is that the Virgin Islands have recovered; America's Paradise is once again open for business, and it's even better than it was because of what it has survived.

We're just a sinner's choir, singing a song for the saints.

—*Kenny Chesney, "Song for the Saints"*

Troubles in Paradise

ST. JOHN

The gossip recently has been as juicy as a papaya, one that gives just slightly under our fingertips and is fragrant on the inhale, the inside a brilliant coral color, bursting with seeds like so many ebony beads. If you don't fancy papaya, think of a mango as we crosshatch the ripe flesh of the cheeks with a sharp knife or a freshly picked pineapple from the fertile fields of St. Croix, deep gold, its chunks sweeter than candy. Like these island fruits, the talk around here is irresistible.

The drama began on New Year's Day with tragedy: a helicopter crash a few miles away, in British waters. One of our own was killed, Rosie Small, whom some of us remember back when she was in LeeAnn's belly. Because LeeAnn's first husband, Levi Small, left the island when Rosie was a toddler, we'd all had a hand in raising her. We sympathized with LeeAnn when the cute Rosie girl we doted on turned into the precocious Rosie teenager LeeAnn couldn't quite control. At the tender age of fifteen, Rosie dated a fella named Oscar Cobb from St. Thomas who drove the Ducati that nearly ran our friend Rupert off Route 107 right into Coral Bay. We were all overjoyed when Oscar went to jail for stabbing his best friend. *Good riddance!* we said. *Throw away the key!* A group of us took LeeAnn out for celebratory drinks at Miss Lucy's. We thought we'd dodged a bullet; Rosie would not waste her life on a good-for-nothing man with shady business dealings like Oscar Cobb.

The man Rosie ended up with was far more dangerous.

After LeeAnn died, five years ago now, Rosie took a secret lover. We called him the "Invisible Man" because none of us had ever caught more than a glimpse of him. But while Paulette Vickers was under the dryer at Dearie's Beauty Shoppe, she let something slip about "Rosie Small's gentleman." Then Paulette clammed up and it was the clamming up that made us suspicious. Paulette was a little uppity because her parents had started the successful real estate agency Welcome to Paradise. She liked to talk. When she stopped talking, we started listening.

The Invisible Man's name was Russell Steele. He was killed in the helicopter crash along with Rosie and the pilot, an attorney from the Caymans named Stephen Thompson. They were on their way to Anegada. The callous among us commented that they should have taken a boat like normal folk, especially since there were thunderstorms. The perceptive among us noted that, while there were thunderstorms on New Year's morning, they were south and west of St. John, not northeast, which was the direction the helicopter would have been flying to get to Anegada.

Both Virgin Islands Search and Rescue and the FBI had reason to believe that the helicopter exploded. Maybe an accident—an electrical malfunction—or maybe something else.

If you think this is intriguing, imagine hearing of the arrival of the Invisible Man's family. For, yes indeed, Russell Steele was married, with two grown sons and one grandchild. And did his wife and sons stroll right down the St. John ferry dock on January 3 and climb into the car belonging to Paulette Vickers, who then whisked them off to whatever grand, secluded villa Russell Steele owned?

Yes; yes, they did.

Would the family of Russell Steele find out about Rosie?

Yes; yes, they would.

It was one of the taxi drivers, Chauncey, who witnessed a determined-looking woman marching down the National Park Service dock calling for Captain Sam Powers (we all know him as Huck), LeeAnn's devoted second husband and Rosie's stepfather, and then talking herself right onto Huck's boat, the *Mississippi*. Chauncey remembers whistling under his breath because he had seen women on a rampage like that before and they always got what they were after.

The two sons appeared out and about in Cruz Bay, going to the usual places tourists go—La Tapa to enjoy the mussels, High Tide for happy hour. We saw these young men (one tall and clean-cut with a dimple, one stocky with bushy blond hair) in the company of two young women we were all very fond of (charming and lovely Ayers Wilson, who had been Rosie's best friend, and Tilda Payne, whose parents owned a villa in exclusive Peter Bay), and that set us speculating, even though we knew that beautiful young people find one another no matter what the circumstances.

When we learned that one of the sons, Baker Steele, took his child on a tour of the Gifft Hill School and that the other son, Cash Steele, had joined the crew of *Treasure Island,* we began to wonder: Were they *staying?*

When we discovered that the Invisible Man's wife, Irene Steele, was working as the first mate on Huck's fishing boat, we thought: *What exactly is going on?*

We couldn't run into one another at Pine Peace Market or

in line at the post office without asking in a whisper: *You heard anything new?*

Sadie, out in Coral Bay, was the one who learned that the FBI had come looking for Paulette and Douglas Vickers, but Paulette and Douglas had taken their six-year-old son, Windsor, and fled by the time the FBI arrived. They went to St. Croix to hide out with Douglas's sister in Frederiksted. Did one of *us* tell the FBI where they were? No one knew for sure, but Paulette and Douglas were arrested the very next day.

We'd barely had time to recover from this shocking news when the FBI sent agents in four black cars along the North Shore Road to whatever secluded villa Russell Steele owned to inform Irene Steele that the villa and the entire hundred-and-forty-acre parcel we called Little Cinnamon was now the property of the U.S. government, since it had been purchased with dirty money.

Whew! We woke up the next morning feeling like we had gorged ourselves. We were plump with gossip. It was, almost, too much.

We feel compelled to mention that this kind of scandal isn't typical of life here in the Virgin Islands.

What is typical?

"Good morning," "Good afternoon," or "Good evening" at the start of every conversation.

Sunshine, sometimes alternating with a soaking rain.

Wild donkeys on the Centerline Road.

Sunburned tourists spilling out of Woody's during happy hour.

Silver hook bracelets.

Hills.

Swaying palm trees and sunsets.

Hikers in floppy hats.

Rental Jeeps.

Turtles in Salt Pond Bay.

Full-moon parties at Miss Lucy's.

Mosquitoes in Maho Bay.

Iguanas.

Long lines at the Starfish Market (bring your own bags).

Cruise-ship crowds on the beach at Trunk Bay.

Steel-drum music and Chester's johnnycakes.

Snorkelers, whom we fondly call "one-horned buttfish."

Driving on the left.

Nutmeg sprinkled on painkillers (the drink).

Captain Stephen playing the guitar on the *Singing Dog*.

Eight Tuff Miles, ending at Skinny Legs.

A smile from Slim Man, who owns the parking lot downtown.

Nude sunbathers on Salomon Bay.

Rum punches and Kenny Chesney.

Afternoon trade winds.

Chickens everywhere.

St. John has no traffic lights, no chain stores, no fast-food restaurants, and no nightclubs, unless you count the Beach Bar, where you can dance to Miss Fairchild and the Wheeland Brothers in the sand. St. John is quiet, authentic, unspoiled.

Some people go so far as to call our island "paradise."

But, we quickly remind them, even paradise has its troubles.

IRENE

Cigarette smoke. Bacon grease. Something that smells like three-day-old fish.

Irene opens her eyes. Where is she?

There's a blue windowpane-print bedsheet covering her. She's on a couch. Her neck complains as she turns her head. There's a kitchen, and on the counter, a bottle of eighteen-year-old Flor de Caña.

Huck's house.

Irene sits up, brings her bare feet to the wood floor. A suitcase with everything she owns in the world is open on the coffee table.

She hears heavy footsteps and then: "Good morning, Angler Cupcake, how about some coffee?"

She drops her face into her hands. How can Huck be thinking about coffee? Irene's life is...over. This time yesterday she'd been steady and stable, which was *no small feat* considering only a little over a month has passed since her husband, Russell Steele, was killed in a helicopter crash and Irene, who'd believed Russ was in Florida playing *golf* and schmoozing with *clients,* discovered that Russ had a secret life down here in the Virgin Islands complete with mistress, love child, and a fifteen-million-dollar villa. Irene handled that news *pretty damn well,* if she does say so herself. Another woman might have had a nervous breakdown. Another woman might have set the villa on fire or taken out a full-page ad in the local paper (in Irene's case, the *Iowa City Press-Citizen*) announcing her husband's treachery. But Irene adapted to the shocking circumstances. She found that she liked the Virgin Islands so much that she's returned here to live—maybe not forever, but for a little while, so she can catch her breath and regroup. Just yesterday she was looking around Russ's villa, thinking how she would redecorate it, how she might turn it into an inn for women like herself who had survived cataclysmic life changes.

Just last night, Irene felt like a teenager falling in love for the first time because, in a plot twist that happens only in novels and romantic comedies, Irene has developed feelings for Huck Powers, the stepfather of Russ's mistress. The universe did Irene "a solid" (as Cash and Baker would say) when she met Huck. He's an irresistible mix of gruff fisherman, devoted grandpa, and teddy bear. What would Irene's situation look like if she hadn't become friends with Huck? She can't imagine.

But entertaining notions of a love life is a luxury she can no longer afford. Last night, FBI agents seized Russ's villa. It's now the property of the U.S. government.

If Irene was painfully honest with herself, she would admit that, once she got down here, she'd realized there was no way the business Russ had been involved in was aboveboard. From the minute Irene set eyes on it, the villa had a bit of a magic-carpet feel: Was it real? Would it fly?

It was a tropical...palace. Nine bedrooms, each with its own en suite bath. The outdoor space featured an upper pool and a lower pool connected by a curvy slide, a hot tub dropped into a lush gardenscape, an outdoor kitchen, a shuffleboard court (which Irene had never used), and, eighty steps down, a small, private sugar-sand beach (which she had). The view across the water to Tortola and Jost Van Dyke was dramatic, soaring. The villa was so over-the-top *luxurious* that Irene was able to get past the fact that it had been the home of Russ and his mistress, Rosie, and their daughter, Maia. She had been looking forward to putting her own stamp on the place—choosing lighter, brighter fabrics, redoing a bathroom in an under-the-sea theme for her four-year-old grandson, Floyd, creating a custom window seat where she or Maia could read or nap.

The far bigger, more devastating development is that, as Agent Colette Vasco of the FBI informed Irene, the authorities were, at that very moment, also seizing her home on Church Street in Iowa City, an 1892 Queen Anne–style Victorian that Irene had spent six years renovating. The Church Street house is Irene's *home*. It's where her photo albums, her cookbooks with the sauce-splattered pages and handwritten notes, her clothes, her teapot, and her Christmas ornaments are. She has the idea that maybe, with luck, some of these items might be returned to her, but how is she to accept the loss of, say, the third-floor landing, paneled in dark walnut with the east-facing stained-glass window, or the mural of Door County on the dining-room walls? Those "moments" in her house are priceless and irreplaceable. Irene thinks longingly of her amethyst parlor, the velvet fainting couch, the absurdly expensive Persian rugs, the Eastlake bed in the Excelsior suite, the washstand, the sepia-toned photograph of Russ's mother, Milly, as a child in 1928.

Thinking about that photograph brings Irene to her feet.

Huck, it turns out, has been watching her every move. "Coffee?"

She casts her eyes around the room and finds her phone plugged into the far wall. That's right; Irene remembers being methodical about packing her suitcase and double-checking for essentials like her phone charger. Agent Vasco had looked on suspiciously, as though she thought Irene might try to slip in a stash of cocaine or blocks of hundred-dollar bills.

When Irene got to Huck's house, they each did a shot—or two? three?—of the Flor de Caña, and Irene only barely recalls plugging her phone in before sleep. She remembers so little about the end of the night that she supposes she should be grateful she woke up on the sofa and not in Huck's bed.

He's a gentleman.

"I need to make a phone call," she says. "Do you have any…aspirin?" She points to her head. "Good morning," she adds, because she has learned the number-one rule of the Virgin Islands: "Good morning," "Good afternoon," or "Good evening" begins every conversation.

"Two aspirin coming right up," Huck says.

"Three," Irene says. *Four,* she thinks. "Please."

"The best reception is out on the deck," Huck says.

Irene slips through the sliding glass door, going from the pleasant air-conditioning of Huck's house (though she gathered last night that he turned it on only because she was there) to the mounting heat of the day. Her phone says seven o'clock, which means it's five o'clock in Iowa City.

Five a.m. Will Lydia be awake at five a.m.? She is going through menopause and complains that now she never sleeps, so maybe. Even if she is asleep, Irene needs to wake her up. Dr. Lydia Christensen is her best friend; she claims she is there for Irene no matter what. The bonds of best-friendship get tested infrequently, especially as Irene prides herself on being self-sufficient.

Today is a different story.

"Hello?" Lydia says. She's laughing. Irene hears the whisper of bedsheets and, in the next instant, a deep male voice. This would be Brandon the barista, Lydia's new boyfriend. Irene doesn't want to imagine what the two of them are doing up so early.

"Lydia, it's Irene." She stops herself. "Good morning."

"Irene?" Lydia says. "Is everything *okay?* Did something happen? Something *else?*"

"Yes," Irene says.

Lydia is there for Irene no matter what. No matter that it's five a.m., no matter that it's negative ten degrees with the wind chill in Iowa City, no matter that Irene interrupted pillow talk. Lydia and Brandon are going to put on their parkas and drive directly over to Church Street to see what's what. She'll call Irene when she gets there.

Inside, Irene accepts the three aspirin and a glass of ice water. The Flor de Caña bottle has been tucked away and in its place is a cup of coffee that Irene understands is for her. There are eggs cooking on the stove.

"I don't want to seem ungrateful, but I just can't eat," Irene says.

"The eggs are for Maia," Huck says.

Right, Irene thinks. Maia has school. For everyone else, it's a normal day. It's Thursday.

"We have a charter," Irene says.

"That we do," Huck says. "I'm going to take it alone. I thought about passing it off to *What a Catch!* but it seems like now we could probably use the money. You stay home and figure out what you need to figure out and I'll be back this afternoon to help you in any way that I can." He gives her a tentative smile. "Maybe with fresh mahi."

Irene bows her head. She notices his use of the pronoun *we,* which she finds both sweet and confusing. What he doesn't understand is that there is no *we.* Irene has lost her house here and her home in Iowa City. She feels like Wile E. Coyote in the old cartoons: suspended over a canyon, running on air, and then looking down and realizing there's nothing beneath him. Irene's problem can't be fixed. It can't be made better by fresh grilled mahi for dinner. Irene's problem is that her husband of thirty-five years, in addition to keeping a mistress and fathering a child and lying about his whereabouts, had been evading tax laws and laundering money.

"Did I ever tell you that Russ sent me flowers on New Year's Day?" Irene asks. "Calla lilies, a beautiful bouquet. He must have arranged it with the florist ahead of time and paid extra because of the holiday. And do you know what I thought when I got them? I thought, *What a lovely man Russell Steele is. I am so lucky to have him.*"

"AC," Huck says. He turns off the heat under the eggs and takes a step toward her, but she holds up her palm to warn him away.

"He was dead by the time the flowers arrived."

"Irene," Huck says. "You're allowed to be upset."

Apparently, Irene hasn't avoided the nervous-breakdown stage after all because what she wants to do is scream, *You're damn right I'm allowed to be upset! It's a good thing the man is dead because if he were alive, I'd kill him!*

But Irene holds her tongue and a second later, Maia walks into the kitchen. She's wearing pink shorts, a gray T-shirt with a hand-painted iguana on the front, and a pair of black Converse.

When she sees Irene, she does an almost comical double take. "Um...hi? Miss Irene?"

"Good morning, Maia," Irene says. She turns the corners of her lips up, which physically hurts. Then, as a demonstration that everything's okay, everything's fine, she takes a sip of her coffee. It's strong. One small mercy.

Maia looks from Irene to Huck and back with raised eyebrows. "Did you...stay here last night?"

Irene nearly laughs. She has no idea what to say. Part of her wants to claim she's here just to pick up Huck for their charter, but in another second, Maia is going to notice Irene's suitcase open on the coffee table.

"I did," Irene says. "Huck was kind enough to let me sleep on the sofa."

"Okay..." Maia says.

Huck spoons some eggs onto a plate and pushes the button on the toaster. "Irene and the boys lost the villa, Nut," he says. "There's some...tax trouble."

Tax trouble is a useful phrase, Irene thinks. It'll put everyone to sleep.

Maia takes a seat at the table. "So you guys can't stay there anymore?"

The toaster dings. Huck pulls butter and jam out of the fridge and sets them on the table along with the plate of eggs and toast. "I have to get ready," he says, and he disappears down the hall, leaving Irene to explain the unexplainable.

"We can't," Irene says. Cash called his friend Tilda and spent the night at her house. Irene asked Cash to call Baker and let him know what had happened. Baker was planning on moving down to the island from Houston with his son, Floyd—though these plans will certainly have to change. Hopefully, Baker hasn't done anything that can't be undone. "The villa belongs to the government now. Because Russ...your dad...he owed the government money for taxes, and since he's not here to pay them, the FBI took the house instead." This isn't quite true, but it's close enough.

"So none of us can stay there?"

"No," Irene says. "They let me leave with only one suitcase. Just my clothes. So the stuff in your room...might be difficult to get back."

Maia's fork hovers over her breakfast. She looks so much like Russ's mother, Milly, in that moment that Irene wants to hug her. Those eyes. Milly's eyes.

"Are you guys leaving, then?" Maia asks in a wavering voice.

"Oh, Maia," Irene says, and her eyes fill with tears. "No? I don't know? The FBI also took my house in Iowa City."

"They did?"

"They did," Irene says. She can no longer stand, she's shaking too badly, so she takes the seat next to Maia. "That house is what's called a Victorian, and it had been a dream of mine since I was a young girl to restore and live in a real Victorian house. When Russ and I were first married, I kept clippings in a file folder of paint colors I liked, sofas, wallpaper, old sinks, light fixtures, doorknobs."

"Like Pinterest?" Maia says.

"Yes, like Pinterest," Irene says. "And once Russ...your dad...took the job down here, I had the money to buy a real Victorian house in a style called Queen Anne, which has elaborate gingerbread fretwork trim..." She looks at Maia. "Do you know what that is?"

Maia shakes her head.

"It looks like a house in a fairy tale, with a deep front porch and a turret and some stained-glass windows."

"Cool," Maia says. Irene thinks maybe Maia is indulging her, but it *is* cool.

"It was as if my entire Pinterest board came to life," Irene says. "The house is filled with antiques and hand-knotted silk rugs. There are built-in cabinets and salvaged fixtures and stained-glass windows and murals on the walls and chandeliers, and I have a doorbell that used to ring in a convent in Italy." She needs to stop. What is she doing, unloading all this on a twelve-year-old? "I would have loved for you to see it." This is true, Irene realizes. She wanted both Huck and Maia to see the Church Street house someday. It was her life's work. In a way, it was an incarnation of Irene herself. "But they're taking it. I'm losing my swimming pool and my rose garden with all my heirloom varietals and my two cars. It'll all be gone. They're taking it because of Russ. And now I have nothing left."

Maia stares at Irene and Irene is just sane enough to feel ashamed.

"You have Cash and Baker and Floyd," Maia says. "You have Huck. He really likes you...he was in a terrible mood when you went back to the States, you know. And you have me." She picks up her toast, butters and jams it, and holds it out to Irene. "And you have this papaya jam from Jake's, which is one of the best things I've ever eaten. Try it."

Irene accepts the toast—how can she not?—and takes a small bite. The jam is...well, it's delicious.

"Good, right?" Maia says.

Irene nods and takes another small bite.

"You can start a new Pinterest board," Maia says. "And the first thing on it can be the papaya jam from Jake's."

If only it were that easy, Irene thinks. She knows Maia is right; Irene still has what matters. Her family. Her friends. Her health. Her good sense, sort of.

"We aren't going to leave," Irene says. She doesn't add

Because we have nowhere to go. This isn't strictly true, anyway. Baker still owns a house in Houston that is untouched by Russ's tainted money. And Irene's elderly aunt Ruth has their family summer home in Door County. But the thought of moving to Houston or living with her eighty-something-year-old aunt isn't at all appealing. "We'll figure something out."

"You can stay here," Maia says. "And you don't have to sleep on the couch—we have an extra room. My mom's room." She takes a bite of eggs and seems to realize what she has just offered.

"The couch is fine for now," Irene says quickly. "And I'll find something. I'm not completely penniless."

Maia swallows. "Gramps told me I could move into my mom's room. That means you can have my room."

"Oh, Maia…"

"It's a mess, I know," Maia says. "But I'll clean it after school. I'm grounded anyway."

That's right; Maia is grounded. She'd pulled a disappearing act last night after lying to Cash to get him to drop her off in town. That drama now seems extremely minor, like running out of dinner rolls on the *Titanic*.

"You don't have to move on my account," Irene says, though there is obviously no way she's going to sleep in Rosie's room. "The couch is fine."

"I want to move," Maia says. "You being here is a good impetus." She scrunches up her eyes. "Did I use that word correctly?"

Irene can't help herself; she halfway smiles. "You did."

"So you'll stay?"

It's not in Irene's nature to accept help from anyone, but she can't turn down such a sweet offer—besides which, she is the definition of *desperate*. "I'll stay until I get back on my feet."

Suddenly, Huck is before them, dressed in his sky-blue fishing shirt and his visor, a yellow bandanna tied around his neck. "I'm glad that's settled," he says.

As Irene is standing at the window watching Huck's truck wind its way down Jacob's Ladder, her phone rings. It's Lydia. Irene hovers her finger over the screen. She would like to stay here, in a space where there's still a filament of hope. Maybe Agent Kenneth Beckett, who came to search the Church Street house a few weeks earlier, has intervened on Irene's behalf. There's always a good FBI agent in the movies, right? One who sees past the letter of the law to what's authentically right and wrong? Irene didn't do anything wrong. She doesn't deserve to lose her home.

"Lydia?" Irene says.

"It's been seized," Lydia says. "They have a sign on the door and a team has just arrived to remove the contents. I asked to see the warrant, and what do I know, but it looked official. The guy called the house the 'fruit of crime.'"

Irene's stomach lurches and she fears she's going to vomit. *Remove the contents. The "fruit of crime."*

"What about the things that are mine?" Irene asks. "What about the things I bought with my salary from the magazine? What about the things we owned before Russ took the job at Ascension?"

"I don't know," Lydia says. "We're sitting across the street in my car. Should I go ask?"

Irene tries to imagine Lydia asking these complicated questions. But the agents must get asked about this sort of thing constantly, every time they dismantle someone's life.

"Please ask if you can get one thing," Irene says. "A

photograph of Milly. It's in the navy-blue guest suite, hanging above the washstand."

"Photograph of Milly, navy guest room, above the washstand," Lydia repeats. "I'll ask right now. You stay on the phone. Here, talk to Brandon."

No! Irene thinks. She is in no mood to make small talk.

"Hey, Irene," Brandon says.

"Good morning, Brandon."

There's the predictable awkward pause. Brandon clears his throat. "So, this is a bummer, huh?"

A bummer is when Iowa loses to Iowa State. It can maybe be stretched to include a flat tire, a loose filling that results in having to get a root canal, and flunking your driver's test. What's happening to Irene is not a bummer. It's a...well, frankly, she lacks the right word.

"Yes," she says. "Yes, Brandon, it is."

Her tone must discourage further conversation because Brandon says, "Hang in there."

A few moments later, Lydia takes the phone. "Here's exactly what happened. First, he asked if I was your lawyer. I should have said yes, but I didn't think fast enough. I told him I was your friend and that all I wanted was one family photograph. I told him I knew where it was and that he could come with me while I retrieved it."

"What did he say?"

"He said no."

Irene needs to hang up. She needs to call Ed Sorley, her attorney, although Ed will be in way over his head with this. She needs to find another attorney. But first, Irene wants that photograph. Out of all the items in her home, that's the one she can't bear to think of being ignominiously tossed onto a pile in some storage unit. "Thank you, Lydia. I appreciate you getting out of bed to check on this for me."

"I wish there were more we could do," Lydia says. "I can't believe how *awful* this is...your beautiful house. You worked so *hard*...remember when they sent the wrong-size pool cover and we thought *that* was a catastrophe?"

"I have to go, Lydia," Irene says. "I'll call you later. Thank you for...I appreciate it." Irene hangs up, hoping she didn't sound rude or, if she did sound rude, that Lydia forgives her. Lydia is too nice to handle the FBI agents in Irene's driveway—but Irene knows someone who isn't too nice.

She scrolls through her contacts until she finds the number of her former colleague Mavis Key.

Irene barely has to explain; Mavis gets it. The FBI has seized Irene's property. Mavis doesn't ask why; she knows about Russ's second life in the Caribbean, so she can surely guess why. Irene tells Mavis that all she wants from the house is the photograph of Milly, Russ's mother, taken in 1928 in Erie, Pennsylvania.

"I'm on my way over right now," Mavis says. "And make no mistake, I *will* get that photograph."

For the first time all morning, Irene feels her shoulders relax. Mavis will get the photograph. Mavis is a thirty-one-year-old dynamo who moved to Iowa City from Manhattan, stole Irene's editor-in-chief job at *Heartland Home and Style,* and is turning the magazine into a midwestern version of *Domino* or *Architectural Digest,* complete with a snappy "social media presence." The magazine's publisher, Joseph Feeney, was correct in hiring and immediately promoting Mavis Key, Irene sees now. The woman is effective.

"Thank you," Irene says.

"Text me your mailing address," Mavis says. "I'll have it packaged properly and shipped with insurance."

"That's above and beyond—"

"And Irene," Mavis says, "I want you to call my twin sister. She's a corporate attorney in New York City, and she deals with white-collar criminals who make Russ look like Mister Rogers."

Irene very much doubts that. "I didn't know you had a twin," she says. Then she realizes she knows next to nothing about Mavis's personal life.

"Well, I'm warning you, she's very tough. I find her a bit intimidating, to be honest."

This gets Irene's attention. Mavis, with her extreme self-confidence, her stylish clothes, her cutting-edge vision, finds her sister intimidating? What must the woman be like?

"I'm not sure what I need," Irene says.

"You need Nat," Mavis says. "Natalie Key. Call her, Irene."

BAKER

Thursday, four in the morning, Houston, Texas. Baker sits straight up in bed. This is it. This is happening. Their flight to St. Thomas is in a few short hours.

His phone shows two missed calls from Cash the night before plus a text that says, Pick up, bro. It's urgent.

Baker still has last-minute packing and organizing to do before Ellen comes to take them to the airport. He doesn't have one spare second to talk to his brother, though he figures Cash must have heard the news: Maia saw Mick kissing Brigid on the beach, Maia told Ayers, and Ayers is going to break off the engagement.

Well, Baker already knows. Ayers texted him right after it happened.

It's a sign from above; this new chapter in his life is going to work. A tropical island, a nontraditional lifestyle, and, most important, Baker's relationship with Ayers Wilson. He's going to win Ayers over or die trying.

"We're going to miss you like crazy," Ellen says. They're curbside at the airport, which is congested with Ubers and taxis and people wheeling their roller bags while talking on their phones, but Ellen insists on getting out so she can give Baker a proper hug goodbye. "Becky is in charge of finding us a new school husband."

"What?" Baker's friendship with his school wives is rare and, he thought, special. He never dreamed he'd be *replaced*.

Ellen shrugs. "She's the one in HR."

"Just as long as it's not Tony," Baker says.

Ellen grins but her eyes are shining with tears. "I'm only kidding, Bake," she says. "You know what? We're already planning a trip to visit you this summer."

"You are?"

"I'm terrible with surprises," Ellen says. "Sorry about that. Yes, we'll see you in a few months."

"You can stay at the villa, you know," Baker says. "It has nine bedrooms."

"You're sweet to offer, but we wouldn't do that to your mom and brother," Ellen says. "I'm going to book rooms at Caneel."

Baker finds himself getting choked up as he shepherds Floyd into the terminal. His school wives are the only people in Houston he's going to miss, and he's touched that they feel the same way, so much so that they're already planning a trip down. Once they see St. John and Irene's villa and meet Ayers, they'll understand why he's making the move. He'd be a fool not to.

When Baker and Floyd check in with all their luggage, Floyd is carrying his copy of *The Dirty Cowboy* under one arm, and the woman at the United desk is so taken with him that she bumps them up to first class. "You're the only child I've seen in years who isn't mesmerized by a screen," she tells Floyd.

Baker wills his son not to mention the iPad that's tucked in Baker's carry-on or the fact that Floyd has watched *Despicable Me 3* ten times in the past week.

"Thank you," Baker says. First class! He's already dreaming of a Bloody Mary and a decent nap.

Turns out, Baker's and Floyd's seats are across the aisle from each other. Is this going to be okay? Sitting next to Floyd is a West Indian woman who is already situated, watching a movie with headphones on. The seat next to Baker is empty. Maybe Baker will ask about switching.

Baker stows his carry-on and Floyd's backpack but tells Floyd not to buckle up just yet. "I'm going to see if we can switch seats. That way you can sit next to me and have a window."

"I want a window!" Floyd says.

There's a guy in a knit cap with a hipster beard getting ready to take the seat next to Baker. He's wearing a T-shirt that reads WASPS OF GOOD FORTUNE—a band, maybe?—and jeans and a Gucci belt and a pair of black Sambas exactly like the ones Baker used to wear to soccer practice when he was nine years old, and on his wrist is a forty-thousand-dollar Rolex Daytona with a light blue pearlescent face. He has AirPods in.

The guy—he looks to be somewhere in his mid-twenties—nods at Baker and goes to lift his duffel into the overhead space.

Baker says, "Hey, man, any chance you would mind switching spots with my son so we can sit together? He's only four."

The guy blinks at Baker and says in a broad Australian accent, "Sorry, mate, I prefer the window."

"No problem, mate," Baker says. He slides out of the way so that Mr. Samba, Mr. Wasps of Good Fortune, Mr. Young Crocodile Dundee can take his seat. Baker tries not to feel put out. It's the guy's seat, Baker has no right to it, but still—who says no when asked to help out a four-year-old child? Baker glances at the woman next to Floyd, but she has fallen asleep.

"Looks like we're staying put, buddy," Baker says, and he fastens Floyd's seat belt.

"Daddy?" Floyd says. "May I please have the iPad?"

Baker doesn't speak to Young Croc during the flight, though he does keep tabs on him out of the corner of his eye. Young Croc orders Maker's Mark straight up (two) to Baker's Bloody Mary (one). Young Croc watches *Deadpool 2* (no surprise there); Baker chooses old episodes of *The Office*. Young Croc declines breakfast; Baker inhales the kale and sausage omelet, the soggy home fries, and even the sad, wrinkled cherry tomatoes. Young Croc does the sudoku puzzle in the in-flight magazine astonishingly quickly, which actually makes Baker like him a little better. He doesn't get up for the bathroom at all, whereas Baker gets up once for himself and twice for Floyd.

As the plane descends, Young Croc finally turns his attention to the window, tapping on the glass with his forefinger in apparent anticipation. And isn't that an emotion he and Baker share?

When the plane's wheels hit the runway, people sitting in coach clap and cheer. Baker checks on Floyd, who is fast asleep, then turns to Young Croc. "You going to St. Thomas?" he asks. "Or St. John?"

"St. John."

"Us too," Baker says. "We're moving down for good."

"Oh yeah?" Young Croc says. "You running a business down here? Doing the EDC deal?"

"EDC?" Baker says.

"Yeah, that's the tax-incentive plan for businesses that relocate to the USVI."

"Legal?" Baker asks, because this sounds like something his father might have been involved in. Anyway, it would explain why the hedge fund was run down here instead of in, say, New York or Chicago.

Young Croc laughs. "Yes, legal. Lots of people do it. I moved my company here from Houston in the fall. I'm saving tons of cash."

"From Houston?" Baker says. "Are you American?"

"Naturalized," Young Croc says. "Originally from Perth."

Perth is in…Australia? New Zealand? Baker should know but he hasn't got a clue and he's embarrassed to ask. "What's the name of your company?"

"Huntley International?" he says, like maybe Baker has heard of it. "Real estate development."

Baker is rendered temporarily speechless. The dude looks twenty-five. But that would explain the watch. It's probably his father's company. Or—he hears his ex-wife's voice in his head asking him to think and act in a way that promotes gender equality—his mother's company. "Baker Steele," Baker says, offering his hand.

"Dunk," the kid says and they firmly—aggressively?—shake. "Duncan Huntley. Nice to meet you, Baker. What do you do?"

Baker isn't eager to admit that he's a stay-at-home dad supported by his superstar-surgeon almost-ex-wife. He could say that he day-trades and has accepted a coaching job at the Gifft Hill School, but does that sound any more impressive? "Investments," Baker says.

"Oh yeah? For whom?"

"I have my own shop," Baker says. "Coincidentally, I've been thinking about getting into real estate myself." By this, Baker means he's considered getting his real estate license because he isn't sure what else he can do that will make a sustainable living on St. John.

"Take my card," Dunk says. "I'm always looking for investment partners."

Baker accepts the card even though he knows he has severely misrepresented himself. Baker has money in the bank—both a healthy brokerage account and a fund that he day-trades with—but he immediately realizes that he's not in a position to be anyone's "investment partner" unless Dunk Huntley is looking for an investment of five hundred dollars.

Still, it can't hurt to know people. DUNCAN HUNTLEY, CEO AND FOUNDER, HUNTLEY INTERNATIONAL LLC.

Founder? Baker thinks.

He's distracted by the business of getting off the plane. He pulls down his carry-on and Floyd's Toy Story knapsack, then he bends at the knees—protect the back—to pick Floyd up without waking him.

Baker gravitates toward Dunk while they're standing at the baggage carousel waiting for their luggage. Baker is sweating despite the air-conditioning. Floyd is as hot as a glowing coal.

Dunk smiles. "Seeing you with him makes me miss my girl."

"Your…" Baker isn't sure if Dunk means his daughter or his girlfriend. He doesn't seem like the paternal type.

"My girl, Olive. She's a harlequin Great Dane."

"Oh," Baker says. "Your dog."

"Yep," Dunk says. "Olive stays here and I fly back and forth to Houston. She weighs a hundred and fifty pounds, so she's too big to crate. I had to fly down private with her when we came initially."

"Right," Baker says, nodding, although, honestly, every new sentence out of this guy's mouth is crazier than the last. "If you don't mind my saying so, you seem pretty young to be a CEO."

"I'm twenty-eight," Dunk says. "I look older without my hat." He shrugs. "Losing my hair."

"Still, that's really young to have your own company. How'd you do it?"

"I went to Baylor, majored in business…I've always sort of had a nose for what's hot. For my senior project, I developed a simple sex app. The user checked in every time she or he did the deed and joined a community of others who were reporting their sexual activity. People could add what positions they'd tried and a few other details." He glances at Floyd. "And then there was a rating system, points they could accrue, status they could gain. I did it as a riff on the swipe-left culture but it took *off*. Especially among the marrieds. Like my sister, Andi. She lives in Bellaire— you know it?"

Yes, Baker knows it. Wealthy Houston.

"Everyone in her neighborhood was on my app. She claims they were all lying about how much action they were getting."

"Well," Baker says. "Yeah." If Baker was ever on a sex app, he would have no choice but to lie. He and Anna got it on approximately twice a year.

"I sold the app for fifteen million and I got into the weed business in Colorado, making artisanal edibles."

"Ah," Baker says. "Now you're talking."

"We made gummies, lollipops, high-quality chocolate bars in nine flavors, cookie dough...we even had pot pasta sauce."

Pot pasta sauce? Who thinks of this stuff? "I can see where that would be popular," Baker says.

"As more states legalized marijuana, the business grew and I sold that company last year for ten times what I'd made with the app."

A hundred and fifty million? Baker thinks. Surely this is hyperbole.

"So I've given up the sex and the drugs," Dunk says. "And now I'm into the rock and roll." He points to his T-shirt. "Wasps of Good Fortune is my band."

"Oh yeah?" Baker says. "What do you do?"

"I sing," Dunk says. "I have kind of a Colin Hay sound, you know, early-period Men at Work?"

Baker blinks. He'd thought there was only one period of Men at Work, the "Land Down Under" period.

He's saved from commenting when the alarm sounds and the conveyor belt starts rolling. "Hey, do you guys want to ride over to St. John with me?" Dunk asks. "I have my driver coming, then we'll hop on my boat."

"Aw, man, that's kind of you, but we have so much stuff, it's just not practical. I'm going to need one of those big taxis all to myself."

"Just come with me," Dunk says. "It'll be way easier. My boat has plenty of room."

"Okay..." Baker says. "If you're sure."

Dunk helps Baker get all the luggage out to the curb, and seconds later, a forest-green G-wagon pulls up. It's unclear to Baker whether the G-wagon belongs to Dunk or a service he hires, but no matter—it's cool and comfortable, and Baker is finally able to set Floyd down. The driver delivers them to the dock at Havensight, where they climb aboard a sixty-five-foot Sea Ray Sundancer called the *Olive Branch*.

"Wow," Baker says. The boat is brand-new and beautifully outfitted; the salon is all leather and gleaming wood. There's a bouquet of fresh flowers, a bowl of tropical fruit. Dunk opens the fridge; one side is lined with bottles of Veuve Clicquot, the other with beer. Dunk grabs two Heinekens, hands one to Baker, and says, "Let's go sit in the cockpit. Charlie will have us to Cruz Bay in fifteen minutes."

Baker kicks back and relaxes in the sun while Floyd sits in the shade of the bimini, still sluggish from his nap. The captain, Charlie, starts the engines and away they go, zipping around the towering cruise ships to open water. They pick up speed and cut a neat seam through the turquoise water to St. John. Baker takes a sip of his beer and thinks: *This is my life now.* He said good-bye to Ellen outside of IAH just this morning, but it seems like eons ago. If he were back in Houston, he would be getting ready to pick up Floyd from the Children's Cottage. The two of them would go home, Baker would fix a snack, and then they'd head to the park or playground, or Baker would bribe Floyd with his iPad so that he could continue to trade until the markets closed, and by then it would be too late to go to the park and Floyd would have conked out anyway and Baker would think maybe he'd take a nap too, why not? And when the two of them woke up, the sun would be setting and Baker would start on one of his gourmet dinner menus as they waited for Anna to come home, and when Anna came home, she would say she had already eaten (pizza) at the hospital, and Baker would either throw half the dinner away or carefully pack it into a Tupperware container for Anna to take for lunch the next day, which she would inevitably forget to do and Baker would throw it away out of anger and disgust because his efforts around the house went unappreciated.

He's so glad he's not in Houston! He's so glad he's no longer with Anna!

Life in the Virgin Islands will be different. After school, Baker and Floyd will go on tropical adventures—to Salt Pond to snorkel with the turtles, to Scoops for ice cream, to the Reef Bay Trail to hike and see the petroglyphs. Even when they simply go home to the villa, they can swim in the dual-level pool or at their private beach. They can play shuffleboard. Baker will invest in field glasses and they'll bird-watch on the hillside. Irene and Cash are both finished with work in the midafternoon, so one or the other can take care of Floyd while Baker coaches at the school. One or the other will be home at night when Baker wants to take Ayers to Dé Coal Pot or visit her at La Tapa or when they just hang out in Ayers's studio apartment.

Here in St. John, he has a support system. Here in St. John, he has everything he needs.

* * *

The *Olive Branch* pulls up to the National Park Service dock in fifteen minutes flat. While they tie up, Baker texts his mother and Cash to see if either of them can come get him and Floyd; if they can't, he'll have to take a cab to the villa.

"Where do you live?" Baker asks. "We own a villa in Little Cinnamon."

"I have a villa in the East End," Dunk says. "I like the quiet."

Baker nods, though he hasn't been to the East End. Has he heard of the East End? He's not sure. It must be special if Dunk lives there.

Dunk points at an island behind them. "That's Lovango Cay," he says. "My next project. I bought the island, and now I'm looking for partners to fund a resort, a beach club, and some world-class dining. In case you're interested?"

Baker laughs. He's drawn to Dunk, no doubt, but he can't wait to get away from him. He shakes Dunk's hand. "Thanks for the ride, man. It was a real treat to meet you. Right, Floyd?"

Floyd shrugs. "You talk funny."

"Floyd!" Baker says, but Dunk just laughs.

"No worries, mate. You have my card, call anytime, we'll shoot over to Foxy's and have a painkiller."

"All right," Baker says. "I'll take you up on that!" He picks up the biggest suitcase and tries to roll it down the dock while holding Floyd's hand. He needs to check his phone to see if his mother or Cash responded.

"You gonna be okay here?" Dunk asks. "Someone is coming to get you?"

"Yep, all set, all set," Baker says. It won't be a G-wagon with a driver but someone will come, he hopes, or if everyone is busy, he'll schlep every gosh-darn thing they own to the dock in the scorching heat and flag down one of the open-air taxis, the driver of which will probably balk when Baker tells him he lives on a hilltop in Little Cinnamon.

He should have returned Cash's call from the Houston airport. Not setting up a ride was very shortsighted.

Floyd starts to cry. "It's hot," he says. "I want a snack and a juice. Where's Grammy?"

Baker pulls Floyd along like a toy on a string. "You were asleep when they served the meal on the plane, honey, but I'll get you something the second we get home. And you can swim in the pool for as long as you want. There are still three whole days until you start school, so we can do some exploring in the Jeep. We'll take the top off and make it a convertible."

Instead of placating Floyd, this agitates him further and a mini-tantrum follows. *I want the pool now, I want a snack now...* Baker swivels his head to check that Dunk Huntley has left and isn't watching Baker. Dunk Huntley has no idea how difficult dealing with a four-year-old can be.

Sex app, artisanal weed edibles, real estate development. Wasps of Good Fortune. Baker wonders if it's supposed to be *WASPs*, as in "white Anglo-Saxon Protestants." That's an obnoxious name for a band, and they probably stink despite the early–Men at Work sound, yet Baker can't deny he finds Young Croc Dunk Samba WASPy Wunderkind Huntley fascinating.

Baker checks his phone. Nothing from his mother or Cash.

He calls Cash. Straight to voicemail.

He calls Irene. She answers on the fifth ring. Her "Hello" is little more than a whisper.

"Mom?" he says.

"Oh, Baker," she says. Her voice is broken; something is wrong. Baker will ask once he's off this dock and in one of the air-conditioned Jeeps.

"Is there any way you can pick us up?" Baker says. "We got a ride over from St. Thomas with this guy on his boat and so we're on the National Park Service dock instead of the regular ferry dock."

"What?" Irene says. "*Where* are you?"

"The National Park Service dock."

"Here?" she says. "On St. John?"

"Yes, here on St. John," he says. "It's Thursday, Mom." He tries not to sound so exasperated because if he's learned one thing about the Virgin Islands, it's that every day feels like Saturday.

"Didn't Cash call you?"

"Yes, he called me—"

"Didn't he tell you?"

"Tell me what?" Baker says.

HUCK

He doesn't understand women—and how is that possible after so many years of loving them?

Huck grew up with a sister, Caroline, who was a scant two years younger than him and who learned to fish from their father right alongside Huck. But whereas Huck was all about sport-fishing— the hunt, the fight, the elation that came from landing a big one— Caroline liked the quiet elegance of fly-fishing. She showed an uncanny talent for it early on, which was unusual for a child that young. She preferred dancing her line over the flats of Islamorada to a trip out to blue water, and to his credit, their father, the original Captain Powers, nurtured her gift. By the time Caroline was thirteen, she had won every youth fly-fishing competition in the state of Florida, competitions in which she was always the only girl.

All through high school, instead of dating or hanging out at the Green Turtle with her friends, Caroline would sit at her desk and tie flies. Caroline Powers became famous for her flies; grown men paid good money for them—*good* money, the price jacked up to an almost absurd level because Caroline didn't want to sell them. Her flies were works of art; she had the patience, the attention to detail, the slender, nimble fingers. She had the love and devotion.

While Huck was in Vietnam at the tail end of the war, 1974 to 1975, Caroline went to college in Gainesville, met a boy from the Florida Panhandle, followed that boy when he went to law school in Tallahassee, married him, and gave up fishing altogether. That, Huck didn't understand. Whenever Caroline and her new husband, Beau, came back to Islamorada to visit, they would go sport-fishing with their father on the big boat, and although Caroline was impressive the way she cast and reeled in the big fish, Huck yearned to see her with her fly rod again. He even suggested it once, the two of them out together on the flats at dawn in the pontoon. She shut him down immediately in a hushed voice: "No, Huck, I can't." As though fly-fishing were something embarrassing she used to do as a kid, like going roller-skating in just a bikini and a pair of red knee socks.

Caroline was diagnosed with a brain tumor the week after her fortieth birthday and was dead by forty-one. Soon after, her husband, Beau, gave Huck a flat tackle box. When Huck opened it, he saw Caroline's flies, one in each sectioned compartment like so many jewels. He has them still.

Before she met Huck, Kimberly Cassel was a bartender at Sloppy Joe's in Key West. In those days, Huck was not yet Huck—he was just Sam Powers—and he was not yet a captain; he was first mate for a guy everyone called Captain Coke. Every Sunday, Coke would invite Sam to go out on the water "just for fun," and nearly every Sunday, Sam said no because Sunday was his only day off and he had to do things like laundry and grocery shopping, and sometimes he hitchhiked up to Islamorada, where his mother would cook him dinner. But one Sunday in March of 1978, Sam said sure and Coke said, "Finally! I've been wanting to introduce you to my sister."

Huck remembers that he'd bristled—he did just fine in the women department on his own and he'd been looking forward to a day of real fishing (instead of baiting clients' hooks and turning back early if someone got seasick), and he wasn't sure he'd enjoy the presence of anyone's sister, aside from his own, on a fishing trip.

But then Kimberly came striding down the dock wearing cut-off army-surplus fatigues, a red bandanna around her neck, and a white visor; her sandy-blond hair was up in a ponytail. Huck recognized her as the bartender from Sloppy Joe's, the famous Key West watering hole where Hemingway used to hang out and where Huck liked to fish for women from time to time. Somehow he'd never realized that the most popular bartender in Key West was his crusty, hard-living boss's sister.

Well, okay, Huck thought. She was nice to look at, but could she fish?

Oh, yes. Like Huck, Kimberly was born and raised in the Keys, on and around boats. During that first trip together, Huck watched her land a one-hundred-fifty-pound sailfish, sitting in the fighting chair, screaming like she was having a baby.

He vowed then that he would marry her.

But first he had to beat out scores of other men—the salty locals and rich, sunburned tourists alike, all calling her name, throwing down money, telling her she was as beautiful as one of Charlie's Angels. It took endurance to get the first date. Huck had to stay at the bar drinking but not getting drunk until Sloppy Joe's closed at four a.m. This was no small feat when his wake-up for the morning charter was only two hours later.

Looking back, Huck realizes that he'd been so dazzled by Kimberly's obvious charms and—he'll just say it—so invigorated by the chase that he ignored the warning signs of a deeply troubled person. Kimberly routinely did shots with customers, sometimes as many as five or six. She never appeared visibly drunk at work, but after her shift ended, there was always a margarita or three or five. Back at the beginning, Kimberly had been happy and pliably good-natured when she was drunk.

Shortly after they were married, things changed. In year three, Captain Coke's own substance abuse got the best of him. He was spending all his money on cocaine and, apparently, none on his business. He'd taken out a line of credit on the equity he had left in his boat and then failed to pay. Just as the bank was ready to claim the boat, Huck stepped in and bought not only the boat but the whole charter business. Kimberly called Huck a savior, though she wanted Huck to keep Coke on as captain. No, sorry— that wasn't going to happen. Huck didn't want Coke anywhere near the boat or the business, though he was happy to pay for rehab. This went over poorly with both brother and sister, but

Huck stood his ground. He took over the charter business, hired a new young mate, and made so much money the first year that he was able to buy a second boat.

Huck wanted to start a family and Kimberly claimed she did too, but she refused to quit her job at Sloppy Joe's. It brought in too much money, plus it was her identity. Huck didn't say that if she had a baby, she would have a new identity.

He wouldn't dare.

Kimberly did go off her birth control but she continued with the shots and the after-shift drinking.

"For God's sake, Kimmy," Huck finally said, "any baby we have will be born pickled."

Kimberly didn't like this one bit, though it did make her slow down a little—and sure enough, she got pregnant. Huck remembers the mixture of giddiness and terror at the news; it was as though someone had told him he could travel to the moon with the astronauts or star in a movie with Clint Eastwood. Did he want to? Hell yes! Did he *really* want to? He wasn't sure. What did Huck know about having a child, about being a father? He was also afraid that Kimberly wouldn't be able to stay on the wagon for nine full months—it seemed impossible—plus both of them smoked like fiends, and that would have to stop.

Kimberly bought prenatal vitamins and went to see an ob-gyn in Miami and she changed her post-shift drink to one white-wine spritzer. She cut down to four cigarettes a day—breakfast, lunch, dinner, and late at night—and Huck thought, *Okay, maybe this will work.* He couldn't expect her to quit everything cold turkey; that was how people failed.

Then, late on the night of December 1, 1983—Huck still remembers the date and probably always will—Kimberly came home stinking drunk, waking Huck up when she slammed into their bungalow on Catherine Street singing "Piece of My Heart" at the top of her lungs and crying.

Huck jumped out of bed. He would never lay a hand on a woman but he wanted to throttle her. He took her gently by the shoulders, pulled her in close, and whispered, "It's not just you anymore, Kimmy. You have to think about our baby."

Kimberly said, "Baby's gone, Sam. I started bleeding at work."

Huck was crushed; Kimberly was worse than crushed. She was riding a pendulum of emotions. When she swung one way, she was fine—it happened to a lot of people; they could try again. When she swung the other way, she was a mess—it was her fault, she was damaged and broken and unfit to be a mother.

Kimberly went back on the pill.

Huck felt like he was on a bike without brakes careening down a mountainside. He was afraid to jump off even though he knew he would crash when he got to the bottom. What followed was three years of Huck fishing and Kimberly drinking, drinking, drinking. This ended only once a beefy, tattooed loudmouth on one of Huck's charters bragged to his buddy that he'd gotten to third base with the bartender of Sloppy Joe's the night before.

"Oh yeah?" Huck said, blood pulsing in his ears. "Blond gal?"

"Ass like a valentine," the loudmouth said, and it took every ounce of Huck's willpower not to stab the guy in the forehead with the gaff.

When Huck confronted Kimberly, she admitted to it right away but said it was more like second base, maybe not even. She couldn't remember and wouldn't have been able to pick the guy out of a lineup. "The men are an occupational hazard, Sammy. They don't mean anything."

"Men?" he said, and he realized then that Kimberly hooked up with her customers all the time, maybe even every night. Was

the baby she lost even his? She had made him a laughingstock, an absolute fool for love.

He told her it was rehab or he was leaving. She agreed to rehab, and once she was safely inside the facility, Huck served her with divorce papers, which broke her heart but broke his heart even worse.

Once Huck left the Keys for St. John, it was only a few weeks before he met and fell in love with LeeAnn Small, who was Kimberly's opposite in every way. Maia liked to throw around the word *queen—Beyoncé is a queen, J. Lo is a queen—*but in Huck's life there had been only one queen and that was LeeAnn. She was statuesque, bronze-skinned, dark-eyed. She had a rich laugh and a slow smile that she shared with Huck like a secret.

On their first real date, at Chateau Bordeaux, Huck told Lee-Ann about Kimberly. LeeAnn tsked him—because who couldn't have predicted how *that* story was going to end—and then said, "If you're looking for more crazy, you're in the wrong place."

LeeAnn didn't fish but she checked the wind, watched the sky, passed along fish sightings from their West Indian neighbors that Huck would never have heard about otherwise. She introduced Huck to the people at restaurants who would buy his catch. She never gave him a hard time about how long he spent on the water or tinkering on the boat. And, man, could she cook—conch ceviche, Creole fish stew, fresh tuna steaks with lime and toasted coconut.

LeeAnn was tough, stubborn, uncompromising, but unlike Kimberly, she stuck to a moral code and was utterly beyond reproach. Huck was a little scared of her at times. She was a nurse practitioner and the most competent person up at the Myrah

Keating Smith Community Health Center, where she treated everything from ankles sprained on the Reef Bay Trail to jellyfish stings to STDs. LeeAnn was strict with Rosie, but despite this— or because of it—Rosie broke the rules again and again and again, eventually getting pregnant by one of the rich men she waited on at Caneel Bay.

There were six golden years when Huck lived in the house on Jacob's Ladder with LeeAnn, Rosie, and Maia. He can remember sitting down to dinner in the evenings and seeing their bright faces and hearing their chatter or their squabbling and thinking how blessed he was to be among them.

He missed that sweet spot in his life now that it was over.

LeeAnn died of congestive heart failure.

Rosie died in the helicopter crash with Russell Steele.

Now here's Huck, five years after LeeAnn's passing and one month after Rosie's passing, in danger of falling in love with Irene Steele, the wife of Rosie's lover.

As his friend Rupert would say, *You can't make this shit up!*

It comes as no surprise to Huck that the Invisible Man, Russell Steele, was just another Caribbean pirate. Evading taxes and laundering money were nearly as common down here as snorkeling and drinking rum. Irene has now lost the villa in Little Cinnamon as well as her home in Iowa City, and the latter, Huck understands, is the greater loss by far. Most people down here are from somewhere else. They have another place they call home. It must feel pretty rotten to have that taken away, to be left with little more than the clothes on your back, the shoes on your feet.

Irene isn't bankrupt. She has twenty thousand dollars in an account down here, money from her magazine job.

"Twenty thousand isn't nothing," Huck says. They're standing out on the deck of Huck's house, elbow to elbow on the railing but not touching, gazing out at the water and the faint outline of St. Croix in the distance. A lot of people would call them lucky— people in Iowa City whose cars were buried under three feet of snow, for example.

"It's not enough to live on for very long," Irene says. "Both you and I know that. I need to find a decent place to live with reasonable rent and I'll need to buy a car."

Huck is relieved that she seems to be talking about staying on St. John, even though they both know that her money would last a lot longer if she lived almost anywhere else. "You can stay here as long as you want," Huck says. This turn of events doesn't seem all that bad to him. He *likes* having her here. He *likes* being the person who can put a roof over her head and food on her plate, though he would never, ever reveal this to Irene.

One trait all the women in his life have shared: They were "born on the Fourth of July." Independent.

Irene bows her head. Her hair is out of its braid; it's wavy and long as it falls around her face, a chestnut curtain shot through with strands of silver. When she looks up, she says, "I'm grateful for your friendship and the job on the boat—"

"You're an asset on the boat, AC," he says. "I *need* you on the boat. Today alone was hell on me." That morning, Huck had a Master of the Universe type on board—guy in his early forties, world by the balls, gung ho, let's go—and his four sons. The older three were complete hellions from the second they stepped onto the boat still in their basketball sneakers.

"Take your shoes off," Huck told them.

The oldest kid, maybe fifteen, said, "These are Cactus Jacks."

"Doesn't matter. Please take them off."

"It's Travis Scott's shoe," the kid said.

"This isn't Travis Scott's boat," Huck said. He didn't admit that he had no idea who Travis Scott was. He hadn't paid attention to basketball since Jordan retired. "It's *my* boat and you are to remove your shoes, please."

The youngest of the kids couldn't have been more than five; he was too little to be out on the boat without a dedicated caretaker, which his father—whose sole focus was catching mahi—most certainly was not. The father mentioned that the mother was having a spa day at Caneel, and he admitted that he wasn't used to having the kids by himself. The father took the first fish (Huck *hated* when grown men did this, ahead of their own kids, in the name of "Let me show you how it's done"), and he also took the fourth fish, forgetting about son number three, who was rightfully pissed off. Kid number three retaliated by grabbing his father's phone out of his pocket and dangling it over the side of the boat. This wasn't the first time Huck had seen this—it happened at least once a month, usually when Huck had a bachelor party on the boat; guys got drunk and bent out of shape or were screwing around—but Huck had never seen anyone flip out the way the father flipped out. He roared so loudly that even Huck flinched, and when the father went to grab the phone from his son, it fell in the water.

You deserved that, buddy, Huck thought.

Chaos ensued. They had to stop the boat, get the diving mask and the bait net, and go fishing for the phone, which was most certainly resting on the seafloor twenty feet below. The littlest kid fell when no one was looking and got a bloody nose but the father was only concerned about his phone. He couldn't live without it. Was there a store on this "stupid little island" where he could get it replaced that afternoon?

"St. Thomas," Huck said, his fists itching.

It had been a terrible charter and Huck was convinced that if Irene had been there, she would have established an order for the fish so that no one got overlooked, no one got angry, no one got hurt, and Huck didn't have to hear his home of the past twenty years insulted by a man-child.

He wants to tell Irene this story and let her know what a joy it is to have a woman in his life who understands the particular texture of his days, but she's in no state to hear it. He'll save it for later, after all this has been resolved and they're back to normal.

Will this be resolved?

Will they be back to normal?

"I appreciate your generosity but I can't impose on you forever," Irene says. "Unfortunately, I have nowhere else to turn right now. I feel like such a burden."

"You're not a burden," Huck says. "Maia wants you here and so do I." He moves an inch closer so that their elbows are kissing, and she doesn't move away. Huck wonders if he should hug her. He places an oh so tentative hand between her shoulder blades and she snaps to attention, ramrod straight. Huck lets his hand drop.

Okay, he gets it. No touching.

"This isn't a fairy tale where I'm a damsel in distress and you're the hero swooping in to save me."

"I know it's not, AC," he says.

"Please," she says. "Stop calling me that."

"Okay," Huck says, and now he's hurt. *AC* stands for "Angler Cupcake," which, she'd told Huck, was what her father used to call her. Huck likes the nickname. It doesn't exactly suit her— Irene is too sensible and straightforward to be any kind of cupcake—but he likes that he has a nickname for her. It suggests intimacy, friendship, something special between the two of them. But fine; she wants him to stop, he'll stop.

"I can't do this," Irene says. "I told you last night that I need more time."

But that was before ten FBI agents showed up to seize the villa, Huck thinks. That was before she learned her Iowa home was gone as well. Huck thought maybe that had changed things. But apparently not.

"I promised I'd give you as much time as you need," he says. "And I meant it."

"Except now I'm living in your house!" Irene says. "Mooching off you, taking advantage of your kindness! Don't you understand how...*confusing* that is?"

"No," Huck says. "I don't. We're friends, Irene. Okay? And coworkers. If you want to keep it just friends and coworkers, I'm good with that. I'm not exactly inviting you to share my bedroom, am I?"

"But you want to, don't you?" she asks.

"Want to what?"

"Invite me to share your bedroom!"

Huck can't figure out if his answer should be yes or no. The truth is yes. Should he be truthful? "I want you to sleep where you're comfortable. You know my feelings for you, AC. Sorry— Irene. But I'm not interested in forcing this along." He's so agitated that he lights a cigarette. This is the kind of conversation he likes the least—murky, ambiguous. They're middle-aged. Why can't they just say what they mean? "If it moves forward, it will be when you're ready. I'm a patient man, Irene. I'm a fisherman."

This gets a smile, though one so fleeting that Huck wonders if he imagined it. "I don't want to be a charity case. And I don't want to feel like I owe you something in exchange for..."

Huck exhales a stream of smoke. Now he's offended. "Please, Irene. Give me some credit."

"I do, but…"

"But you were married to a fella for thirty-five years who turned out to be a cheat and a liar and a criminal," Huck says. "So I understand how maybe you're hesitant to trust the very next man you meet. But I promise—Irene, I promise you on my precious granddaughter's life that I am pure in my intentions and my feelings. I've been hurt before too. Hurt badly." Huck pauses. At some point, he'll tell her the story about Kimberly, and she'll understand they're more alike than she knows. "I'm not going to use kindness to leverage something from you. Do you understand me?"

"Yes."

Are we okay, then? he wants to ask. Irene steps toward him and puts her hands on his shoulders, then moves closer and clasps her hands behind his neck. She rests her head on his chest.

Two things are apparent in that moment. One, they *are* okay. And two, Huck doesn't understand women.

Irene's phone rings, snapping them back to reality. Happiness is a butterfly that lands and then just as quickly flies away.

Irene answers the phone. "Hello?" There's a pause. "Oh, Baker." Another pause. "What? *Where* are you? Here? On St. John?" She turns to Huck, her eyes wide with alarm, and mouths: *He's here.*

Huck stubs out his cigarette. He imagines his buddy Rupert doing his best Chief Brody imitation: *Huck, my friend, you're going to need a bigger boat.*

AYERS

Treasure Island has a blown powerhead. It needs to go all the way to Puerto Rico to be worked on and won't be back in commission for a week.

Ayers is relieved. As usual, she wakes up facedown on her bed at the crack of dawn when her coffeemaker starts gurgling, but Ayers can barely even lift her head. She has to go to the bathroom but it's ten feet away, which might as well be a country mile.

Depression is setting in. Because of Mick.

Fool me once, shame on you.

Fool me twice, shame on me.

After Maia called to tell Ayers that she saw Mick and Brigid kissing on the beach—*They were all over each other, I saw it with my own two eyes*—Ayers nearly smashed her phone against the tile floor of her apartment. But she was stopped by her pragmatism (it would take seven hundred and fifty dollars and a trip to St. Thomas to replace it) and her skepticism. Maia must be mistaken. She'd thought it was Mick and Brigid, but it had to be another couple.

Mick had proposed only *two days before.* He'd planned the whole thing, luring Ayers out onto his boss's boat, *Funday,* rafting up in Christmas Cove near Pizza Pi among all their friends in the St. John service industry, asking Captain Stephen from the *Singing Dog* to play "Southern Cross," which was Ayers's favorite

song. *My love is an anchor tied to you, tied with a silver chain.*
He'd proposed in front of everyone, but aside from that, Ayers
couldn't have executed it better herself. And maybe part of her
did appreciate the public nature of the proposal. All of their
friends knew that Mick had cheated on Ayers with Brigid and
had then dated Brigid for two months, one week, and three
days. (Yes, it was painful enough that Ayers kept track.) So it
was *validating* to have everyone bear witness to Mick's ultimate
choice.

It was Ayers. Ayers, not Brigid.

Or so she'd thought.

She wanted to dismiss what Maia had told her. Maia was only
twelve. Could she really be trusted?

But Ayers trusted Maia more than anyone else she knew. Maia
wouldn't have said it was Mick and Brigid unless it was Mick
and Brigid. Ayers had to admit that Mick kissing Brigid on the
beach wasn't out of the realm of possibility. She could only too
easily imagine how it had unfolded. Brigid wanted "closure," she
needed to have "a talk," she "deserved at least that." And then
she gazed at him a certain way or she nudged her knee between
his legs or she stroked his earlobe—and Mick broke. Mick might
have thought that since he'd proposed and would be with Ayers
the rest of his life, he had one last pass.

He did not have one last pass.

Ayers had decided to verify Maia's sighting with a second
source. She'd texted Lindsay, another server at the Beach Bar,
someone she considered a friend, to ask if she'd noticed Mick
and Brigid slip away during service.

The response: TBH, yes, B. stranded me tonight with all her tables
for…half an hour? She's been crying since Monday, and I assumed
Mick was going to talk with her about it because it's been distracting

for all of us. But they were gone an unusually long time and when they came back, B. looked much happier.

Ayers pulled the ring off her finger and nestled it back into its little velvet box. She wondered about the happy bride-to-be who would eventually wear it.

She sent Mick a text: I know you kissed Brigid. I'm leaving the ring in the box under the big rock at the end of my driveway.

Mick texted back: K.

K? Ayers thought. What kind of response was *that?* Didn't he want to know how Ayers had found out? Didn't he want to try and *deny* it? Wasn't he going to *fight* for her?

Apparently not.

The engagement was over; it had lasted slightly more than forty-eight hours. Ayers should never have taken Mick back. Brigid was some kind of narcotic for him.

She sent a second text: Best of luck to you two.

She wanted to say something else, but *You deserve each other* was too cliché and *Just remember—once a slut, always a slut* seemed too mean. In the end, Ayers wrote, Poor Gordon. Because Ayers felt sorry for Mick's dog. She'd miss him.

And then Ayers had texted Baker to let him know what was up. Maia saw Mick kissing Brigid on the beach tonight. I'm giving the ring back.

Baker responded: Can't wait to celebrate your newfound freedom!

Ayers is so tired. She's flattened. She lies in bed until three thirty, which is the last possible moment she can get up and make it to La Tapa on time, but she still can't muster the energy to move. She picks up her phone—there's no word from Mick, or from Baker either, for that matter—and calls La Tapa.

Tilda answers.

"Til," Ayers says. "I can't make it in tonight. I know it's trash of me to bag on you so late but honestly..." Honestly, the mere idea of lifting trays, opening wine, remembering orders—nope, it's beyond her today.

"Don't worry about it," Tilda says. "We have only thirty on the books. Besides"—here, Tilda lowers her voice—"we all know what happened with Mick."

"You do?" Ayers says. She's not sure why she's surprised; it's a tiny island, the coconut telegraph and all that. Brigid is probably crowing about her triumph all around town. Ayers wonders if Mick came by to get the ring. Maybe he gave her ring to Brigid; he is just enough of a cheeseball to do exactly that.

"Yeah, he's staging a sit-in at Cruz Bay Landing. Him and Gordon."

"A what?"

"He's been at the bar at CBL since it opened this morning. He has the ring in front of him. He's stinking drunk and he claims he's not moving until you take him back. Gordon is tied to his bar stool."

"You're kidding me," Ayers says.

"Not kidding, saw it myself," Tilda says. "I think AK is going to cut him off soon, but he might have to call the police to get Mick out of there."

Ayers is slightly revived by the news that Mick is staging a sit-in at Cruz Bay Landing, crying into his beer. So he *is* upset after all.

"He gave me this whole song and dance about how Brigid was taking a new job at Island Abodes, something *he* arranged to get her away from him. And not two days later, they're making out on the beach. I don't care if he sits at CBL for the rest of his life, I don't care if he turns into petrified wood and moss grows on him and a bird builds a nest in his hair, I'm not taking him back."

"Good girl," Tilda says. "You're on the schedule Saturday night. I'll see you then?"

"Yes," Ayers says. "Thanks, Til."

Thursday passes in a blur. Friday comes and Ayers doesn't feel any better. She feels worse—dull, leaden, sluggish, and dizzy. Her coffee tastes sour; food holds no appeal. She doesn't have to work at La Tapa but she's supposed to hang out with Maia in the afternoon.

She can't imagine getting in her truck and driving to Gifft Hill, much less doing some kind of fun, enriching activity. Waterlemon—they were supposed to snorkel at Waterlemon. If Ayers tried to snorkel, she would end up sleeping on the sandy floor of the Caribbean.

She sends Maia a text even though Maia is at school and (technically) not allowed to check her phone: I can't pick you up, Nut. I'm sick.

Two seconds later (so much for the rules), there's a response: It's okay, I'm grounded anyway, plus there's been drama at home.

Drama? Ayers texts. *At home* meaning with Huck? This is unusual.

Too much to text, Maia says. Call me later.

Later is Saturday at noon. It takes everything Ayers has to get out of bed, take a shower (her hair is in the first stages of dreadlocks), and make herself eat a piece of toast at her tiny kitchen table. She fights to keep the toast down. Something is up with her; this isn't just emotional distress. After all, Ayers hiked the Reef Bay Trail only two days after Rosie died.

Ayers checks her arms and legs, praying that she has overlooked some kind of weird bite or sting that would explain this. She'd gone backpacking all over the world with her parents when she was growing up, and she'd witnessed travelers in the throes of all kinds of exotic ailments. There was a pretty, blond college student doing a gap year in Nepal who nearly died of giardia, a couple of Israeli kids in India who had leishmaniasis that they thought they'd gotten from sand flies on Goa, and in Thailand, they'd met a family who had been infested with sea lice.

Leptospirosis? A guy Ayers knows down here contracted that from cleaning palm rats out of traps.

Ayers is making herself sicker just thinking about this. *Stop thinking about it!* She texts Maia. You busy?

A second later, Ayers's phone rings; her screen says Nut and lights up with a picture of Maia at Carnival a few years ago, her face painted royal blue and crimson.

"Hi," Ayers says. "Whatcha doin'?"

"Decorating my new room," Maia says. "Or, as Gramps calls it, 'moving the mess.'"

"New room? Are you..."

"Taking Mama's room," Maia says. "I've slept in here the past two nights." She pauses. "The sheets still smell like her. How long do you think that will last?"

Ayers's heart feels like a dying rose shedding its petals. "Oh, Nut," she says.

"I worry I'm gonna make the smell disappear faster by sleeping in the bed and that one night it won't smell like her, it will smell like me. But I don't have a choice because Irene is sleeping in my room."

"Irene?"

"Yeah," Maia says. "Have you not heard? Baker didn't call you?"

Baker has *not* called her, which she finds strange, since he's supposedly so keen on celebrating her "newfound freedom," but she figures he's been busy getting settled in, and, frankly, she's relieved that he hasn't asked to see her. "No," Ayers says. "Heard what?"

Maia sighs like an adult. "Well, they lost the villa in Little Cinnamon."

This news propels Ayers out of her chair and over to the front window. It's another beautiful day in paradise; things are happening out there while Ayers convalesces. "Lost the...lost the villa? What are you talking about?"

"Gramps said it was tax trouble. But I heard him and Irene talking about the FBI. I think my dad was into something illegal."

Ayers's stomach lurches. She collapses onto the sofa. Hidden underneath it are all of Rosie's journals. Ayers had discovered the journals buried in Rosie's dresser and she'd...absconded with them, taking them from Huck's house. They were Ayers's own private archaeological find, no less precious or revelatory to Ayers than the Dead Sea Scrolls or dinosaur bones. These journals *told Rosie's story,* one Ayers didn't know, and Ayers was Rosie's best friend. Ayers found herself compelled to binge on them but she'd made herself read slowly and carefully. She'd made herself *savor* them.

In the final two volumes are passages in which Rosie described Russ telling her outright back in 2016 that his company, Ascension, sold the lots in Little Cinnamon to fictional entities—shell companies. He admitted to Rosie that Ascension was in the business of hiding money, laundering money. And then, in the very last pages of the journal, Rosie wrote about how Russ had informed his boss, Todd Croft, that he was leaving the company and how Todd Croft had shown up at La Tapa and threatened Rosie.

Six weeks later, both Russ and Rosie were dead.

Now the FBI knows and the villa is gone? Ayers's thoughts are all over the place. Do the FBI agents think Todd Croft killed Russ and Rosie, or do they think it was, in fact, a lightning strike? Ayers remembered hearing thunder that morning. So it was a lightning strike—simple, impossible bad luck. But the scene Rosie described with Todd Croft was...alarming.

The villa is gone.

Ayers can't help but wonder what this means for Baker. Obviously, if there's no place for him to live, then he's going back to Houston.

Ayers feels a deep, crushing disappointment, worse even than her pain about the broken engagement. Baker will leave—if he even arrived in the first place. And what about Cash? Will he leave too?

Ayers brings her mind back to the present. "So Irene is living with you guys?" she says. "For how long?"

"Until she gets back on her feet," Maia says. She lowers her voice. "I think Gramps is happy. He cut my grounding down to a week."

"Won't Irene go back to Iowa?"

"She can't," Maia says. "The FBI took that house too."

"You're kidding."

"I told you, there's been drama."

"What about Cash?" Ayers says. Because *Treasure Island* is out of commission, Ayers hasn't spoken to Cash since Tuesday night. "Is he staying with you guys?"

"He's living with Tilda," Maia says.

Living with Tilda? Ayers knew they were kind of seeing each other; they'd been together the afternoon that Mick proposed at Christmas Cove. That was five days ago. Now they're living together? "Wow," Ayers says. The toast won't settle in her stomach; she feels like it's on a seesaw. Is it coming up or staying down? "Where's Baker?"

"He and Floyd are at the Westin," Maia says. "I'm actually headed there in a little while to watch Floyd while Baker looks at some rentals."

"You are?" Ayers says. She feels a tiny arrow of optimism shoot through her, though she's too lethargic to even smile. "So they're staying?"

"Yes, they're staying. Floyd starts at Gifft Hill on Monday," Maia says. "Wait until I tell everyone he's my nephew."

Oh, boy, Ayers thinks. *The Gifft Hill mothers will have a field day with that.* "Have fun," Ayers says. "I love you; you're my number-one girl. Let's hang out next week."

"We can..." Maia says. "But I might be busy with my friends or babysitting for Floyd."

"Right," Ayers says. "Only if you can fit me in."

"I'll have my people call your people," Maia says, and she hangs up.

Baker is staying! For a second, Ayers's happiness is greater than the dread that she feels about the rest of the story—the lost villa, the FBI, Russ's illegal business dealings.

She should tell someone about the journals; it feels like they're smoldering beneath her. But...they're personal, private. Rosie wouldn't want anyone to see them, of that Ayers is certain. Ayers plans to give them to Maia when she gets older.

The FBI knows Russ was laundering money, so the journals

wouldn't offer anything new. But what about the mentions of Todd Croft? *Was* there foul play with the helicopter?

Argh! Ayers doesn't want to hand the journals over. It's her own private line of communication with Rosie. And if Huck read them, or, worse, *Irene* read them—well, that wouldn't be good. And yet to *hide* them...no, Ayers has to show someone.

She'll show Huck. Or Baker? No, Huck.

I'm sorry, Rosie, Ayers thinks—and then she races to the bathroom to throw up.

CASH

I'm sure you understand my concerns," Granger Payne says.

Before Cash can respond, Granger dives into the T-shaped pool and powers out six laps. Then he lifts himself out of the pool, triceps flexing, and dries his face with one of the fluffy white Turkish towels. Over the past week, Cash has become very familiar with all the luxuries on offer here at Tilda's parents' house in Peter Bay.

Which is precisely Granger's point.

"I do indeed, sir," Cash says. He's relieved that the *Treasure Island* is back up and running and that he's dressed for work. Every day for the past few days, while the boat was being repaired, Cash woke up late with Tilda, and over banana pancakes and mango smoothies, they picked a beach or a trail or both to hike. On Tilda's day off, the two of them climbed into Tilda's Range Rover and drove out to Hansen Bay in the East End. They rented a kayak and spent the entire afternoon drinking grapefruit margaritas and eating the sublime tacos—rum rib with chipotle slaw, green chicken curry—at the floating-barge restaurant Lime Out. Lime Out had bar seats attached to the barge, which Cash and Tilda sat in before claiming a floating table. They reclined on inflatable chaises, faces to the sun, drinks in hand, toasting the good life, which they were undeniably enjoying. Cash had to actively fight off encroaching guilt. His family had just undergone a huge financial crisis and what was Cash doing? Drinking cocktails that his brand-new girlfriend was paying for with her black American Express card.

Granger wraps the towel around his waist. He's about Cash's size, five nine or so, and is in extremely good physical shape, possibly even better shape than Cash, and he's fifty-six years old. The villa has a full gym with two Peloton bikes; Granger and Tilda's mother, Lauren, get up at five thirty every morning to ride together, then Granger does his weight regimen, then he swims.

"Want some green juice?" Granger asks Cash. On the counter of the outdoor kitchen is a carafe of liquid the color of shamrocks. It was most likely put there by Virgie, the housekeeper, who moves around the villa with the stealth of a ninja and who, this past week, has refused to let Cash do so much as take his own dishes to the sink.

Guilt—his mother; Baker; Floyd. If they knew how Cash was living, what would they think? "Sure," Cash says. He accepts a glass of green juice, takes a sip, and immediately wants to spit it out. It's liquefied kale, he suspects, with maybe a thin slice of apple or one green grape thrown in.

"Lauren and I are very protective where Tilda is concerned," Granger says. "She tends to show all her cards. She doesn't have much of a poker face, I'm afraid." Granger gulps down the entire glass of juice and Cash shivers just watching; he's unsure he can manage even one more sip. "It's clear how much she likes you. She says you have other places you can go, so it's not like you're using her to avoid being homeless."

"Right," Cash says quickly. "That's right, sir."

"Please, call me Granger."

"Granger, sir," Cash says. He can't help it; the *sir* comes automatically. Granger Payne is a *sir* as surely as Johnny Cash or Muhammad Ali would be a *sir*. "I could move in with my mother or my brother. And I'll do that if it makes you more comfortable." Here, Cash holds Granger's gaze, willing the older man not to call his bluff. Irene is presently living in Maia's bedroom at Huck's house, and Baker is still at the Westin hemorrhaging five hundred dollars a night while he looks for an affordable year-round rental. Cash told Baker that if he found something big enough, Cash would happily move in, share the rent, provide child care for Floyd.

"Okay," Baker said. "But you'd better have a backup plan."

Cash had initially considered asking Ayers if he could take over her lease, since she had gotten engaged to Mick and would likely move in with him. He wasn't sure how much she paid but if she could afford it, then he could, right? They worked at the same place. But Ayers had a second, very lucrative job waiting tables at La Tapa. Cash would likely need to get a second job as well. He should be looking now instead of goofing off every day with Tilda.

The plan of taking over Ayers's place vanished when Tilda came home from La Tapa with the news that Ayers was no longer engaged. She had given the ring back to Mick.

"Stay here for the time being, please," Granger says. "I have to admit, I like the idea of having another man around. Tilda and her mother tend to gang up on me. I could use some support."

"Thank you, sir," Cash says. He needs to excuse himself so Tilda can drive him to work. He's dependent on her for everything, and she has been a total rock star, accommodating him and never making him feel bad. *I have more than enough privilege for both of us.*

"Tilda tells me you used to be in the outdoor-supply business in Colorado," Granger says. "What happened?"

"Ah," Cash says. He has any number of responses ready: *I got tired of the cold, the lack of oxygen, the stoner teenagers who worked for me stealing from the register.* But he suspects that Granger Payne has run a background check on him and maybe also investigated his credit. "I blew it. My father bought me the stores and expected me to know how to run them. But I didn't learn how to manage them properly until it was too late. I got behind with the bank and they went under. It was quite a learning experience."

"I'm happy to hear you learned something," Granger says. "Because I have an exciting business proposition on the horizon, and Tilda is dead set on having you be a part of it. Sweat equity, boots-on-the-ground type of stuff. You're good with people, I can see that, and you seem to have personal integrity. Another man might have lied to me about the stores or tried to blame the failure on someone else."

Cash nods. Integrity he has. It's everything else he's lacking.

"How well do you handle unexpected setbacks?" Granger asks.

"Um…" Cash says. "Pretty well. I mean, yeah, my life has been one unexpected setback after another recently, but I'm still standing. So I'd say I can deal with just about whatever life throws at me."

"Good," Granger says. "Because although Lauren and I are happy to welcome you with open arms, your dog has to go."

Cash feels like Granger has just taken him into a headlock and is squeezing his windpipe. "Winnie?" he squeaks.

"Winnie," Granger says. "Lauren and I are far too peripatetic to have pets, and the way she decorated the house—"

"In white," Cash says. "Right, I get it." He swallows. "We've kept Winnie mostly outside…"

" 'Mostly outside' won't cut it with my wife," Granger says. "And it's not fair to the dog. So best to find another place for her to wait out this time of transition you're in."

"Yes, sir," Cash says. He's saved from breaking down in tears in front of Granger when Tilda honks the horn of the Range Rover. "Steele, let's go!" she calls out.

"Exactly like her mother," Granger says. He claps Cash on the arm. "All right, Cashman, glad we understand each other."

On the steep, twisting drive from Peter Bay to town, Tilda says, "How was the inquisition?"

"Most of it was okay. But—"

"But it was a complete ambush," Tilda says. "I know. I'm sorry. They normally text or call to let me know they're coming so I can go to Starfish and get their soy milk or whatever. This is highly unusual. I think after I told them you were staying here, they wanted to catch us unawares."

They succeeded, Cash thinks. The night before, Tilda got home from La Tapa bearing goodies from the kitchen in to-go boxes—a gorgonzola Caesar, pork belly, and wood-grilled sirloin. They lit the candles on the patio table; Tilda opened a good bottle of cabernet from Granger's wine collection—the Lail 2016 Blueprint—and after she tasted it, she winked at Cash and said, "Notes of fire coral, DEET, and the Tide Pod challenge."

"Good one!" Cash said. Nonsensical wine descriptions had become a verbal tic of Tilda's ex, Skip, the bartender at La Tapa, and Tilda and Cash couldn't stop themselves from riffing on it.

They had just picked up their forks to dig in when they heard voices, and Cash, for one panicked moment, feared another FBI raid—were they coming for *him?*—but then Tilda scooted back her chair and said, "Well, hello, parents!"

"Don't you two look cozy," Lauren Payne said. She was tall with a slender yoga physique like Tilda, but while Tilda sported a pixie cut, Lauren had long golden-brown hair that she'd pulled up in a ponytail. She wore a white linen dress and a pair of leopard-print wedge sandals. She was...pretty. And looked way younger than Cash had expected.

Granger followed close on Lauren's heels. He wore a tan suit, white shirt, and no tie; he had his hair slicked back, and reading glasses were perched on top of his head. His handshake was brutal, but somehow Cash had anticipated this and gave his firmest effort, complete with eye contact and smile. On the inside, however, Cash felt his confidence evaporate. Her parents were here. What would they think about Cash moving in? Did they know what had happened to his father? His mother? The optics weren't great; Cash realized this. His father, now dead, had been revealed to have a second family hidden down here, and his sketchy—indeed *illegal*—business practices had been uncovered. His mother was newly destitute and worked on a fishing boat.

It wasn't exactly the platinum pedigree that the elder Paynes no doubt wanted for the romantic partner of their only child.

However, the only thing Tilda's parents had objected to in that moment was her opening the 2016 Blueprint. Granger fetched two balloon goblets from the crystal cabinet (Tilda and Cash were drinking the wine out of regular tumblers) and poured wine for himself and Lauren, then they retreated to the master wing, which was so far from Tilda's wing that it was like a separate house.

When Cash asked how much Tilda's parents knew about his situation, she said, "I tell my mother everything and she tells my dad."

"And do they...care?"

"Granger will probably have questions in the morning," Tilda said.

But neither Tilda nor Cash had thought about the dog.

"So *most* of it was okay," Tilda says now. "But not all of it?"

Cash thinks back to the first time Tilda brought him to the Peter Bay villa. Tilda and Cash were caring for Tilda's very drunk friend Max, and Cash had noticed the villa's terrifyingly white furnishings because he was afraid Max might vomit on them. And then later, at dinner, Tilda told Cash she volunteered to walk dogs at the shelter because *her parents wouldn't let her get a dog of her own.*

But Tilda hadn't balked for even one second about Cash bringing Winnie with him, though she did suggest Winnie stay only in Tilda's wing of the house. (The line about Winnie living mostly outside was a lie.) And Virgie, the housekeeper, had seemed not only unbothered by Winnie but downright delighted by her. She had even brought Winnie treats!

"Your dad told me Winnie has to go," Cash says.

They have reached the parking lot across from Mongoose Junction. Tilda pulls in. "I was afraid of that."

"I'm not sure what to do," Cash says.

"Your mom?" Tilda says. "Baker?"

"Maybe?" Cash says. Baker is at a hotel, so the answer is no, or not yet. His mother...argh. She loves Winnie, but she's a guest herself, just like Cash. He manufactures a smile. "I'll figure something out. Can you come pick me up at four? If not, I'll hitch."

"If you think I'm going to let someone else pick you up, you're crazy," she says, and she leans over for a kiss.

"Thank you," Cash says.

"You're not allowed to thank me."

"I know, but...I want you to know that I'm grateful. The timing on all of this was so...bad. Our relationship is still so new and you've done so much."

"All I've really done is save you from pining after Ayers," Tilda says. "I told my mother you used to have a crush on her."

"You did not," Cash says. "Why did you do that? It wasn't even a thing."

"It *was* a thing," Tilda says. "But it's over now."

"Over before it began," Cash says. "Please don't tell me you're worried about Ayers."

"She's newly single," Tilda says, shrugging. "And you're with her every day."

Cash takes Tilda's face in his hands. He did have quite an intense crush on Ayers when he first got down here—he and Baker both did—but she ended up with Mick, and Cash's feelings for her vanished as quickly as they'd appeared. He can still see she's attractive, but all he feels for her is a brotherly fondness.

"I like *you,*" Cash says. He looks into Tilda's hazel eyes. She's so young, and yet so self-possessed and clearheaded and *unspoiled* despite her parents' wealth.

"You'd better."

"I do."

"I feel bad about Winnie," Tilda says. "But my parents will not be moved on the topic of a dog. I'm so sorry." She kisses him again. "See you at four."

*   *   *

What is he going to do about Winnie? What is he going to *do?*
He feels unreasonably angry at Tilda's parents. Winnie is such a
good dog—the best of dogs. She's more human than dog. They
would realize that if they took the time to get to know her.

My parents will not be moved on the topic of a dog.

It's their villa, they make the rules, and they aren't bad people
just because they aren't dog people. What Cash is angry about is
that he has no power. He's at the mercy of others.

Peripatetic. Cash Googles it: "Of or relating to traveling or
moving frequently; in particular, working or based in various
places for short periods. Synonyms: *nomadic, itinerant.*"

Fortunately or unfortunately, there's no time to ruminate on
the situation with Winnie. *Treasure Island* has a completely full
charter today since the boat has been out of commission for over
a week, and the first person Cash sees is the captain, James, who
does not look happy.

James is six foot six, West Indian, and though he's only a little
older than Cash, Cash thinks of him as a *sir.*

It's seven thirty on the dot, so being late isn't the issue,
though there's already a line of passengers waiting to check in,
including a group of forty-something women who, Cash can tell,
are ready for a good time. He thinks back to the charter when
he babysat Tilda's drunk friend Max and decides then and there
that he's not opening the bar until the snorkeling part of their
trip is over.

"Hey, bruh," James says and he shakes Cash's hand. "Ayers
isn't coming. She called in sick."

"Called in sick?"

"Yeah, bruh, so you're on your own today." James glances over at the group of women, who are making no secret of checking out James and Cash. "Good luck."

Cash can't believe Ayers called in sick on their first day back. She had all of last week to be sick. He wonders if maybe "sick" has something to do with her broken engagement. Maybe she's depressed? Should Cash be worried? He'll text her later. Right now, he has to check in twenty-seven people, record their passport information (since they're heading to the British Virgin Islands), and collect their money. Mr. and Mrs. Bellhorn from Coral Gables would like to talk to Cash about getting a partial refund since the boat's mechanical issues pushed this trip back five days, which was quite an inconvenience.

The phrase *partial refund* spreads like a virus. Everyone in line starts to repeat it because every single person—except for the group of women, who are from Wichita, Kansas—was originally scheduled to come on a different day.

Cash nearly makes a stern announcement that he isn't the person who handles refunds and if they want to explore that possibility, they need to call the office, but then he realizes that without Ayers, he has an opportunity to shine—and by *shine* he means "make some serious tip money." In an instant, his attitude changes. He's not going to be grouchy Cash who has been left to do the paperwork and make the breakfast and wash the snorkel equipment and check the lines and make sure no one goes overboard and give the historical and ecological details of the Virgin Islands by himself. He is going to be warm, funny, solicitous, helpful Cash. He is going to go out of his way to ensure this is the best charter these twenty-seven people have ever been on.

"This is the number for the main office," Cash says, sliding Mr. and Mrs. Bellhorn a card. "You want to ask for Whitney. I certainly hope she offers you a partial refund, though of course I can't guarantee it. I'm very sorry about the inconvenience. I'm a planner myself and I do appreciate your patience."

Cash smiles. The Bellhorns smile back.

Okay, then. Next!

Somehow, Cash gets it done—everyone present, documented, paid up, and on board enjoying the fruit platter and the coconut-banana bread. People are applying sunscreen. Cash puts on Kenny Chesney's "Get Along." The ladies from Wichita belt out, *"We ain't perfect but we try!"* That's Cash's motto today as well. No matter that he's flying solo, no matter that he's been on this job only a few weeks, no matter that his father is dead and his mother broke and his dog homeless. He's in the Caribbean; the turquoise water is smooth, and the emerald-green islands create an artistic landscape. He doesn't want to leave St. John, ever. He needs to find someone to take Winnie, at least for a while. He needs to find a way to make his life work.

Granger has a business proposition "on the horizon" that Tilda wants Cash involved in. Yes, Tilda has been talking ambitiously about opening a business—adventure ecotourism, which would be right in Cash's wheelhouse. Boots on the ground, sweat equity. He doesn't have to front any money; he just has to show up. Cash wishes that *on the horizon* meant next week or even tomorrow.

Cash is the only crew member and James thinks the planned itinerary—a trip to the Baths, snorkeling at the Indians, and then two hours of merrymaking on Jost Van Dyke—will be too much for Cash to handle alone. Instead, James says, they're going to Smuggler's Cove, on the western tip of Tortola, followed by stops at Sandy Spit and Willy T's.

"Oh, man," Cash says. "Are you sure about that? I've never been to any of those places."

"They'll snorkel first thing in Smuggler's Cove," James says. "There's a beautiful beach and they can have lunch at Nigel's. Then back on the boat to Sandy Spit. Then Willy T's for an hour, then home." James starts the engine. "Trust me."

What choice does Cash have?

He's afraid the passengers will rise up in protest. Not only have many of them had this trip rescheduled, but now they're not even going where they were supposed to go. They aren't going to the Baths on Virgin Gorda, which is an experience like no other, and they aren't going to the world-famous Soggy Dollar.

He expects a mutiny.

But then he gets an idea.

He heads up to the top deck where the nine women from Wichita are sitting. Midwesterners are *nice,* they're *helpful*—Cash knows this because he is one. When Cash checked the women in—Christine, Stephanie, Kelly, Amy, Jennifer P., Jennifer A., Michelle, Tracy, and Donna—he learned that it was Donna's fiftieth birthday. Over their bathing suits, the women all wore navy T-shirts that read DONNA, DO YOU WANNA?, which Christine told him was a private joke.

"Ladies," Cash says. "I need a favor."

He tells them what the favor is and they fall all over themselves assuring him that they've got his back. He's so cute, he's so hot, they say, and all they want in return are some pictures with him for their Instagrams and a promise that he'll hold Donna's hand as she jumps off the Willy T. (Michelle read on Tripadvisor that jumping off the Willy T is a bucket-list item, which is news to Cash.)

"Yes, I will, I got you," Cash says. "Thank you, ladies."

Cash gets ready to announce the change of itinerary over the microphone; it's his first time wearing the headset, and he has to admit, he kind of likes the authority. "The captain is allowing us a rare and exciting opportunity today, ladies and gentlemen," Cash says. "We're heading over to Smuggler's Cove on Tortola, where we will snorkel in the crystal-clear water and then you'll have ample time to enjoy the secluded white sand beach. If you'd like lunch and cocktails, you can visit Nigel's Boom Boom for a taste of the authentic Caribbean. When we leave Smuggler's Cove, we'll swing by Sandy Spit for a terrific photo op. We'll end our day at the world-famous Willy T's, a decommissioned freighter that has been reimagined as a beach-bar mecca. How does that sound to everyone?"

From the top deck comes the sound of ecstatic screaming and everyone looks up to see Donna, Christine, and company jumping up and down as though they've just been picked as contestants on *The Price Is Right.* The other passengers do high fives and cheer like they can't believe their good fortune.

Cash relaxes. He's good at this.

James is right; this itinerary is extremely easy for Cash to manage, even alone. They arrive in Smuggler's Cove in just half an hour. The beach is a crescent of white sand fringed by palms, and it's deserted, as though it has been ordered up and is waiting just for them. James asks Cash to drop the anchor and then he runs through the snorkel spiel. *Defog your mask with this simple solution of dish soap and water; stay away from fire coral and the spiny black sea urchins, nothing else in these waters will hurt you.*

"And after you finish your snorkel," Cash says, "we'll open the bar."

Cheers. Zac Brown sings "Chicken Fried." *There's no dollar sign on a peace of mind, this I've come to know.*

The day unfolds without a hitch. Cash joins his new lady friends from Wichita at Nigel's Boom Boom, where Nigel himself makes the best hot dog with griddled onions Cash has ever tasted. The ladies ask him questions that he avoids answering in detail, but they're into Nigel's rum punch, so they don't really notice. *My first winter in St. John, I came down here to be with my mother after my father died* (the ladies *love* this; he's so sensitive, such a devoted son). *I used to be a ski instructor in Breckenridge, then I lived in Denver for a while, but I've traded in my ski boots for flip-flops, my poles and goggles for a mask and snorkel, and I'm staying here. Yes, I have a girlfriend, Tilda, the relationship is pretty much brand-new.*

"Well," Amy says, "I hope she knows how lucky she is!"

They leave Smuggler's Cove and head to Sandy Spit, which is half an acre of pure white sand with light foliage, including a couple of palms, making it look like a Corona ad. Everyone jumps off the boat to swim ashore, and Cash takes pictures with his ladies for their Instagrams.

Then it's off to the Willy T, properly the William Thornton, the floating bar named for an infamous nineteenth-century pirate. They tie up, and the nine ladies head directly upstairs to the bar and order the shot ski, something Cash is only too familiar with from the bars in Breckenridge. The "ski" has four holes for four shot glasses and on the count of three, four of the ladies lift the ski to their mouths and do the shots in unison. Because there are only four shots per ski, this has to be repeated a number of times so the other passengers from the *Treasure Island—*

including the inconvenienced Mr. and Mrs. Bellhorn—can take turns as well.

The ladies want Cash to do the shot ski—it's a bar trick that never gets old—but no, sorry, he says, he's on the clock. He can, however, fulfill his promise to step out onto the jumping platform, twelve feet above the water's surface, and jump off while holding Donna's hand. Cash won't lie; he's a little nervous, even though he'd think nothing of a ski jump this steep.

He checks in with the birthday girl when they're standing on the platform. "Donna, do you wanna?" he asks, thinking he's the epitome of wit, but she doesn't answer, just flings herself forward, and Cash has no choice but to follow.

Shot skis, jumping from high ledges—what could go wrong? Nothing, as it turns out. It's exhilarating. Everyone loves it, everyone's happy. The day is a resounding success.

It's only after Cash has mixed up the last batch of painkillers and the charter is on the way home that he thinks to text Ayers.

Missed you today, he says. This is true. Today went well but it would have been easier and more fun with Ayers. You okay?

A couple of seconds later, she sends the thumbs-up emoji, which tells him nothing but the bare minimum: she's alive. Cash is debating whether or not to ask a follow-up question—emoji answers sort of discourage longer text exchanges—when she texts again.

I'm taking a leave of absence from the boat.

What? he writes. Why?

I heard about your mom, she says. How're you doing?

Cash feels like sending back a thumbs-up emoji as a little *Screw you,* because what does she mean, she's taking a leave of absence from the boat? But what he says is I'm living up at Tilda's but today her parents said Winnie has to go so I'm scrambling.

There's a pause. Then three dots. Then: I'll take Winnie if you want?

Cash quickly checks on everyone. They're happy, the sun has mellowed, Jimmy Buffett is singing "Nautical Wheelers."

If you wouldn't mind for a few weeks? I would be so grateful.

Happy to, Ayers says. I'll pick you up at the boat and we can go get her.

Ahh! Cash feels an overwhelming sense of relief. Ayers will take Winnie; Winnie is crazy about Ayers, she's going to think she's died and gone to heaven. This is a good solution, much better than asking the housekeeper, Virgie, to take the dog home, which was Cash's only other idea.

Cash texts Tilda: I don't need a ride, Ayers will bring me to Peter Bay, she's going to take Winnie.

Tilda texts back: Kk. There is no heart-eyes emoji, her signature signoff, which is odd.

Cash texts, Are you okay? He thinks about what Tilda said about Ayers that morning: *She's newly single.* But come on, Tilda can't be *that* sensitive. And the bald fact remains that Cash needs someone to take Winnie.

Tilda texts, I'm fine. I have a meeting anyway. I was going to tell you to hitch.

Okay...should Cash be offended? Because he's feeling a little offended. A meeting with whom?

No time to wonder because the boat is pulling in. And yes indeedy, the tip jar is filling up.

*   *   *

Cash is standing in front of Mongoose Junction three hundred and ten dollars richer when Ayers arrives in her little green pickup.

"Hop in," she says. She really does look sick—pale, washed out, heavy-lidded. She's wearing cotton sleep shorts and a St. John Concrete T-shirt (STAY LEFT, POUR RIGHT), and her curly blond hair is a mess. Not a sexy mess, just a mess.

"I hope whatever you have isn't contagious," Cash says, getting in.

She hits the gas.

"So...you broke things off with Mick?" Ayers nods but doesn't offer anything else. Fine, she doesn't owe him an explanation. "How did you know about my mom?"

"Maia told me."

"Oh, right," Cash says. He hates to be a talker but he feels like there's something going on. "Have you seen Baker?"

"He called once but I didn't pick up," Ayers says. "I'm not feeling great and I need some time."

"Right, right," Cash says. He will stop talking even though he wants to brag about how smoothly the charter went.

They swoop and dive around and over the hills—past Caneel, past Oppenheimer and Jumbie, past everyone packing up from a day spent at Trunk Bay—and then begin the climb up to Peter Bay. Cash speaks only to direct Ayers to the correct house. They careen down Tilda's driveway, and when Ayers stops, Cash hops out. "I'll go get Winnie, her food, her bowl, her leashes. Be right back."

He returns with Winnie in tow and there's a bit of a long goodbye because although Winnie is going to the best possible home, Cash is still going to miss her like crazy. "I'll come see her tomorrow after work," he says. "I can't thank you enough."

"You don't have to thank me," Ayers says. She sighs, and if

Cash isn't mistaken, her eyes glaze over like she might cry. "The more the merrier."

The more the merrier? Cash thinks. He wonders if maybe Mick has left Ayers with his dog—that would be weird—and then he wonders if maybe Ayers plans on letting Baker and Floyd move in with her.

"Are you...do you have company?" Cash asks.

"Kind of," Ayers says. "I'm pregnant."

MAIA

Her grounding lasts six days instead of two weeks, but even so, Maia misses the first meeting at the new clubhouse. She arrives at the second meeting early, by herself; everyone else is getting a ride but because Huck and Irene have tripled up on their charters, Maia has to take the bus and then hike. The new clubhouse is *very* inconveniently located in the middle of nowhere— but that's the point. It's Par Force, the great house of the Reef Bay plantation, and it can be accessed only by a spur of the Reef Bay Trail. Maia hikes down the trail, and when the three tourists ahead of her veer to the right to see the petroglyphs, Maia goes left up a steep hill that switchbacks up an even steeper hill. Par Force is engulfed in vines and coral creeper; the brick walls and stone columns are barely visible. There's a low hum surrounding the house that sounds like some kind of electrical force field. It's bees, Maia realizes, feasting on the pretty pink flowers of the creeper. Maia heads up the staircase to the main entryway. Unlike most of the ruins of houses on the island, this one still looks like a house. It has arches and columns and window openings, and the walls and roof are still mostly there.

But—Maia's not gonna lie—it's spooky, even during the daytime, and she wishes someone else were here. They all agreed they would meet at two thirty on Saturday; earlier today, Bright had basketball practice, Colton guitar lessons, and Shane an orthodontist appointment over on St. Thomas. Joanie is getting a ride from her mom, who's happy Joanie and her friends are "finally taking an interest in hiking."

Maia tries to text Joanie to ask if she's OTW, but she has no signal. In her backpack, she has three bottles of water, a peanut butter and jelly sandwich, and a banana, so she won't die, but the idea of hanging out here alone much longer doesn't appeal. Maia's mother, Rosie, had brought her to Par Force only the year before. *I can't believe I've never shown you this place,* she said. Then, once they were inside: *I probably avoided it because it's haunted.*

Now that Rosie is dead, ghosts aren't as scary as they used to be. Maia would welcome a visit from Rosie right now, in any form. Because where is everyone? She worries that this is some kind of prank, that while she was grounded, the rest of the group decided to trick her into going alone. Or maybe at the first meeting, they picked a different clubhouse location—Annaberg or Catherineberg, somewhere easier to get to—and forgot to tell Maia. Maia scrolls back through her texts with Joanie. Meet you at the place. Leaving for the place now.

Snap, Maia thinks. What if *the place* Joanie is talking about isn't *this* place?

But then Maia hears voices. She pokes her head through one of the crumbling stone window openings to see Joanie, Colton, and some girl Maia doesn't recognize all climbing up the hill together.

"Hey," Maia says. She's relieved to see her friends but she wishes it were Shane. Shane is a year older than Maia and he goes to the Antilles School; he's her crush, and recently he's become more than just a crush. They have held hands on three separate occasions. Joanie has a crush on Colton, but Colton likes Joanie only as a friend. For now. Both Maia and Joanie are hoping the clubhouse—where they're going to hang out without any adults watching them—will change this.

"Maia!" Joanie cries out. She runs up the stairs and gives Maia a hug, which seems a little strange since they just saw each other at school the day before, then gives Maia's hand an extra-hard squeeze. It's a message of some sort about this unknown girl. Friend or foe?

Colton and the girl follow.

Maia says, "Hey, I'm Maia." The girl has milky-white skin, long red hair, and a pointy nose. She's wearing white shorts and a regular pair of beach flip-flops that show off her green-polished toenails and silver toe rings. How did she hike all the way here in flip-flops?

"I'm Lillibet," she says, shrugging. She peers around the dank inside of Par Force. "I'm in seventh; I go to Antilles. Is Shane here?"

"Not yet," Maia says. "He had the ortho—"

"Yeah, I know, but he said he'd be here waiting."

"You know who Lillibet's sister is, right, Maia?" Colton says. "Dusty. Dusty Beck."

Maia tries to hide her surprise. Dusty Beck is a bona fide St. Thomas celebrity. Maia—along with twelve million other people—follows Dusty on Instagram. Dusty was on the cover of last year's *Sports Illustrated* swimsuit issue, and Shane has a copy that she signed; he'd said he got it from "a kid in my class." Which must have been the sister, Lillibet. What is she doing here?

"Cool," Maia says. Joanie, behind Lillibet, has her arms locked across her chest and is rolling her eyes. Not cool with Joanie. Okay, then, not cool with Maia either. "Shane invited you?" Maia asks.

"Hey!"

They all turn to see Shane and Bright Whittaker racing up the hill. Maia tries to harden her facial expression, form it into some kind of shell. They created this club the night they met on the beach in Frank Bay because Colton was upset about his parents' divorce. Colton is staying on St. John with his mom, but his dad is moving back to the States—to North Carolina, the Outer Banks—and Colton will see him only half the summer and at Christmas. As they were talking to Colton that night, trying to make him feel better, it came out that they all had stuff to deal with at home and no one to talk to about it. (That was really true for Maia—her mother had died and a new family had appeared out of nowhere!) So they'd decided to form a club and have meetings in person, not online, which felt old-fashioned in a cool way. They weren't allowed to discuss club business on their phones. They weren't allowed to take any pictures or post about the club. It would be a secret society, like the kind they had at Harvard and Yale.

Maia didn't realize they were allowed to invite outsiders to join. She'd thought it was supposed to be just them—Maia, Shane, Joanie, Colton, and Bright. But five is an odd number, so Maia supposes adding another girl makes sense. She had sort of figured they would discuss it first and vote. But this isn't Congress or Parliament; it's a bunch of middle-school kids in the Virgin Islands.

Maia decides to give Lillibet the benefit of the doubt. Maybe Shane invited her for a reason—maybe her sister the model is addicted to drugs, or maybe Lillibet is being bullied at school, or maybe Lillibet's parents ignore her because Dusty is so pretty and famous.

"Shane!" Lillibet screams. She goes flying down the steps in her stupid flip-flops, and forget the benefit of the doubt—Maia wishes for her to fall flat on her face. But she doesn't. She goes up to Shane and says, "Let me see."

Shane smiles. His braces are off.

Whaaaa? Maia thinks. She knew Shane had the orthodontist but she didn't know he was getting his braces off. Unfair! He looks hotter now than he did before by, like, a *lot.*

Lillibet squeals and gives Shane a side hug and Shane leans into her.

They all head deeper into Par Force and wander through different rooms until they come to what must have been the kitchen—there's a giant fireplace opening. There are a bunch of piles of bricks that they can sit on.

Shane turns to Maia. "Are you surprised the braces are off? What do you think?"

She shrugs. She isn't going to fawn all over him like Lillibet.

Lillibet is touching the columns, poking her head through the window openings. "This place is sublime," she says. "What's it doing here?"

"This was the main living quarters of the family who owned the sugarcane plantation," Maia says. She gives an ironic laugh. "So two hundred years ago, someone who looked like me would have been working in this kitchen as a slave."

Everyone is quiet. Maia has made her friends uncomfortable, but oh, well—the history of the Virgin Islands is uncomfortable.

Lillibet says, "Maybe we should meet somewhere else? Do you want to pick a different place, Maia?" Her voice is concerned without being patronizing, and the benefit of the doubt resurfaces. Is Lillibet *nice?*

"It doesn't bother me," Maia says. "My mom brought me here." She hopes that mentioning Rosie will lead them into the kind of soulful conversation that they had on Frank Bay, but nobody is paying attention to Maia except Lillibet.

"Shane told me that your mother was killed in that helicopter crash on New Year's," Lillibet says. "I felt so bad for you. And honestly, you're kind of famous at Antilles now. I knew Shane was your friend, so I asked to meet you."

Lillibet is here because of Maia? This *sounds* like a compliment, but it also makes Maia feel like a circus sideshow. *Famous* at Antilles? Because she tragically lost her mother?

"It's too bad we can't meet at the villa in Little Cinnamon," Shane says. He turns to Lillibet. "Maia's dad...it *was* your dad, right? Your real dad that nobody knew about? Yeah, he was really rich and owned this huge villa with a two-story pool. Maia gets to hang out there whenever she wants."

"A two-story pool?" Lillibet says.

Maia feels like her heart is being stung by a swarm of bees. She has confided a lot to Shane, but the things she told him were private, and here he is, telling everyone.

Maia shrugs. She isn't about to admit that the villa has been seized by the FBI. She can't afford to be any more "famous" at Antilles than she already is.

Colton and Bright are watching a YouTube video of surfing in Portugal on Bright's phone, and Joanie joins them. Maia nearly says, *I thought we said no phones,* but she doesn't want to sound like a teacher or a parent.

"I have no service," Maia says—to no one, because Shane is now telling Lillibet the gory details of getting his braces off. Maia could join in and say, *That sounds like medieval torture,* but she knows three's a crowd. She takes a minute to study Shane and Lillibet together. They're just two kids talking, right? Or does Shane *like* Lillibet? They move on to the topic of their math teacher, then to something that happened at morning meeting the day before, and then Shane relates all the near-death experiences he's had taking the shuttle to Antilles from the Red Hook ferry. Maia smiles to herself, pretending to be deep in thought. If Lillibet is here because she wanted to meet Maia, then why is she talking only to Shane? Maia doesn't go to Antilles. She wants to, but her mother said not until ninth grade.

Maia wonders if there will be enough money to pay for Antilles, or college—Irene had said she'd handle it, since Russ was gone, but now Irene has no money. What if Huck hasn't saved enough and Maia can't go to college in the States like she wants to?

She feels like demanding everyone's attention so she can bring up this monumental issue—her entire future hangs in the balance—but looking around, she realizes no one will care. Colton and Bright are engrossed in the video; Joanie is shamelessly hanging over Colton's shoulder (later, Maia will suggest Joanie stop being so obvious). Lillibet and Shane are talking, and maybe they've inched closer together, maybe Lillibet is flipping her hair for Shane's benefit.

Here is the group the five of them created because they had no one to talk to about the important stuff, and Maia still has no one to talk to about the important stuff.

She sits unnoticed for five minutes, ten—then the boys' interest in the video ends and Colton says, "This clubhouse sucks. There's nothing to do."

Maia can't help herself. "We were supposed to *talk*," she says. "Remember?" *Remember crying on the beach about your parents and remember who was there to listen?*

Lillibet checks her phone. "I've got to go," she says. "My dad's coming to get me in our boat in twenty minutes and I have to get down to the beach." She looks at Shane. "Do you want a ride back to Chocolate Hole? It's on our way."

Shane raises his eyebrows. He seems like a different person without his braces. Older. Out of Maia's league.

"Can you take..." he starts, casting his eyes around.

"I live in Coral Bay," Joanie says. "Wrong direction."

"It should probably be just you," Lillibet says. "My dad knows you."

Say no, Maia thinks. She and Shane can hike back up to the Centerline together. She'll share her sandwich with him, her banana. They can help each other up the steep parts. It's frightening how bad she wants this.

"Okay," Shane says. He stands up and gives the rest of them a wave. His eyes linger on Maia and she looks down into her lap. She knows it's unreasonable to expect Shane to turn down a boat ride home. It's a ten-minute walk downhill to the beach—Lillibet will be fine in her flip-flops after all—and then he'll be back in Chocolate Hole ten minutes after that. But still, it feels like Shane is choosing Lillibet over Maia.

There are goodbyes but they don't pick another day and time to meet. Shane and Lillibet race each other down the trail, with Lillibet, predictably, shrieking. Maia's insides have become crumbling ruins. Ahhh—but just like Par Force, she has a sturdy foundation. It's a nice thought that doesn't make her feel any better.

"I'm leaving too," Maia announces.

"Well, wait for us," Joanie says.

"Yeah," Bright says, and he tugs on Maia's ponytail. "Wait for us."

Maia backhands Bright against the chest. She dislikes anyone touching her hair. Bright grabs her arm and pokes her in the ribs, then tries to tickle her. She shoos him away.

"My mom can probably give you a ride home," Bright says to Maia. "It's not that far."

Bright lives on Gifft Hill, across from the school. It's not that far but it's not close either. Bright probably has a crush on her. He used to like Posie Alvarez, but that's over. Maia thinks about how easy it would be if she could just transfer the feelings she has for Shane to Bright. Bright is in her grade and he goes to Gifft Hill. He's tall and he's good at sports and his parents own a rental-car company, which is cool because he gets driven around in all these brand-new Jeeps in juicy colors. But Maia likes Bright only as a friend. Probably because she knows him too well; she remembers when he threw up during library time in second grade.

Colton and Bright run up ahead, leaving Maia and Joanie to eat their dust.

"Hey, wait up!" Joanie says. "Cole!"

Her mother was right, Maia thinks. Love is messy and complicated. And, most of all, unfair.

IRENE

Because she no longer has a vehicle of her own, Irene joins Huck on his errands after their fishing charter. This means going to a few places:

1. Starfish Market for (most) groceries. It's BYOB—bring your own bag. Huck keeps a stash of reusable shopping bags behind the driver's seat of his truck, which Irene finds charming. Russ rarely (if ever) shopped for groceries, and the idea of him remembering reusable shopping bags is laughable.

2. Papaya Café and Bookstore for a Vietnamese coffee and a browse through the stacks of used books. Huck is a particular fan of the coffee (he has turned Irene on to it as well) and of Michael Connelly. He's patiently waiting for some tourist to turn in a copy of *Dark Sacred Night*. In the meantime, he buys a James Patterson novel, one of the Women's Murder Club series, which he says aren't half bad.

"I'll take your word for it," Irene says.

"Why don't you pick out a book?" Huck says. "My treat."

It's kindnesses like this that make Irene emotional. She thinks back to New Year's Day, her dinner at the Pullman Bar and Diner with Lydia followed by a trip to Prairie Lights, where Irene thought nothing of buying whatever books struck her fancy. Now it feels like an unreasonable luxury to spend ten or twelve dollars on a used book. Irene shops carefully. What will help her escape? She finds a well-loved copy of *The Vacationers* by Emma Straub for six bucks. She hands it to Huck. She wishes they were merely vacationers.

"Thank you," she says.

Huck studies the cover. "Maybe I'll read it when you're done. Do you want a coffee too, AC?"

She has stopped trying to get him not to use the nickname. She likes it more than she cares to admit. "Please," she says.

3. Pine Peace Market for beer, wine, and a fresh bottle of Flor de Caña. Best prices.
4. St. John Market for anything they didn't have at Starfish. St. John Market is right across from the Westin resort and time-shares, so it's heavily populated by fish-belly-pale tourists buying groceries. (It's to be avoided at all costs on Saturdays, when families arrive for the week; Irene learned this the hard way.)

A few days earlier, Irene bumped into her own son at St. John Market. Baker was buying a jar of peanut butter and a loaf of white bread, for Floyd's school lunches, Irene assumed. He had been too busy considering the ingredients on the peanut butter jar to register any surprise at seeing Irene. (Maybe he wasn't surprised, Irene thought. It was a small island.)

"This isn't organic," he said. "And it has a lot of sugar." He held up the bread. "This isn't sprouted whole-grain spelt or whatever. If my school wives from Houston saw this, they'd stage an intervention."

"They'll never know," Irene said, and she and Baker shared a smile for the first time in what felt like forever.

Irene and Huck had also bumped into Ayers Wilson at St. John Market. They were walking in while Ayers was untying Winnie from the railing outside.

"There's my granddog!" Irene said, crouching down to rub Winnie's silky butterscotch head. Winnie's tail was going nuts. Winnie was happy to see Irene—but Ayers seemed to be another story.

"Hey," Ayers said flatly. She didn't look good. Her hair was unbrushed, her eyes puffy, her skin sallow. Cash had told Irene that Ayers had taken a leave of absence from the boat and also that her engagement had ended, leaving her free to care for Winnie.

"I owe you a huge thank-you for helping Cash out," Irene said. "I'm not sure what would have happened otherwise."

"It's no big deal," Ayers said. "I like having her around...good distraction and all that. It gets me outside a couple of times a day, anyway."

"Are you okay, honey?" Huck asked. "If you don't mind my saying so, you look like death on a stick."

"Huck!" Irene said.

"It's okay," Ayers said. "I'm just...going through some stuff right now." She frowned at Huck. "And I've been meaning...there's something I need to talk to you about. Later. I'll call you later."

"Anytime," Huck said.

Irene wanted to ask Ayers if she knew that Baker was staying at the Westin or if she knew Baker was moving to the island permanently if he could find a suitable rental, but she couldn't get into everything that had happened while they were all there at the store, so Irene said, "We're on the hunt for mangoes for Maia," and Ayers led Winnie back to her little green truck.

Huck said, "Did she seem off to you?"

"Yes," Irene said. "But you should never tell a woman she looks anything less than radiant."

"Oops," Huck said.

5. St. John Business Center. This is where Huck picks up his mail. There's always a long line of people who need to scan or make copies or ship something back to the States. Last time, Irene went inside with Huck. Candice, the woman in charge, asked Huck if Irene was his new lady friend, and Huck said, "Irene is my business partner," and Candice said, "Okay, if that's what you want to call it."

This time, Irene stays in the truck. She has now been living with Huck for nearly two weeks, and everyone on the island must think they're a couple. Irene has far bigger worries than what other people think, but she has decided it's best to maintain a bit of distance by letting Huck get his own mail. There are still condolence letters about Rosie that arrive, and there are bills for the house. Irene has tried to contribute to the household but Huck says, *Absolutely not.*

And, frankly, Irene is relieved.

Huck emerges from the business center holding a square, flat package and grinning. He's got his sunglasses on and his visor; he wears a navy bandanna around his neck. *He's handsome when he smiles,* Irene thinks. *He's handsome all the time. He's strong, he's kind, he's trustworthy, he's honest.*

But she's not ready.

He comes to her window and hands her the package. "For you."

"Me?" She studies the package. It's from M. Key in Iowa City.

Mavis Key has sent Irene...what?

Milly's picture! Irene opens the box, slides out the bubble-wrapped bundle inside, untapes it, unfolds it, and yes—there's Milly's portrait. Irene's eyes fill with tears. Mavis got it back. Amazing. Simply amazing.

"Look," Irene says, showing the picture to Huck. "This is Russ's mother, Milly, back in 1928 in Erie, Pennsylvania. Who does she remind you of?"

Huck takes the picture. "God*damn*," he says. "Maia is her spitting image."

Irene leans back against the seat and closes her eyes. "I'm going to give that picture to Maia. Thank God Mavis got it back."

"There's a note here," Huck says.

Irene opens her eyes and Huck pulls a card from a corner of the frame.

Call Nat! the note says. There's a number.

Irene already has Natalie Key's number—Mavis texted it to her back on day one of the Destitution—but Irene hasn't called her yet because...well, because she can't afford a lawyer, especially not a big fancy lawyer in New York City. And yet Irene knows she has to do something. She has been so busy trying to make it through each day—working on the boat, helping out around Huck's house where she can, checking in with Cash and Baker and Floyd—that she has been able to avoid thinking of all her worldly possessions in the custody of the FBI. If she ever wants to see them again or figure out what the hell is going on, she needs to do exactly what this card says and call Natalie Key.

"I think we should celebrate," Huck says. "What do you say we go to Candi's for some barbecue?"

Irene places the photograph in her lap. It does feel like a victory, having Milly back. Maybe Milly will be good luck. Maybe Milly will help them.

"Yes, please, and thank you," Irene says. She'll call Natalie tomorrow, she decides. Tonight, she's going to eat some ribs, pasta salad with peas, and coleslaw with raisins and pretend she's a vacationer.

"Before we get started," Natalie says, "I want you to know that a guardian angel of yours has already sent me a retainer for ten thousand dollars."

"What?" Irene says. "Who did that? Was it Mavis?"

"I'm not supposed to tell you, but I don't play games," Natalie says. "It was your former boss, Joseph Feeney."

Joseph Feeney, Irene thinks. The big boss at *Heartland Home and Style*. "Mavis must have told him what happened," Irene says.

"No doubt—and she probably strong-armed him," Natalie says. "Mavis is tough, as I'm sure you know."

"Mavis told me that *you* were tough," Irene says.

"Ha!" Natalie says. "I guess we're both tough. We had three older brothers who were state champion wrestlers, so we learned how to get out of a headlock and a half nelson at a very young age. Now, normally I charge nine hundred dollars an hour, but for you, I'm dropping my fee to three hundred—again, that's at Mavis's request, and I always honor her requests when I can—so

I'm really hoping, Irene, that we can get this done without any out-of-pocket expenses on your end."

Irene is so relieved, she feels dizzy. *Thank you, Joseph Feeney,* she thinks. *You underpaid me for twelve years and essentially demoted me when you hired Mavis, and I called you all kinds of ugly names in my head. But when I needed you, you came through.*

Thanking him should be done by phone but she can't risk the follow-up questions. She'll e-mail. "Wonderful," Irene says.

"Now that that's out of the way," Natalie says, "I need you to tell me everything."

Irene expects that, because Natalie is charging only a third of her usual fee, Irene will receive a third of Natalie's usual attention. But in only a matter of days, Natalie calls and gives her some answers.

1. The helicopter that Russ and Rosie took to Anegada was privately owned by Stephen Thompson, the third principal in Ascension. This particular helicopter had no black box, so there's no voice recording of the ride or the moments before the crash. Irene is relieved. There's a limit to what she can handle.

2. The people from VISAR—Virgin Island Search and Rescue—told the FBI that they had reason to believe the helicopter was *not* struck by lightning but rather exploded due to an electrical issue or, possibly, foul play. They are still investigating. The helicopter presently belongs to the British authorities because it went down in British waters.

"In theory," Natalie says, "the Americans and the Brits work together, but after talking to both sides, my guess is that there's an intentional withholding of information by the Brits, which always has to do with money. The Brits will hold the copter hostage until they get some kind of recompense." Natalie pauses. "Hard to know if this is all aboveboard or if there's bribery going on." She chuckles. "Actually, there's definitely bribery going on. Just so you know, even the good guys aren't good all the time."

3. Todd Croft had been arrested north of Trinidad and Tobago the same day that Irene lost the villa. There are a lot of charges against him, but the only one that they're presently holding him on is resisting arrest. Apparently, he gave the Feds quite a chase. The other charges, Natalie says, might not stick. Most of the paper trail that ties Ascension to money laundering and tax evasion has Russ's signature only; a few documents also include Stephen Thompson's name. Although Todd is the founder of the company and the last remaining principal, without any concrete evidence tying him to the illegal activity, he might soon go free, and, if his lawyer is good, he'll avoid jail time.

"He's telling the FBI that it was your husband and Mr. Thompson who ran the illegal business dealings, that he was involved only in the legitimate side of things—the soccer stars and casino owners who used Ascension to avoid taxes by residing in legal gray areas. He claims he didn't learn that Mr. Thompson and your husband had 'ventured to the dark side' until September. Ascension is, technically, Mr. Croft's company and he says those two threatened to take it down if Mr. Croft contacted the authorities. He cited the fact that Russ and Mr. Thompson were scooting off to Anegada without him as proof. And yet the FBI found him heading for Venezuela, where there are no extradition laws. Among Ascension's clients are entities that are into, among other things, narcotics trafficking, human trafficking, explosives, cybercrime, underground gambling, organ trafficking, and good old-fashioned counterfeiting. According to the paper trail, these entities gave their money to Russ, and Russ created shell companies at offshore banks in the Cayman Islands. He then invested that money in legitimate businesses on St. John and in the BVIs, where regulations are looser than they are in the U.S. They bought and sold a lot of land over on Anegada. They used SGMT, an offshore bank with a reputation for secrecy. That's the bank your personal finances were drawn on. Stephen Thompson joined the company only a year before Russ. Now, I did a little poking around on him. He was a British citizen, worked for Barclays out of law school, then disappeared for a few years, only to resurface down in the Caymans. But Mr. Thompson also held a passport from Suriname."

"Where's that?" Irene says.

"It's a country in South America," Natalie says. "They have a pay-for-citizenship policy. Invest two hundred thousand in the country's economy and receive a passport. That would have allowed Mr. Thompson to move around more freely, without the oversight of the British government."

"I'm sorry," Irene says. It's nearly seven o'clock; Natalie called just as Irene and Huck were driving home from a double-charter day. They are both exhausted and irritable. "I'm sorry, Natalie, but there is no way Russ was the mastermind behind all this." Irene laughs. "He—I swear to you—didn't have it in him. Let's start with…we lived in Iowa. Russ was a member of the Rotary.

He was on the school board. He liked puns, for Pete's sake." *Underground gambling?* Irene thinks. *Human trafficking?* Russ's definition of *underground gambling* was the office football pool, and he would have thought *human trafficking* was something a crossing guard took care of. "He was a decent man. I do still believe that. He must have been bribed by Todd Croft and that was why he was the one who got his hands dirty." Irene turns and looks out the open window. They're climbing Jacob's Ladder. It's one steep switchback after another and the engine of Huck's truck wheezes like an out-of-shape geezer on the StairMaster. But they make it, they always make it, and they're treated to a magnificent sunset—brilliant orange, like a wildfire across the sky. The beauty of these islands is completely at odds with the news Irene is now hearing. Or maybe it's not at odds. Maybe this beauty was what seduced Russ. Irene knows better than anyone that once you experience life in this paradise, you'll do anything to keep it. "Todd Croft offered Russ more money than he could possibly imagine," Irene says. "Russ made fifty-seven thousand dollars a year selling corn syrup. We were *always* struggling before he took this job. All I can think is that Todd offered him millions, and in exchange, he agreed to be the fall guy if they ever got caught." Irene swallows. "He was that desperate, that eager to please me. I was hard on him."

"Maybe it was bribing at first," Natalie says. "But I'm going to guess that, as things progressed, it became blackmail."

"Blackmail."

Natalie lowers her voice. "If Todd Croft knew about Rosie...and about Maia...well, he could have gotten Russ to do anything."

Huck pulls into the driveway. Irene sees Baker and Floyd out on the deck with Maia. She can't continue a conversation that involves organ trafficking—and not the church kind of organ—while she's looking at her grandchild. She has to end this call. "Right," Irene says.

"But we have no way to prove Todd did that," Natalie says. "Yet."

AYERS

Baker must have had a sixth sense that something was going on because he'd called Ayers while she was in the bathroom holding the pregnancy test with a shaky hand.

Positive.

Ayers had stared at the screen of her ringing phone. Baker was listed in her contacts as "the Tourist" with a photo of a leatherback sea turtle.

She'd declined the call.

She was pregnant? Well, yeah. Obviously. Of course.

Ayers wasn't a complete idiot; *pregnancy* had been her first thought, but she'd dismissed it immediately because it was too awful and Ayers had had so much *awful* piled on her recently that there wasn't room for any more. Rosie dying, a broken engagement, and now...

When Ayers got back together with Mick, she'd insisted he use a condom because of Brigid. He'd been good about this. Not happy, but conscientious. Even the night of their engagement, he'd used a condom.

The only time Ayers had had unprotected sex was with Baker

on their single night together. It was just that one night. A couple of times, but still.

Still, that was all it took. One egg and one sperm—baby.

Well, she couldn't have a baby. She could barely take care of *herself*. She lived in a studio—cute, but unsuitable. Her houseplants were dying. Where would she put a crib? A high chair? A Pack 'n Play or a bouncy chair or a swing or any of the other large, noisy paraphernalia that babies required?

She could, maybe, have had Mick's baby, because Mick was a known quantity to Ayers. But to have a baby with Baker, a person she had been on exactly one date with and slept with twice?

She wasn't prepared for any kind of conversation with Baker. She sent him a text: I've come down with something. It's bad and I wouldn't want you or Floyd to catch it. I'll call you when I'm better.

Rosie had been in this exact same predicament. No, Rosie had had it worse. Rosie found herself pregnant by a man she thought she'd never see again. She'd kept the baby—and who was that baby now? It was Maia, the most wonderful human Ayers knew. Didn't Ayers want a Maia of her own? A child who was wise and sweet and smart and funny? A child who would love her the way that Maia loved Rosie?

Theoretically, yes; Ayers wanted children. She had always pictured herself with children, and she even knew what kind of mother she wanted to be—the kind of mother who dressed up with her kids for Halloween, the kind of mother who let the kids have hot fudge sundaes for dinner on their last day of summer vacation. She wanted to be a Scout leader. She wanted to be fun and involved and reliable, a buoy during the unpredictable currents and undertow of growing up.

Just like everyone else, she wanted to be exactly like and completely different from her own parents.

Oh, jeez, Ayers thought. She had to tell her parents the news. But first, she would need to find them.

Treasure Island was fixed, but Ayers couldn't handle an all-day boat charter either physically or mentally. She called Whitney in the office and told her that she needed some time off—a couple of weeks, she thought, but maybe longer.

"But you're not quitting on us, right?" Whitney said. "No pressure, girlfriend, but you're the heart and soul of this operation. Cash is good but he's brand-new."

"I'm coming back?" Ayers said. "I mean, I'm coming back. Of course I'm coming back."

At La Tapa, Ayers was shaky and sweaty and distracted. Tilda covered for Ayers's lethargy and her mistakes. Tilda thought the problem was Mick, both the broken engagement and his week-long sit-in at Cruz Bay Landing. It had become a *thing.* Mick had been going to work, but directly afterward, he sat at the bar at CBL with the ring in front of him and Gordon tied to his bar stool, and he drank. He was there on his days off as well, from open to close. Tourists had started posting pictures of #heartsick-mick with the beer and the ring box in front of him and Gordon snoozing dutifully at his feet.

Mick had managed to make the breakup all about himself; he'd cast himself as the victim, and he'd gotten his own hashtag in the process. Meanwhile, Brigid was still working at the Beach Bar and *not* at Island Abodes like Mick had promised, so frankly Ayers didn't care if *60 Minutes* came to do a segment about his broken heart—Ayers wasn't going back.

"I feel bad for the guy," Skip, the La Tapa bartender, said at the end of service. "I'm going over to have a drink with him."

"Birds of a feather," Tilda murmured.

Ayers needed to confide in someone—and that someone should have been Baker. However, on Wednesday afternoon, Ayers got a text from Cash, and the next thing she knew, she had offered to adopt Winnie for a while because Tilda's fancy, type A parents didn't "do dogs."

This, at least, felt right. It was the least she could do after abandoning Cash on *Treasure Island.* It would also be nice to have a warm body around, one who wasn't going to ask her any questions.

Ayers had picked Cash up from the boat and driven to Peter Bay to collect Winnie. Ayers had never been to Tilda's fancy, type A parents' villa before—she had never been to any of the homes in Peter Bay; it was exclusive, private, gajillionaire territory—and when she drove down the steep chute of Tilda's driveway, she got vertigo. It felt like they were driving off a cliff into the sea.

Whooooooo! When Ayers parked, her heart was slamming against her chest.

She watched Cash as he strode into the house.

Uncle Cash, she thought. *My baby's uncle.*

She was about to leave—she had Winnie's leash in one hand and her bowl in the other—but then…*then* she blurted it out. Without intention, without planning, without warning.

I'm pregnant.

"Whoa!" Cash said.

"It's Baker's," Ayers whispered.

Cash's eyes bugged. "It is?"

Ayers nodded.

"You're sure?"

"I'm sure."

"You haven't told my brother yet, have you?"

Ayers shook her head. The mere thought made her want to hurl. She'd inhaled the scent of the frangipani bushes that surrounded Tilda's fancy, type A parents' villa. She needed to get out of there. The last thing she wanted was for Tilda to come home and ask what was wrong.

"I haven't told anyone," Ayers said. "Not even my parents."

"That explains your leave of absence."

"Just for a couple weeks," Ayers said. "Until I get a better grip on things."

"I'm sure it seems scary," Cash said. "But I'll help. We'll all help. Baker has his flaws, but he's an excellent father."

Ayers wasn't ready to hear this; she wasn't even sure she was going to go through with it. "Don't tell a soul," she said. "Not Tilda, not your mom, not Baker."

"Are you kidding?" Cash said. He bent down to rub Winnie's head. "I'm giving you my best friend. The last thing I'm going to do is cross you."

"Thank you."

"I'm here," Cash said. "And you know what? I'm psyched."

To track down her mother and father, Ayers clicks on the Wandering Wilsons Facebook page. Her parents share a cell phone and they call her when they're in a place with reliable service, which isn't often. Ayers's parents—Phil Wilson and Sunny Ray—have never married, though they've been together for thirty-five years. Each refers to the other as "my partner," and they call each other "my love." Their relationship is nontraditional—and enviable. They have a shared vision of seeing the world on its own terms, abiding by the old adage "Take nothing but photographs, leave nothing but footprints." Phil and Sunny met during a semester abroad in the Canary Islands in 1984; Phil was at Berkeley, Sunny at the University of Wisconsin. After that semester, they both dropped out and hopped on a freighter headed for Portugal, starting a life of wanderlust that has continued to this very day. Ayers's earliest memories are of walking between her parents down the dusty streets of one foreign country or another, the smell of diesel fuel, the sound of unfamiliar languages. Phil was the navigator; he had the map. Sunny was the ambassador; she did the talking, learning the words for *Hello* and *Thank you* in the language of every place they visited. They stayed in hostels or cheap hotels, Ayers and her parents sometimes all sharing a bed. They cooked in communal kitchens, showered in communal bathrooms. They slept on trains. They hiked and camped, snorkeled, tubed, ziplined, canoed, rafted, spelunked. They shopped at local markets, napped in botanical gardens, hopped on and off the goat-and-chicken bus, lit candles in churches, swam with dolphins and whale sharks, ate from street carts, bathed in hot springs, climbed to the scenic lookout at the crack of dawn, rode the elephant or donkey or camel, awoke to the call of the muezzin from the local mosque, swapped paperbacks, hand-washed their laundry and hung it to dry stiff as cardboard in the baking sun. As soon as they stayed somewhere long enough to feel comfortable, they packed up and moved on. Ayers had seen it all: the Pyramids, the Taj Mahal, Torres del Paine, the Galápagos, the northern lights, the Monteverde Cloud Forest, the Amazon River, the fjords, the glaciers, the mountain ranges, the deserts, the lakes, all of the oceans.

That must have been so cool, people say when Ayers describes her upbringing. *You're so lucky.*

We all want what we can't have. Ayers wanted a house. She wanted a subscription to *Seventeen* magazine that would arrive reliably on the first of the month. She wanted parents like Coach and Tami Taylor. She wanted siblings.

Every week or two someone aboard *Treasure Island* asks Ayers, "What do your parents think about you living on a tropical island?"

The true answer: *They think it's boring.* "Oh," she responds. "They're proud of me."

Ayers's parents have money now—inherited from Ayers's paternal grandmother—and so their travel has become far more comfortable. They stayed at the Shangri-La in Paris, which must have been interesting. Phil and Sunny still travel with large backpacks instead of proper luggage. Sunny wears pants and dresses made from khaki cotton; both of Ayers's parents wear Birkenstocks. While in Paris, they had dinner at La Tour d'Argent—because, as Sunny said, it was a classic Parisian experience they'd yet to have in their half a dozen visits to the city. Had Sunny worn her Birkenstocks to La Tour d'Argent? Ayers was afraid to ask.

The last time Ayers spoke to her parents, they were in Morocco, staying with friends they'd met in Ibiza in the 1980s, before Ayers was born; these friends now own a home on the coast in Essaouira. All of Phil and Sunny's close friends are people they met on one adventure or another—hiking around the crater of Mount Batur in Bali or shopping for an authentic Panama hat in Montecristi, Ecuador. That conversation with her parents was on the morning of Rosie's funeral, and a *lot* has happened since then. It feels like nearly everything important in Ayers's life has happened since then.

A Facebook post from yesterday puts Phil and Sunny at Fairmont the Norfolk in Nairobi. A scroll back through their pictures shows they've been on safari in the Maasai Mara.

Bah! Ayers thinks. They never took *her* on safari! They always said it was too expensive. There are the requisite pictures of giraffes, zebras, lions, elephants. And some of a hot-air balloon ride they took at sunrise. Cheetahs, leopards, rhinos, baboons, hippos. A Maasai warrior posing with Phil and Sunny in their Birkenstocks.

Ayers sighs. Her parents are in Africa. They couldn't *be* any farther away. Still, she tries their cell phone. What's the time difference? She doesn't care. She calls.

Her mother answers on the first ring. "Freddy!" Sunny says. "Your timing is perfect! The front desk just sent us a bottle of champagne. They think we're travel bloggers." She laughs. "I may have misled them a bit—"

Suddenly, Ayers's father is on the phone. "She misled them a *lot,*" he says. "Though it works. We've gotten free stuff every place we've checked in since your mother started referring to her 'blog.'"

"Great," Ayers says weakly. Her parents are in high spirits; they're about to open a bottle of champagne at a five-star hotel after having been on safari. In other circumstances, Ayers might have made a sarcastic comment about the "good old days" when they drank river water that they'd purified with iodine tablets and stayed at a hotel in Borneo where the sheets were crawling with tiny golden ants.

"We've been expecting your call for over a week." Her mother again. In the background, Ayers hears the cork pop—the mere sound makes her stomach lurch—and the Tubes singing "Talk to Ya Later," Phil and Sunny's favorite song, straight out of the early eighties. Ayers's eyes water. Despite the fact that she can't remember the last time she saw her parents, Ayers knows them well. They're her family.

But why were they expecting her call? She never calls them; it's always the other way around. "You have?"

"There's something you want to tell us, isn't there, Freddy?" It's her father again. Freddy is their nickname for Ayers; it's short for "Ready, Freddy," which was apparently what Ayers said non-stop when she was little.

"I do..." Ayers says.

"You're engaged!" Her mother blurts it out; the champagne must have gone to her head already. "Mick sent us a Facebook message asking for our blessing."

"He *did?*" Ayers says. She's taken aback by this news. Mick has met Phil and Sunny three times—the two times they swung through St. John to visit and then at Ayers's cousin's destination wedding in San Juan. Phil and Sunny like Mick. Phil and Mick are both craft-beer fanatics and they have a friendly rivalry in the sunset-picture-taking department (#sunset; Ayers doesn't miss this habit of Mick's one bit). Mick won Sunny over by dancing with her at Brinley's wedding and by agreeing to tour Castillo San Cristóbal at seven o'clock the next morning. But even so, asking for her parents' blessing isn't something Ayers ever thought Mick would do. It seems too formal and old-fashioned.

It also seems unfair. If Mick was so invested in the engagement, why did he blow it less than two days later? Who *does* that?

"When we did an overnight in the Maasai village," Sunny

says, "we told the elder that our daughter was getting married, and he insisted on roasting a goat, which is a very big honor."

Ayers falls facedown across her bed. Mick asked for her parents' blessing without her knowledge. Her parents celebrated her engagement with Maasai villagers without even hearing if she'd said yes, which feels vaguely dishonest of them, just like intimating they wrote a travel blog. And yet this is typical of her parents. When they travel, living is done in the moment. The strangers they're with become friends. The particulars of their lives can be stretched and even distorted without any consequence because tomorrow, they'll be gone.

Ayers lifts her head from the bed. "Why didn't you call *me?*" she asks. "You had goat with the Maasai but you didn't call to say congratulations?"

"It was your news to share," Phil says. "We've been waiting for this call. Frankly, it took so long that we began to wonder if something had happened."

Ayers hesitates. She feels bad about ruining her parents' happy champagne drinking. "Something did happen. Maia saw Mick kissing Brigid a couple days after he proposed. I gave the ring back."

On the other end, there's silence. Who has the phone now? Did they drop it? Ayers can ever so faintly hear Fee Waybill sing, *I'll just see you around!*

"Mom?" Ayers says. "Dad?"

"Sorry, Fred, it's just we're..." Phil says. He clears his throat. "The Maasai assured us killing the goat would mean a long and happy union."

The goat lies, Ayers thinks.

"Darn it," Sunny says. "I liked Michael."

"I liked him too, Mom," Ayers says. "But I'm not going to stay with someone who cheats on me; sorry." She pauses. "Anyway, I have more news, and I'm sure it will come as an even bigger shock, so sit down."

"Go ahead, Freddy," Phil says. "Your mother says she needs her drink."

Yes, Ayers thinks. *Yes, she does.* "I'm pregnant."

"She's pregnant!" Phil shouts.

In the background, Sunny shrieks.

"But wait," Ayers says and she silently curses Mick for being thoughtful enough to contact her parents and despicable enough to cheat on Ayers two days later. "It's not Mick's baby."

"It's *not?*" Her mother. "What do you mean? Whose baby is it?"

"Mom, stay on the phone, please." They always do this, pass the phone back and forth like they're playing a game of hot potato. "I'll explain it to you and you can explain it to Dad." Ayers rolls onto her back. The spinning ceiling fan above makes her nauseated, so she closes her eyes. "While Mick and I were broken up, I met a man named Baker Steele."

"Baker Steele?" Sunny says. "That sounds like a name from a soap opera. *Baker Steele.*"

"I liked him a lot but he lived in Houston—"

"And you don't date tourists."

"That's right. But he has...family ties here, so he came back and I slept with him and now I'm pregnant."

"Oh, Freddy," Sunny says.

"I haven't talked to Baker about it yet, but I...I think I'm going to have the baby, Mom."

Phil gets on the phone. "Your mother is crying," he says. "Happy tears? Yes, happy tears, happy champagne tears. We're going to be grandparents."

Ayers sighs. "The baby isn't Mick's, Dad, it's this other guy's—Mom will explain. Anyway, I called because I was feeling overwhelmed and alone and I wanted to hear your voices."

"We love you," Phil says. "And guess what, Freddy—you weren't exactly planned either."

"I know, Dad," Ayers says. Her parents were living on Wineglass Bay in Tasmania when Sunny realized she was pregnant. They figured out the baby had been conceived a few weeks earlier at Ayers Rock, and they decided that would be the official name, boy or girl.

"But out of all the good things we've experienced in our lives," Phil says, "becoming your parents is on the top of the list."

"We'll be there as soon as we can," Sunny says. "Remember what we taught you to do when you get to the end of your rope?"

"Make a knot and hang on," Ayers says.

The next day, Ayers steps out of St. John Market—she bought lemons, a knob of ginger root, a two-liter bottle of ginger ale, and white bread, hoping one or all of these would cure her nausea—and bumps into Huck and Irene.

Irene comes right over to hug Winnie. "My granddog," she says.

Grandmother, Ayers thinks. *My baby's grandmother. Or one of them. The other one is probably flying over the Congo right now on her way here.*

Ayers thinks about how surreal it is that she's pregnant with Irene's grandchild and Irene has no idea, but when Ayers sees Huck, she starts thinking about Rosie's journals and what they say. This makes her even queasier.

When Ayers gets home, she pulls the journals out from under

her sofa, and Winnie sniffs them, tail wagging. Ayers moves them to the center of her kitchen table to be safe. She should photocopy every page in case the FBI confiscates them as some kind of evidence and they vanish into the black hole of bureaucracy. But to copy them requires a trip to the St. John Business Center, and Ayers lacks the energy for that, plus she's bound to see people there she knows, people who will peer over her shoulder and ask what she's doing.

The journals contain relevant information about Russ. Ayers will give them to Huck and let him deal with contacting the FBI.

But…she needs to do this when Irene isn't around. And now Irene works with Huck on the fishing boat *and* she *lives* with him. She drives everywhere with him. They're joined at the hip.

Ayers sends Huck a text: That thing I need to talk to you about is sensitive and confidential. Any chance you can swing by La Tapa after service tomorrow?

Past my bedtime, Huck says. But yes, I'll see you tomorrow night.

Huck shows up at La Tapa at nine thirty and Ayers still has three tables lingering, so he takes a seat at the bar and orders a beer from Skip.

Ayers goes over and tells Skip, "That's on the house. You remember Captain Huck, Rosie's father?"

"Captain!" Skip says, reaching a hand across the bar. "It's an honor to have you in. We all miss Rosie very much. We have customers asking about her every day."

"Well," Huck says. He clears his throat. "Thank you. She was…yeah."

"I'll get your beer," Skip says.

*　*　*

Ayers lavishes her last tables with extra love and attention—*Can I get you a box for that? Would you like another decaf latte?*—because suddenly, she questions what she's about to do. The journals are private. They're intimate. And no one except Ayers knows they exist. What if she holds on to them for ten years and gives them to Maia when she's in her twenties, long after this whole mess has blown over?

Her tables pay their bills and wander out to the street. Skip cashes Ayers out.

"You look better today," he says. "Peppier."

Huck throws back what's left of his beer. "Skip was telling me what a fixture Mick has become over at Cruz Bay Landing. I hear they're planning on having him bronzed."

Ayers gives Huck a weary smile. "Walk me to my truck? I have something for you."

When they're out on the street, Huck says, "I must admit, my interest is piqued."

They walk past the Tap and Still, up by the baseball diamond of the Sprauve School, and around the traffic circle to Ayers's truck. Ayers says, "Back when we cleaned Rosie's room and you asked me if I found anything, I lied to you."

"Money?" Huck asks. He sounds hopeful. "More money?"

"Not money," Ayers says. "Rosie's journals about her relationship with Russ." She forages under the passenger seat of her truck, then hesitates ever so slightly before she hands the journals over. Is this the right thing to do? "I intended to save them for when Maia's older. But this whole thing with the FBI has me spooked." Ayers pushes out a breath. "They're pretty detailed, Huck, about how the whole relationship unfolded. There's stuff in there about Irene, and Russ's boss, Todd Croft…"

"Oh, jeez," Huck says.

"Yeah, exactly. It's sensitive." Ayers pauses. "Which is why I wanted to talk to you alone. Irene…she probably shouldn't see these. But the FBI might be interested."

"Agent Vasco said she'd hoped there were diaries," Huck says. "I'll probably just call her and hand them over. I'm sure Rosie wouldn't want me reading them."

"I should have told you sooner, though. I'm sorry."

"You did the right thing in telling me now," Huck says. "And I'll make sure we get them back."

Ayers nods. She feels as flat and insubstantial as a paper doll. Giving away the journals is like having an arm ripped off.

Huck leans over and kisses Ayers on the cheek. "You handled this just right, honey. I'll take it from here."

"Thank you for not being angry," Ayers says.

"It's no wonder you look so worn down," Huck says. "You have your crazy ex over at Cruz Bay Landing making a public spectacle of himself and you've been carrying the burden of these journals. Plus you miss Rosie. We all miss Rosie."

Plus I'm pregnant, she thinks.

"Have you seen Baker yet?" Huck asks. "Apparently, he has a good lead on a rental."

"So he's definitely staying, then?"

"They're all staying," Huck says. "Is that crazy or what?" Huck stretches out his arms in a gesture that takes in the hibiscus bushes lining the sidewalk, the sound of steel drums wafting over from Tamarind Court, the velvet sky filled with stars above them. "Then again, who ever wants to leave paradise?"

CASH

He and Tilda are eight minutes late to meet Granger and Lauren at Extra Virgin Bistro for dinner, which makes Cash crazy. Tilda has changed her top three times and spent half an hour putting on makeup, including some kind of sparkly silver stardust around her eyes. Cash can't fully appreciate the effect of the makeup because Tilda is beautiful even without makeup and because he hates being late for anything but especially for a work meeting, which this dinner technically is. Tonight, Granger and Lauren want to discuss the "exciting business opportunity" with Tilda and Cash.

Extra Virgin is a sexy restaurant. Outside, there's a spacious deck surrounded by tropical vegetation; in the dining room, there's a horseshoe-shaped bar backed by a glowing wall of bottles. There are leather banquettes, huge open windows, and low lighting. The buzz is high; stepping inside feels like arriving somewhere important. Cash has eaten in plenty of fine establishments in his life, though he consciously avoids any restaurant that can be called "a scene"—he prefers a taco and a beer, to be honest. Also, he doesn't like to eat in places he can't afford.

Granger and Lauren are already sitting, and a bottle of red has been decanted. (This is a phenomenon Cash has learned about in detail in the past week, how certain fine vintages of cabernet and Syrah and pinot noir need to be "aired out"— poured from the bottle into a glass carafe—so that the wine can breathe and become even more complex and sublime than it was when it was just wine in the bottle.) Granger is wearing one of his limited-edition Robert Graham shirts, another fancy thing Cash has recently been schooled on. Robert Graham designs, among other things, colorful, whimsically patterned sport shirts with dazzling contrasting cuffs. Granger collects Robert Graham shirts, registering each one like it's a Thoroughbred horse. After he bought his one hundredth shirt, the creative geniuses at Robert Graham designed a shirt specifically for Granger, called—unsurprisingly—"the Granger." Granger showed it to Cash the other evening at the house. It's vivid green and embroidered on the back with a psychedelic palm tree, only instead of a cluster of coconuts at the top, there are skulls, skulls being a popular Robert Graham motif.

The thing Cash likes about the Robert Graham shirts is that you can look dressed up without wearing a coat or tie. Cash could probably use one in his wardrobe, but again, he can't afford it; he can't even afford a knockoff of one. To this dinner, Cash is wearing a red polo shirt, a pair of Dockers, and flip-flops because his only other shoe options are sneakers and hiking boots. He's worried he's underdressed; he looks like he's been hired to park cars.

Oh, well—it's the Virgin Islands.

Granger and Lauren stand up; they're all smiles as they greet Cash and Tilda, though Lauren says, "We were wondering what became of you two!" The elder Paynes run a tight ship; one needs to watch them for only five minutes to see why they're successful. They do things impeccably—they get the best table at the most sought-after restaurant and then they welcome you into the place like it's their home. Cash's parents had money for years, but they never quite acquired the easy confidence that the Paynes exude.

Tilda instructs Cash to scoot over so he's across from Lauren. Maybe Tilda is trying to save Cash from an evening of tough face-to-face interaction with Granger, or maybe she would like to be her father's focus in this discussion. Granger pours them each a glass of wine. It's the Archery Summit pinot noir, "just to get everyone started." Cash sees from a quick check of the menu that the Archery Summit costs a hundred and twenty-five dollars a bottle, or roughly twenty-five bucks a glass. He tries to sit up straighter.

Granger says, "We'll wait until Duncan arrives to order."

Duncan? Cash thinks. *Who's Duncan?* Then he notices a fifth seat at the end of the table, between Granger and Tilda. He feels better about being eight minutes late because this Duncan is even later.

In a moment, Granger and Lauren are back up on their feet again, beaming, and Tilda stands, and Cash, a beat later than he probably should have, also stands to shake hands with a guy—maybe Cash's age, maybe younger—who's wearing jeans, a Gucci belt, a Revivalists T-shirt, and a forty-thousand-dollar watch.

"Hey, I'm Cash," he says.

"Hey, how you doin', mate, I'm Duncan Huntley, call me Dunk, nice to meet you." Dunk has an Australian accent, which puts Cash at ease a bit. Cash has never met an Aussie he didn't like. It seems to be a country filled with friendly, outgoing, well-adjusted people.

They all sit and pick up their menus. Granger says, "We ordered a bottle of the Archery Summit to start." He checks the bottle; there's less than a full glass left. "But we are definitely ready to move on."

"Let's go with a couple bottles of the Penfolds Shiraz," Dunk says. "I love a good Shiraz and Penfolds is the best in the Barossa—the best in the world, if you ask me."

"The Lewis reserve cab is pretty good too," Granger says. "Lauren and I visited the estate in Napa in January."

"Don't brag," Tilda says.

"You were invited," Granger says.

"I have a *job,*" she says.

"You can't compare the two—sorry, mate," Dunk says. "Penfolds is head and shoulders above." He waves over their server, a pretty young woman with long dark hair. "Jena, would you please bring us a couple bottles of the Penfolds Shiraz? We'll need to decant it."

"The Lewis will be drinkable right out of the bottle," Granger says. He turns to Jena. "One bottle of the Lewis reserve as well, please." He looks across the table. "What about you, Cash? Are you more a cabernet guy or a Shiraz guy?"

Cash would very much like to admit that he's an Island Hoppin' IPA guy. He has the wine list open in front of him. The Lewis cab is $240 a bottle, and the Penfolds Grange Shiraz is...Cash blinks. Is he seeing things? No; it's $700 a bottle. Which is, what, $140 a glass? Cash has a list of things as long as his arm that he would do with $140 before he blew it all on one glass of wine.

Dunk draws a circle with his finger. "So, Cash, how do you fit in with these bludgers?"

Cash would like to ask Duncan Huntley the same thing. "I'm a friend of Tilda's," he says. He doesn't use the word *boyfriend* because he is already having some manhood issues.

"Well, then," Duncan says. "That makes two of us."

The wine arrives, there's an enormous amount of theater involved in the tasting and decanting, and then Jena runs through the specials. She asks if it's anyone's first time eating at Extra Virgin, and Cash admits that he's an Extra Virgin virgin—only Jena laughs—and she tells them that they have a rooftop garden where the herbs and vegetables are grown, that they use local farms for eggs, and that they get their seafood from local fishermen.

"The mahi for the special tonight was caught just this afternoon by Captain Huck of the *Mississippi.*"

"Hey," Cash says. That's cool, right? Huck caught tonight's fish? But nobody is paying attention and Jena is off describing how the pasta, the stracciatella cheese, and the sausages are all made in-house.

"Would you ask Chef to do the tuna preparation I like?" Granger asks. "I don't see it on the menu tonight."

Cash expects Tilda to give her father a hard time—ordering off the menu is a gratuitous flex—but Tilda seems unbothered. She orders the lamb, Cash the mahi, Lauren the gnocchi. Dunk has a bunch of questions about the short rib preparation and Cash wonders if Dunk will be the first Aussie he'll ever hate.

He wants to go home—and by *home* he means...he's not sure where. He now lives under Granger's roof.

He throws back several mouthfuls of the cabernet, which is the most incredible wine he's ever tasted. All other wine hasn't been wine; it's been Kool-Aid, lacking the layers of this complex liquid. No, Cash is kidding. The wine is fine, nothing special. The best thing about it is it's getting him buzzed.

And once he's buzzed, he notices that Tilda is sitting with her chair pivoted toward Dunk; Cash has a fine view of the back of her shoulder. Is she into him? he wonders. Or just mesmerized by his accent, like a typical American? Tilda and Dunk are discussing *something* in depth, though it's hard to tell what exactly because Lauren, gracious, wonderful Lauren, is thoughtfully asking Cash about his years skiing in Breckenridge. How does it compare to Aspen? she wants to know. Deer Valley? Jackson Hole? Cash has answers for her because if there's one thing he knows about, it's the ski resorts of the Rocky Mountains. Cash is probably saying too much; he's had a large, seemingly bottomless glass of wine, and although Tilda and her mother ordered salads and Granger the hand-pulled stracciatella, Cash didn't order an appetizer. He lifts his empty glass and says, "I'll try some of the Penfolds. See what all the fuss is about."

Dunk eyes his glass, and for one instant, Cash thinks he's going to say no, that Cash isn't worthy of a $140 glass of wine. Dunk is going to call him out for what he is—a wine hack.

"Let's get you a clean goblet, mate," Dunk says in the most patronizing way possible.

The Penfolds Shiraz is heavier on the tongue, thicker; it's the consistency of ink. Everyone is watching Cash as he tastes. Even Tilda has swiveled toward him.

"Notes of goose fat," Cash says. "And the rain in Spain. And Russian interference in our elections."

"Now, now," Granger says. "No politics at the table."

"It's a joke, Dad," Tilda says. She rolls her eyes. "An old, tired joke."

Is it old and tired? Cash wonders. Because he thought it was *their* joke.

As soon as their entrées arrive and they all toast "to the next step," Granger says, "I guess it's time to talk particulars about what that next step is. Cash, you need some background about the meetings that Tilda and Lauren and I have been holding with Dunk."

Dunk has the short rib in all its gorgeous, umami glory in front of him but he makes no move to eat. "I bought Lovango Cay, the island just across the way from Cruz Bay, and I'm partnering with Granger, Lauren, and sweet Tilda here to build an eco-resort. We're thinking of selling off a number of lots for private homes, and then we'll build both hotel units and glamping tents. We'll have a world-class restaurant and a beach club with an oceanfront pool."

"That's ambitious," Cash says.

Tilda bubbles over like a glass of champagne. "It's exactly what I've always wanted. And Lovango is the perfect location. We'll run ferries to Red Hook and Cruz Bay, but because it's a separate island, it'll have built-in exclusivity."

"A boaters' paradise," Granger says.

"We've needed a destination like Lovango for a long time in the USVIs," Lauren says. "Just think about all the people who spend their money at the Baths and Jost and the Willy T."

"Yeah—I mean, you're right," Cash says. Tour stops in the USVIs versus the BVIs is another topic he knows something about. "I had a woman the other day who booked a trip on *Treasure Island* with her husband and their kids but she forgot her passport and couldn't go." Cash drinks some wine; he wonders if he has blue teeth like everyone else at the table. "We offer our USVI itinerary only once a week, and it's never as popular because there aren't as many destination stops."

"You work on *Treasure Island*?" Dunk says. "I guess I should apologize. I make a bit of a habit out of bouncing you blokes around in my wake."

"What's the name of your boat?" Cash asks, though he fears he already knows: the *Olive Branch*.

"Olive Branch," Dunk says.

Yep, it's the sixty-five-foot Sundancer that not only routinely buzzes by at top speed but also cuts *Treasure Island* off. James, the captain, *hates* the *Olive Branch*.

"The boat is named for Dunk's dog," Tilda says. "He has a harlequin Great Dane."

"We love Olive," Lauren says.

Cash turns to face Lauren. She loves Olive? Is this the woman who doesn't do dogs? "Harlequin Great Danes are...quite a breed," Cash says.

"It's not a dog," Granger says. "It's a horse!"

"She's so sweet," Tilda says.

"That face," Lauren says.

They have obviously all met Olive and fallen in love with her—after casting Winnie out onto the street. Cash stares at his mahi. It's a beautiful piece of fish, and the pan sauce is probably heaven, but Cash can't eat. He's furious with Tilda for not telling him that Duncan was coming to dinner. This is why she was being so extra with her outfit and sparkly makeup—it's all for Duncan. She has already met with him, maybe with her parents or maybe alone, but when Cash asked about her meeting last week, she claimed it was top secret.

Dunk says, "I guess my question for Cash is, what position are you qualified for? Do you have any management experience? What do you do on *Treasure Island*?"

"I'm the mate," Cash says. He holds Duncan's gaze, just daring him to smirk. Cash wishes he'd chosen a different shirt, one that makes him look less like Gilligan. He's tempted to throw his napkin on his plate and leave. He doesn't belong here. But he likes the idea of an eco-resort on Lovango. *Treasure Island* passes Lovango Cay every day, coming and going. It's just sitting there, beautiful, lush, undeveloped, filled with potential. What a great opportunity to build something from the ground up.

"I'm a Colorado guy, actually," Cash says. He nods at Dunk's T-shirt. "I saw the Revivalists at the Mission Ballroom before they hit it big."

"Cool, cool," Dunk says. "I saw them in Austin. Great show, probably best show I've seen in a while."

"Duncan, *eat* something," Lauren says. "You haven't touched your food."

Tilda glares at her mother and mouths, *Mom, stop!*

"I'm a people person," Cash says. "I enjoy the interface on *Treasure Island,* and I'm good at it. Before I moved down here, I taught skiing in Breckenridge."

"Love Breck," Dunk says. "We'll have to talk about *that* after we get into the whiskey."

Cash relaxes enough to take a bite of mahi. His mother might have caught this fish.

"We'll find a place for Cash," Granger says. "I'm already conferring with engineers about the desalinization plant. We greased the palms we needed to grease for the permitting." Granger leans forward. "How much time can you take off work, Til? Will the restaurant shut down if you're away for a week?"

"Ayers owes me a bunch of shifts, so, yeah, I can probably take a week. Why, are you flying me to Napa?"

"I'd like to send you on a reconnaissance mission," Granger says. "Island hopping. Three high-end resorts. I want a report on everything from the kind of ice they serve in their cocktails to the brand of toiletries in the bathrooms to the temperature they keep their fitness centers."

"Oh my God," Tilda says. "Can Cash come?"

"Obviously your mother and I would feel more comfortable if you weren't alone," Granger says. "And we have to be in LA next week for work." He pours Cash the last of the Shiraz. "What do you say, Cash? Can you swing it?"

A week away? Cash thinks. He would be a fool to turn the opportunity down, but he's the only crew member on *Treasure*

Island right now. Whitney in the office and the boat's owners, who live on St. Croix, are desperately looking for someone else. Any warm body will do; all they need is someone without a criminal record who can pass the required drug test. But even if they do miraculously find someone, Cash won't be able to leave for a week. Ayers is too sick and exhausted to come back, and she has seniority; she shouldn't *have* to come back because Cash wants to skip like a stone across the Caribbean.

"I can't," he says.

"But—" Tilda says.

"I just can't leave them in the lurch, Til. You know that."

"Dedication," Granger says. "Personal integrity. Frankly, if you'd said you could go, I would have wondered if you were the right person for our project."

Cash drinks what's left of the precious wine. He's passed a test.

"I can go," Dunk says. "I have zero personal integrity." He laughs. "Kidding, of course. But I am free and I would love to put my eyes on a few places, gather some intel."

Cash opens his mouth to protest. Does Dunk understand that Cash and Tilda are dating?

"Great idea," Granger says. "Til, is that okay with you?"

Say no! Cash thinks.

"Sure," Tilda says.

The drive home is tense. Cash isn't sure what to say. He and Tilda have been together a couple of weeks. They haven't said *I love you;* they aren't even close to that. They're still in the gaga-infatuation stage, which was, admittedly, rushed along a bit by Cash's circumstances. But he likes Tilda. A lot. They're exclusive. They're *living together.* So what will happen while Tilda's gone?

Is Cash going to just stay in her villa as she's gallivanting around the Caribbean with another guy?

"Thank you for being so cool about this," Tilda says, which is rather ingenious of her because Cash is not feeling cool at all. "If it puts your mind at ease, I'm not attracted to Dunk—like, not even a little bit. He's too intense."

Intense. She's making this sound like a flaw, but is it?

"Who *is* he?" Cash asks. "How does he have the money to buy an *island?* He's my age. Do his parents have jack?"

"He hasn't mentioned parents," Tilda says. "He was born in Australia, moved to the States when he was twelve…"

"Twelve?" Cash says. "Wow, he really milks that accent."

"I believe accents develop when you learn to talk," Tilda says. "Why are you being ungenerous?"

"I'm not," Cash says, though he is.

"Dunk is self-made, he's built and sold a couple of companies, and now he does real estate down here. He has a palatial home out in the East End. It's bigger than my parents' place—six buildings, including a pool house, two guesthouses, a gym, a theater, the whole enchilada. But as far as I know, it's just him and Olive."

"So he's single?" Cash says. "No girlfriend? Aren't guys like him required to run around with the supermodels from Fyre Festival?"

Tilda doesn't laugh.

"Is he…gay?" Cash asks. If Dunk is gay, Cash can relax. Somewhat.

"No idea," Tilda says. "It doesn't matter. I'm not interested in him. I'm interested in you."

Cash finds little comfort in these words. It sounds like Tilda has been to the villa in the East End. When did that happen and why didn't she tell him? And how to explain the makeup and sexy outfit? She didn't get all dolled up for her parents.

"Did you notice he didn't eat his dinner?" Cash says. "Not one bite. He asked Jena all those questions and then he didn't even touch it. He told me he was taking it home for his dog. That short rib cost forty-five bucks. Who does that?" Out of all the uncomfortable moments at dinner, the worst was when Jena dropped off the check and Dunk and Granger fought over it. It felt like a test of manhood, one that Cash couldn't even pretend to compete in. He'd just looked on with Tilda and Lauren while Dunk and Granger threw down their credit cards, which were radioactively glowing with money.

"He fasts," Tilda says. "I mean, he drinks, obviously, but he goes for days at a time without solid food."

"What?" Cash says. He thinks about living in the East End, which is within shouting distance of Lime Out, and denying himself the pleasure of a rum rib taco.

"It's a willpower thing."

"He sounds like a sociopath," Cash says. "Be careful while you're away, please."

"I'll text and call and we'll FaceTime every morning and every night, and when I get back, we'll skinny-dip at Hawksnest and go to the pig roast at Miss Lucy's and get drunk one night at Skinny Legs and do all the things we haven't done as a couple yet."

"I'll miss you," Cash says. Tilda is a beacon for him, and a buoy. They have gotten so close so fast, he can't imagine a week without her.

"Awww," she says. "You're sweet."

Cash perks up a little. "The project sounds amazing. I'm honored your parents are including me."

"They would do anything to make me happy," Tilda says.

Cash doesn't love the implication of this statement—that Cash's involvement on Lovango is due solely to his relationship with Tilda. If Tilda comes home from St. Lisa or St. Roger and announces that she's fallen in love with Dunk, Cash will be heartbroken, but will he be out of luck on the project as well?

Yes. If the whole mess with Cash's father has done nothing else, it has prepared him for the worst.

BAKER

Every now and then, when Baker is sitting by the pool at the Westin watching Floyd play with Aidan/Nicholas/Parker/Dylan/Maddie/Eli—it's a revolving cast of best friends for the day when you live at a hotel—he wonders if things are really as bad as they seem. The room—garden-facing with two queen beds and a balcony that is off-limits to Floyd—is five hundred bucks plus tax plus resort fee plus service charge, which is obviously a lot. But if Baker can ignore his mounting bill, he's able to appreciate the fine weather and all the amenities on offer—the pool, an excellent gym, daily housekeeping, the playground, kayaks and paddleboards, a private beach featuring a water trampoline, and a plethora of organized kid-centric activities, like movie nights and ice cream socials. Temporarily, anyway, Baker and Floyd are living the life.

The villa is gone. Russ was laundering money using offshore accounts and shell companies to hide profits for some of the most evil human beings on earth. According to Irene's lawyer, Russ's is the name that shows up most often on the incriminating paper trail, and his boss, Todd Croft, is claiming Russ and the third principal, Stephen Thompson, masterminded the illegal under-belly of his legitimate business without Croft's knowledge. This assertion is outrageous. And yet, what does Russ have to recommend him in the way of personal character? Zero, zip, and zilch. He had a second family—a mistress, a love child. Plus, he's dead and not able to defend himself.

Baker's determination faltered for a moment when he and Floyd arrived and he heard the news. He checked into the Westin thinking he would have to turn tail and run back to Houston. He couldn't make a life here without a place to live and without a car. Anna had agreed to let him bring Floyd down only because she had seen the villa—and even then, she had expressed reservations.

The second Floyd fell asleep their first night at the Westin, Baker had taken a cold beer (thirteen dollars for a six-pack of Island Hoppin' IPA at St. John Market, which was nearly the same price as a single beer from room service) out to their balcony and called Anna. She was, technically, still his wife, and she would forever be Floyd's mother, and Baker couldn't hide their reduced circumstances from her. He figured Anna would insist they return to Houston or else make a plea for Baker and Floyd to move to Cleveland, where she and Louisa would be living.

But Anna surprised him. "First of all, you need to know it wasn't me who sent you that text," she said.

Louisa and I have some concerns about you uprooting Floyd.

"Louisa stole my phone," she added.

"Sounds like you're finally in a healthy relationship," Baker said.

"Please stop," Anna said. "Weez was concerned. Once I tell her the villa is gone, she'll go ballistic."

"You do realize that Louisa isn't Floyd's parent," Baker said.

"I do realize that," Anna said. "Which is why I'm not going to tell her."

Baker took a nice long pull off his beer. For the first time in a long time, he felt like he was talking to his wife. "Thank you."

"I never expected you to move to Cleveland with us," Anna said. "But the job offer was too good to turn down. It's the top job in my field in the whole country."

"Anna, I get it. I'm proud of you. Floyd is proud of you."

"Since I'm chasing my dream, you should too," Anna said. "Give it a try down there. You have a lot of potential, Bake, and it's gone untapped for a while now. Put Floyd in school, then follow your passion."

"I'm supposed to be coaching," Baker said. "Which pays approximately five dollars an hour. So I'll need to find something else."

"I believe in you," Anna said. "You're a hands-on, involved father, an eleven out of ten. Maybe I didn't tell you that as much as I should have."

You didn't, Baker thought.

"You're incredibly smart and you're wonderful with people."

"Not as wonderful as Cash..."

"Every bit as wonderful," Anna said. "The two of you always claim to be polar opposites, but you do share similar strengths—and shining in social situations is one of them. You both have a magnetism. People gravitate toward you. All those mothers at Floyd's school, for example. They *love* you."

"Well, thanks," Baker said. He was surprised at how this little bit of validation boosted his spirits. He'd assumed Anna left him because she thought he was a slacker, weak and useless, good for nothing except taking care of their child, a job that she felt was beneath her.

"Just remember that this isn't the end of the world," she said. "Ischemic heart disease—now, *that's* the end of the world."

"You're right," Baker said. Anna saved lives every single day. Losing a villa that wasn't his to begin with fell into the no-big-deal category.

"I'm getting an absurd signing bonus at this new job," Anna said. "I'll wire you half in the morning. Buy a Jeep. And rent a place, something comfortable."

"Oh, Anna, I can't—"

"Sure you can," she said. "You helped me get where I am. You were the wind beneath my wings." She cracked up in a way that was very unlike her. "And, yes, I have just had a glass of wine." She sighed. "Kiss Floyd for me."

The next morning, there is a hundred and twenty-five thousand dollars in Baker's bank account.

The wind beneath her wings, he thinks. *Hot diggity dog.*

His first order of business is to buy a Jeep. Why not ask right there at the Westin? They have a rental-car concern that must have turnover. And yes, sir—he scores a 2017 four-door soft-top bluebird-colored Jeep Wrangler with 1,200 miles on the odometer for half its original price.

Next up is getting Floyd settled in school. Floyd had loved the Gifft Hill School when they'd visited and Maia was there to show him around, but this, of course, is different. This is for real. Floyd is now the new kid; he doesn't know a soul, and it's the middle of the school year.

Floyd takes getting ready in stride. He protests about the shower but submits and then eats four bites of Cheerios. (They have been eating like paupers. Baker bought Cheerios and milk, a carton of OJ, a loaf of white bread, a jar of peanut butter, a package of hot dogs, and a twenty-four-pack of ramen noodles at St. John Market, and even those low-end groceries had cost him thirty-five dollars. It has been a week in his life that he's not anxious to repeat.)

When Baker pulls the Jeep into the parking lot of Gifft Hill with the other parents, *he* feels nervous. "It's going to be fine, buddy," Baker says. "You've already met your teacher. She knows you're smart, and you're going to meet new kids."

"I know," Floyd says. He has his lunch box with the peanut butter sandwich that Baker made that morning in their hotel room.

A rental, he needs to find a rental—and a real job.

Being with Ayers was Baker's primary motivation in moving down to St. John, but he has to push thoughts of her away for now. Food, clothing, shelter—then love. He called her; she didn't answer, but she sent a text: I've come down with something. It's bad and I wouldn't want you or Floyd to catch it. I'll call you when I'm better. Frankly, this was a relief; it bought him some time. He assumes she knows what happened from talking to Cash or Maia. As soon as Baker gets settled, he's going to swing by La Tapa and see her. He'll ask her out to dinner. They'll start fresh, as though the whole fraught way they met (at Rosie's memorial reception, where Baker lied about who he was) and their bizarre first date (they had sex in a beach chair that ended when the chair collapsed) and their one night together (which took place only hours after Ayers had broken up with Mick and two days before she became engaged to Mick) never happened.

They need a clean slate. They'll get to know each other gradually, without any heavy emotional baggage weighing them down. Everything will be aboveboard, out in the open, uncomplicated.

"Hey there!"

Baker and Floyd have just climbed out of their new Jeep when Baker sees a tall, rail-thin blond woman in expensive yoga clothes (Baker's eyes land on the woman's nipples completely by accident) walking toward them and smiling.

"You must be the new dad," she says. "I'm Swan Seeley. My older son, Colton, is friends with Maia, and my little boy, Ryder, is in kindergarten just like Floyd." Swan bends over, hands on knees, and looks at Floyd. "Everyone has been waiting for you to get here, Floyd. There's already a cubby with your name on it and a chair right next to my son Ryder at the blue table, which is where the cool kids sit."

Baker tries to imagine his school wives' reaction to the term *cool kids*. One of them would point-blank tell this woman not to project her own insecurities about social status onto children. Which one would say it? Debbie, he thinks. Unless Ellen beat her to it.

"Blue is my third favorite color," Floyd announces. "Green first, then red, then blue." He glances up at Baker. "Can we go in, Dad?"

"Yes, of course," Baker says. He holds out his hand to Swan and is careful about looking her in the eye. "Thank you for the words of encouragement. I'm Baker Steele."

She grasps his hand and lays her other hand on top. "Oh, I know who you are. We've all been waiting for you to arrive too."

Floyd has a good first day, then a good second day. All the kids are cool kids. Floyd is happy. Baker is getting there. He has a new Jeep and money in the bank. He checks in with his mother and his brother. Irene is living with Huck, working on the fishing boat, driving around with Huck in his truck like a local. She seems fine…better than fine. Her former boss at the magazine is paying for a real lawyer, a woman who is unraveling the tangle of Russ's deceits. Cash, meanwhile, is living high on the hog with Tilda from La Tapa, but that hardly seems like a sustainable arrangement.

Maybe, just maybe, Baker will be able to find a place that's big enough for all of them.

Welcome to Paradise Real Estate, which was owned by Paulette and Douglas Vickers, is now out of business, so Baker decides to try an agency called the Love City Villa Experience, which sounds sort of like an adult film from the 1970s—but maybe that's a good sign?

Baker walks into the agency and approaches the desk of a middle-aged West Indian woman wearing a cantaloupe-colored blouse and glasses on a chain. The nameplate in front of her says FRANCES.

"I'm looking for a villa rental," Baker says.

"Good afternoon," Frances says, sounding like a teacher correcting a student's grammar.

"Good afternoon," Baker says quickly. He chastises himself; the most important thing when speaking to anyone in the Virgin Islands is a proper greeting. Frances has probably already pegged Baker as a tourist from a busy place like New York—or Houston—where civility and manners don't exist. "How are you today? My name is Baker Steele."

Frances blinks. "Oh," she says. "Hello."

Does Frances know who he is? Does she know who his father was? Something about the way she said those two words conveys a *yes* on both counts. Will she work with him anyway?

He tells her his budget and says he'd like a villa with four bedrooms. She gives him the death stare. He says three. She shakes her head, tsks him. He says, "Two?" She picks up her keys and says, "Come along, son. Let's find you a home."

Baker has spent enough time lounging on the couch watching HGTV to know that the places you love are always too expensive and the places that are within your budget are always under-whelming for one reason or another. Frances takes him to look at an apartment on the first switchback of the Centerline Road. It's fine but the traffic noise is a problem, plus the place looks run-down and the communal pool is green with algae. No. They look at a tiny cottage all the way out past Salt Pond in Coral Bay. It's a forty-five-minute drive from town, which means ninety minutes spent commuting each day. No. There's a place near the Cinnamon Bay campground that smells like rot and is swarming with mosquitoes and doesn't have air-conditioning. No.

Well, Rome wasn't built in a day. Frances says she'll make a comprehensive list; they'll look again on Saturday. In the meantime, Baker will continue to hemorrhage cash at the Westin. It's starting to feel like home. There's a young woman at the front desk named Emily who flirts with Baker, and he flirts back. It's harmless! The morning after Baker's fruitless house search, he's getting his coffee in the lobby when Emily says, "I heard my aunt Fran is helping you find a place to live. And here I thought you were planning on staying with us forever."

"I'm moving here," he says. He wonders how his name came up in conversation with her aunt. He wonders if the entire island is whispering about him behind his back. "And I need to find a job."

"Got a minute?" Emily says. She leads him outside and

then across the Westin property to the building where they sell time-shares.

"Oh, I can't afford to buy a time-share," Baker says. "Though, don't get me wrong, I'd love to live at the Westin permanently. It'd be a dream come true."

"I didn't bring you here to buy," Emily says. "I brought you here to sell."

What is she talking about? She's talking about an opening they have for a sales associate in the time-share office. Emily leaves Baker with a woman named Jacqui who plops him down for an informal interview. There's no experience required for the job, though Jacqui loves that Baker has a degree from Northwestern and an MBA. He's personable. And he now knows the Westin property very well and can extol its many virtues. Baker wanted to get into real estate anyway, didn't he? This is one way in. There's a built-in clientele, Jacqui tells him. People show up at the hotel and fall so in love with St. John that they buy time-shares so they can keep coming back. The commission scale is generous—it's real money—and the hours are flexible. He can work seven thirty to two thirty and then pick Floyd up from school. The job comes with full benefits, and he'll be good at it. He knows he'll be good at it.

"I'm a team player," Baker says. "Sign me up!"

And the hits keep coming! On Baker's next outing with Frances, they look at a villa called the Happy Hibiscus. It's a beautiful stone home with cathedral ceilings, two bedrooms, two baths, a modern kitchen, a laundry room, and a small jewel of a pool out back in the garden. It has a gas grill, cable TV, and a yard planted with bismarckia trees. It's a bit beyond Baker's budget but he likes it so much, he bends. The house is on the flat part of Fish Bay and has no view; frankly, looking at it, you wouldn't even know you were on an island. Is Baker going to let this bother him? He's not. The house is *directly* across the street from Ayers's place; he can see her little green truck in the driveway when he stands at his front door. This is more of a downside than the price or the lack of a view; Baker doesn't want to crowd Ayers or have her think he's stalking her. How will he ever explain that he's now renting the house across the street? She's going to think he's psycho. It's a small island, but not that small. If he rented any other house, it would give her more breathing room.

Frances must sense his momentary hesitation because she chimes in, "You'd be a fool not to take it, son."

"I'm no fool," Baker says, though he suspects he'll feel like one when he tells Ayers they're neighbors. "I'll take it."

Baker and Floyd go out to dinner to celebrate. Baker stays away from La Tapa. It's too fancy for Floyd, plus Ayers works there, plus Swan Seeley was lurking in the school parking lot that afternoon (waiting for him?), and she told Baker that she would be having dinner at the bar at La Tapa that evening around seven and why didn't he join her? The invitation had unmistakable romantic intent, so now Baker has to avoid Swan at all costs.

They try the Banana Deck, but from the bottom of the stone steps, Baker can see Cash sitting at the bar by himself. It's surreal, bumping into his family around the island (Baker saw his mother at the market). Under other circumstances, Baker might say, *What the heck, let's eat with Uncle Cash and catch up.* But the truth is, he's not quite ready to fill his brother in on everything that's been happening, meaning that he doesn't want to break the news to Cash that he's renting a two-bedroom place that doesn't have space for him (except a sofa to crash on in case of emergency) and that is directly across the street from Ayers's house. Ayers might not call him a stalker to his face, but Cash most certainly will.

"Let's go, buddy," Baker says, wheeling Floyd around. They check at Lime Inn, but there's a forty-five-minute wait, and that won't work—Floyd is four years old; Baker has to get him fed. The Longboard has a line, and High Tide is still filled with happy-hour revelers.

What about Cruz Bay Landing? Someone at the Westin pool this past week was raving about the shrimp appetizer, which sounds good to Baker, and he can get Floyd a burger. They go over, and there are a couple of seats at the bar and a guitar player singing "Waiting on a Friend."

"Ooh, making love and breaking hearts, it is a game for youth," Baker sings quietly. He orders a beer for himself and a ginger ale for Floyd and checks out the menu. He's so happy to not be eating ramen noodles with hot dogs again tonight that it takes him a minute to realize that he knows the guy sitting a few stools away with a rum punch and a Corona and a velvet ring box in front of him, a bucket-headed American Staffordshire terrier leashed to his bar stool.

It's Mick.

Baker is halfway off his bar stool, ready to leave—they can just go to Ronnie's for pizza—when Mick sees him.

"Hey," Mick says. "Banker! It's Banker, right?" Mick sounds like the town drunk, his voice overly loud and his speech slurred. The guitar player ends the song; the bartender says, "Easy, Mick," as though he's expecting a scene. But there's not going to be a scene. Floyd is there. Does Mick see Floyd, Baker's little boy?

"Baker," Baker says, extending a hand. "How've you been, man?" Baker asks the question in earnest, though anyone can see Mick has not been well. What's with the velvet box? (Baker can guess.) And the poor dog. Floyd clambers down off his bar stool and stands a respectful distance away, regarding the dog.

"Can I pet him?" Floyd asks Mick.

"Sure!" Mick says. "His name is Gordon. Old Gordie-Gordo. You can take him for a walk around the park if you want. He could use the exercise."

"Is it okay, Dad?" Floyd asks.

No! Baker thinks. It's getting dark and Powell Park is cast in shadows. But the park is only a couple steps away from the restaurant patio and what kind of father tells his son he can't walk a dog? "Why not?" Baker says. "Once around only, okay? Stay on the path. Don't let him go."

"Gordie won't run off," Mick says. "He's a good dog. Likes to sniff things."

Floyd takes Gordon's leash and, looking self-important and three inches taller, leads him a few steps away. Baker puts in an order with the bartender for the shrimp appetizer, a grilled mahi sandwich, and a kid's burger.

Then Baker drains his beer and pretends to watch the basketball game on TV, Duke against North Carolina. Mick is here, and Floyd is walking Mick's dog, so there are no hard feelings. Everything is fine. Is everything fine?

"Word on the street?" Mick says.

"Excuse me?" Baker says.

"Word on the street is that Ayers is pregnant," Mick says.

Baker flags down the bartender for another beer, then puts his eyes on Floyd. Floyd has stopped to let Gordon sniff. Ayers is pregnant.

"Really," Baker says. He thinks of the text she sent him. I've come down with something. It's bad and I wouldn't want you or Floyd to catch it. I'll call you when I'm better. She's pregnant?

"That's what I heard," Mick says. He raises his Corona to Baker. "So I guess congratulations are in order."

Baker feels like he's suffered a grave injury—lost a limb, maybe—but has yet to feel the pain. "Yeah, man, congratulations." He would like the congratulations to be accompanied by giving Mick a sock in the mouth or pouring Mick's drinks over his head. Mick doesn't deserve Ayers. He sure as hell doesn't deserve to have a baby with Ayers. But that's the way the world always works, isn't it? The jerks win.

"Congratulations to *you,*" Mick says. "The baby's not mine."

"What?" Baker says.

"It's not mine," Mick says. He drains his rum punch in one long swallow and bangs the empty glass on the bar. "It's yours."

HUCK

He sees the Jeep with the tinted windows idling at the base of Jacob's Ladder in the morning when he and Irene take Maia to school, then he sees it again in the National Park Service lot when he and Irene are letting off their charter clients. The clients were a couple, the husband reeking of weed and high as a kite and the wife spending the entire six-hour offshore trip glowering at him from under her wide-brimmed sun hat. Irene had tried to draw the woman out, tried to put her on a mahi, but the wife was having none of it. That was fine; Irene cut bait and left her alone. It wasn't her job to make friends or play marriage counselor.

"Some people like being miserable," Irene murmurs to Huck as the couple head off the dock like two of the Seven Dwarves—Dopey and Grumpy. "It's what brings them joy."

I love you, Huck thinks, and that's when he notices the Jeep again. Black Jeep, tinted windows. He checks the license plate and repeats it in his head—*TP 6756*—but two seconds after the Jeep drives away, he's forgotten it.

Could be just a coincidence, a tourist driving around. Tinted windows are legal, though you don't find them on rental vehicles.

He shakes his head. He's thinking of Oscar Cobb, Rosie's old boyfriend, the one with the Ducati motorcycle who, after he was released from prison, drove a Jeep with tinted windows. Oscar's Jeep called attention to itself; it was jacked up, sitting on top of thirty-five-inch BFG mudders.

Huck is thinking of Oscar Cobb again because even though he promised himself he wouldn't, he has been reading steadily through Rosie's journals. It was as simple and irrevocable as Eve taking the first bite of the apple; one taste and Huck was damned.

The journals were a trip back in time. Rosie was single, working at Caneel Bay, living with Huck and LeeAnn. Oscar Cobb came sniffing around, and Rosie resisted. (LeeAnn, Huck thought, would have been so proud of how Rosie resisted!) Russell Steele had stepped between Rosie and Oscar one night. He put Oscar into some kind of death grip, and despite himself, Huck cheered for the guy. That was the beginning of the relationship; it was damn near accidental. Russ hadn't been on the prowl looking to hook up with anyone. He'd seen a person in trouble and he'd helped out. The affair lasted the weekend, and that, Huck supposed, would have been that—were it not for Maia.

There are two places in the journals where Huck choked up. The first was the description of the morning Rosie announced she was pregnant. If Huck had had to remember this on his own, he would have come up blank. But reading the scene in Rosie's handwriting carried him back to the exact moment—his own kitchen, a typical morning. LeeAnn was wearing her raspberry scrubs, her nails painted to match. She was drinking the cup of coffee that Huck always made for her, awaiting her egg and toast. Huck had been dressed for a charter. He wonders now who he'd taken out on the boat that day and what they'd caught and if he'd seemed distracted because of the news his stepdaughter had dropped at breakfast. What Huck does remember is his fear about LeeAnn's reaction. LeeAnn's number-one priority since the day Huck met her had been keeping Rosie from messing up her life in exactly this way. She had gotten Rosie through high school and through college without her becoming pregnant with Oscar's baby.

That day, Rosie swore the baby wasn't Oscar's. She said it was a white fella's, a businessman who'd stayed at the hotel. A pirate. Huck was skeptical. LeeAnn was more than skeptical.

"We'll know the truth when this baby is born," she said.

The second place Huck tears up is at Rosie's description of Maia losing her first tooth. Again, the breakfast table, again toast, because at some point, Huck began making an egg and toast for Maia as well as for LeeAnn. The tooth popped out and skittered across the kitchen floor. Huck found it after a few minutes of hunting— Maia had been worried, the Tooth Fairy and all that—and when he held it up, she'd wrapped her arms around his legs. That was right before LeeAnn got sick and died. The end of the golden days, though of course, none of them had any idea it was the end.

And that, Huck supposes, is why it makes him emotional. His life was blessed and he hadn't appreciated it like he should have.

Rosie got back together with Russ after LeeAnn died; she was vulnerable—and she was free.

The journals mention Irene, the wife at home in Iowa City, a woman Rosie saw as a rival. Was Russ planning on leaving Irene and moving down to the islands permanently? It's anyone's guess. Starting in 2015, there are mentions of Russ's business dealings—the villa and land in Little Cinnamon, the business trips to Anegada, to Grand Cayman. There's mention of Russ wanting to get out of his business dealings and Todd Croft not allowing it; Todd Croft showed up at La Tapa to threaten Rosie.

He killed them, Huck thinks. They were headed to Anegada on New Year's Day and Todd Croft blew them up.

What did Irene say? That the charges might not stick; Croft might be released.

The journals have to go to the FBI. Huck has Colette Vasco's number programmed into his phone. He should call her; she needs to see these.

But...maybe not yet.

Huck believes in honesty. In this situation, does that mean that he should tell Irene he has these journals and that he's planning on handing them over to the FBI? Should he ask Irene if she wants to see them? Or, out of regard for her emotional well-being, should he spare her? Should he give the journals to Vasco and when Irene finds out say he didn't read them and didn't think she should read them either? Is this reasonable? This sounds reasonable, but it's not honest. Is it better? Will it save Irene's heart from breaking again?

Irene is adjusting to their new circumstances better than Huck expected. She's now sleeping in Maia's room. They have developed a routine. Irene worries about money, he knows, but guess what—so does everyone else in the world.

Irene's attorney in Iowa City calls and leaves a message while they're out on a charter. Her mother-in-law's estate is through probate and Milly Steele has left behind "assets," though in the message, the attorney doesn't say what kind.

"Do you think it's money?" Irene asks Huck. "Do you think it's a lot of money? Do you think Russ used Milly's account as a place to hide cash? Do you think Milly knew what Russ was doing? Was she in on it?"

Most of these questions sound rhetorical, so Huck just answers the first. "*Assets* could mean money," Huck says. "Or it could mean a pile of crocheted afghans and used bingo cards."

"You're making an old-lady joke," Irene says. "By definition, *assets* are worth something. Maybe Milly owned real estate I don't know about?" Her voice is hopeful, then, sounding defeated, she says, "I'm actually hoping that Russ hid money with his ninety-seven-year-old mother and that now it will be mine and somehow the FBI won't find out."

"And you won't tell them?"

"I'm not sure," Irene says. She fiddles with the end of her chestnut braid, worrying the band that keeps it together, which is something Huck has noticed her doing a lot recently. This gives Huck hope that Irene Steele is just a regular gal after all and not some kind of superhuman who elegantly copes with whatever life throws at her. "I hate to say it, but I might be tempted to keep it." She honks out a laugh. "But you're right. It's probably afghans. Or her cane. Or a fifty-percent-off coupon for an order of wings at the Wig and Pen."

*   *   *

Two days later, Huck sees the Jeep with the tinted windows parked outside the minimart in front of Rhumb Lines just as someone is climbing into the front seat. The "someone" appears to be a white female, small in stature. Huck chuckles. Probably just some local concerned about the sun. Although...if it were a local, he would have seen the Jeep before. Maybe she just bought it. It's not impossible.

Irene gets hold of her Iowa City attorney, Ed Sorley. The assets are a collection of blue-chip stocks that Milly has apparently had for decades; converted to cash, they will net Irene one hundred and seventeen thousand dollars.

Irene is jubilant. "The assets are clean!" she says. "They were investments Russ's father made years and years ago that Milly never touched."

"And she left it all to you?" Huck says. "You're rich!"

"It's breathing room," Irene says. "I'm going to split it four ways—me, Cash, Baker, and Maia."

"Maia?"

"For her education."

"AC..."

"Just let me do it, please," Irene says. "She's Russ's daughter, Milly's granddaughter. I'm not arguing with you about it."

"Okay," Huck says. "Should we celebrate? Maia is with Ayers tonight, so it's just the two of us."

"Shambles?" Irene says.

Huck chuckles. Shambles is Irene's new obsession. It's a brightly painted local bar at mile marker two on the Centerline Road that overlooks the Paradise Lumberyard and a mechanic's car-strewn lot. The place puts the *loca* in *local,* which is maybe what Irene likes about it, along with the drinks. The first time they went, the bartender, Nathan, made Irene a rum punch that she claimed was "magic" (or maybe just strong). The food is better than it needs to be; it's downright delicious.

Huck and Irene grab two bar stools, then order a couple of rum punches and pulled pork sandwiches with fries and slaw. They chat with the mechanic and his wife and a couple visiting from Toronto. Nathan slips Irene a second rum punch and, Huck suspects, maybe even a third, because by the time they're ready to leave, Irene has talked the couple from Toronto into booking a fishing charter.

"Ha!" Irene says as they climb into the truck. "That was fun. And I made it rain! We have a full-day charter on Friday."

"Good job, AC," Huck says. When he pulls into the driveway at home, he turns off the ignition but he stays in the truck, and Irene stays in the truck, and it feels for all the world like he's taking her home after a date. Should he kiss her? He promised to let her make the first move.

She places her hand on his thigh. She takes off her seat belt and scoots closer to him. She raises her face to his cheek; he can smell the rum and fruit on her breath. How magic were those rum punches? he wonders.

"AC," he says. "There's something I have to tell you."

He warns her they'll be difficult to read.

"It's the story of their relationship," he says. "Start to finish. I can give you the CliffsNotes version, if you'd rather?"

Irene shakes her head, clutching the journals to her chest. Instantly, he wants to snatch them back. Rosie never intended those journals for Huck's eyes and she *definitely* never intended them for Irene's eyes.

"When I found out about Rosie and Russ, I told myself that I would find a way to forgive them," Irene says. "Maybe understanding how it all unfolded will make that easier."

No, Huck thinks. *It won't.* "Maybe," he says.

She's standing in front of her bedroom door. The air between them is charged—yes? Maia is away overnight for the first time since Irene moved in.

"I appreciate you giving these to me," Irene says. "I'm sure it was a hard decision."

"Torturous," Huck says. He needs a cigarette, badly. "Well, good night, AC."

"Wait," Irene says. She opens the bedroom door, sets the journals on the nightstand, and reemerges to give him a kiss. It's a real kiss, long and delicious, that leaves Huck breathless and aching. She pulls away for a second, then comes back in for more. Huck is very careful with his hands. One is on her shoulder, one on the side of her face. Her fingers are linked through his belt loops. He forgets about the cigarette, about the journals, about the FBI, about the Jeep with the tinted windows, about Rosie, Russ, LeeAnn. He's here with Irene in this moment. It's all he wants in the world.

She reels him in; she lets him go; she reels him in a little closer. He's hooked. She is the Angler Cupcake.

She lets him go. Pulls away. Smiles at him. "That's all for tonight," she says.

Huck raises his palms. He can't speak.

She disappears into her room. Huck grabs the Flor de Caña from the shelf in the kitchen and his pack of Camels and goes out to the deck.

*　　*　　*

The next day, Irene is fine, she's normal. She tells the boys about the money from Milly. Baker says he doesn't need his share; he got a windfall from Anna. He tells Irene to split his portion three ways.

And Cash is...

"He seemed more relieved than anything," Irene says. "Thirty-nine grand is a big boost for him, so I thought he'd be more excited. He sounds preoccupied. Tilda has just left on a work trip with an investor in this project her parents have cooking and he's bothered by that."

"Women," Huck says. "They'll get you every time."

Irene's expression is inscrutable. Has she read the diaries? Huck is afraid to ask, but his gut tells him the answer is no.

The next day, they have the charter with the couple from Toronto whose names, Huck sees when he checks the confirmation text from Destiny, are Jack and Diane Boyle. *Little ditty,* Huck thinks, *'bout Jack and Diane...* He wonders how many times those poor folks have heard people sing that to them. Huck makes coffee for himself and Irene, makes an egg and toast with papaya jam from Jake's for Maia. Irene has yet to come out of her room, which is unlike her.

"Is Irene okay?" Maia asks. "I thought I heard her crying late last night."

Crying? Huck's heart sinks. "Hurry it up, Nut. I'm going to run you to school a little early, then come back and scoop up Irene."

Maia shovels in her egg, takes her toast to go.

Huck calls out, "Be right back, AC!"

The black Jeep with the tinted windows is waiting in the elbow joint of Jacob's Ladder, a step closer than it was the last time. Huck stares at the place where the driver would be. If the Jeep is still there when he comes back, he's going to knock on the window.

As soon as Huck and Maia pass, the Jeep follows them. In his rearview, Huck can see the woman—brown hair pulled back, round face. He doesn't recognize her. When he turns left, the Jeep turns right, toward Cruz Bay.

Okay, Huck thinks. The driver doesn't seem particularly villainous, but there's no denying she's watching them. Who is she?

When Huck gets back to the house, Irene is out front. Her hair is braided, she has her sunglasses on, her face is grim. She climbs in the truck and slams the door a little harder than necessary.

"I take it you read the journals."

"I don't want to talk about it until after this charter," Irene says. "But you should know, today will be my last day working for you."

"What?" Huck says. "Irene..."

"I don't want to talk about it," Irene says, "until after this charter. This charter was my doing and although I would rather be anywhere else today, I'm honoring my commitment. But after today, Huck, no, I'm sorry."

She's angry, Huck thinks. *She's hurt.* He's an idiot. He should have handed the journals over to Agent Vasco, honesty be damned.

What makes matters worse is that the charter with Jack and Diane is magnificent from start to finish. Diane is a nurturer—she's the mother of six, she tells them—and she has brought treats for the entire day, starting with a thermos of coffee and sausage-and-egg sandwiches from Provisions, which Huck knows Irene loves, though since losing the villa, she can't spare the money for them. Jack is a terrific guy, a regional manager for a Canadian bookstore chain called Indigo. (Huck has never heard of it but Irene has. Apparently, it's like the Barnes and Noble of Canada.)

Jack and Diane are hearty; they're excited to go offshore and try their luck with the fish. "We're here, aren't we?" Jack says. "Let's go for it."

Huck cranks the music. He starts with John Cougar just for fun and they love it, singing along, arms raised in the air and then wrapped around each other. In his mind, Huck changes "Jack and Diane" to "Huck and Irene." *Hold on to sixteen as long as you can.*

Amen, Huck thinks.

The water is smooth, and the boat skates along with barely a bump. Right before they reach Tambo, they get a hit on the outrigger line. Huck stops the boat. Irene is already handing the rod to Diane, who, after a short fight, brings in a respectable-size wahoo, bright as a bar of sterling silver. Irene handles the gaff like a pro now. As Huck watches her he thinks there's no way she's leaving; she loves this boat too much, this job, him—that kissing the other night was real stuff. Nothing that's in the journals—things that happened years ago—can dismantle that.

They move on to Tambo. The birds are out; there are fish around. They get another bite and Jack takes it. Mahi, a beauty. Then they get another hit, and another. Diane takes one rod, Irene the other, while Huck helps Jack with his fish. Diane brings in a barracuda, Irene another wahoo.

Then there's a lull, the best kind of lull, Huck thinks. Jack cracks open a beer and Diane and Irene settle down to talk about books. Irene says she just finished *The Vacationers*. Diane says she loves Louise Penny.

"I'm probably biased because she's a woman and she's Canadian, but I think she's the best mystery writer alive."

"Huck likes mysteries," Irene says at exactly the same time that Huck says, "I read mysteries."

"How long have you two been together?" Diane asks. She smiles from under the brim of a Blue Jays cap. "Jack and I have been dating since eighth grade."

"My one and only," Jack says.

Huck waits for Irene to answer Diane. They've been asked this before, of course, and Irene normally handles it by saying they're not together, that she is just the mate, and everyone is always surprised because they seem like a couple. They finish each other's sentences.

"I'm just a hired hand," Irene says. "And today is my last day. I'm moving on. You guys will be my last clients on the *Mississippi*."

"Saved the best for last," Jack says, raising his beer.

Huck has a lump in his throat. She said it out loud to strangers—she's leaving. Today is her last day. This doesn't mean it's carved in stone, he tells himself. She'll calm down. She'll reconsider. She has to. Please, God. He can't believe he's being punished for telling the truth.

"Will you leave the island?" Diane asks. "Go back to..."

"Iowa," Irene says.

Huck lights a cigarette in the stern. His nerves are splintering.

"No," Irene says. "I'm going to go for my captain's license and get my own boat."

What? Huck thinks. *What?*

"Good for you," Diane says. "Girl power!"

The line whizzes. "Fish on," Huck says, though he couldn't care less.

Wahoo, mahi, barracuda, mahi, then lunch (sandwiches from Sam and Jack's) and a bottle of champagne that Diane brought.

"It's the forty-fifth anniversary of our first date," Diane says. "Way back in 1974." She pours the champagne into four paper cups and passes them around. "But we had no idea you had something to celebrate as well, Irene. Captaining your own boat!" Diane raises her cup. "Hear, hear!"

Somehow, Huck makes himself sip the champagne. He sees Diane grinning at him.

"You must be an excellent teacher."

"She's a natural," Huck says. He's directing his words at Irene, willing her to look at him. "She's the Angler Cupcake."

When Jack and Diane disembark at the National Park Service dock, there are hugs and handshakes all around. Great day, perfect weather, tons of fish, highlight of their vacation; they'll post their pictures on Facebook and write a five-star review on Tripadvisor.

Huck's heart is broken.

Irene is silent in the truck and Huck knows not to make any stops on the way home. When he pulls up Jacob's Ladder, he looks for the Jeep with the tinted windows, but it's not there.

He says, "There's a strange Jeep that's been lurking around here. Black, with tinted windows. Female driver."

Irene says nothing.

Maia is at Joanie's, which is good, Huck thinks, because they can talk freely. Irene hops out of the truck and goes around to grab the smaller cooler out of the back like she always does, leaving Huck to handle the bigger cooler. Jack and Diane took four pounds of the mahi, but there's a lot of fish left. Huck needs to call the restaurants—La Tapa, Morgan's Mango, Extra Virgin, Lime Inn.

But first.

"Irene," he says.

She disappears inside and when Huck comes in, she's standing in the hallway with the journals in her hands. She reads aloud. " 'I'm sex and lobster and champagne-drinking under a blanket of stars. Irene is home and hearth, mother of the boys, keeper of the traditions that make a family.' "

"Irene," Huck says. "Please stop. I tried to warn you—"

" 'Can I lure Russ away from her? Can I make him feel his family is here? I can try. In the new year, I decided, I'm going to introduce him to Maia.' "

"I know, Irene. I read them."

"You don't know," Irene says. Her voice wavers. "He was my *husband.* I *trusted* him. Rosie knew I existed, Huck. She knew about me, she knew about the boys from day one, minute one. She knew about the house I was building, she knew how I was decorating it. She thought I was some kind of...*shrew* who didn't appreciate Russ, didn't respect him or honor his sacrifices, didn't love or worship him the way he deserved." In a move so uncharacteristic that Huck can't believe it's happening, Irene throws the journals down the hall. They land at his feet, splayed open, like birds shot out of the sky. "She wanted him to leave me. She wanted him to propose."

"For the record," Huck says, "at the time, I had no idea any of this was going on."

"Your wife did," Irene says. "LeeAnn!"

"Watch it," Huck says. "Please."

"LeeAnn knew I existed. She knew my *name!*"

"Yes, and if you read carefully, LeeAnn said that if Rosie didn't stop seeing Russ, she would call you." Huck clears his throat. "LeeAnn didn't condone the relationship for one second, Irene. She never would have. She wasn't like that."

"What about *you,* Huck? You expect me to believe that LeeAnn didn't tell you what was going on? You weren't informed that Rosie was seeing a married man?"

"LeeAnn kept her business with Rosie between herself and Rosie."

"But you were her husband."

Huck gives Irene a hard stare. "I'm not sure I owe you an explanation." He sighs. "LeeAnn and Rosie's relationship was tumultuous, Irene. It had deep fault lines that weren't visible to the casual observer. Although most of the time things were fine between them, there would be tremors. And some of those tremors turned into earthquakes. I didn't get in the middle. So, no, I didn't know Rosie was seeing a married man."

"And when she started seeing Russ after LeeAnn died? The Invisible Man, Huck? You didn't ask questions?"

"After LeeAnn died...I was lost for a long time. I was self-absorbed. I knew Rosie was dating someone; I asked to meet him, and Rosie was dead set against it. I didn't push. Maybe I should have, but she was a grown woman."

"She was living under your roof! She was your—"

"Daughter," Huck says. "Yes, yes, she was. But you have two

grown children of your own, Irene. Are you accountable for their actions?"

"My sons are good people," Irene says. "I raised them right."

"Fine, I agree, you did. That's not my point. My point is you can't control how they act. Cash lost the stores in Colorado. Was that *your* fault? Both Baker and Cash lied to Ayers about who they were when they first got here. Was *that* your fault?"

"No," Irene says.

"Rosie made a mistake, Irene, but as the saying goes, it takes two to tango. That affair was fifty percent her fault." Huck feels his blood pressure rising. "I could just as easily be furious that Russ led Rosie on for so many years. That Russ's business dealings *got her killed.* Leaving my granddaughter *without a mother!*" He's losing control—and it feels good! Irene isn't the only one allowed to feel angry and hurt. The affair was 50 percent Russ's fault, but the illegal business was 100 percent his fault.

Irene stares at Huck for a long second, her eyes narrowed. "'Love is messy and complicated and unfair,'" she says. "Quote, unquote, from Rosie herself, and I agree. It's not fair that I have feelings for the man who should be my enemy. Your words just now crystallized our problem. You *should* be furious with Russ. He *was* to blame for their deaths, at least indirectly. We're on different sides of this, Huck. And because of that, I can't work for you and I can't live here. I'm sorry."

"So—what?" Huck says. "You're quitting and you're moving out? Where will you go?"

"To Baker's for the time being, then I'll figure something out," Irene says. "It's none of your concern."

None of your concern. How can she *say* that? "What you told Jack and Diane is true?" Huck asks. "You're striking out on your own? Getting your captain's license? Starting your own charter?

Any idea how difficult that's going to be? You don't know anyone on this island except for me." This comes out all wrong; he sounds like a complete bastard when what he really wants to say is *Please don't leave me.*

"I'm going to pack my things," Irene says. "Which shouldn't take long, but I'd appreciate it if you weren't here when I left."

"Oh, that's rich," Huck says. "You're ordering me out of my own house. After I took you in and gave you a *home* and gave you a *job* and..." He wants to say *Gave you my love*—but no, he won't let her have the satisfaction. She wants to leave? Fine, she can leave. She wants to throw away the relationship? Great. Maybe she's right, maybe they are on different sides of this goddamned situation, maybe the stupidest thing he ever did was let her on his boat that first day.

But even as Huck is thinking this, he knows it's not true. They are on the same side because they're alive. They're the survivors. "I'll leave," Huck says. "But just remember what you told me yesterday, Irene."

She cocks an eyebrow. Her expression now is more sassy than angry; she looks like a rebellious teenager.

"You said you would find a way to forgive them."

Irene retreats to the bedroom and slams the door behind her.

When Huck gets out to his truck, he lights a cigarette and flies down Jacob's Ladder faster than he should. He checks the spot where the black Jeep with the tinted windows was waiting that morning, but it's not there. Too bad, because he's in the mood for a confrontation. He wonders if the woman is a reporter. Or someone sent by the FBI to watch them. Or...someone sent by Croft to watch them. Maybe it's good that Irene is leaving. He doesn't need strangers lurking around him and his granddaughter.

When Huck reaches the bottom of the hill, he has to decide

where he's going. He could pick up some barbecue from Candi's but he won't be able to eat a thing and Maia would be just as happy with peanut butter and jelly.

Her own charter boat. Ha!

He should have passed the journals on to Vasco. People think they want the truth but they can't handle the truth! Huck supposes it's possible that Irene would have reacted like this if he'd given the journals to the FBI without telling her about them. He was damned either way.

He toys with the idea of going to a bar for a beer and a shot, something to calm him down, but that's not the answer tonight. He could only too easily end up like Mick, chained to a bar stool at CBL making a spectacle of himself.

Huck drives through town, past Mongoose Junction, and up the wide, sweeping hill to the sunset-view spot over Cruz Bay. He pulls over and parks. There are a dozen or so people, several couples and one family, waiting for the sun to drop into the ocean. They have their cameras out—of course. These days, a picture of a thing is more important than the thing itself. But Huck is old enough to remember otherwise. He's old enough to watch the sun go down and the fiery pink brush-stroking the clouds and do nothing but think.

At first he's melancholy. The sun is setting on the last day he will ever spend with the Angler Cupcake, Irene Steele.

But then he thinks, *No, that won't do.*

He's a pretty smart guy, resourceful. He's going to find a way to get her back.

AYERS

The phone rings at midnight but Ayers doesn't wake up until she feels Winnie's cold nose pushing against the back of her hand. The dog has proven to be eerily in touch with the human world. *Your phone is ringing!* Yes, Ayers hears the muffled tone; she digs it out from under the rumpled covers of her bed.

The screen tells her it's Mick.

Ayers huffs and hits Decline. She was so tired after her shift at La Tapa that she face-planted on her bed still in her uniform, still in her *clogs,* and when Winnie jumped onto the bed with her, she didn't protest. The phone goes dark for a second, then lights up again, and again Winnie nudges Ayers.

"Argh," Ayers says, but she answers. "What? What, Mick, what?"

Mick is crying.

"What's wrong?" Ayers asks, then remembers that she no longer cares what's wrong.

"Can I come over?" he asks.

"No," Ayers says.

"Please?"

Ayers summons her resolve. It would be only too easy to relent. *Okay, fine, you can come, but you're not staying long.* Mick would step inside, bringing their nine-year history with him. It's not that Mick is even that attractive, but he's attractive to her. He has that something. Ayers loves his hands, and the tattoo of Gordon's paw print under his left rib, and the way he squints when he looks at her like he's looking at the sun. They have good memories, years of them—snorkeling and hiking and partying on the water and on land. How many times had Mick anchored a boat off Water Island so they could swim ashore and get bushwackers from Dinghy's? How many times had they played the brass-ring game at the Soggy Dollar or rolled the dice at Cruz Bay Landing? How many times did they stand in line together at the post office or at the bank to deposit their paychecks, pinkie fingers entwined? How many brunches up at the Banana Deck, how many hikes to Ram Head, how many times had Mick dropped Ayers off at Drift-wood Dave's on their way home from the beach so she could run in for two rum punches to go while he drove around the block? How many times had Mick saved Ayers the corner seat at the Beach Bar while he was working so she could have a front-row view of the band? He used to sneak up behind her and kiss her shoulder, take a surreptitious sip of her drink.

"I'm asleep," Ayers says. "Go home to bed, Mick. Or call Brigid."

"I don't want to call Brigid. I don't care about Brigid. That night at the beach, she trapped me."

"You kissed her, Mick," Ayers says. "Right?" They haven't had a conversation since Ayers broke their engagement, so she hasn't heard Mick admit his guilt.

"Yes," Mick says. "I kissed her. We kissed."

Something inside Ayers zips shut, a tiny compartment where she held out hope that maybe it wasn't true. "Thank you for telling me. We're done. I gave you a second chance, and you blew it. I have self-worth and self-respect and you, my friend, have a problem with commitment, fidelity, and honesty." Ayers runs her hand down Winnie's back for comfort. "This theater production you've been starring in at Cruz Bay Landing is a pathetic plea for attention but it's also a subtle way to make everyone we know think that this is my fault. You're playing the injured party when *you're* the one who screwed it up." Ayers's anger energizes her; she sits up, kicks off her clogs. "You're making an ass of yourself. You've become the village idiot."

"I kissed Brigid," Mick says. "I own that. But even if I hadn't kissed Brigid, the engagement would be over. And why? Why, Ayers? Because you're pregnant with Banker's baby, that's why."

Ayers falls back. Winnie gets to her feet and stands over her. "Who told you that?"

"It's all over town," Mick says.

"No," Ayers says. Did Cash tell Tilda, who then told Skip, who then told Mick? "I haven't told anyone."

"You didn't have to," Mick says. "You took a leave of absence from the boat, you missed shifts at La Tapa, Skip said he heard you retching in the ladies' room before service. It doesn't take Sherlock Holmes to figure it out. Skip actually congratulated *me,* thinking I was the father. But I'm not. Both you and I know that I'm not."

"No," Ayers says.

"And now Banker knows too."

Ayers feels dizzy, like she's on some kind of crazed rocking horse. "What?"

"He and his little boy sat next to me at CBL earlier tonight," Mick says. "I told him."

Ayers is so addled that she's certain there's no way she'll be able to fall back to sleep.

But she does, immediately.

When she wakes up in the morning, there's a text from Baker.
Good morning! You feeling any better?

He knows.

Does she tell him that she knows he knows? Or should she just pretend the phone call with Mick never happened and tell him herself?

The latter. Mick is irrelevant.

She thinks about sending a text back, something along the lines of *Not sick, pregnant. It's yours!*

Whoa! The room is spinning. Ayers races for the bathroom and throws up. When she emerges, Winnie is stationed outside the door.

"Do you need to go out?" Ayers asks. Winnie trots over to the front door and waits. "I can't walk you this second, I'm sorry. Just do your thing and come right back, okay?" Ayers opens the door and Winnie obeys, taking care of business efficiently and then slipping back inside past Ayers's legs. She's such a good dog; much better than Gordon, if Ayers is being honest. Gordon would have sniffed around for twenty minutes and couldn't be trusted if a car or another dog came past. Of course, Winnie is female, so that alone explains it.

Ayers takes a four-seven-eight breath and pours herself half a glass of warm ginger ale. She calls Baker, who answers on the first ring.

"Good morning!"

"Good morning?" Ayers says. He sounds awfully chipper. It occurs to Ayers that maybe Mick lied about telling Baker that Ayers is pregnant. "Listen, Baker, there's something I need to talk to you about."

"If you want to talk in person, I can be there in two seconds," Baker says.

What she wants is to hang up and go back to bed. She sighs. She can't put this conversation off much longer. "Okay."

One Mississippi, two Mississippi, three—there's a knock at the door. Winnie shoots over and starts barking.

"Just a minute!" Ayers says. Is that *him?* Had he been standing outside when she called him? Ayers hurries to the bathroom, takes in her pasty complexion, her bed-mussed hair, her rumpled uniform shirt. Does she stink? Probably. She tries to rub deodorant on without taking off her shirt. She piles her hair on top of her head. Better? Worse? Worse, she decides. She lets it go. Oh, well.

When she swings the door open, there's Baker, looking tan and relaxed. He's gorgeous—tall, broad, smiling in that gee-whiz midwestern way. Ayers is struck by something she has willfully ignored until now. She *likes* Baker. A lot.

Winnie barks. She wants to jump on him, Ayers can tell; her slender golden body is shimmying with energy, her tail is going nuts. It's not her daddy, but close—his brother.

"Hey, I recognize you," Baker says to Winnie. And then, to Ayers, "Hello, beautiful."

If Ayers weren't pregnant, this moment would be so sexy. She would be wearing a bikini or a sundress or hiking shorts and they would be heading out into the sunshine to start their relationship.

"I'm pregnant," she says.

"I know," he says. "Can I come in?"

Ayers figures she's about six weeks along. A check of the internet reveals that her baby is likely the size of a pea.

Will there come a day twenty-five or thirty years from now

when Ayers tells Sweet Pea about the morning she invited Baker Steele inside her tiny, disheveled home to discuss Sweet Pea's very existence? What will Ayers remember? Baker's handsome face may be forgotten, but what will stick with Ayers is her own sense of bewilderment. She's attracted to Baker, but she doesn't know the first thing about him. He might as well be a stranger at the airport who asks her to travel with a mysterious piece of luggage.

They settle on the sofa. Winnie is at Baker's side now—fickle girl.

"It's your baby," Ayers says.

"I heard."

"I want to make that clear. It's yours, not Mick's. Also, I'm finished with Mick."

"You're sure? Because you said that last time and it didn't end up being true. I was gone for two days and you got engaged to the guy."

When he says it that way, it sounds awful. It *was* awful. In agreeing to marry Mick, Ayers was unfair to all parties involved—Baker, Mick, and, most of all, herself. "I thought it was what I'd been waiting for," Ayers says. "It was validating after what happened with Brigid to feel like he was choosing me, to feel like I'd won."

"You told me that story about your parents in Kathmandu. The hiccup, your mother with another man." Baker's gaze wanders over to the travel photographs Ayers has on her wall. "In telling me that story, you made me feel like the hiccup."

Ayers can't believe she told Baker the story about her parents in Kathmandu. Her mother had had a brief affair with a British expat bar owner...or she hadn't; Ayers isn't sure to this day. Ayers pulled that story out, she supposes, because she wanted to justify forgiving Mick. She was making excuses for him. But she was finished with that now.

"This doesn't have to look any certain way," Baker says. "First question: Do you want to keep the baby?"

"Oh. Yes. Yes, I do."

"Great. Second question: Do you want to have the baby and still be with Mick, Ayers? If the answer is yes, I will understand."

"You will?"

"Yes. Is that what you want?"

"No," Ayers says. "I told you, I'm finished with Mick. That's my final answer, in the name of self-respect."

Palpable relief emanates from Baker.

"But," Ayers says.

"But?"

"I don't know that I can be with you either, not right away. I think I need to be alone for a while."

"Alone."

"Romantically alone, yes. I need some time and I need some space." This is something Ayers has given a lot of thought to. If she weren't pregnant, she might have climbed right into bed with Baker, forging ahead without any introspection. On to the next guy! She would have used Baker like a bandage, plastering his love and devotion over the wounds that Mick left. But being pregnant changes things. Ayers needs to be alone. She needs to worry less about falling in love with someone else and instead fall in love with herself. It's the best gift she can bestow on this child: a mother who is happy and capable and whole.

Ayers puts a hand on Baker's arm. "But we can be friends."

"Friends."

"Until I feel like I'm ready to start something new. I don't want this baby to dictate my love life. I want my heart to dictate that."

"We're not exactly starting from ground zero," Baker says. "We have something to work with. I fell in love with you the second I saw you—"

"Don't say *love*." Ayers collapses back into the cushions. "Before I found out I was pregnant, I figured we could just start over, go on some dates, take things slow, do it properly."

"That's what I thought too."

"Nothing says *taking it slow* like instant family."

They laugh. It's funny for a few seconds.

"You heard we lost the villa?" Baker says.

"Maia told me. She said you were looking for a rental?"

"Yep, yep. I stayed at the Westin for so long that they offered me a job selling time-shares, which I accepted."

"Seriously?"

"I start Monday," Baker says. "And I got Floyd settled at Gifft Hill with the cool kids."

"All the kids at Gifft Hill are cool," Ayers says.

"My feelings exactly," Baker says. He gives her an uncomfortable smile. "And I found a villa."

"You did?" Ayers says. "Where?"

"Across the street," Baker says. "The Happy Hibiscus."

At this, Winnie barks in a way that sounds like a laugh.

"The Happy Hibiscus? *Right* across the street?"

"Yes," Baker says. "Floyd and I are moving in…today."

"Today?"

"I was just over there dropping off groceries."

"Ah," Ayers says. She rubs Winnie behind the ears. *So much for space,* she thinks. She and the Steeles are becoming one big extremely nontraditional family. She casts her eyes skyward. Rosie is either laughing or crying up there. Or both.

CASH

The night before Tilda leaves on her weeklong research trip with Dunk, she and Cash drink a bottle of Granger's Cristal while skinny-dipping in the pool (Granger and Lauren are gone, off to LA) and then Cash makes love to Tilda on the round sun bed under a crescent moon. Later, when they're wrapped in the luscious Turkish towels, gazing at the twinkling lights of Tortola, Tilda cries a little. She doesn't *want* to go away without him, she says. She's going to *miss* him.

"It's only a week," Cash says. His casual attitude is an act. He can't believe this is happening. Tilda is going to Anguilla, St. Lucia, and a tiny private island called Eden, home to a resort so exclusive that you have to be invited to stay there; management curates its guests as though it's selecting art for a museum. (How did Tilda and Dunk make the cut? Cash wonders. He hopes it was through Granger's prodigious network and not Dunk's influence.)

Tilda and Dunk have separate rooms at Midi et Minuit, the resort on Anguilla, and at Emerald Hill on St. Lucia. But of the dozen freestanding villas at Eden, only one is available during Tilda and Dunk's stay. So they'll be sharing.

"You'd better behave yourself," Tilda says, resting her head on Cash's chest. "No picking up women at the Soggy Dollar."

"What about you?" Cash asks. "Are you going to behave yourself?"

"Oh, please," Tilda says. "You never have a thing to worry about with me. But especially not with Dunk."

The next day, as Cash is aboard *Treasure Island* heading for Virgin Gorda, a boat cuts in front of them going at least sixty knots— it's coming from the direction of the East End and heading for St. Thomas. It's the *Olive Branch,* of course. Tilda and Dunk are sitting in the stern, laughing. Cash hears the captain yell out and Cash wonders if this will finally be the time James calls the Coast Guard to complain. Or maybe Cash will call the Coast Guard himself. Dunk did this on purpose; is he trying to make a point to Cash? *I'm taking off with your girl.* Tilda is wearing a black sundress Cash has never seen before; it's sleek and sophisticated, possibly borrowed from her mother's closet. She's also wearing a pair of dark cat's-eye sunglasses, Tom Ford, that Cash knows she lifted from Lauren.

When Tilda sees Cash, she waves and blows a kiss. She seems older and more glamorous, as though she outgrew him overnight.

"Hold on!" Cash calls to his passengers as the boat slams into the *Olive Branch*'s wake.

With Tilda away, Cash has the villa in Peter Bay to himself; Virgie, the housekeeper, has been given the week off. Another guy might revel in the freedom, might make a list of all the ways to push the envelope. Cash can borrow liberally from Granger's wine fridge and make a trip to Starfish Market for thick, marbled steaks and charge them to the house account. He can snoop through the master wing—Granger and Lauren's bedroom, sitting room, closets, offices, and bathroom—and see what secrets he can dig up. Money? Pills? He can bring Winnie back; he can let Winnie swim in the pool. Of all these ideas, only the last one holds any appeal—although Cash suspects that the villa has cameras placed so strategically that he can't even find them and block them.

The first night alone, Cash cracks a beer and checks his phone frequently to see if Tilda has texted or called. She and Dunk were taking his boat all the way to San Juan and flying to Anguilla from there. Tilda sent the full itinerary to Cash's phone and when he looks at it, he sees that she was supposed to land in Anguilla at three o'clock. At seven, he still hasn't heard from her and so what is he to think but that she has forgotten all about him? She and Dunk landed on the tiny airstrip and were whisked away by a private car—Cash pictures a vintage Peugeot—to the lush tropical entrance of Midi et Minuit. Midi et Minuit, built in the 1920s, was the private beachfront estate of French perfume heiress Helene Simone until the early 1980s, when it was transformed into a resort. In those days, it attracted guests like John and Cristina DeLorean and Burt Reynolds and Loni Anderson, and it was famous for its midnight disco parties. The owners went bankrupt in the crash of 1987, and Midi et Minuit closed until the year 2000, when it was bought by a businessman from Monte Carlo who poured fifty-five million dollars into the property and turned it into the epitome of "low-key luxury" and "barefoot chic."

Cash wonders if Tilda and Dunk were greeted with welcome cocktails and chilled towels while the hotel's most famous resident, Bijou, a Yorkshire terrier, yipped around Tilda's ankles until she scooped him up and gave him kisses. Were Dunk and Tilda mistaken for a couple? Undoubtedly yes, despite the reservation for separate rooms. Or maybe during their day of travel, Tilda and Dunk had bonded over their excitement about this new venture; maybe they'd had drinks on the plane, and maybe Tilda fell asleep with her head accidentally leaning on Dunk's shoulder. Maybe by the time they reached the resort, they asked to share a room. But no, not yet, not the first night. Cash has enough faith in Tilda to know that nothing has happened between them yet.

Why hasn't she called? Or at least texted to let him know she arrived safely?

Cash's fingers hover over his phone. Should he text her?

No, he won't. And he's not going to sit around the villa pining away either. He doesn't have money to waste on going out to dinner, but, oh, well, he's doing it anyway. He drives Tilda's Range Rover into Cruz Bay and sits at the bar at the Banana Deck. He orders the shrimp curry and chats with the bartender, Kim, who immediately says, "You hang out with Tilda Payne, right? I saw you two at Christmas Cove a few weeks ago. Is she working tonight?"

"She's...away," Cash says. Kim seems friendly enough for Cash to spill his guts to. He could tell her that Tilda is away for a week with some millennial millionaire who lives out in the East End, but how pathetic would that sound? Instead, Cash raises his beer glass. "I'll have another one, please."

He stops at two beers, eats his curry, and chats a little more with Kim, telling her that he works on the *Treasure Island*.

She says, "Oh yeah?" and studies him for a second. "You know, rumor has it that Ayers is pregnant."

Whoa! This is unexpected. Cash's face must register genuine shock because Kim leans across the bar. "I shouldn't have said that, it's probably not true, please don't tell anyone."

"Oh, I won't," Cash says. Kim moves down the bar to help another customer and Cash realizes their conversation is over. He scans the place to see if anyone looks familiar or even promising to talk to; he needs some *friends*. He thinks about stopping by La Tapa on his way home to give Ayers a heads-up that her secret is out, but that will only upset her, and swinging by Tilda's place of work while Tilda is away feels weird and desperate. Besides which, Skip will be working, and he hates Cash's guts.

Cash pays the bill, waves to Kim, and tries to look like a man who has important people to meet. He could check out Beach Bar, see if a band is playing tonight, or he could try his luck at the Parrot Club, though he definitely does *not* have money to gamble away. Another drink sounds appealing—maybe at the Dog House Pub, where he can watch basketball on TV? But he's driving Tilda's Range Rover, it's a seventy-thousand-dollar vehicle, and two drinks is a wise limit.

He checks his phone, which he miraculously avoided doing all through dinner (there is nothing more pathetic than a dude alone at dinner looking at his phone) and finds nothing from Tilda. For an instant, he wonders if she's okay. Did her plane crash? Was she kidnapped? Or, a more likely possibility, did something happen to her phone? Did she leave it in the airport restroom? Did it fall into her personal plunge pool? If anything dire had happened, Cash assumes he would have heard from Granger or Lauren. If something happened to her phone, she would have simply texted from Dunk's phone.

Tomorrow, maybe he'll see if James the boat captain wants to grab a drink. James will say no; he has a wife and a baby girl out in Coral Bay, and he likely gets his fill of Cash while they're on the boat.

Well, it's not like Cash doesn't know anyone else on the island. He calls his mother—gets her voicemail. Then he calls his brother—gets his voicemail.

Cash tosses his phone onto the seat beside him and yells as loud as he can. The sound, desperate even to his own ears, is absorbed by the expensive leather.

Cash wakes up in the morning to a new day—chirping geckos, singing birds, blue sky, pearlescent sunlight. There's a text from Tilda. Finally. Cash opens it.

It says: Arrived! Followed by a single kissy-face emoji. Sent at...12:47 a.m.

Cash stares at the text, willing it to say something else, something more. She was supposed to land yesterday at three in the afternoon. Why is she only texting him at a quarter to one the following morning? He checks to see if there's a missed call from her. Nope. So this is it. Technically, it checks the box—she's let him know she made it safely—but it feels perfunctory, like an afterthought. *Oops, forgot to text Cash.* Does she miss him? If the answer is yes, why doesn't she say so? She used to text that she missed him if the *Treasure Island* was a few minutes late pulling into Cruz Bay or if he got held up in the customhouse coming back from the BVIs. This feels like a blow-off. Why did she wait so long to text and what was she doing up so late?

Cash texts back: Glad you made it safely. I miss you!

He waits to see if she responds, but there's nothing. She must still be sleeping.

While Cash is driving to work, his phone rings and his whole body relaxes. There she is.

He's on the dicey curve above Hawksnest so he answers without checking the display. "Hello?" He has the radio up, 104.3 the

Buzz out of San Juan, which is playing Michael Franti, and he makes no move to turn it down. He wants to sound happy, busy, unconcerned.

"Cash?"

It's not Tilda. It's his mother.

Cash is so crushed, he nearly hangs up.

"Hey," he says, and he does turn down the music. He's no longer in a "Sound of Sunshine" mood.

"Cash? It's Mom. Listen, I have some good news."

Good news at this point would be Tilda calling to say that Dunk's picture should be next to *douchebag* in the dictionary and that she can't stand him another second and is on her way home, hotel research be damned. He can't believe how strongly he feels about Tilda. He knew the relationship was promising but his feelings have ratcheted up to the next level now that she's gone. Gone with Dunk. "Oh, really?" Cash says. He wonders briefly if Irene's attorney somehow managed to get the villa back. What a major relief *that* would be! He could leave Peter Bay and regain at least a little of his self-respect.

"Milly's estate is through probate," Irene says. "She had stocks that your grandfather bought back in the late 1970s that were sold for us. To the tune of a hundred and seventeen thousand dollars. Now, I wanted to split that four ways—you, your brother, Maia, and myself."

"Good call including Maia," Cash says. "That's really decent of you, Mom."

"Well, just listen. It turns out Baker doesn't need the money. He got money from Anna. So Milly's money will be split three ways. By next week, you'll be thirty-nine thousand dollars richer."

Thirty-nine thousand dollars. Cash knows he should be grateful but all he can think is that Dunk has enough money to buy an island. Buy! An! Island! This little jaunt Tilda is on must be costing nearly thirty-nine thousand dollars, if not more.

"Thanks, Mom," he says. "That is good news. I can buy a truck." *Used,* he thinks.

"Your brother bought a Jeep," Irene says. "And he found a rental."

"He did?" Cash says, perking up. "How big?"

"Two bedrooms," Irene says. "In Fish Bay."

Cash's mood darkens. "I thought he was looking for something bigger. I can't stay at Tilda's forever, Mom. And what about Winnie? She's living with Ayers."

"The villa Baker rented is across the street from Ayers," Irene says. "I forgot to ask Baker if he's allowed to have pets. He might be."

Which means that Winnie might have a home—but Cash does not. "Thanks for the call, Mom. I'll get you my bank information but I'm at work now, so I should go."

"Honey?" Irene says. "Is everything okay?"

Cash sighs. His mother knows him; his mother loves him. They have always been allies, and if anyone on this earth can relate to feeling abandoned, it's his mother. Except she seems pretty happy with Huck. "Tilda went away for a week with another guy," Cash says. "Some super-wealthy investor who's funding this eco-resort that Tilda and her parents want to build on Lovango Cay."

"They went away together? Like, *together*-together?"

"Supposedly all business," Cash says. "Tilda said he turns her stomach." *Had* Tilda said this? No; this is how Cash feels. Dunk turns *his* stomach. "Whatever. I guess we'll see."

"If it makes you feel any better," Irene says, "she'd be a fool to leave you."

Cash shakes his head. "Thanks, Mom."

*   *   *

On the second day, Tilda texts Cash a selfie. It's just her face. She has her mother's sunglasses on; she's lying back on a chaise in the sun.

Cash responds by texting her a selfie he takes on the bow of *Treasure Island,* his sunglasses and headset on, wind blowing his hair. He feels like a jackass.

The third day, Tilda sends a text that says, Off to St. Luscious! With a kissy-face emoji.

Cash texts back: Have fun. He can't believe the minimalist nature of her communication. One text a day? No calls at all? Of course, Cash hasn't called her either. Should he? No, he thinks. But an instant later, he does call her. The phone rings six times, he hears the funny tone that means she's in another country, then her voicemail picks up. She texted only two minutes earlier; is she so busy that she can't say a quick hello? Maybe she's on the plane, or maybe she's frantically packing, trying to get out of the hotel room to meet her car to the airport. There could be lots of reasons she can't talk. Cash hangs up.

Cash realizes he hates being trapped in the villa in Peter Bay and—hidden cameras be damned—he starts flagrantly breaking the rules. Okay, maybe not *flagrantly,* Cash doesn't have a rule-breaking bone in his body. He *cautiously* breaks the rules. He drinks six of Granger's Island Hoppin' IPAs and samples the whiskey in the crystal decanter that he finds in Granger's study. Granger's study is dark and serious—there's a portrait of Abraham Lincoln on the wall. Then again, the Payne family *is* from Illinois, so maybe this makes sense. The desk is backed by a wall of books, nothing leather-bound, though they're all hardcovers; fiction, it looks like—Tilda mentioned that Granger is a prodigious and serious reader. Cash sees they're alphabetized by author, like in a bookstore—Nabokov, Nesbo, Ng. The surface of Granger's desk is clear, and the drawers are all locked (Cash checks; he's looking, of course, for notes, some record of Granger's impressions of Duncan Huntley or possibly even their financial arrangement), so Cash takes only the whiskey, but even that feels like getting away with something.

Before going to sleep on the third night, Cash moves out of Tilda's wing and into the guest wing, which is where Cash brought Tilda's friend Max after Max got drunk and sick on *Treasure Island*. Tilda's wing of the house is cluttered with Tilda's clothes, books, magazines, sunglasses, bikinis, hair products, a bunch of half-burned Nest scented candles, corkscrews, the cheap vinyl drawstring backpacks she likes to carry, and pairs of hiking boots, water shoes, and work clogs as well as receipts and piles of cash, her tips from various nights that she doesn't ever bother to count or deposit, but the guest wing is immaculate. The wing is two stories connected by a floating staircase that appears to be magically suspended in air. Upstairs is a comfy sitting room with a huge television and a perfect little palm-green-and-white-tiled kitchenette that has a petal-pink minifridge filled with soft drinks and beer. How did Cash not know about this? He takes an Island Hoppin' IPA, thank you very much. The bedroom is downstairs. There's a four-poster mahogany bed draped with white sheers that looks like what a bed in heaven must look like. Out a sliding glass door is a private garden and a deep, circular plunge pool.

Home for the night, Cash thinks. He doesn't have to go into the main house at all.

He's getting thirty-nine thousand dollars free and clear. After he finishes his beer, he feels happy about this. He can buy a truck and stop driving Tilda's Rover around like he's the errand boy.

Cash has a difficult time falling asleep in the guest wing. The bed is too soft and it doesn't smell like Tilda. It's quarter to eleven; he could still go out. Cruz Bay isn't exactly a late-night town but Cash knows the Parrot Club will be open. He can take what's left in his bank account and gamble, now that he knows there's more money coming.

Cash gets all the way out to the driveway before he comes to his senses. He's been drinking; he should not get behind the wheel of the Rover and he should *not* piss all his hard-earned money away at the Parrot Club. He has a full charter tomorrow. He should go to bed.

He does go to bed—back in Tilda's wing, his face buried in her pillow.

Working on *Treasure Island* has been a good distraction. There's nothing like being responsible for thirty people as they swim, snorkel (often for the first time), and drink copious amounts of alcohol to keep one in the present moment. But on day four of not talking to Tilda—honestly, what's going on? Has she not thought to call Cash even once?—Cash finds himself short on patience. It doesn't help that he has a guest on the boat who reminds him of Duncan. This guy, Bradley, is an aggressive, in-your-face hipster. He's exactly Dunk's height and build, and he's wearing jeans—jeans, on a trip to the BVIs!—and a plain white T-shirt that looks like it came out of a three-pack of Hanes but probably was made by Rick Owens and cost four hundred dollars. And he's wearing a flashy gold Omega. Cash notices the jeans and the watch when Bradley checks in but not his Versace slip-on loafers, which he refuses to be separated from when it's time to board the boat.

Cash says calmly, "Take your shoes off and put them in the basket or I will leave you here."

"Oh yeah?" Bradley says, squaring his shoulders.

Cash lifts the rope from the bollard. Everyone is aboard except for Bradley, who remains in his shoes on the dock.

"Yeah," Cash says.

Reluctantly, Bradley removes his precious shoes and hands them over to his girlfriend, who, Cash remembers from check-in, is named Gretchen Gingerman. She puts them in her oversize Fendi bag.

Bradley stays in the shade of the wheelhouse while Gretchen fetches him drinks. Gretchen has golden hair, is three inches taller than Bradley, and has the face and body of a supermodel; Cash tries not to look too closely but Gretchen Gingerman seems pretty damn perfect. And unlike Bradley, she's cool. She leans across the bar and apologizes about the shoes, then says, "Bradley has a thing about people seeing his feet," which is a statement so bizarre that all Cash can do is laugh, and Gretchen Gingerman laughs right along with him. Then Gretchen's phone rings and she checks the display and says, "That's him. He must be wondering where his drink is."

"He called you?" Cash says. He takes his time making two painkillers. Let Bradley wonder.

Bradley stays on the boat during their trip to the Baths, since it can't be done in jeans. Gretchen goes (she's wearing a gold-lamé string bikini; Ayers would have had a field day, but Cash is inclined to cut Gretchen some slack, and besides, she looks amazing in it) and has a wonderful time. Gretchen also goes snorkeling at the Indians. Cash shows her his favorite staghorn coral formation, where they see a school of parrotfish and a baby barracuda, and when they get back to the boat, Bradley is glowering.

He says to Cash, "You trying to make time with my girl?"

Cash holds up his palms. "Just showing her the fish, man."

They go to Pirates Bight on Norman Island for lunch; it has a dock, so Bradley can finally disembark. Cash always sits at the bar and orders the mahi sandwich (he isn't required to socialize during lunch), but he can't keep from seeking out the two-top in the corner where Gretchen and Bradley are sitting by themselves. This seems a little sad. By this point in the trip, most people have bonded with other guests and all sit at nearby or connecting tables so they can chat. Cash knows he shouldn't... but he heads over to Gretchen and Bradley's table. Gretchen is eating the fish and chips like it's her last meal on earth, swiping her fries liberally through the tartar sauce, but Bradley has only a painkiller in front of him.

"Not hungry?" Cash asks. He's poking the bear, he knows this, but he can't help himself. "Did being on the boat make you nauseated?"

"He's fasting," Gretchen says. "He's like Jack from Twitter. It's a control thing."

"A *productivity* thing," Bradley says. He shoots his watch to the end of his wrist; it actually looks a little big, like it's his father's watch. "Not that it's any of this squid's business whether I eat or don't eat."

Squid? Cash thinks. Did *Bradley,* who came on an all-day swim-and-snorkel charter in a pair of skinny Calvin Kleins like he's Brooke Shields, just call *Cash* a squid?

Gretchen is giving Cash big apologetic eyes, probably

imploring him not to engage, an expression that doesn't escape Bradley's notice. "Don't ogle him," Bradley says. He drains the painkiller top to bottom in one long gulp like it's some kind of party trick. *Guess what, Bradley,* Cash wants to say. *I see it all day, every day. Chugging a painkiller does not make you a badass.* "Don't you have to go swab the decks?" Bradley asks.

He's small, Cash tells himself. *And he's insecure, even though he probably makes millions and has a smoke-show girlfriend.* "Yes," Cash says. He grins because Bradley is so mired in his own pointless misery that this seems like the response that would irk him the most. "See you on the boat at one thirty sharp."

Their last stop is White Bay on Jost Van Dyke. On the way over to Jost, Cash mans the bar and Gretchen comes in for two painkillers.

"I'm sorry about Bradley," she says. "I made him come on this trip when he didn't want to. He agreed just to make me happy."

So is *it making you happy?* Cash wants to ask. He believes that if you agree to do something you'd rather not do for someone else's sake, then you should do it *graciously,* with some *enthusiasm,* like a *good sport.*

"I told him I'd stay on the boat with him when we get to Jost," Gretchen says. "He can't get onto the beach without getting wet?"

"No," Cash says. "We anchor about ten yards out and people wade ashore." He laughs. "There's a reason the bar is called the Soggy Dollar."

"We'll stay on the boat, then. I just wanted to tell you in advance."

"You do you," Cash says. "But I would be a terrible first mate if I didn't warn you that you're making a mistake. Leave your boy-friend on the boat and come ashore, just for a little while. White Bay is the most joyous place on earth. You have to experience it. I can't let you be a bystander."

"Aww," Gretchen says. "You're sweet to look out for me like that, but I'd better stay with Bradley."

"Okay…" Cash says.

Gretchen comes over to Cash's side of the bar, snakes an arm around his shoulders, and holds her phone up for a selfie. "Smile," she says. "I'm going to make you famous."

Late that night, Cash's phone rings. He grapples around in the dark until he finds it on the nightstand. He is, once again, in Tilda's wing.

The screen says NO CALLER ID.

Great, he thinks. Just what he needs, an anonymous call in the middle of the night. "Hello?"

"Cash?"

It's Tilda. Now, on night four, she decides to call. At—he checks the bedside clock—2:17 a.m. Man, he would love to just hang up, but he's been waiting a long time for this, and besides, he *is* living in her house. "Hey," Cash says. "What's up?"

"What's *up?*" She sounds…angry for some reason. *She* sounds angry. That's rich, Cash thinks. She was supposed to call him days earlier, was supposed to call and text and FaceTime, and she said she'd send pictures of every cool detail so he would feel like he was right there with her. Has any of that happened? No, it has not.

"How's your trip?" Cash asks. "You having fun?"

"My trip *was* great. My trip *was* the best four days of my life until just now, when I logged on to Instagram and saw a picture of you cozied up with Gretchen Gingerman!"

"Who?" Cash says, though he obviously knows who Gretchen Gingerman is. What he doesn't know is how or why Tilda knows who Gretchen Gingerman is. Are they *friends?*

"Gretchen Gingerman, Cash, don't play dumb. She was on *Treasure Island* today and she posted a selfie with you for her sixteen million followers."

"What?" Cash says. Sixteen million followers? "Who is she?"

"An influencer," Tilda says. "One of the biggest in the country. Literally every single person I know follows her, and hence, *everyone* saw you drooling over her in her Lisa Marie Fernandez bikini."

"I wasn't drooling," Cash says. He can't believe Gretchen Gingerman is an influencer with sixteen million followers. That's...insane. He can't quite wrap his mind around that. "She was just a guest on the boat, Til. Her boyfriend was a world-class jackass and I was nice to her. Not extra-nice, just regular nice."

"Her boyfriend, Bradley?" Tilda says. "The one whose father invented Bitcoin?"

"Yeah, that was him." Cash doesn't care about Gretchen, and he cares about Bitcoin Bradley even less, though he's unsurprised to hear Bradley is a spoiled rich kid without any identifiable talent or skills of his own. "So I've been wondering why you haven't called," Cash says. "I guess you were just waiting for me to turn up on some famous chick's Instagram." He tries to keep his voice light, but actually, he's furious.

"This is a work trip," Tilda says. "My parents laid out a lot of money for this and I'm trying to be mindful of that and do a good job here. You know how distracting the phone can be. It's black magic that sucks you right out of the present moment."

"All right." Cash closes his eyes and tries to be mindful about enjoying the sound of Tilda's voice. "How's it going? Tell me everything."

"Our first stop was Midi et Minuit on Anguilla. It was very chic, very French. Edith Piaf was playing over the speakers in the lobby; we were greeted with glasses of Taittinger—that's their house champagne, hello—and these tiny, airy gougères. The place was so elegant and gracious, it was like we were visiting a fantastically wealthy French aunt with impeccable taste. The rooms were minimalist in the best way. The linens...don't get me started on how divine the linens were. I sourced everything with their GM. And the lighting in the bathroom was so flattering— I will never look as beautiful as I did in the Midi et Minuit bathroom. The pool was huge and had different areas. It was the perfect temperature, twenty-six degrees—that's Celsius, I have to convert that. It was cool enough to be refreshing but not chilly. But...the service...well, I thought it was fine, excellent even, but Dunk found it obsequious."

Dunk found it. Cash gets out of bed and goes out onto Tilda's deck. At the mention of Dunk's name, Cash wants to throw his phone into the pool. "Nothing worse than obsequious service."

"Yes, there is, Cash. Slow, careless service is worse. Island time is worse."

"I was kidding, Til. I don't even know what *obsequious* means."

"It means there's a person fawning over you, trying to anticipate your needs every time you turn around. Like I said, it doesn't bother me; these people are simply doing what they're paid to do. Dunk got bent out of shape when he was helping me with the headrest of my chaise and the pool guy nearly took him out."

Cash now has to picture Dunk helping Tilda with her chaise,

which necessarily puts Dunk and Tilda side by side in chaises, Tilda in one of her skimpy bikinis.

"How was the second place?" Cash asks.

"I'm getting there, hold on. So, our two days on Anguilla are sublime, we feel pampered, the place is elegant as hell, and I'm thinking nothing can possibly top it. Then..."

Then? Cash thinks.

"We get to Emerald Hill on St. Lucia. Now, Anguilla is a flat white sandbar, no topography to speak of. But St. Lucia is volcanic, like St. John only...much prettier."

Cash feels offended by this statement, which is funny, seeing as how he has lived here only a couple of months. "I don't believe it."

"Believe it. St. Lucia has these tapered volcanic spires called the Pitons, and Emerald Hill is positioned to display their fifty shades of green to maximum advantage. Now, you want to talk about an eco-resort? You won't believe how committed to minimizing ecological impact this place is, but in the most aesthetically jaw-dropping way. Listen to this..."

Cash drifts in and out of Tilda's monologue. *Twenty species of tropical hardwood harvested in environmentally sustainable ways...bloodwood, locust, purpleheart, cabbage wood...walls of crushed coral plaster quarried in Barbados...and the food...mahi banh mi, conch tacos, guava pulled pork...*

"It was so delicious, even Dunk ate."

Cash snaps to attention. "He did?" Cash is dismayed to hear that Dunk loosened up enough to let food pass his lips and that he exhibited the behavior of a normal human being.

"He's been eating three squares. I mean, I had to work on him for a few days but nobody could resist the breakfast buffet that Emerald Hill lays out. The fruit alone! They have a secret chilled drawer filled with champagne mangoes, but you have to know about it to request them."

"I take it our resort will have a secret chilled-mango drawer?" Cash says. *Our resort* sounds a little too presumptuous, so he quickly says, "The Lovango resort."

"You bet," Tilda says. "But the best part of Emerald Hill is the spa. Dunk and I went for massages and before you enter the treatment room, they ask you to sit in this round shallow pool that's inlaid with iridescent rainbow tiles. It's like sitting inside a kaleidoscope."

"Wait a minute," Cash says. "Go back. You and Dunk had massages...together?"

Tilda pauses. "We each had a massage, yes."

"Together? Were you naked under a sheet side by side while you got massages?"

"Technically, it *was* a couples massage, but that's not what I requested. I requested two massages at the same time so that our schedules were aligned and I wasn't sitting around waiting for him to go to dinner. But the woman in the spa misunderstood and booked it as a couples massage and once I figured that out, I'm sorry, it was too awkward to fix, so I rolled with it." Tilda pauses. "I kept my bikini on."

"Did Dunk keep his shorts on?"

"I have no idea, Cash. I didn't check to see what Dunk was doing. I promise you, the massage wasn't a big deal."

"But me in a selfie with Gretchen Gingerman was?" Cash says. "Why don't you explain what the dynamic between you and Dunk has been?"

"It's been...better than I expected, I guess. At first, he was a little over the top with his hokey Australian shtick—*Crikey! Good on ya! Bob's your uncle!*—but he's toned that down and I have to admit, I'm impressed by how informed he is. He did his research on these islands before we got down here—the history, the culture, the industry, the hidden treasures. So, for example, today we had the resort pack us a picnic and we hiked into the rain forest to see this fifty-foot waterfall in the middle of a natural garden. It was like something out of a fairy tale."

Cash clears his throat. Does she realize what she sounds like? She "worked on" Dunk and got him eating the chilled champagne mangoes and the conch tacos; he adjusted Tilda's chaise; they had a couples massage (no big deal!); they hiked with a picnic to the fairy-tale waterfall. Cash can, maybe, accept all that (no, not the massages, sorry), but what about the things Tilda *isn't* telling him? Has Dunk touched her? Reached for her hand? Kissed her good night? Rubbed sunscreen into her back? Held her in the water? Played footsie under the table? Has Dunk told Tilda he had a dream about her? Have they had heart-to-heart conversations? Has Tilda talked about Cash, and, if so, what has she said?

"They have live music at all meals," Tilda says. "A classical piano player at breakfast, a jazz combo at lunch, a guitar player who sounds exactly like Zac Brown at dinner. The Zac Brown guy is named Ezra, we sort of befriended him and he took us to this local bar in Gros Islet tonight where they had real reggae music, not just warmed-over Bob Marley, and we danced. That's why I'm home so late. I told Dunk I wanted our resort to have live music at every meal but I didn't think we could afford it and Dunk said we have carte blanche and everything is possible." She sighs. "Tomorrow we go to Eden by private seaplane."

"Private seaplane?" Cash says. "I thought it was commercial to St. Vincent and then a prop plane."

"Dunk arranged for a private seaplane," Tilda says. "We save half a day that way."

Cash has heard enough. The signs are all right in front of him: Tilda and Dunk are a "we" now. If they haven't slept together yet, they will on Eden when they're sharing a villa. This thought—that it hasn't happened yet but will imminently—is gut-wrenching.

"You haven't asked about me or things here, but you should know that I won't be living at your parents' when you get back."

"Wait," she says. "How come? Did you find a place, or—"

"No."

"Did...oh, jeez, did Granger say something about you going into his study?"

Cash feels a hot flush creep up his neck. Granger knows Cash was in his study? He told Tilda? Cash is being monitored, his every move watched and questioned, while Tilda is free to do as she damn well pleases! Couples massage! It was a misunderstanding! Too awkward to fix!

"Listen, Tilda," Cash says. "Staying here isn't working out for me. Enjoy the rest of your trip. I'll see you around."

He hangs up and feels extremely proud of himself—for approximately sixty seconds.

His phone pings with a text from Tilda: Are you breaking up with me, then?

No! he thinks. *I want you to come home. I want to wake up to-morrow and have things back to the way they were before Duncan Huntley walked into Extra Virgin and ordered his pretentious Australian wine.*

Yes, Cash types. Sorry. His finger hovers over the Send button.

Picnic at a waterfall, like something out of a fairy tale?

He squeezes his eyes shut and presses Send, and the swoosh sound marks the end of his relationship with Tilda Payne.

Tilda called to accuse him of drooling over a social media influencer? That wasn't jealousy, he sees now. That was a manifestation of her own guilty conscience! Cash was the one who did the right thing; he stayed on St. John to work so that he didn't leave *Treasure Island* in the lurch. Why is he getting kicked in the balls?

Dunk arranged for a seaplane? Bah! What Tilda means is that Dunk is rich and ordered a seaplane as a flex, whereas Cash swabs the deck and doesn't know the meaning of the word *obsequious*.

First thing in the morning, Cash calls Baker.

"Does your new place have a sofa?" Cash asks. "Because I need to crash with you for a while. This thing with Tilda blew up."

"It has two sofas," Baker says. "Which is a good thing, because one sofa is already taken."

"What?" Cash says. "By whom?"

"Our mother," Baker says.

ST. JOHN

The Gifft Hill mothers among us are the first to notice the black Jeep with the tinted windows. It drives slowly past the school at drop-off one morning, then the next. None of us have ever seen it before, but for a second we think maybe it belongs to Janine Whittaker. She and her husband own the Beach Bum Car Rental company and it feels like she gets a new Jeep every week.

The Gifft Hill School mothers who are romantically available—

Swan Seeley (divorcing), Bonny Kizer (divorced for years), and Paula Morrow (open marriage)—have taken to loitering in the school parking lot, pretending to share parenting woes while they wait for Baker Steele to drop off his son, Floyd. Swan is a natural flirt so she always finds a way to engage Baker in conversation, and Paula Morrow is a pleaser, a flatterer, and touchy-feely—on those occasions when Baker climbs out of his Jeep to chat, she squeezes his biceps and compliments his legs. We can all agree: Baker Steele has very fine legs. Bonny Kizer inevitably mentions that she is the only one of the three who is technically free. Swan and her husband, Brent, are in the throes of a nasty custodial and financial battle (Swan has family money and Brent has a gambling problem), and Paula Morrow *has a husband who lives with her on Pocket Money Road* (although he travels to the States for work and they have an "arrangement").

Swan, Bonny, and Paula are all standing in the school parking lot on the day that the bluebird Jeep pulls in and it's *not* Baker driving but rather some other man—cute, with blond surfer hair.

When Floyd gets out of the car he fist-bumps this man and says, "See ya later, Uncle Cash."

"That must be Baker's brother," Paula says.

"Maybe he has two brothers," Bonny says.

"I've seen that guy before," Swan says, and Bonny and Paula mentally roll their eyes. Swan has an acute case of Been There, Done That. "He goes out with Tilda Payne from La Tapa."

"I don't think so," Paula says. "Mark and I were out to dinner at the Terrace over the weekend and we saw Tilda there eating with someone else. Mark said it was that Australian guy, Duncan Huntley, who just bought Lovango Cay."

"Is that guy *single?*" Swan says. "I could use a boyfriend with money."

The three of them watch Floyd's uncle Cash back out of the parking lot. He notices them and waves—he's friendly!—but then Julie Judge pulls into the lot in her falling-apart RAV4 with the duct-taped soft top to let Joanie out, and the three women disperse. "Judgy Julie" is a marine biologist and a vegan and a stick-in-the-mud. She wouldn't approve of them checking out Baker Steele or his cute brother.

But who cares what Judgy Julie thinks?

A few days later, the three women are once again gathered, drinking chai lattes from Provisions, when the bluebird Jeep pulls in and a woman is driving. She's too old to be Baker's love interest, they think (though look at Emmanuel Macron!).

Floyd says, "Bye, Grammy!"

"It's Baker's mother?" Bonny says.

Grammy Steele is just about to pull away, when Captain Huck's truck swings in and lets Maia out. Maia notices the bluebird Jeep and waves to Floyd's grammy. Captain Huck calls out, "Irene!" Grammy Steele throws the car into reverse and hightails it out of there.

"That only makes sense," Swan whispers. "Because you know, girls, that Baker is the Invisible Man's son, which means Irene was the Invisible Man's wife..."

"And Rosie was the Invisible Man's lover," Bonny says. "No wonder Grammy doesn't want to talk to Huck."

"For some reason, I thought they were friends," Paula says. "I thought they worked together?"

"Take off the rose-colored glasses, Paula," Bonny says. "Would you work with the father of your husband's lover?" Then Bonny realizes she's talking to Paula Morrow. Who knows what kind of rules are bent in that household? "Never mind. Don't answer that."

None of those mothers are in the parking lot when the little green truck named Edie pulls in to pick up Maia from school—but Julie Judge is there and she goes over to say hello to Ayers. The poor woman has been through so much—losing Rosie, taking over mom duties with Maia, breaking up with Mick from the Beach Bar, and enduring his antics at Cruz Bay Landing.

"Ayers," Julie says. "How're you doing?"

Ayers places a hand on her abdomen. "I'm pregnant," she says. "Due in September."

Ayers Wilson is pregnant? No wonder Mick is so despondent! He's losing not only a fiancée but also a child.

No, no, no, Brigid tells first her coworker Lindsay, then Skip from La Tapa, then anyone who will listen—Mick isn't the father of Ayers's baby. Baker Steele is.

"What?" Swan Seeley yells when she hears this. "Are you kidding me?"

"There's always his brother," Paula says dreamily. "Uncle Cash."

With all this drama and excitement going on, it's a wonder they notice the black Jeep with the tinted windows. But they do, and then there it is again a day or two later, rolling by the school—at pickup this time.

"Creeper," Swan Seeley says. She cups her hands around her mouth. "Take a picture, it lasts longer!"

"It looked like a woman," Bonny says.

MAIA

The group has fallen apart; nobody wants to meet anymore. Maia and Joanie can occasionally talk Huck into dropping them off in town, and they get ice cream from Scoops, then hang out in Powell Park until the Antilles kids get off the four o'clock ferry. Maia sees Shane climb into his dad's truck but she's never brave enough to call out to him. One awful day, both Shane and Lillibet get off the ferry and hop into his dad's truck. Maia still Snapchats with Shane at night and he hasn't said anything about Lillibet being his girlfriend, but he also hasn't asked to hang out with Maia after school.

Things between Joanie and Colton aren't much more promising. All Colton wants to do is play Fortnite at Bright's house.

Boring.

They need to arrange another meeting, but where? Par Force is too hard to get to, and although it's private, it's just an old abandoned house where there's nothing to do but think about the people who lived there who are now dead and maybe ghosts.

Maia has an idea for a meeting spot but she's not sure she's brave enough to go through with it.

She has more freedom than ever. Irene has moved in with Baker and Floyd at the Happy Hibiscus in Fish Bay. Huck said that Irene wants to be with her family—yes, this makes sense—but what he hasn't explained is why Irene is no longer working on the *Mississippi*. Huck is in such a foul mood all the time that

Maia's afraid to ask. He says he doesn't want to find another mate; he'll just do all the work himself. He's almost never around to give Maia a ride home from school, but Joanie's mom and Ayers pick up the slack.

The good news is that Huck isn't paying much attention to Maia. He still makes her eggs and toast in the mornings but the eggs have been dry, which is *no bueno*. He doesn't bother checking one Saturday when Maia says she's going to Cinnamon Bay to swim with Joanie and a few other friends. They all meet in the parking lot—Maia, Joanie, Colton, Bright, and Shane (but happily, happily, not Lillibet; she's been grounded for talking back to her parents)—but instead of heading to the beach to swim or watch the volleyball game that is always happening on the eastern end, they walk down the Centerline single file to the turnoff up the hill to Little Cinnamon.

This is how Maia persuaded the boys to show up: they're going to hang out at her father's villa, the one with the two-story pool.

The one that has been seized by the FBI.

Shane says he can't believe Maia is letting them do this. She's too clever to show her hand; if she wants to get Shane back, she needs to come up with something irresistible. Which in this case is also something illegal.

Maia feels anxious on the Centerline Road. It's a short walk, but at any moment, one of their parents or teachers could drive by and see the five of them. Once they turn onto Lovers Lane, Maia's nerves fray with anxiety. The FBI have seized the house. There's no way Maia should be going anywhere near the place.

They climb up the hill past the dummy driveways, and Shane grabs Maia's hand.

This makes the whole plan worth it. Maia doesn't care if she goes to federal prison!

At the top of the hill is the villa. The gate is wide open. Maia had assumed it would be closed but she knows the code— her mother's birthday—and if that didn't work, she knows a way around the gate through the dense landscaping, which isn't great but would work as a last resort.

They walk up the empty driveway. A piece of yellow police tape hangs limply across the stairs up to the deck. Maia ducks under it and the others follow suit. Colton and Bright, who usually never shut up, are silent.

Maia climbs the stairs. The deck looks…the same. The furniture is all there. The pool is full but the water down the slide has been shut off. Maia goes over to the control panel and flips the switch, and water starts flowing down the slide.

She's going to get arrested for sure.

"Can we go in?" Bright whispers.

Maia holds up a finger. "Let me check out the house first." The outdoor kitchen is the same; there are fancy Italian sparkling waters in the fridge—and they're ice-cold! "Help yourself," Maia says.

There's a sign on the sliding glass door into the kitchen: PROPERTY OF THE UNITED STATES GOVERNMENT. NO TRESPASSING. VIOLATORS WILL BE PROSECUTED. The door is locked. Maia cups her hands around her eyes and peers inside.

It looks…the same. The kitchen counters, the sink, the cabinets, the fridge, the living-room furniture, the television. Everything is exactly where it was. But what about her room?

"Do you know where there's a key?" Joanie asks.

Maia says, "Follow me." They go across the deck, past the hot tub, and down the stairs to the shuffleboard court. The cues are hanging on the rack and the black and red disks are stacked in a milk crate. Maia reaches around to the back of the crate and feels the key taped just under the lip. *Ha!* She pulls the key loose. This is the key her mother used when she and Maia arrived before Russ got here (sometimes Rosie brought home-cooked meals—her jerk chicken with beans and rice—or pints of coconut ice cream from Scoops, which was Russ's favorite), and this was where they put the key when they stayed after Russ left (which was sometimes very, very early in the morning). This means the last person to touch this key was Rosie. Maia brings the key to her lips.

She leads Joanie to the door that the key fits. It pulls right open, and seconds later, they're up in the kitchen, opening the slider.

"Hey, guys," she says to Shane, Colton, and Bright. "Who's hungry?"

There's still food in the fridge, though all of the fresh stuff has grown mold or gone bad. The cabinets and pantry, however, are a treasure trove. The boys dive on the bags of chips while Joanie unearths a package of hot dogs from the freezer (Joanie's parents are vegan; for her, a hot dog is the ultimate forbidden treat). Maia opens three cans of SpaghettiOs and dumps them in a pot.

Ten minutes later, they have a feast: bowls of SpaghettiOs, hot dogs with yellow mustard and relish, Cheetos and dill-flavored potato chips—all washed down with Italian sparkling water.

Maia thinks maybe now is the time to start a conversation. "Does anybody have anything they want to talk about?" She looks at Colton; it was his parents' divorce that brought the group together. But Colton and Bright are tussling on the banquette; Colton bumps up against Joanie, who must love it.

"Let's go back in the pool," Bright says.

"Should I turn on the hot tub?" Maia asks.

"Yeah!" they all say. The afternoon is sunny and very hot but there's still something alluring about the bubbles and all of them close together.

"I'll do it after I clean up," Maia says.

Colton, Bright, and Joanie head outside. Shane stays to help Maia bring the plates and the bowls to the sink. He throws the empty bags and cans away.

"The FBI owns this house now?" he says.

Maia shrugs. "I guess so."

"It doesn't look like anyone's living here." He gazes upward. "Do you think they installed cameras?"

"I think..." Maia tries to remember if she overheard Huck and Irene saying anything about the fate of the villa. *Gone* was all they said. *It's gone.* "I think maybe the government will sell it? And take the money and put it into their budget?"

"Yeah," Shane says. "You're probably right. When do you think the new owners will move in?"

"Probably not for a while," Maia says. "Everything looks the same. It's almost like the FBI locked it up and then forgot it was here."

"So maybe we can use it again?" Shane says. "Because this is an awesome hangout. What's upstairs?"

"There are nine bedrooms," Maia says. She knows this is an outrageous number because she heard her mother say so. "Want to see my room?"

Shane's eyebrows shoot up. "Sure."

Sure, sure, sure, Maia thinks. Is this happening? She should *not* be doing this, she's twelve and a half, too young to have a boy in her bedroom. If you listen to Huck, twenty-five is too young. But this is an opportunity she may never get again. What if the new people move in next week, or tomorrow?

The upstairs is unpleasantly hot and stuffy; the air-conditioning is off. Maia leads Shane down the long hallway past the other bedrooms, all of them the same as Maia remembers, with their camel cashmere blankets and fluffy white duvets folded at the bottom of each bed and the arrangement of six pillows plus bolster at the head. She wonders briefly about the people who will end up buying this villa. Will they be older with a lot of children and grandchildren? Will they be young with a lot of friends they invite for weekend house parties? Will they ever learn anything about Maia—or Russ and Rosie?

Maia reaches the end of the hallway and opens the door to her room. It's a swirl of turquoise and purple tie-dye; pillows that spell out her name hang on the far wall.

"Wow," Shane says. "This is way cooler than my room."

"It's way cooler than my room at home." Maia feels disloyal to Huck in saying this, but it's undeniable. Here, she has bean-bag chairs and a dressing table with a lit mirror. She remembers her mother handing her the Pottery Barn Teen catalog and telling her to "go crazy." Maia had pointed to her favorite picture in the catalog, and the next time Russ came back to the island, her room looked like this. He had thought of the name pillows himself, he said. Maia picks up her copy of *The Hate U Give.* "I forgot I left this here. I'm taking this home." She sits on the bed and Shane sits next to her. He kicks at her foot and then their two legs are intertwined. She's afraid he's going to kiss her. But isn't that what she wants? The door is halfway open. She's safe here, safe with Shane.

She falls backward on the bed and he does the same. When she looks at him, he smiles. He's so cute without his braces. He inches his face closer and she thinks, *This is it.* She closes her eyes. His lips touch hers and they kiss. He lingers and she thinks, *Is this where we open our mouths? Yes; yes, it is.* They are, suddenly, tongue-kissing, which makes Maia feel like she's flying down the pool slide upside down and backward.

"Maia!" Joanie shouts from somewhere.

No, Joanie, please, Maia thinks. *Go away! Don't ruin this!*

"Maia, where are you?" Joanie calls. "Someone's here!"

Shane jumps to his feet. "Someone's here?" he says. "Should we hide?"

Should they hide? Maia opens her bedroom door wide and sees Joanie's stricken face; Colton and Bright are right on her heels, trailing pool water down the hall.

"There's a woman here," Joanie says. "She pulled up in a black Jeep."

"With tinted windows," Bright says. "It's a four-door Sahara Limited, plate TP six-seven-five-six."

"She asked to talk to you," Joanie says. "By name. She said, 'Is Maia here?'"

"What?" Maia says. She can't hide if they know her name. "Did she show a badge? Is she with the FBI?" Maia can't even fathom the massive amount of trouble she's in. And maybe not only her, maybe Huck as well. She feels her SpaghettiOs repeat on her; she's going to hurl.

Shane comes up behind her and squeezes her hand. "I'll go down with you."

"We'll all go down with you," Joanie says.

"We're just kids," Colton says. "We can say we didn't know we weren't allowed to be here."

Maia is trembling when she gets down to the bottom of the stairs. "You guys stay here," she says. She steps out to the deck.

The woman is gazing at the view across the water to Tortola and Jost Van Dyke. She's short and has brown hair that's pulled back in a ponytail; she's wearing white capri pants and a beige linen shell and sandals, and when she turns around, Maia sees she has a round, pale face with wide brown eyes. She doesn't look like the FBI, but maybe this is how they trick you. They send someone who looks like the person who cleans teeth at the dentist's office.

"Hello, Maia," she says.

"Hello?" Maia says. Who is this woman? "Am I in trouble?"

"Oh," the woman says. "Not with me, but I'm sure you kids realize you're not supposed to be here."

"We're leaving," Maia says. "We were just…I left some personal things behind that I wanted back." She wishes she'd thought to bring the Angie Thomas book out. "I mean, it's okay to take personal items? That have no value?"

"I'm not going to report you," the woman says, but it sounds like there's something else coming. "I just have one question. Something I need help with."

"Okay…" Maia says.

"I'm a friend of Irene Steele's," the woman says. "An acquaintance. And I know she was living with you and your grandpa, correct? Up on Jacob's Ladder? Has she moved? Left island, maybe?"

"Irene?" Maia says. "She lives in Fish Bay now with my brother Baker." Maia absolutely loves using the phrase *my brother*. "And my nephew, Floyd. They live in a house called the Happy Hibiscus."

Irene's friend nods and brings her hands palm to palm up to her heart like a yoga person. "Thank you. That's all I needed to know."

"Do you…want her phone number?" Maia says. She wonders if it's okay to give out Irene's number, but this woman does not look threatening. She looks like someone from Iowa.

"No, thank you," the woman says. "I'd like to speak to her in person." She moves toward the stairs. "You kids should probably skedaddle. And don't forget to lock up."

*   *   *

Maia goes into the kitchen, where everyone is huddled in the far corner by the trash.

"Let's go," Maia says. "She wasn't the FBI."

The boys and Joanie shoot out the door and Maia does a check—lights out, stove off, everything put away. She locks the sliding glass door and turns off the water on the slide.

Goodbye, villa, she thinks. *Site of my first kiss.*

Together, they run down Lovers Lane shrieking with heady joy. Maia can't believe they got away with it.

BAKER

He feels like he's starring in a sitcom about a single dad who moves from the big city to a tropical island to woo the girl he fell in love with on vacation. In episode 2, he finds out this girl is pregnant. Twist: It's his child. Twist: She is just out of a long-term relationship and needs time alone. Twist: He moves in across the street.

In episode 3, his mother moves in. There's no room for her but she's adamant and says she has nowhere else to go.

"What about Huck's?" Baker said when Irene showed up on his doorstep with her suitcase. "That was working out. You had your own bedroom. You drove to work together."

"I quit the boat," Irene said. "I need to be with family. Huck isn't family."

"You quit the *boat?*" Baker said. "You like the boat."

Irene stared at him. She was impossible to read but he couldn't just let her stand outside so he held the door open. She set her suitcase behind one of the sofas in the living room.

"So you're here for a while?" Baker said. "Why don't you take the second bedroom. Floyd can sleep with me."

"I'll be fine on the sofa," Irene said. "I'll use Floyd's bathroom. I hope he won't mind."

"Mom," Baker said. "I insist. Floyd will sleep with me. Are you kidding? He'll be thrilled."

"I'm not putting either one of you out," Irene said. "I feel horrible about this as it is. The sofa is fine."

He decided that after she spent a few nights on the sofa, he would offer again. "What are you going to do for work now? Do you have a plan?"

"I'm going to get my captain's license," Irene said. "I have that money coming from your grandmother. I'm going to buy my own boat and start my own charter."

"Your own charter?" Baker said. "Here?"

Irene nodded. Wow, she did not look happy.

"You're going into direct competition with Huck?" he said.

"Oh, yes," she said.

Something had happened, but what? She would tell him when she was ready. Or she wouldn't. It would be nice to have his mother around, but he needed to catch her up. "That house across the street is where Ayers lives," he said. He considered asking Irene to sit down—but if anyone could handle the news standing up, it was his mother. "She's pregnant."

"You're kidding."

"With my baby."

"*Your* baby?"

"Yes." Baker paused. "We aren't together. I mean, we *were* together, I suppose that's obvious, but then she got engaged to Mick, then she broke the engagement with Mick because he was unfaithful, then she found out she was pregnant."

"But the baby's not Mick's?" Irene looked dubious. Baker's private fears were written all over his mother's face. "You're sure? She might just be telling you that because...well, because you're you, by which I mean a wonderful father."

"She insists the baby is mine," Baker said. "Don't women have a sixth sense about things like that?"

Irene frowned. "I'm not sure. I never had any doubts about the paternity of my children."

The last thing Baker wanted was for Irene to take issue with Ayers. "Here's the thing. I want to be with Ayers eventually. The cart came a little before the horse—"

"You think?"

"And she needs space right now and I'm giving it to her."

"She's across the street."

"Emotional space. We're building a friendship first." What Baker didn't tell Irene was that Ayers resisted every attempt at friendship that Baker made. On Saturday morning, he and Floyd had gone to Provisions for coffee and scones. When they knocked on Ayers's door with the offerings, she hadn't answered, even though her green truck was in the driveway.

Baker had said, "She's probably still asleep, bud."

"But we waited until ten," Floyd said. He was eager to open the door because he wanted to play with Winnie.

They wandered back across the street and although Baker told Floyd they'd try again later, he ate Ayers's scone and drank her coffee. The second coffee made him feel so unhinged that he became convinced she hadn't answered the door because she had Mick over. Or maybe she wasn't home. Maybe she was with Mick at his new villa, Pure Joy. (Baker had scoped out the villa once—okay, twice—on his way to work at the Westin. It wasn't as big as the Happy Hibiscus but it had an unbeatable view and an outdoor shower.)

Speaking of the Westin, Baker had asked Ayers if she wanted to join him and Floyd at Greengos after Baker's first day of work and she said no, thank you, she had the night off from La Tapa and was looking forward to getting takeout from Dé Coal Pot and streaming *The Marvelous Mrs. Maisel.*

She had waved to Baker from her driveway once. They passed each other at the steep, tight curve by Ditleff Point and the hoods of their cars almost kissed, but that was as close to physical contact as Baker had gotten.

So now he's at episode 4: His brother moves in. Baker has to go pick Cash up at Tilda's villa in Peter Bay. The place is like something plucked off the cover of *Architectural Digest.* During his downtime in the Westin time-share office, Baker has been researching the St. John real estate market. Peter Bay fetches top dollar. It's a private community on the north shore with a prime location between Trunk Bay and Cinnamon Bay. While Tilda's villa doesn't have as many bedrooms as their villa in Little Cinnamon did, it has nearly exactly the same amount of square footage. Cash gives Baker a tour of the place. The three wings are connected by covered walkways bordered on either side by lush landscaping—hibiscus, frangipani, birds-of-paradise. The T-shaped pool is unique. The kitchen has a curved island topped with white marble and three light blue suede bar stools that look like egg cups. Baker sits in one and swivels. Cash will be getting a serious downgrade at the Happy Hibiscus.

*   *   *

"Explain to me again why you're leaving," Baker says as they pull out of the extremely steep driveway. The views are ridiculous! From the top of the driveway, Baker can see the entirety of Tortola and beyond. Beyond!

"Tilda went on a work trip with someone else," Cash says. "Her parents are building an eco-resort over on Lovango Cay so they sent her on a three-stop tour of the fanciest, most expensive resorts in the Caribbean." He stares out the window. "Today, for example, she's on an island resort called Eden where management decides what guests are allowed to stay there."

"Who'd she go with?" Baker asks. "A guy?"

"This dude named Duncan Huntley," Cash says. "He bought Lovango Cay. Bought the entire island. And this guy is, like, our age."

Duncan Huntley? Baker opens his mouth to say, *I know that guy. He gave Floyd and me a ride on his boat from the airport.* But for some reason, Baker stops himself. "So he and Tilda are a thing, then? Or they just went on this trip as business partners?"

"They went as business partners," Cash says. "But Tilda didn't call me at all for the first four days, which I found fishy because she cried when she left and promised to be true, blah-blah-blah. When I asked her what she thought about Dunk, she said, 'He's too intense.'"

Intense is a good choice of word, Baker thinks.

"He fasts," Cash says. "Which is apparently a lifestyle we've been missing out on. Starving yourself brings better focus and productivity."

"I'll never know," Baker says, thinking about the scones from

Provisions and the container of Red Velvet Cake ice cream he has hidden in the freezer.

"So, anyway, after four full days away, she hits me up at two thirty in the morning and all she can talk about is Dunk this and Dunk that. Dunk adjusted her chaise by the pool, she and Dunk took a picnic to a waterfall, Dunk arranged for a private seaplane, and—get this—she and Dunk had a couples massage at the spa."

"Couples massage?" Baker says. "I'm sorry, bro. You were right to leave."

Episode 5: Baker, his brother, his mother, and Floyd all cohabitate in Baker's villa, which, although blessed with cathedral ceilings, a spacious laundry room, and a picturesque backyard with sapphire pool, has only two bedrooms. Irene and Cash each take a sofa; every morning, Irene folds up their bedding and hides it away in the closet. Irene shares a bathroom with Floyd, and reluctantly, oh so reluctantly, Baker lets Cash share his bathroom, which makes them both feel like they're teenagers again. Cash spends sixteen thousand dollars of his inheritance from Milly on a silver Dodge pickup with only eight thousand island miles on it. Irene borrows Cash's truck or Baker's Jeep, alternating between the two, which would be annoying, except she occasionally drives Floyd to school and picks him up, and she takes over all the grocery shopping. Baker does the cooking; he finally has an appreciative audience— or sort of. Cash gets home from *Treasure Island* each night so spent and hungry that he ravenously shovels in whatever Baker puts in front of him without even seeming to taste it, and Irene helps herself to doll-size portions, then eats half. She's losing weight again, just like she did when they first got here, right after they'd received the news of Russ's death.

Baker shows Irene his secret stash of Red Velvet Cake ice cream—he was hiding it from himself, and now he's hiding it from Cash—but Irene just shakes her head. "I'm not hungry."

Something happened between Irene and Huck—but what?

One afternoon while Baker is in the Gifft Hill School parking lot waiting for Floyd, he sees Maia and her little friend Joanie emerge. Maia zips right over and offers Baker a fist bump. "Hey, bro."

"Hey, sis," Baker says. Joanie is now hanging back, talking to a boy, so Baker seizes the moment. "Do you know what happened between Huck and my mom? Did they have a fight?"

Maia shrugs. "He told me she just wanted to live with you guys. She thought she was imposing."

"Fair enough," Baker says. "But why did she quit the boat?"

"Gramps won't talk about it," Maia says. "But he refuses to hire another mate. So he's doing two jobs by himself and he's never home." A beat-up RAV4 pulls up. "That's Joanie's mom. I have to go, bro."

That night over dinner, Baker says, "I saw Maia at school. She said Huck refuses to hire another mate."

Irene freezes with her fork suspended over her plate. They're having pineapple fried rice with grilled shrimp, and Irene has helped herself to one spoonful of rice and one shrimp. "Well," she says finally. "That's his prerogative, I guess."

"Why don't you go back, Mom?" Cash says.

"I want to do my own thing," Irene says. "I bought the study materials for the captain's license, and I've been working my way through. I'll go to St. Thomas to take my test, and while I'm over there, I'm looking at a boat. I just need a marketing plan, advertising, some way to get my new venture out there."

"What's the name going to be?" Cash asks. "Of the boat?"

"*Angler Cupcake,*" Irene says. Her lips hint at a smile. "That was what your grandfather used to call me."

Why shouldn't Irene have her own fishing boat? Baker wonders. Why shouldn't *Angler Cupcake* be every bit as successful as the *Mississippi*? Well, he suspects his mother will have a challenging time attracting male clients with a boat called *Angler Cupcake*. Which means she'll be going after a female clientele. Are there enough women who fish for her to sustain a fishing-charter business?

Baker decides to ask his Gifft Hill School–mom friends. They're not school wives, not yet, but Baker, Swan, Bonny, and Paula are bonding. Whenever Baker drops Floyd off or picks him up, those three are reliably waiting for him.

He broaches the fishing-boat question one afternoon while Floyd plays for a few extra minutes on the jungle gym with Swan's son Ryder.

"I think she could be very successful," Paula says. Baker has learned that Paula is a bit of a Suzie Sunshine; she says whatever she thinks will make someone happy, regardless of whether or not she believes it's true.

"I don't," Bonny says. Bonny balances Paula out; she's a nay-sayer. "Women don't fish."

"Some women fish," Swan says. "Your mother could start a trend, Baker. Lots of women with money are planning girls' trips, and your mom's fishing boat would be perfect. Plus, she could market to families with young children. And…bachelorettes?"

"Families, maybe, but bachelorettes do *not* want to fish," Bonny says. "Do you even watch the show? The girls on *The Bachelor* will fish or bungee jump or go to the machine-gun range, but only to seem cool and beat out the other girls. It's never their choice."

"I majored in marketing at Florida State," Swan says. "Have your mom reach out. I'm happy to help her, free of charge."

"You are such a kiss-ass," Bonny says.

"Maybe we could all help?" Paula says, and Swan gives her a withering look. These women make Baker miss Ellen, Debbie, Becky, and Wendy because they were relaxed, stable…and not after him.

"I'll run it past my mom," Baker says. He needs to get out of there before they come to blows. "Thanks, ladies."

Episode 6: Baker is *killing it* at work! He feels like the host of a new HGTV show called *Do You Want to Buy a Time-Share?* He's aware that most people take the tour only because they want the free breakfast (with bottomless mimosas) or the free appetizers (with free-flowing rum punch), plus the hundred-dollar resort credit. But Baker finds that the clients he interacts with at least consider the *possibility* of buying.

One day, he puts two units under contract, a one-bedroom and a three-bedroom! He experiences a surge of pure, unadulterated confidence that feels like mainlining a drug. Nothing is going to happen with Ayers until he makes it happen. It's ludicrous that she's right across the street and they almost never see each other. *Cash* sees Ayers more than Baker does because he goes over every day to visit Winnie. Floyd sees more of Ayers than Baker does because he tags along with Cash. Baker told Cash that the property manager of the Happy Hibiscus explicitly stated there were no pets allowed—but this was a lie. Pets are fine. Baker just wants Ayers to keep Cash's dog so there is still one filament connecting Ayers to Baker. And anyway, the household is crowded enough as it is. (Sorry, Winnie.)

Baker swings by Our Market to get Ayers a pineapple-mango smoothie, then he stops at Sam and Jack's for a bag of their home-made potato chips. This is the perfect afternoon snack. He still has an hour and a half before school pickup. He can bring Ayers these goodies and stay for a visit—catch up, see how she's feeling, ask if she wants him to go with her to her prenatal appointment at Schneider Hospital. This will show he's thinking of her. He's never *not* thinking of her, but it won't be overbearing.

Her green truck is in the driveway—wonderful. He strides up to the door and knocks. The pineapple-mango smoothie is sweating in his hand, and while he waits, he worries that her favorite type is pineapple-banana, not pineapple-mango. He should have written it down the second she mentioned it. This is the kind of thing that Mick knows by heart and Baker doesn't.

He hears voices. A man's voice. Is Mick there? The voice is very deep. Not Mick's. Mick has a reedy voice that reminds Baker of some pimply adolescent playing the oboe. So someone else is here. Another man. Someone who took advantage of the broken engagement to make a move?

Baker turns to leave. He doesn't want to know who it is. Naturally, as Baker is retreating, the door swings open.

"Hello there, young man, can we help you?" The deep male voice is attached to a very tall, very thin older gentleman with a high forehead and curly silver hair sticking out in tufts on either side, like an aging Bozo the Clown, although Bozo might be an ungenerous comparison. Baker immediately knows that it's Ayers's father.

"Hello," Baker says, retracing his steps back to the front door. "I brought some things for Ayers. A smoothie. And chips."

"Wonderful!" the man bellows. He holds the screen door open. "I'm Phil Wilson and my sweetheart, Sunny—Ayers's mom—is here as well. You must be the infamous..." Phil turns and calls to someone who is out of Baker's field of vision. "What's the soap opera guy's name again, Sunny?"

"Baker Steele," a woman's voice says.

"Baker Steele!" Phil says.

This isn't exactly the way Baker was hoping the afternoon would go, but he steps inside because he sees no other choice. "Yes, sir," he says. "Nice to meet you."

Ayers and her mother are sitting cross-legged on the sofa. Sunny is beautiful; she looks just like Ayers, only older. She's slender with curly blond-silver hair; she's wearing a beige jersey dress and lots of silver jewelry. Ayers doesn't look unhappy to see Baker, which he supposes he should take as a win. "Mom, Dad, this is Baker," she says. Her expression is neutral, as though she's introducing her parents to the pizza-delivery guy.

"You're the one who impregnated my daughter?" Phil says.

"Um..." Baker looks to Ayers to see if she confirms this.

"Dad, please," Ayers says. "Yes. Baker and I were together. This is his baby."

"We're over the moon," Sunny says. "We flew all the way from Nairobi to be here."

"Nairobi, wow." Baker looks at the photographs hanging on Ayers's living-room wall—her at the Great Pyramids and the Taj Mahal—and he picks out younger versions of Phil and Sunny. "You're world travelers."

"Nomads," Phil says. "The earth is our home."

"Where are you staying?" Baker asks. He looks around Ayers's studio; Winnie is asleep on Ayers's bed. "Not here?"

"We have a room at Caneel Bay for now," Phil says. "We're planning on staying a few weeks, then maybe spending some time in Jamaica, the DR, Antigua and Barbuda, St. Vincent and the Grenadines..."

"Bequia is supposed to be relatively unspoiled," Sunny says. "We've avoided the Caribbean for the most part because it's so tacky."

"Gee, thanks, guys," Ayers says.

"St. John is different," Phil says. "It still has that rugged-nature-lover vibe."

"With spots of luxury," Sunny says. "Like Caneel."

"There aren't any all-inclusives," Phil says. "Just the term *all-inclusive* makes me shudder."

"They're travel snobs," Ayers says.

"Anyway, once we complete our little jaunt, we'll come back here and wait for the baby to be born," Sunny says.

"That wait could be weeks or months," Phil says. "So I was going to look into buying a time-share at the Westin."

"We'll need a home base here if we ever want to see our grandchild," Sunny says.

Baker hates to be opportunistic, but... "If you decide you do want a Westin time-share, I can help you," he says. "I'm working at their sales office right now."

"Great!" Phil says. "We'll take one."

"Dad," Ayers says. "Don't tease."

"Who's teasing?" Phil says. "I'll be by to see you in the morning."

"Free breakfast with mimosas," Baker says. "And a hundred-dollar resort credit."

"Hear that, gorgeous?" Phil says to Sunny. "She loves free stuff. We got a discount on our room at Caneel because she told them she's a travel blogger."

"We should ask Baker some questions," Sunny says. "We know nothing about you. Freddy told us the two of you are just casual acquaintances."

"Mom!" Ayers says.

"Freddy?" Baker says.

"That's my daughter's nickname," Phil says. "Short for 'Ready, Freddy,' which was something she used to say often as a child. I can't believe you don't even know her nickname."

"Nobody knows my nickname," Ayers says. "No. Body."

Baker is still holding the chips and the smoothie, which is turning his hand numb. He's afraid to make himself any more comfortable until he's invited to do so. "Well, I grew up in Iowa City, went to Northwestern, graduated with a business degree, worked on the commodities exchange in Chicago for a few years, and then my soon-to-be-ex-wife, Anna Schaffer, got a job offer in Houston. She's a cardiothoracic surgeon."

"A cardiothoracic surgeon?" Sunny says. "That's impressive!"

Yes, yes, story of Baker's life—the most impressive thing about him is his wife's career. "We're in the process of getting a divorce," Baker says. "She fell in love with a coworker of hers, a doctor named Louisa Rodriguez"—Baker glances at Ayers's parents; they seem unfazed by this—"and I have custody of our son, Floyd, who's four."

"We'd like to meet Floyd!" Phil says.

"Another time," Ayers says. She checks her phone, which is sitting in front of her on the coffee table, and what can Baker think but that he's overstaying his welcome.

"My brother, Cash, and my mother, Irene, are also living with me right now," Baker says. He takes a breath. He *has* to put down the smoothie. "Here." He sets it down in front of Ayers. "I brought you this. It's pineapple-mango. Your favorite."

"My favorite after pineapple-banana," she says. Baker deflates and hands over the chips without adding that he made a special trip to Sam and Jack's for them.

"You don't know her nickname or her favorite smoothie?" Phil says. "I can see we still have some work to do."

"Please stop, Dad," Ayers says.

"It was very thoughtful of you to bring these," Sunny says, opening the chips and helping herself to one. "How interesting that you live with your family of origin."

"Yes, well..." Baker says. He glances at Ayers. Has she not explained *any* of his situation to her parents? "My father died in a helicopter crash on the first of the year..."

"So did Rosie," Phil says.

"We adored Rosie," Sunny says.

"Was the fella she was with...your father?" Phil asks.

"Yes," Baker says. Ayers is staring at her own crossed legs. Why didn't she give her parents the thorny background? "And so my mother and brother and I all flew down here to figure out what was going on."

"What *was* going on?" Phil asks.

"Well, we learned about his relationship with Rosie..."

"Had your mother suspected anything?" Sunny asks.

Baker can't believe he's being put on the spot like this. But it's refreshing, in a way, to answer questions that everyone must be asking in his or her head. "She had no idea," Baker says. "It came as a complete shock. Jaw-dropping. For days I think we all believed there'd been a mistake, that it was a different Russell Steele. But then, yeah, we accepted it was my dad. He owned a giant hilltop villa that we knew nothing about. He had a whole life. A second life."

"You'll forgive me for saying so," Phil says, "but it seems unusual that you stayed on the island where your father had a second family."

"Dad!" Ayers says.

"It wasn't our *plan* to stay," Baker says. "Each of us ended up back here for his or her own reasons. I can only speak for myself. I was living in Houston, my marriage fell apart, my almost-ex-wife took a job at the Cleveland Clinic—"

"Impressive!" Sunny says.

"—and I met Ayers. I decided I wanted to try to make our relationship work." He can see the warning in Ayers's eyes but he ignores it. "I came down here without knowing about the baby. But I'm excited—no, thrilled about the news, and I plan to be a hands-on father, just like I am with Floyd."

"Well," Sunny says, "I'm overcome. What a beautiful thing to say."

"We ended up losing my father's villa a few weeks ago," Baker says. He clears his throat. "There was tax trouble. Legal trouble. And that was a hurdle for all of us—my mother, brother, and me— because we had all planned on living there. It was...spacious."

"Um, yeah," Ayers says.

"It's almost better that we aren't at the villa anymore." Baker realizes these words are true only as he's saying them. "It was...tainted. Don't get me wrong, it was luxurious, the wow factor was high, but I think that masked the truth, which was that we didn't belong there. I've rented the place right across the street from here, and although it's a tight fit right now, I'm confident my mom and brother will find their own spaces in time."

"Across the street from *here!*" Sunny says. "How convenient."

Phil leads Baker to the door. "You've made a very fine first impression, Baker Steele."

Baker raises his eyebrows at Ayers. *Your parents like me!* Ayers whistles, and Winnie lifts her head, jumps off the bed, and joins Ayers on the couch.

"We must arrange a dinner with your mom and brother," Sunny says. "A family affair! But we can't do it tonight because we're taking Freddy and Michael out."

"To the beach bar at Caneel," Phil says. "Supposedly, they have decent sushi."

"We spent nine months traveling through Japan in the early aughts," Sunny says. "And do you want to know where we found the best sushi?"

"Gate thirty-five at Narita Airport," Phil says. "The tuna special. I dream about it."

Baker is still trying to figure out who "Freddy and Michael" are. Friends of theirs? A gay couple? Then he remembers that Ayers is Freddy. But who's Michael? "Who's Michael?" he asks.

"Mick," Phil says. "We're taking out Ayers and Mick."

"'Mick' makes him sound like an Irish hoodlum or a horny rock star," Sunny says. "I prefer to call him by his given name."

Ayers rubs Winnie's head. Is she even listening to this conversation?

"You're taking out Ayers and Mick?" Baker says.

"It's been so long since we've seen him," Sunny says.

Somehow, Baker makes it through the door, saying graciously, *Enjoy the sushi, hope it's decent, come see me in the morning, we'll look at one-bedrooms and two-bedrooms, nice to meet you, all righty, will do, yep, yep, yep, bye-bye.* And then, mercifully, Phil closes the door.

Taking out Ayers and Mick?

Baker heads across the street, limping like he has an old sports injury—Mick is the old sports injury, the one Baker can't seem to recover from—until he's at his front door and can safely disappear into what should now be known as the Heartbroken Hibiscus.

HUCK

He calls Agent Vasco to tell her about the diaries.

"Have you read them?" she asks.

"Yes," he says.

"Are they going to give me what I need?"

They better, Huck thinks. *Because I sacrificed my relationship with Irene for them.* "Only you would know," Huck says. He's on his deck, smoking. He's been going through half a pack a day since Irene moved out. "Should I mail them to you or are you on the island?"

"We're on the island today," Vasco says. "Can I swing by around eleven?"

"I have a charter," Huck says. "I'll leave them on the mail table just inside my front door. You remember where I live? Up Jacob's Ladder?"

"You don't lock up?"

"I have nothing to steal," Huck says.

"Fine, we'll be by," Vasco says. She pauses. "Thank you for calling me."

"I want to cooperate," Huck says. "Can you tell me what's up with Douglas and Paulette Vickers?"

"In the vault?" Vasco says.

"Of course."

"We offered them a deal if they gave us something tangible on Croft, but they refused, insisted he was no part of it, that it was only Steele and Thompson."

"Wow," Huck says.

"So the Vickerses will serve time for fraud and money laundering. They allowed Ascension to buy and sell land from one fictional entity to another using their real estate concern. Welcome to Paradise Real Estate was as dirty as they come."

"They'll both serve time?" Huck says. "What about their son?"

"Staying with Douglas's sister on St. Croix." Vasco sighs. "Those diaries are my last shot. Croft is a slippery bastard. I'd love to nail him."

Vasco is tough; Huck likes that about her.

Huck is distracted on his charter. He has three lawyers from Philadelphia on board who are going out on the boat only so they can escape their wives, smoke the Cuban cigars they scored in the BVIs, and enjoy a day on the water. They don't care if they catch any fish. All good; less concentration required from Huck. He hates to phone it in but he can't get his mind off the question of whether or not to call Irene when they get back to the dock. Would she want to know about Paulette and Douglas Vickers? He normally would say yes but now all bets are off; she has been radio-silent since she left. He thought she'd come to her senses and that one of these mornings, he would find her waiting by the *Mississippi* with two sausage biscuits and two cups of strong black coffee. But no such luck.

He won't call her, he thinks. She made it clear she didn't want to talk about those diaries ever again.

He misses her at work. He misses her at home. He tries to maintain for Maia's sake. He continues to grill mahi or he stops at Candi's for barbecue, but more often than not, he feeds Maia and drinks his own dinner, smokes his dessert. He doesn't make any move to hire a new mate because he can't handle the idea of breaking someone in—and, too, he thinks Irene will return if he waits her out.

Without a mate, he often can't pick Maia up from school so he leans on Julie Judge more than he should. He feels like he's losing his grip on where Maia goes, how she spends her days. Well, she needs food on the table. And she likes to be able to order new clothes from Amazon. Her bath-bomb business seems to have stalled; something new has her attention. Boys, probably.

One night over dinner—it's not even Candi's, it's *leftover* Candi's, that's how sorry a state Huck is in—he says, "Maybe you could make some extra money babysitting for Floyd."

"Floyd has plenty of babysitters now," Maia says. "Irene is there. And Cash moved in too."

"Cash moved in?" Huck says. "I thought he was living over in Peter Bay with what's her name."

"Tilda," Maia says. "They broke up. Tilda is dating some super-rich guy who bought Lovango Cay. Tilda's parents are building an eco-resort there."

Yes, Huck has heard whisperings about this around town. A resort on Lovango will bring in some high-end clientele, which everyone is excited about. It means more potential fishing clients.

Huck would be excited too if he could only summon the energy. "How do you know all this?" Huck asks.

"Ayers," Maia says. She finishes her coleslaw and eyes Huck as she sets down her fork. "If I tell you something, can you keep it a secret?"

All he can think is that she's going to tell him something about Irene—she bought a boat, she signed on with rival fishing boat *What a Catch!*, she's moving back to the States. "I can, yes," he says.

"Ayers is pregnant!" Maia says. "With Baker's baby!"

Huck would have said he was too old and jaded for anything to bowl him over, but Maia just proved him wrong. He thinks back to the last time he saw Ayers—when she gave him the diaries. She looked...peaked. To say the least. "You're kidding."

"Nope. She told me the other day."

"And Baker is the father? Baker, not Mick?"

"Isn't that crazy?" Maia says. She lifts a rib off Huck's plate that he didn't have any appetite for. "Their baby will be my niece or nephew. And if Ayers and Baker get married..." Maia's eyes light up. "Ayers will be my sister-in-law! We'll all be related!"

Huck wonders if Irene knows. She must. What the hell does she think about that? Well, there is one silver lining: Irene Steele isn't going anywhere with a new grandbaby on the way.

The next morning, Huck sees Irene pull into the Gifft Hill School parking lot to drop off Floyd. Even the sight of her—chestnut braid, white scoop-neck T-shirt, the blocky sunglasses that look like what an elderly person with cataracts wears—addles Huck.

"Irene!" he calls out through his open window. He wants to talk to her about Ayers and Baker, a baby coming, her new grandchild. Forget the FBI and Russ and the diaries—the pregnancy is good news, beautiful news.

He catches Irene by surprise. She glances over, sees it's him, and, without missing a beat, throws Baker's Jeep in reverse, backs out of the lot, and goes screaming down Gifft Hill, which is in the opposite direction of her house. She must really want to get away from him.

After dinner that evening, Huck smokes two cigarettes in rapid succession on the deck. He passes through the kitchen, then hits reverse, pulls the Flor de Caña off the shelf, does a shot, then a second shot. He checks on Maia. She's at her desk studying, not on her phone, a small miracle.

"I'm going to read for a bit, Nut," he says. "Good night."

He goes into his bedroom and sits at his desk, which is where he keeps his laptop and a paper calendar listing all his charters as well as files for bills and boat maintenance. He pulls a piece of paper from the tray of his printer, finds a pen that works, and thinks, *Here goes nothing.*

He writes a letter to Irene. He doesn't worry about his spelling or word choice; he doesn't start over when he wants to change his phrasing, just crosses things out. It doesn't have to be perfect; it just has to be true.

When he's finished, he reads it through, folds it in thirds, sticks it in an envelope. He's probably the only fool on earth who's still handwriting letters, but what he had to say shouldn't be texted and she won't talk to him. A letter is outdated, but it will also be difficult to resist reading. He hopes.

He just has to figure out how to get it to her.

*   *   *

A few days later, Maia stays overnight with Ayers. It's the first time Huck has been alone since Irene left. He could easily go out and spend a few hours tinkering on the boat, then grab a burger from the Tap and Still on the way home. Or he could buy some good beer, grill some tuna, lie down in his hammock, and finally crack open the Patterson book. But when he pulls up to the National Park Service dock and lets out his charter guests—a perfectly nice couple from he can't remember where and their three boys, who were all in boarding school; they obviously didn't see one another very often because they were so happy to be together—he hears steel-drum music coming from Mongoose Junction blending with strains of Kenny Chesney over at Joe's Rum Hut: *Save it for a rainy day!* And he decides he doesn't want to be alone. He calls Rupert. "You out?"

"Yes, sir."

"Skinny?"

"Aqua."

Good, Huck thinks. He's been craving the Aqua Bistro's onion rings for a while now. "I'll be there in an hour," he says.

"I'll be waiting," Rupert says. "But I gotta meet Sadie at Skinny at nine and Dora at Miss Lucy's at ten thirty."

Typical Rupert; he has a woman at every watering hole. No doubt Josephine will be singing tonight at the Aqua Bistro. Huck will hurry and shower. He loves Josephine's voice.

Forty-five minutes later, Huck is seated at the round open-air bar of Aqua Bistro next to Rupert. Josephine is playing the guitar, lulling everyone into a sense of well-being with her sultry rendition of "Come Away with Me." Rupert orders tequila shots with beer backs.

"Don't forget, I have to drive home," Huck says.

"Ha! That's no excuse on this island. Stay left, go slow, tell the donkeys to get out of your way. You and I both know you could do it blindfolded."

They click shot glasses and throw the tequila back. Huck feels okay. He slaps down five bucks and asks for the roll. The bartender hands him a leather cup filled with dice. He shakes it and lets them spill—nothing.

Rupert laughs. "Might as well have taken out your lighter and set your money on fire."

It's something to do. Only locals can roll. Irene can't roll. The Invisible Man couldn't roll. Huck's luck has been so damn awful this week that it'll surely take a turn soon. Why not now?

He throws the dice. Three threes, five, six.

"The pot is over a thousand bucks," the bartender says. "Nobody's won since before Christmas."

Josephine sings "Do You Know the Way to San Jose," only she changes "San Jose" to "Coral Bay."

"I love that woman," Rupert says.

"You love a lot of women," Huck says. Part of him wishes he were built this way, but he isn't. He loves Irene. *I love you, Irene,* he thinks and he throws the dice one last time. Two fours, two ones, and a six.

The bartender sweeps up his money. Rupert says nothing but Huck can sense him wanting to blurt out *I told you so.*

"Heard you and the Invisible Man's wife are shacking up," Rupert says.

"You're behind on your gossip. She moved out."

"Any fool off the street could have told you that wasn't

going to work," Rupert says. "There's too much tangled up between you."

Huck wants to tell Rupert he knows nothing about it but he doesn't like to bicker with Rupert, and also the phrase *tangled up* feels like a bull's-eye. Huck and Irene have always communicated on the level. But beneath all that was a mess both of them had willfully ignored—because neither of them had created it. Those diaries must have been salt in a wide-open wound. Huck should never, ever have showed them to her. It must have seemed like he *wanted* to hurt her, when the truth was, he assumed she was so strong and resilient that Rosie's words wouldn't matter.

Why would they matter when she has me? Huck had thought. He was there for her day in, day out, waiting, adoring, offering whatever support and encouragement she needed. Wasn't that enough? Why did the events of thirteen years or six years or two years earlier matter?

Huck spins his finger at the bartender. Another round— more shots, more beers. He found a way to get Irene the letter, ingeniously, or so he thought. He hasn't heard from her. Yet.

"You're right," Huck says to Rupert. "It was never going to work."

Josephine takes a break and comes to sit between them. Onion rings arrive, compliments of the kitchen. Huck admires them—fat, golden, glistening with oil, stacked on a dowel like so many rings in a game of quoits. (Did he eat any? He couldn't say. He might have waited for them to cool and then forgotten about them.)

Another beer.

Rupert says, "Jojo, you have any lady friends you could intro-duce to Huck here?"

"I hear Huck's taken," Josephine says, but Huck is saved from explaining that he's not, because it's time for her second set.

"Let's get out of here," Rupert says. "I'm late for Sadie."

Huck follows Rupert around the road in Coral Bay over to Skinny Legs. The place is crowded but there are two bar stools empty in the corner—how is this possible? Rupert must have called in on the way.

They take the seats; Huck orders a margarita with salt. Rupert says, "Who are you, Jimmy Buffett?" He asks for Cruzan Gold over ice. Heidi is bartending. She's in the weeds but she takes one glance at Huck and Rupert and says, "How 'bout a couple of burgers, fellas?"

Burgers, yes, sure. There's a band playing songs that Huck doesn't recognize and a bunch of kids in their twenties dancing. Tourists, spring-breakers. Huck and Rupert are geezers in this crowd but it doesn't matter, they're having fun, Heidi is taking good care of them. Huck feels a hand on his back and he turns to see Sadie. She pulls Rupert up out of his chair, and he claps a hand on Huck's shoulder, which is his way of saying he won't be back, please cover the check, Rupert will get him next time.

Fine, fine, Huck thinks. Good for Rupert. Sadie is Huck's favorite of the women anyway.

He should leave—but it's been so long since he's been out like this and it's working like a tonic against the ache in his heart. He orders a beer in an attempt to sober up.

He sees a familiar-looking blonde across the bar. She's one of the mothers from the Gifft Hill School, he figures out that much, though he couldn't in a million years come up with her name.

She's waving at him like crazy, and he raises his beer in a way he hopes says, *Yes, I see you, please don't come over here.*

The band plays one last song, and when it's finished, the bar empties out somewhat. Finally, Huck can hear himself think.

Heidi comes over and says, "Woman over there wants to buy you another drink. Beer?"

"Please," Huck says. "Which woman?" He assumes it's the Gifft Hill mother whose name he can't remember or never knew in the first place.

"Behind you," Heidi says.

Huck turns to see a redhead in a pale green dress sipping what looks like a painkiller over at the side bar. She's by herself, gazing out at the people drinking on the back deck. Is that who Heidi means? Well, yeah. She's the only woman behind him.

The beer arrives. Huck takes a swallow, then checks behind him again. The woman is gone.

Huh, he thinks. *Strange.*

A second later, someone takes Rupert's stool. It's the redhead in the green dress. "Good evening, Captain," she says.

Huck has had one—or a few—too many, perhaps. He has to back up a few inches to get a look at this woman. The mother on the boat today had red hair but no, no, no...this is...

The woman smiles.

Holy shit, he thinks. "Agent Vasco?"

"Colette, please."

Colette. Tonight, she looks like a Colette. Her hair is sleek and shiny. The green dress has buttons down the front; the top button has been undone to reveal a modest bit of her cleavage. She's wearing lipstick.

"Thank you for the beer," he says.

"I'm happy I bumped into you."

He wonders for a second if she followed him here. She's an FBI agent; is any contact accidental? "Are we breaking the law?" he asks.

"I'm off duty," she says. "And you're not under investigation." She orders another painkiller from Heidi. "I will break protocol to tell you a few things, though. First of all, those diaries didn't give us enough to lock up Croft."

Huck spins his beer by the neck. All that for nothing? "What about the stuff Russ told Rosie about the dummy driveways? About the illegal business dealings?"

"Hearsay."

"What about the end, where Croft shows up at La Tapa to threaten Rosie?"

"It isn't enough," Colette says. "The person who's implicated is Steele. And even Rosie. You turned over the cash you found in the dresser drawer, but I had to persuade my superiors not to go after the money in Rosie's accounts. I made the argument that the amounts were consistent with what she might have saved from her job." Colette takes a healthy pull of her drink. "But we could easily have called those tainted assets."

She did him a favor, and he's not ungrateful. He has that money to send Maia to college. "Thank you," Huck says.

She dips her head and gazes up at him. "I don't want you to think of me as the bad guy."

"You're just doing your job," Huck says. "I get it."

"Secondly, I got a call from the police in Charlotte Amalie. Apparently Oscar Cobb's girlfriend reported him missing. We watched Oscar a few years back because we knew he was selling drugs aboard the cruise ships—though ultimately he was too small a fish for us to pursue. I was surprised, though, to see his name show up in Rosie's diaries."

"Oscar Cobb," Huck says. "Not one of my favorite people. My wife, LeeAnn, wanted to disappear Oscar herself. He was terrible for Rosie—although I guess 'terrible' is all relative."

Colette says, "The police were wondering if we had any leads, which we didn't, but here's the thing: the girlfriend admitted that Oscar actually went missing on January first. She said they were at a New Year's Eve celebration and that Oscar left the party between two and three a.m., saying he had 'work' over on St. John."

This gets Huck's attention. He thinks about the black Jeep with the tinted windows—but no, it wasn't Oscar driving, and that woman didn't seem like a girlfriend of Oscar's. She was old enough to be his mother and, as Huck had learned, Oscar preferred his women much younger. "Did she say what kind of work?"

"She wasn't sure what he did exactly, but in the police report, she used the word 'investments.'"

"So Oscar Cobb disappears the same day that Rosie and Russ die in the crash. Could be a coincidence. Rosie doesn't mention Oscar again in the diaries and I haven't seen him around here. Believe me, I would have noticed."

"I don't believe in coincidences," Colette says. "But I also don't have anything that ties Cobb to Croft. I'll follow up with the girlfriend—she said she didn't report it earlier because she was scared, and I guess Oscar had a habit of disappearing for weeks at a time..."

Of course, he did, Huck thinks. He flashes back to the first time he laid eyes upon Oscar Cobb—at the Rolex Regatta in the late nineties. Rosie had been so young, only fifteen, and infatuated, completely blind to the fact that Oscar Cobb was bad news.

Though "bad news" is all relative.

"If I don't get anywhere with the girlfriend, I do have one last hope," Colette says. "Someone left a message at the field office saying she wants to talk to me about Croft. It was all very mysterious; she didn't leave a name, only a number. She might be a crackpot. Or she thinks there's money in it for her. The only thing is, she asked for me specifically. So she might be for real."

"You'll follow up?" Huck asks.

"I'll follow up," Colette says. "That's enough talk about work."

Huck has another beer and buys Colette Vasco another painkiller, and then he can't wait another second. He has to have a cigarette. He says, "I'm going out to smoke. I'll be right back."

"We share a vice," Colette says. "I'll come with you."

Huck tells Heidi they're coming right back and the two of them go stand in the grass past the back patio. There are a few crooked palm trees, then the lip of Coral Bay. Huck lights Colette's cigarette. It feels a little weird; the last woman he smoked with was his first wife, Kimberly.

She points to his left hand. "What happened to your finger?"

"Barracuda," he says.

"I love a man with scars," Colette says.

Huck lets that comment slide, though it's starting to feel like she's flirting with him, maybe more than flirting, which he can't deny is good for his battered ego. How old is she? Maybe closer to forty than he'd thought. "How did you end up in the Caribbean?" he asks.

She tells him she's originally from New Jersey, around Manasquan, Brielle, Belmar. Springsteen territory, she adds, because he's never heard of any of those places. Colette's father was a policeman; she went to Rutgers. The FBI recruited her. She spent years working the ports, fell in love with her boss, got married, and when he was transferred to the field office in Puerto Rico, she went with him. She got promoted, they split (it's unclear to Huck if these two things are related), he went back to New Jersey, she stayed in Puerto Rico. The FBI acknowledged the need for a bigger white-collar crime investigative team in the territories.

They're dangerously close to their original topic. Huck is still trying to process the news about Oscar Cobb. *Investments*? By "investments" the girlfriend must have meant "dealing drugs," because what kind of investments needed to be tended to at three o'clock in the morning on St. John?

"Time for me to call it a night," Huck says. They wander back inside and Huck flags Heidi for the check. "I have a charter bright and early."

"I should go too," Colette says.

They end up walking out to the parking lot together. It's dark and unpaved so Huck does the gentlemanly thing and offers Colette his arm.

"You didn't drive the Suburban out here, did you?"

"I'm staying out here," she says. "Company digs. I can't disclose the exact location but it's close enough to walk."

Huck is relieved. He's spared having to offer her a ride home. "Well, this is me," he says, nodding at his truck. He lifts his arm in an attempt to reclaim it from her and Colette grabs his hand, then winds her arms around his midsection and hip-locks him.

Whoa! Huck isn't sure what to do but he has to make a decision right now. Colette Vasco is pretty and there can be no mistaking her body language. She's ready to go—all the way.

Kiss her! Huck thinks. *Take her home. What's stopping you? She's divorced, you're single, you're both lonely, and admit it, there's been something between you from the beginning.*

He places his hands on Colette's shoulders, then cups her face and bends down. He kisses her once, gently, and is overcome by a strong wave of the worst emotion that exists in the world: guilt. He pulls away.

She presses farther into him. "Huck."

"Agent Vasco," he says. He reaches behind his back and unclasps her hands, holds them in both of his. "You're a very attractive woman. But I'm…involved with someone else." He stops. Is he doing the right thing? Is he? "And although it is quite tempting to take you home and let things unfold as they may, that wouldn't be fair to her. Nor would it be fair to you. So I'm going to say good night. Please get home safely."

Colette Vasco stares at him with half a smile—incredulous? embarrassed? drunk?—and then disappears into the dark.

Huck climbs into his truck, lights another cigarette, and blows the smoke out the window. *I hope you're happy, Irene Steele,* he thinks. *You've ruined me.*

He starts the engine, thinking, *Go slow, stay left. Donkeys, get out of my way.*

AYERS

During the first week of their stay on St. John, Ayers's parents cover a lot of ground. On the very first day, they meet Baker and then take Mick and Ayers out to dinner. On their second day, they buy a two-bedroom time-share at the Westin from Baker, and Ayers experiences predictably mixed feelings. On the one hand, she's comforted by this. On the other hand, she feels suffocated.

In the following days, Phil and Sunny hike the Reef Bay Trail, charter the *Singing Dog* with Captains Stephen and Kelly to the BVIs (no *Treasure Island* for them; they want to sail), experience happy hour at both Woody's and High Tide, snorkel with turtles at Salt Pond, dance to Miss Fairchild at the Beach Bar, buy matching hook bracelets at Bamboo, and kayak to Lime Out for tacos.

And yet somehow, they're still underfoot. They wake Ayers up with chai lattes from Provisions, they swing by with containers of sesame noodles and spinach-artichoke dip from the North Shore Deli, they appear at La Tapa while Ayers is working and introduce themselves to the guests at Ayers's tables until she has to ask them to either sit at the bar or leave. They choose the bar and end up getting into a deep conversation with Skip about his trust issues with women.

How is she ever going to survive them? When will they leave for Barbuda, Bequia?

The dinner with Mick was...illuminating. Ayers wonders if, in her parents' minds, Mick is still her boyfriend. Maybe they haven't yet fully absorbed the news of the breakup or the idea that Ayers is pregnant by someone else. At dinner at the Longboard—which unfortunately evoked the evening of their engagement—Mick was his most charming self, sucking up to Phil and Sunny in every possible way, asking about their travels, begging to see their pictures, giving Sunny too much encouragement about her prospective blog. Ayers bit her tongue and thought, *Fake it to make it,* all the while hoping the staff at the Longboard weren't getting out their phones in the back to broadcast the news that Mick and Ayers were together again.

What Ayers realized while being smushed up in a booth next to Mick was that her feelings for him had changed.

She'd broken the engagement because she was smart—Mick would never stop cheating—but it hadn't changed the fact that she loved him. Being pregnant with Baker's baby hadn't canceled out her feelings for Mick either. It was amazing the things that love could endure; nothing demonstrated this more than her ups and downs with Mick had. But at dinner with her parents, Ayers had been pleasantly surprised to find that she felt nothing for Mick other than a mixture of mild annoyance and nostalgic fondness. After Phil and Sunny headed back to Caneel, Mick walked Ayers to her truck and tried to kiss her. She ducked out of the way; she felt no attraction to him. *Finally,* she thought. The vine Mick had wrapped around her heart was withering. She had spent much of the previous six months hating Mick for what had happened with Brigid—but hate was not the opposite of love. Indifference was the opposite of love, and for the first time, Ayers felt like she could take Mick or leave him. Tonight, she would leave him.

"Good night," she said.

Later, when Ayers was home in bed with Winnie snoring softly at her feet, she'd texted Baker. Survived dinner with Mick. Sorry about that; my parents wanted to see him.

There was no response, which was unusual. Ayers wondered if maybe she'd blown it. At noon the next day, Baker still hadn't responded, and she nearly sent a second text asking if he wanted to grab lunch—but she decided this would be confusing. She was the one who had asked for space; he was giving it to her.

When their visit enters its second week, Phil and Sunny decide it's time to introduce themselves to Irene Steele. Ayers tries to dissuade them; Irene is reserved. She may not appreciate being ambushed without warning. But Sunny waves Ayers's concerns away like incense smoke. They see Baker and Floyd get back from school, and the instant Irene arrives home with Cash, they gather up Winnie, a bottle of champagne, and a charcuterie platter from Island Cork.

"Come over after you shower, Fred," Sunny says, which bugs Ayers. She doesn't want to shower and she doesn't want to socialize.

She says, "I'm tired, Mama. I'm going to lie down for a little while."

Sunny immediately changes her tune. Yes, Ayers should sleep, the first trimester is so taxing on the body. Sunny starts talking about being in western Australia on an ostrich farm that was owned by a woman who was also a potter, she made the most beautiful bowls...

"Mama, please," Ayers says. She lies down on her bed and pulls the comforter over her head. The last thing she hears is Sunny saying to Phil, "Leave her be, honey."

When Ayers awakens, it's dark outside and her parents are back, laughing, whispering, bumping into things, shushing each other. Ayers checks her phone—ten thirty. They went across the street at five. "Mom?" she says. "Dad?"

They erupt in giggles. Ayers feels like she's the parent right now. "Have you been across the street this whole *time?*"

"Oh, Freddy," Sunny says. "It's going to be so great!"

"What is?"

"Irene took a while to warm up," Phil says. "But by the fourth bottle of wine..."

"Fourth?"

"Plus the champagne," Sunny says. "So, technically, five."

"Irene likes her chardonnay," Phil says.

"*What* is going to be so great?" Ayers asks.

"Our family!" Sunny says. "The family we're creating with the Steeles. And that Cash—what a cutie!"

"Your mother has a crush on him," Phil says. "She made that much obvious."

"He's single," Sunny says. "I'm surprised you didn't end up with him, Freddy. He's much more your type. Outdoorsy."

"Cash and I are friends, Mom. We work together." Ayers sits up in bed and pats the comforter. Winnie leaps up. "So you all had a great time and you drank the night away..."

"Baker made fish tacos," Phil says. "That guy can really cook."

"Floyd let me read to him before bed," Sunny says. "I feel like a real grandma already."

"We discussed our grandparent names," Phil says. "Irene is Grammy, so Mom will be Mimi. I'm torn between Pop-Pop and Granddaddy." He clears his throat. "It's a big responsibility, being this child's only grandfather."

"We heard the whole story about Russ," Sunny says. "Very interesting."

"If by *interesting*, you mean 'tragic,' then yeah," Ayers says.

"I think what's interesting is the way Irene has come to terms with the situation. She blames Russ, but she also blames herself for taking Russ for granted, for not paying attention to the marriage, for all kinds of things."

"Wow, you guys really got into it," Ayers says. "Did you talk about me?"

"When we first got there, we told them you were tired," Sunny says. "And we talked about the baby."

"But other than that, your name didn't come up," Phil says.

Ayers is both relieved and bothered by this. Her parents and the Steeles are out forging a new family together but somehow the most important person—the person carrying the baby that will unite them—doesn't matter.

Her parents gather their things to return to their room at Caneel—in two short days they're off on their Caribbean adventure, thank goodness—and as soon as the front door closes, Ayers sends Baker a text. Thank you for entertaining my parents; I'm sure they overstayed their welcome. Baker doesn't respond. Well, maybe he's asleep. But when Ayers gets up to check, she sees a light on in what she knows is Baker's bedroom.

She has a strong impulse to tiptoe over and knock on his window. Maybe even encourage him to come over. Maybe even...

She climbs back into bed. *Space,* she thinks.

Two nights later, Ayers is working at La Tapa. Her parents left that morning on the ten o'clock ferry; they'll be gone for six to eight weeks. Ayers is relieved; happy, even. They'll be back, but she doesn't have to deal with them right now.

Tilda approaches Ayers at the back service station. "I assume you've heard?"

God alone knows what Tilda is going to drop on her. *Heard you left Cash for some wealthy guy who doesn't eat?* Yes, Ayers has heard about that, in gory detail, from Cash. Ayers won't lie—it has colored her opinion of Tilda. Tilda is entitled to see whomever she pleases but going away with a rich boy and leaving Cash in the dust seems crueler than your average breakup.

"Heard what?" Ayers asks.

"Mick quit the Beach Bar," Tilda says. "He's leaving island."

"That must be a mistake," Ayers says. "He told me at dinner last week that he signed a one-year lease at his new place, Pure Joy."

"He's trying to find someone to take over his lease."

"Really," Ayers says. "Where's he going?"

"You should probably ask him that," Tilda says.

Tilda is back to being very annoying, even more annoying than when she had a crush on Skip.

On her way home, Ayers calls Mick. "Word on the street is that you quit the Beach Bar? You're leaving island?"

"Yes," Mick says. "And yes."

"Wow," Ayers says, though she still doesn't believe him. He's been at the Beach Bar a Caribbean eternity—eleven years.

"I can't live on this island and not be with you," he says.

Ayers knew it. This is all a ploy to get her back. He *planned* this with Tilda; they're in *cahoots!* "Well, I'm never coming back to you. I'm not in love with you anymore. So I guess you'd better go."

"Yeah." He clears his throat. "Any chance you want to take over the lease on Pure Joy?"

"Damn straight I do," she says. He may be bluffing but she's dead serious. Pure Joy is a one-bedroom with incredible views across Great Cruz Bay over to St. Thomas, views that are best enjoyed sitting at the cute bar counter on the front porch. Ayers is sure her parents will help her with the rent.

"I thought you might move in with Banker and his kid. Play house, happy family, and all that."

"No plans to," Ayers says. "I definitely want your place."

"Cool," Mick says. "I want to leave as soon as I can. I've been offered a position as food and beverage director at Tucker's Point in Bermuda."

Ayers hoots. "Will you wear knee socks?"

"I think I might have to," Mick says. "The resort is five-star, so the job has more responsibility. The only downside is the shorts-and-knee-socks look. My legs are so stubby."

"So you're doing this?"

"Yes," he says.

Things move fast, so fast! The next day, Ayers meets Mick at the real estate office to sign paperwork for the lease. Mick is leaving this weekend; Ayers can move in as soon as he's out.

"What are you doing with your place?" Mick asks.

"Cash is taking it," Ayers says. This whole thing is almost too easy; Cash can move off his brother's couch right into Ayers's studio apartment across the street. He and Winnie will be reunited. Ayers isn't sure how Baker feels about her leaving Fish Bay, but it's not like she's leaving for St. Thomas or even Coral Bay. She'll be on Great Cruz Bay Road, halfway between the Happy Hibiscus and the Westin time-share office. And it's only for a year.

It will be a big, scary year, but Ayers isn't going to let that stop her. She loved the cottage when Mick showed it to her. Now it's hers!

On Saturday when Mick is scheduled to leave, Ayers drives down to the car barge to say goodbye. She can't quite figure out why she wants to do this. She supposes that part of it is to witness the milestone—the moment her boyfriend of nine years moves on. Part of it is to make sure he actually goes. And part of it is to kiss Gordon one last time.

The car barge is, as always, a whirl of activity with a snaking line of cars and Jeeps and pickups and huge Mack trucks waiting to board and a notoriously unflappable West Indian woman named Sheila overseeing who goes where. More than once, Ayers has witnessed Sheila letting her friends and sweethearts jump the line, which isn't fair—but nobody ever questions Sheila.

Sheila is a cousin of Rosie's on her father's side and because of this, Sheila likes Ayers. "You getting on, doll?" she asks.

"Saying goodbye to someone," Ayers says.

"And good riddance?" Sheila asks.

"Kind of, yeah," Ayers says and Sheila chuckles.

Ayers almost doesn't recognize Mick's blue Jeep because it has the top on. Has she ever seen his Jeep with the top on? She doesn't think so. She and Mick got caught in rain showers in that thing probably a hundred times. The seats held a damp smell and Mick eventually pulled up the rugs so that water emptied through the holes in the floorboards. Ayers parks her truck over by Sheila's guardhouse. As she strides toward Mick's Jeep, she hears Gordon barking. Automatically, she tears up. She promised herself she wouldn't become emotional, but that dog was like her first child and she's going to miss him.

They're loading the boat; she has to hurry. She runs up behind the Jeep and goes to the driver's side, where Gordon is hanging his head out the window.

"Who's a good boy?" she says.

"Hey!" Mick says. "What are you doing here?"

"Came to say goodbye to my pup—" Ayers is at the window, her hands cradling Gordon's bucket head, when she realizes there's someone in the passenger seat of the Jeep.

It's Brigid.

"Hey, Ayers," Brigid says. "Thanks for seeing us off. Good luck with your *baby*." She says the word like it's something imaginary and she holds up two fingers in a peace sign.

Ayers is…she's…she looks at Mick. "Brigid's going with you to Bermuda?"

He nods. "Yeah."

Ayers kisses Gordon between the eyes, then leans in past Mick. "Goodbye, Brigid," she says. She returns the peace sign—ironically, but Brigid will never know this.

Sheila whistles, windmilling her arm; it's time for Mick to go.

Ayers watches the blue Jeep drive up the ramp of the barge.

"And good riddance," Ayers says.

The very next day, Ayers wakes up feeling like a new woman. She got a long luxurious night's sleep, and for the first time in weeks, she feels hungry. She makes not only buttered rye toast but also cheesy scrambled eggs. She takes her prenatal vitamin, drinks a glass of juice, eats a banana.

She figures she needs two days to pack her things and one day to move them. Then she'll be back in action.

She calls Whitney at the *Treasure Island* office. "I can work again, starting on Wednesday," she says.

It's as though Ayers has crossed an invisible boundary. Her body was her enemy, but now it's a friend. She has energy; she has vitality. The tiny life inside her might as well be a supercharged battery. Ayers moves into Pure Joy. While Ayers's studio was funky and bohemian but gloomy, with a view only of the Happy Hibiscus, Pure Joy is bright and airy, filled with sunlight. She has actual rooms—a living/dining/kitchen area, a brand-new bath with gleaming white subway tile, a bedroom with a king-size bed, and a bona fide walk-in closet. The cottage has a gas grill and an enclosed outdoor shower and Ayers will spend every spare minute on one of the stools at the bar counter gazing at the dreamscape across her new front yard—the striated blue and green shades of the Caribbean.

Ayers sets her mugs and plates and wineglasses on the fresh white shelves in the kitchen; she puts new sheets on the bed; she hangs her photographs; she sets her houseplants in the sun. During her last check of her old studio, she discovers the hidden pack of cigarettes on top of the refrigerator and throws them away.

Her first night in the new place, she gets barbecue from Candi's—ribs and chicken and pasta salad and coleslaw and plantains—and she sits at the bar counter on her front porch to watch the sun sink into the Caribbean. *Hashtag sunset,* she thinks. Mick is gone, she's pregnant, and she has a new place to live— it all feels like a fresh start. She picks up her phone and nearly sends a text to Baker saying, *Want to see my new place?* But it's only her first night. There's plenty of time.

A leave of absence from *Treasure Island* was exactly what she needed because she comes back rejuvenated. Virgin Gorda Baths, snorkeling at the Indians, White Bay on Jost Van Dyke, where Leon, the bartender at the Soggy Dollar, makes her a virgin painkiller.

"Congratulations, love," Leon says. "When will I meet this child's daddy?"

"Soon?" Ayers says. She wonders if she should invite Baker and Floyd out on the boat so they can experience the BVIs and see her in action. Yes, they would like it. When they get back to Cruz Bay, Ayers checks the schedule and sees there are plenty of spots on Saturday's charter. She texts Baker. BVI trip Saturday, you and Floyd, my treat?

The response comes: Nice offer, thank you. Floyd doesn't have a passport.

Ah, bummer, Ayers thinks. He's only four, but yeah, he still needs a passport. How about just you, then? Leave Floyd with your mom?

I shouldn't, he says. Weekends are my time with Floyd. Sorry about that.

He's a good dad, she thinks. *He's a really good dad.*

A few nights later, Ayers leaves La Tapa after service and she's so tired that she drives to Fish Bay without thinking. It's only when she pulls into her former driveway and sees Cash's new-used truck that she realizes she's on autopilot.

Ugh! She might need Tilda to close from now on so she can get out of the restaurant earlier. Tilda won't like this. She has been the one slipping out early, rushing her tables, neglecting to offer dessert, coffee, or aperitifs, snapping at Skip for change—all because her new beau, Dunk, likes to linger across the street outside the Tap and Still, vaping and waiting for Tilda to emerge. Ayers has studied him. He's always in jeans and a T-shirt and a baseball cap and Sambas, looking more like a guy with an online-poker habit than a multimillionaire with an estate out in the East End, but Ayers supposes that's part of the appeal. Dunk looks shady, which Tilda has mistaken for mysterious; she finds his fasting intriguing rather than ridiculous. She's young. She'll learn.

As Ayers is backing out of her former driveway she sees, in her rearview mirror, two people coming out of the Happy Hibiscus. It's Baker and...a woman. Tall, blond.

Wait a minute. Ayers pulls back into her former driveway, turns off her lights, cuts her engine. She squints into the mirror. Do they see her? No. Baker and the woman are standing by an ivory Land Cruiser that Ayers recognizes as belonging to Swan Seeley.

Baker is walking Swan Seeley out to her car at ten thirty at night. Are they *seeing* each other? Is this why he hasn't responded to her texts?

No, Ayers thinks. *No!* She can't let this happen. And yet this is all her fault. She told Baker she needed space; she told Baker she wanted to be friends. Friends! After he moved his entire life down here, after he handled the news of the pregnancy like a hero. Has he complained? No. Has he been even a little bit of a jerk like literally any other guy in America would have been? No. He stopped by with a smoothie and chips. She had seen him another time, with Floyd in tow, bearing coffee and a bakery bag, and she'd burrowed into her bed, not even answering the door. She'd skipped the impromptu visit by her parents. She had been so certain that Baker would be there when she was ready that she had never considered another woman might step in, a woman such as Swan Seeley, a Gifft Hill mother who is going through a divorce and who *told* Ayers the afternoon that Mick proposed that she thought Baker was hot. And now here they are, Baker and Swan, standing by the driver's side of Swan's car, about to have a moment.

They're talking, but not touching. Swan tosses her hair, leans her head back, raises her face to his. She lays her palm on Baker's strong chest, and Ayers feels a pang of longing. The first time she saw Baker was at Chester's Getaway, when he crashed Rosie's funeral reception. He had seemed such a stunning, fresh presence in that sea of all-too-familiar faces, some of which were also all too unpleasant (Mick had had the gall to bring Brigid).

At first, Ayers thought Baker was a tourist. Learning he was the Invisible Man's son had been shocking, but on later reflection, she'd known there was *something about him.* She sensed that meeting him wasn't random luck. Rosie, in a way, had sent him to her.

Then he went back to Houston.

Then he returned. They'd slept together. It had felt...right. They clicked. There was light, heat, chemistry.

Then he left again. For only a few days—but a few days was a few days too many. Mick proposed.

Then Baker came back. He's here now. He has a job, a Jeep, a villa. Floyd is in school. Baker is a tourist no longer.

Swan takes hold of Baker's arms and stands on her tiptoes.

No, Ayers thinks. She gets out of the truck, slams the door. Both Baker and Swan turn toward the noise. Swan's heels hit the ground.

"Hey," Ayers calls out. She crosses the street and strides up the driveway to the two of them. They're standing farther apart now.

Swan looks...miffed. "Ayers?"

Baker says, "Ayers, hey!" He takes a step away from Swan.

"Sorry I didn't text or anything," Ayers says to Baker. "But I just got out of work and I was wondering if you wanted to come see my new place?"

Swan emits an audible breath and Ayers thinks, *I know. This is brazen. You will rewind and replay this moment for your school-mom friends dozens of times until they're all sick of hearing it, and maybe none of you will ever speak to me again. Maybe you'll boycott La Tapa and post anonymous nasty comments on the* Treasure Island *Tripadvisor page, but I don't care. Baker is the father of my baby and although I've treated him carelessly, I'm not giving him up without a fight.*

Then she thinks, *The good news is, Skip is still available.*

"Yeah," Baker says. "My mom can watch Floyd, and Swan was just leaving." He takes Ayers's hand and squeezes it. "I'd love to come with you."

IRENE

Baker sees Maia at school while he's picking up Floyd and invites her over for dinner.

"I hope that's okay?" he says when he tells Irene. "I'll go get her and drive her home."

"Of course," Irene says. She still isn't ready for a détente with Huck—nope, not at all. Rosie's relationship with Russ happened while Rosie was *living under Huck's roof.* He said he'd never met Russ—Irene believes this—but could he not guess the man Rosie was involved with was married? Obviously, the Invisible Man was married. That was why he was invisible!

Huck should have asked more questions. He should have followed Rosie to the villa. He should have *put an end to it.*

Are these unreasonable expectations? Maybe. But the bald fact remains: Huck stood by and did nothing. For years.

He's the only one left for Irene to blame. She can't summon the same ire or resentment toward Maia. Maia is a child. Russ's daughter. The boys' sister.

"Maia is always welcome," Irene says, and she sees relief cross Baker's face.

Maia arrives bearing two large square packages—one light, which she carries, and one heavy, which Baker carries.

"These came for you," Maia explains. "To Gramps's post box."

While Maia and Floyd take a predinner swim in the pool, Irene slices the packages open. One of them holds her Christmas ornaments, still carefully wrapped up in tissue. Irene sighs, recalling her *industriousness* on New Year's Day before her dinner with Lydia at the Pullman Diner, before the phone call when she learned Russ was dead.

On New Year's Day, she had been a different person—irritated and hurt that her husband was traveling for work over the holiday but determined to make the best of it and be productive. She'd wanted to wake up on January 2 and have all traces of Christmas gone. Back then, nothing had annoyed Irene more than lazy neighbors who left their outside lights up until Martin Luther King Jr. weekend, their wreaths up until Valentine's Day. She had carefully removed and wrapped all the ornaments because she was a methodical person who believed God was in the details. She would be grateful for the effort the following Christmas when she opened the box and everything was just so.

She'd never imagined she'd be opening the box that spring in the Virgin Islands.

The most precious ornaments aren't her collection of intricate and clever Christopher Radkos or the vintage ornaments she picked up at estate sales across the country but rather the ornaments the boys made in elementary school. A cardboard disk covered in green foil decorated with beads and dried macaroni, CASH written in glitter on one side. A puffy painted Santa face with cotton glued on for a beard. Irene is happy to have these back, even though they belonged to that other lifetime.

The other box holds photo albums and the framed family photographs that Irene had had on display around the house on Church Street. The photo that greets Irene is the last picture taken of her and Russ together. They're side by side on the front porch swing at her aunt's house in Door County, Wisconsin. They're smiling at Cash, who took the picture. Russ's arm runs along the back of the swing behind Irene, and Irene's hand rests on Russ's thigh, lightly but proprietarily. Why wouldn't it? He was her husband of thirty-five years. She would characterize Russ's expression as content. Irene then flashes back to the photograph she found of him and Rosie lying in the hammock. He had looked ecstatic, as though he had no idea how he'd gotten so lucky. A girlfriend whose beauty was as rarefied as the Mona Lisa's.

Irene had wanted to smash the photograph of Russ and Rosie but she feels an even greater violence toward this picture of her and Russ. The audacity of him to smile at the camera as though nothing is amiss. As though he doesn't have a mistress and a child waiting for him down in the Caribbean!

Irene steadies her breathing and checks out the window. Baker is drinking a beer, his legs dangling in the water. Maia is carrying Floyd around the pool on her shoulders. He's shrieking with joy. He adores her.

Irene digs a little deeper in the box and finds the navy leather photo album and the red vinyl photo album. These hold pictures of the boys growing up. She can see the snapshots without looking at them: Baker on the pitcher's mound in his green and yellow uniform, all spindly arms and legs; Cash on the ski slopes, goggles resting on top of his helmet, braces glinting in the glare off the snow; both boys in khakis and navy blazers escorting Milly out of church on Easter.

Beneath these is a photograph of Baker and Anna on their wedding day. Anna is stunning in her sleek ivory silk, but she's not smiling.

Irene closes up the box and puts it in the closet. When she's had a chance to properly go through it, she'll show some of the pictures of Baker and Cash to Maia. But for now, it's important that Maia not see any of the photos. What would she think if she saw the picture of Russ and Irene on the swing? Irene shudders. She would never put a child through what she has just experienced—being starkly confronted with evidence that she was being lied to.

At dinner, Maia says, "So what was in the boxes?"

"Christmas ornaments," Irene says. "And other knickknacks from my house in Iowa."

Maia takes a knife to her fried chicken. "I had to give up being a vegan," she says. "It was too hard."

"How's the bath-bomb business?" Irene asks.

"I kind of gave that up too," Maia says. "I'm busy with other things."

"What kinds of things?" Baker asks. "Not sports? I was supposed to coach the upper-school baseball team but only four kids signed up—three girls and a boy."

"Not sports," Maia says. "I hang out with my friends mostly. Joanie, Colton, Bright, and...Shane. Shane is sort of a special friend." Maia's face shines and for a moment, her beauty takes Irene's breath away. She's Milly, she's Russ, and she's someone else—Rosie, Irene supposes.

Maia makes it through the entire meal talking about her life without mentioning Huck even once. This must be on purpose; maybe Maia thinks Huck is a forbidden topic.

Irene clears her throat. "How's your grandfather?" As soon as the words are out, she feels like she's lost a test of wills.

"Oh," Maia says, shrugging. "He's good." This seems to be all Irene is going to get. *He's good. He's good?* Then Maia locks eyes with Irene and says, "He misses you."

Irene is startled by the simple frankness of this statement.

I miss him too, she thinks—and it's the first time she's allowed herself to admit it.

"He gave me this to deliver," Maia says. She pulls an envelope that has been folded in half out of the back pocket of her shorts.

"Oh," Irene says. Her name is on the front in Huck's handwriting. Maybe it's an accounting of what she owes him for rent and utilities—but she knows Huck wouldn't ask for money even if he were angry. "Thank you." She takes the envelope. "Who wants dessert?"

She would like to throw the envelope away unopened, but she isn't strong enough. She waits until Baker returns from running Maia home and starts giving Floyd a bath, then she takes the envelope to the back deck and opens it.

It's a letter.

Dear AC,

Maybe you'll read this, maybe you won't. In the event you are reading this, I want to start by saying that this is not an apology because I didn't do anything wrong.

When LeeAnn died and Rosie got back together with Russ, she was nearly thirty years old. She described Russ as "this man I'm seeing, Russell Steele"—she said his name to me only that once—and I had no idea that this was the same man as "the Pirate," the one who had gotten her pregnant. She very deliberately led me to believe it was someone new.

I asked the usual questions: Where was he from, what did

he do, when could I meet him? Rosie provided no answers. She wanted to keep the relationship private; she was concerned that the island would poke its nose into her business. After the way that LeeAnn rallied every single one of her friends and relations against Oscar Cobb, I couldn't blame Rosie for feeling this way. Rosie told me that, just like certain plants, some relationships do best with a lot of sunlight, and some thrive hidden in the shade, and her new relationship was the latter. It concerned me, I made that clear, but I also want to explain that I was lonely without LeeAnn and my greatest fear was that Rosie would take Maia and move out. I wanted to avoid that at all costs.

If you read the diaries closely then you know that Rosie didn't start taking Maia with her to see Russ until 2016. Once this happened, my questions grew more insistent. I didn't like the idea of Maia spending time with any adult I hadn't met.

Again, I was shut down.

There were whispers around town about the "Invisible Man," and some of it reached my ears. I learned he was white, he was wealthy, he had a villa somewhere on the north shore. Did I think he was married? It crossed my mind, but again, Rosie was in her thirties, old enough to know what she was doing.

To be honest, AC, I was worried about Rosie—and Maia— getting hurt. I didn't give a thought to any woman Russell Steele might have been betraying. When I think of it this way, I understand what you mean about us being on "opposite sides" of this thing.

Although this isn't a letter of apology, I do want to say that I'm sorry. I'm sorry this happened to you. I'm sorry you were betrayed and I'm sorry you were hurt. I also want to tell you something about my past that you might not know.

Before I moved to St. John and met LeeAnn Small, I was married to someone else, a woman named Kimberly Cassel, whom I met when I lived in Key West. Kimberly was a hot ticket—a star bartender and one hell of a fisherwoman. She was also a serial philanderer and an alcoholic. Before our marriage ended, Kimberly revealed that she had fooled around with hundreds, maybe even thousands, of the men who came into the bar where she worked. Kimberly got pregnant and miscarried at fourteen weeks, which was devastating to me at the time and felt even worse when I discovered the child might not even have been mine.

I put Kimberly in rehab and divorced her, which might sound like a door that shut clean and firm, but I assure you, the hurt lasted for a very long time after.

I tell you this only because I want you to feel less alone and to know that I do have some idea of what you're battling.

If you made it this far in the letter, AC, then I'm grateful— and not only grateful but hopeful that, at some point in the future, we can have a conversation and mend things between us. I miss you for many reasons, but mostly I miss our friend- ship. As unlikely as it might be, the friendship is genuine.

With love,
Huck

Irene clears the emotion from her throat and reads the letter again. Then she folds it up and returns it to the envelope. She heads back into the kitchen to unload the dishes from the drying rack and she holds the letter over the kitchen trash. It feels like

Huck is, once again, rushing her. If he'd learned anything from watching and listening to her the past couple of months, he would have known that what she needs is time.

She can't bring herself to throw the letter away. She tucks it into the front pocket of her suitcase.

As she's falling asleep, she thinks, *Huck wrote me a letter.* And she smiles.

The next day, Irene e-mails Natalie Key to thank her for the boxes. She doesn't call because she knows Natalie is handling a new, highly sensitive, high-profile embezzlement case and is very busy. She's surprised when the phone rings.

"I'm sorry I couldn't get you more," Natalie says. "Your books and clothes will be returned eventually, once they've been documented and it's been determined that they have minimal resale value. Certain other personal items as well—your teakettle, kitchen utensils. But no antiques, and not the rugs. Not your cars. I'm sorry."

"It's okay," Irene says—and the strange thing is, she means it. She owned a house filled with *things,* some of them very expensive. But none of it matters. She's doing just fine without *things.* Why had she put so much time and energy into them in the first place?

"Also…" Natalie says. Her voice takes on a sober tone and Irene assumes she's about to say that Irene's retainer has run out. "I heard from the Feds. There were personal journals of Rosie Small's that were discovered—but unfortunately, these didn't contain enough hard facts to incriminate Todd Croft."

Irene closes her eyes. All of that pain…for nothing? Huck

should have buried the diaries in a drawer and given them to Maia ten or fifteen years from now. In ten or fifteen years, the love affair between Russell Steele and his Mona Lisa wouldn't hurt Irene the way it does now.

"That guy Croft," Natalie says. "He's the mastermind. There's no other way."

"He's such a mastermind, he managed to walk away unscathed," Irene says.

"Fined," Natalie says. "Heavily fined. But make no mistake, that guy has money hidden."

"He killed Russ," Irene says. "And Rosie. And Stephen Thompson. And he's getting off scot-free."

"I thought for sure we were going to help send him to jail," Natalie says. "I'm sorry, Irene."

She received the study materials for her captain's test, but when she starts reading the introduction, she sees that, in addition to passing the test, she has to have at least three hundred and sixty days logged on the water as a mate or crew member.

Three hundred and sixty days!

She has, maybe, thirty.

Irene sags at this news. She chastises herself for not realizing this would be the case. If it were just a little studying and a test, then every clown out there would have a captain's license. She feels so naive. Here she announced her grandiose plan—her own charter, *Angler Cupcake,* direct competition for Huck. She had cinematic fantasies of standing proud at the helm of her own boat with a full charter, puttering past the empty *Mississippi.* In some versions, she waves to Huck. In others, she ignores him.

He must have known she didn't have enough hours on the

water when she mentioned her plans to Jack and Diane. How embarrassing.

How will she get three hundred and thirty more days on the water? Who would hire a fifty-seven-year-old woman as a mate?

Treasure Island? she wonders. Maybe. Cash and Ayers could definitely use a third crew member to cover their respective days off, and once the baby is born...Cash says all they're looking for is a warm body, and Irene is much more than that. She's good with the clients. It's a little babysitting, a little psychology. Irene has the touch.

How would Cash feel about working all day with his *mother?* Not great, she predicts. Living together is taxing enough.

She could approach a different fishing boat, like *What a Catch!* But those guys are young, single, wild. They don't want Irene on their boat.

Could she work on Pizza Pi as a delivery person, zipping the pizzas to yachts on a little Zodiac? Would that count? What about asking at Palm Tree Charters or the *Singing Dog?* There's a new charter Irene heard about, a Midnight Express called *New Moon* owned by a very cool couple named Brian and Michelle Zehring— *that* boat might be too sexy for Irene, but she could always ask.

Even if she can cobble something together, it's still going to take an entire year for Irene to realize her dream. She has an appointment to see a 2006 forty-five-foot Hatteras on St. Thomas next week. The asking price is fifty thousand, but on the phone the guy said he's willing to work with her and she can hopefully take out a loan at FirstBank.

Baker's new friend Swan Seeley is scheduled to come over tomorrow after dinner to talk to her about a marketing strategy. Irene considers canceling but this woman Swan might be well connected and could have leads on where Irene might look for work. Irene confirms with Swan, then texts Lydia to see if Brandon the barista is willing to part with his recipe for lemongrass sugar cookies. Irene needs to have something to offer the woman. Other than wine, of course.

Swan arrives right on time. She's tall, blond, and stunning; Irene puts her at thirty-five or thirty-six. She's wearing white pants, a formfitting white T-shirt, a slender gold watch, and gold hoop earrings. Irene peeks behind her in the driveway and sees an ivory Land Cruiser.

"Hello, Mrs. Steele, I'm Swan Seeley." Nice handshake, smile; she's wearing makeup and she smells divine, some kind of expensive perfume. Maybe Swan thought tonight was going to be more formal than it is?

They sit at the dining-room table. Swan pulls a Moleskine notebook out of her supple leather hobo bag. This woman is smooth, polished. Wealthy. She's the Mavis Key of St. John.

Irene offers Swan wine—"Yes, please"—and sets out a plate of the lemongrass sugar cookies, which turned out splendidly. (Brandon's suggestion to undercook them by two minutes was spot on; they're pale golden and have alluringly crinkly tops.) Irene offers the plate and Swan takes not one but two—oh, Irene likes this woman already.

Irene says, "I'm not sure what Baker told you..."

Swan's head swivels around. "Is Baker *here?*" she asks. "I saw his Jeep out front."

"He's reading to Floyd," Irene says. "He'll be out in a minute."

"He's *such* a good father," Swan says. "Not just a good father but a good *parent.* My ex...well, this time of night you could usually find him in front of the slots at the Parrot Club."

Irene suddenly understands that Swan's presence here has little to do with Irene and much to do with Baker. Does Swan know that Ayers is pregnant with Baker's baby? Maybe that doesn't matter. Baker and Ayers have hardly seen each other at all. The week before, Ayers's parents came over and Ayers stayed home. Irene figures she'd better state her case before Baker comes downstairs and distracts Swan.

"I want to start my own fishing charter," she says. "Here's what I've found out..."

Swan agrees the three-hundred-and-sixty-day requirement is a bummer and means it'll be another year before Irene's charter is up and running.

"I would hire you as a mate on my boat," Swan says. "But it looks like I have to sell it to pay off my ex."

"Divorces are tricky," Irene says. She's had a glass and a half of wine, so she nearly adds, *But better than staying married and finding out your husband has a secret family!*

"I'm confused about why you're not working for Huck anymore," Swan says. "He's *such* a great guy. *Such* a wonderful grandfather. Completely devoted to Maia."

"That he is," Irene says.

"You know, I saw him on Friday night out at Skinny Legs." Swan sips her wine. "He was with a woman, a very pretty redhead. I saw them leave together, so I think maybe Huck got lucky!" She leans in conspiratorially and bumps Irene's shoulder.

Irene nearly falls over in her chair. "A redhead?" she says. "Was she his age?"

"Younger," Swan says. "Closer to my age, I'd guess. Go, Huck!"

The wine and cookies churn in Irene's stomach. Her neck flushes. She has to get out of there.

"Hey, ladies." Baker saunters into the kitchen. "I don't mean to interrupt—"

"Baker!" Swan says. She jumps up from the table to give him a hug. Here is Irene's way out.

"Thank you for all your help, Swan. I'll let you two kids chat. I need to hit the hay."

"Hit the hay," Baker says. "Can you tell we're from the Midwest?"

"Are you sure, Irene?" Swan says. "We didn't get to talk about my marketing ideas. I have a bunch."

"We've got plenty of time," Irene says. "I hope you'll come back once I buy a boat and get closer to my hours…"

"You don't have to run off, Mom," Baker says. His expression seems to be asking Irene *not* to run off.

Sorry, Baker, she thinks. *You're an adult. You deal with your romantic entanglements and I'll deal with mine.* "Enjoy the cookies," Irene says.

Very pretty redhead. I think maybe Huck got lucky! Go, Huck!

The living room, where Irene is sleeping, is too close to the kitchen to be private. Irene slips through Floyd's room to the bathroom and sits on the edge of the tub in the dark.

Huck was out with Agent Vasco. She's a redhead, about Swan's age, very pretty. Well, Irene thinks, *very pretty* might be overstating things, but yes, she's attractive. She's also the person who took away Irene's house. *She took my house, Huck, and you two are out canoodling at Skinny Legs!*

Just as Irene was starting to soften a little and wonder if she should let him know she read his letter.

Vasco!

I think maybe Huck got lucky!

Did he take her home? Did he *sleep* with her? Irene can't let herself imagine this. The night she and Huck went to Shambles, he kissed her. It could have gone further but Irene stopped him. She was right to stop him, because when she read the diaries, she realized how wrong it was that she had become friends with Rosie's father!

Irene's face is wet. She's crying. She quit the boat and moved out of Huck's house because she was hurt by *Russ,* angry at *Russ.* And now Huck is with someone else. He's had the hots for Vasco this whole time; he'd admitted as much, this could hardly come as a shock. The letter said he missed their friendship. Apparently, he's getting his "friendship" somewhere else now!

She'll never speak to him again, she decides.

Should she call him right now? It's nine thirty. He's asleep.

Irene cracks the door of Floyd's room; she hears Baker and Swan talking. She lies down on the other half of Floyd's king bed and falls asleep.

When she wakes up in the middle of the night, she has no idea where she is. Then she hears the steady purr of Floyd's breathing and remembers.

Her mouth is cottony; she's still in her clothes. She brushes her teeth in the bathroom and applies her nighttime moisturizer. Her reflection in the mirror is unforgiving. *You messed up.*

The house is now dark and quiet. Irene grabs her pillow and blanket from the closet and heads to the sofa.

She needs to see Huck tomorrow, she thinks. She isn't going to lose him to Vasco. Nope, sorry. She has lost too much already.

She wants to be waiting for Huck by the *Mississippi* in the morning but there are the logistics of cars. Baker needs his Jeep to drop Floyd off at school and then get to work. Cash has to be at *Treasure Island* by seven. If Irene had let Cash know the night before, he would have dropped her at the National Park Service dock first, but she can't spring it on him now.

She says to Baker, "Is it okay if I borrow your Jeep after you pick up Floyd from school? I have errands."

"No problem!" Baker says. He's unusually chipper. He has made Floyd banana pancakes for breakfast. "Would you mind watching Floyd tonight? I have plans with Ayers."

"Ayers?" Irene says. "What about Swan?"

"Swan?" Baker says as though he isn't sure who Irene is talking about. "Oh, we're just friends."

Just friends. Maybe Huck and Vasco are just friends as well. Maybe Swan misunderstood the situation at Skinny Legs. *Oh, please. Oh, please!* Irene isn't sure how she's going to make it until three o'clock. She would text Huck right away but she knows he's out on the boat. She'll be waiting when he pulls back in. If, God forbid, Agent Vasco is also waiting for Huck on the dock, Irene will...push Vasco in.

I'm crazy, Irene thinks. *Crazy about him and just plain crazy.*

She sits by the pool with her captain's-license study materials but she can't concentrate on characteristics of weather systems or lifesaving equipment. She heads to the kitchen.

She isn't hungry, but what about a drink? The bottle of wine she opened with Swan is gone, but Irene has plenty of other bottles. What if she starts drinking now, at eleven o'clock in the morning, and shows up at the dock completely blotto?

This is so out of character, she's tempted to try it.

She still has a few Ativan left. Should she take an Ativan?

I think maybe Huck got lucky! Go, Huck!

She hears a car in the driveway. Yes? No. Yes—a car door slams. Did Baker come home for lunch? Irene goes to the front door and sees a black Jeep with tinted windows in the driveway and a small woman with a limp brown ponytail approaching. Probably she's lost. Hikers come out this way looking for the start of the Reef Bay Trail coastal walk, but that's up the hill.

"Can I help you?" Irene says.

"Irene Steele?" the woman says.

Irene blinks, looks again at the Jeep. Didn't Huck say something about a black Jeep with tinted windows? Yes. He saw one loitering on Jacob's Ladder.

"I'm sorry," Irene says. "Do I know you?" The woman is wearing a plain white short-sleeved blouse and khaki capris. She has a pale, round face and brown eyes. FBI? Irene wonders. They've taken everything she has. If they ask for anything more, she'll give them the Christmas ornaments.

"Irene." The woman checks their surroundings as though she thinks they're being watched. "May I come in? I need to speak to you confidentially."

"About?"

"Your husband," the woman says. "And Todd Croft."

"Are you with the FBI?" Irene asks. "I'd like to see some ID."

"I'm not with the FBI," the woman says. She takes a step

closer to the screen door and lowers her voice. "Irene, we've spoken on the phone. I'm Marilyn Monroe."

Irene's hand flies to her mouth. Marilyn Monroe was the person who called Irene on New Year's Day to tell her Russ was dead. She was Todd Croft's secretary, but it seemed like she'd dropped off the face of the earth.

She looks *nothing* like the famous Marilyn Monroe. Under other circumstances, Irene might find this amusing.

Irene holds the door open, then locks both the screen and the solid wood door behind Marilyn. Turns the dead bolt.

"Yes," Marilyn says, as though this is a necessary measure.

"Can I offer you anything—"

"We just need a quiet place to talk," Marilyn says. She looks around the Happy Hibiscus. "He hasn't gotten in here, so it's safe."

"Who?"

"My husband," Marilyn says. "Todd."

"Todd Croft is your *husband?*" Irene doesn't mean to sound incredulous but she'd thought Todd Croft, with all his money and power, would have a trophy wife. Someone like…Swan Seeley. Polished, put together, a woman who wears five-hundred-dollar-an-ounce perfume and carries a two-thousand-dollar bag, someone who owns a cigarette boat so she can zip over to Virgin Gorda for a facial at Little Dix. This woman looks like she drives in a carpool, then heads home to scrapbook. She's neither fat nor thin, neither pretty nor ugly. How would Irene describe her to the police? Round face, clear skin, a nice straight part in her brown hair. She wears a gold wedding band next to a diamond engagement ring; her nails are filed into pretty ovals, though they're unpolished. She has leather thong sandals on her feet and a gold anklet so thin it's almost imperceptible. Irene can't recall the last time she saw anyone wearing an anklet. Her sorority sister Sandra, maybe, back in 1985. She must be Irene's age, maybe a few years younger. Fifty-two or fifty-three, Irene would guess.

"Yes," Marilyn says. "We've been married for twenty-five years."

"So before all this started."

"Todd started Ascension the year after we got married," Marilyn says. "My family owns marinas and boat-building concerns in Florida. My father got Todd set up in business." She nods at the sofa. "Okay if we sit down?"

Yes, yes. Irene leads Marilyn into the living room but the midwesterner in her will not be quieted. "Are you sure I can't get you any coffee, tea, or . . . will we be needing wine?"

Marilyn doesn't smile at that, and Irene starts to worry. "I've been trying to talk to you alone for a while now. But you were always with the captain."

"Huck," Irene says. "Yes."

"And then, suddenly, you weren't. I thought I'd lost you. I thought you left the Virgin Islands."

"No, I moved in here with my son. You found that out somehow?"

Marilyn nods. "I asked someone close to you."

"That narrows it down," Irene says. "I know only five people."

"I have things to tell you, things I wanted you to hear directly from me. When I leave here, I'm meeting the FBI to turn state's evidence against Todd."

Irene lowers herself down to the sofa inch by inch, as though Marilyn has a gun trained on her. Where is Irene's cell phone? She wants to record this conversation but she doesn't want to frighten Marilyn away. "You are?"

"After I do that, I'll go into protective custody—assuming he doesn't find a way to kill me first. But it's been eating at me since I spoke to you on the phone in January, the wrongs that have been done to you. And your sons. And the captain. And the girl."

"Maia."

"I feel like I've been carrying all of you around on my back," Marilyn says. "But I don't want to get ahead of myself."

"No, by all means," Irene says, "start at the beginning." *Where is the beginning?* she wonders.

Marilyn takes a deep breath like she's about to jump into cold water. "Back when my father gave Todd the seed money, ten million, Todd's investing business was legit. Todd is...good-looking and quite charismatic, so his main strategy in building a client base was to court new widows, especially the gold diggers who'd hit it big, and there are an endless supply of those women in Florida. Todd was a savvy investor, and it was the heady first days of the internet bubble. Cisco, Oracle—everyone was printing money. Todd brought me to the Virgin Islands on vacation, we stayed at Caneel, and while he was chatting with someone at the bar there, he heard about the EDC, the Economic Development Commission, which offered tax incentives to lure businesses down to the territories. Todd immediately applied. He could work from virtually anywhere, and he wanted the tax break because it freed up that much more capital for him to invest. And, too, he loved the Virgin Islands."

She pauses, checks that Irene is still with her. Irene bobs her head: *Yes, yes.* She can't believe Marilyn Monroe is sitting here. She can't believe she is hearing all of this in what would look to an observer like a regular social visit.

"I was ambivalent about the EDC. I thought it sounded shady, though now I know it's perfectly legal, but also, I wanted to start a family, and I wanted to do that at home, in Miami, where the schools were good and my parents were nearby. No problem; Todd had to spend only a hundred and eighty-three days per year in the islands, according to the EDC guidelines, so he bought a simple villa on Water Island, which is undeveloped, deserted, overlooked. That's the way Todd wanted it, and he traveled to and from Florida by himself.

"Well, I didn't get pregnant, probably because we rarely slept together. I quickly realized Todd was using his time down here for more than just business. I also became aware that Todd had one client who, among his legitimate business interests, owned marijuana farms. This gentleman had a high net worth, and Todd didn't want to lose him as a client, so he found a way to shuffle the dirty money deep into the deck. That, as far as I know, was the first time he hid a client's money."

"Marijuana farms seem nearly quaint," Irene says.

"They call marijuana the gateway drug, which was true in this case," Marilyn says. "In 2005, Todd hired Stephen Thompson, an attorney from the Cayman Islands who had a lot of experience with offshore accounts. Stephen brought along clients who were big dirty-money guys—the human traffickers, the exotic-animal dealers, the gem smugglers—but both Todd and Stephen were looking for a third partner." Marilyn clears her throat. "A fall guy."

Russ, Irene thinks.

"Todd bumped into you and your husband at the Drake Hotel in Chicago. He remembered Russ from college and the arrangement they had where Todd sold alcohol to the underclassmen while Russ looked the other way in exchange for a part of the profits. He ran a background search on Russ. He found out Russ's salary with the Corn Refiners Association, learned about his membership in the Rotary Club and his position on the school board. He got information about your house, your cars, what they were worth, what you owed, and even the ages of your sons, who he assumed would be heading to college in a few short years. Todd decided Russell Steele would be the perfect front man. He was both respected in your community and strapped for cash—overextended beyond what you probably even knew. And he had that history with Todd. Todd knew Russ would be willing to look the other way while someone else broke the rules.

"Todd called Russ, brought him down to the Virgin Islands, wined and dined him on his new yacht, *Bluebeard,* and at Caneel." Marilyn stops. "Todd had a local man working for him named Oscar Cobb."

Irene's breath catches. *Oscar Cobb!* Oscar Cobb worked for Todd Croft?

"I know of him," Irene says. "He was Rosie's former boyfriend."

"Well." Marilyn shakes her head. "Is it okay if I continue candidly?"

Irene nods. It can't be worse than what she read in Rosie's diaries. She hopes.

"When Todd and Stephen brought Russ down to the Virgin Islands, they didn't mention any of their sensitive clients. They let Russ believe that Ascension's dealings were on the up-and-up—which they were, for the most part—and that Russ's job would be to capitalize on his natural charm as a salesman and his trustworthy persona as a midwestern husband, father, and citizen. Ascension's clients were investing tens and sometimes hundreds of millions of dollars. They wanted a friendly face who would answer when they called, who would lose to them at golf, who would make them feel safe and comforted."

"Yes," Irene says. "This is exactly the way Russ explained the job to me."

"They planned to ease into the black money so gradually

that Russ would become acclimated to it bit by bit." Marilyn shakes her head. "Like the old frog-in-a-pot-of-water myth where supposedly if you raise the temperature a few degrees at a time, the frog won't realize it's boiling."

Irene understands the simile—it's apt—but she hates thinking about Russ that way.

"The marijuana farmer was already on the books, and next might be someone who moved cocaine, heroin, oxycodone. So... on that first trip down here, they set Russ up."

"Set him up?"

"Oscar Cobb was in the restaurant at Caneel on their first night. He'd told Todd that his former girlfriend, Rosie Small, would be working as a cocktail waitress. He also told Todd that Rosie was single, vulnerable, and extremely beautiful. Oscar staged a situation where he followed Rosie out to her car and harassed her, allowing Russ to step in and save the day."

Irene gasps. "You mean the part...I'm sorry, I read about this in Rosie's diaries...Russ put Oscar in some kind of headlock. That was *staged?*"

"Yes," Marilyn says. "Rosie left the restaurant, Oscar followed, and he knew Russ would be heading back to his room along the same path. He let Russ get the better of him. If you knew Oscar, you'd understand that a headlock from someone like Russ wasn't going to stop him. Once Oscar told Todd that he'd been successful, Todd and Stephen took *Bluebeard* over to the BVIs, leaving Russ alone for the weekend. That was all by design."

Russ had been set up. Irene felt almost embarrassed for him.

"But Rosie had no idea?"

"None."

"Russ still could have acted like an upstanding and faithful husband," Irene says. "But he didn't."

"That's right," Marilyn says. "Todd and Stephen saw Rosie in Russ's hotel room and they knew he could be blackmailed. He certainly wouldn't want the news getting back to you in Iowa City. And then Rosie reached out to Russ using Todd's e-mail, and Todd suspected she was pregnant. Todd flew down to confirm this and saw with his own eyes that it was true. He told Russ, and Russ confirmed with Rosie that it was his baby. She said she didn't want to see him again and he honored that, but he started sending money."

Marilyn leans forward; her pretty nails gently scratch at the knees of her khaki capris. "Does this come as a surprise?"

"I'm aware he sent her money."

Marilyn purses her lips, sighs, shakes her head. "Because both Todd and Stephen knew about Rosie and the baby, there was nothing they couldn't ask Russ to do. They put all of the 'sensitive' business deals under Russ's supervision, in a whole separate sub-division of the company. They made it seem like this offshoot was independent of Ascension. Russ's name alone was on the paper-work as the principal for all of the money laundering, all of the tax fraud, even things that weren't so bad, like hiding money for a European soccer star who owed alimony. He couldn't object, and Todd paid Russ handsomely to keep him happy. You had plenty of money at home? For the renovation of the Victorian?"

"Yes," Irene whispers.

"In 2014, Rosie's mother died, and Russ and Rosie reunited. Because there had been no oversight on any of the company's deals, Russ grew bolder. He wanted property down here, a villa. He couldn't very well keep bringing Rosie to Caneel; someone would find out about them. Through a tip from Oscar Cobb, Todd approached a failing real estate concern, Welcome to Paradise, owned by Douglas and Paulette Vickers. They'd bought a hundred and forty acres in Little Cinnamon with the intention of developing the hillside, but they ran out of money. They were about to lose the whole thing to the bank when Todd paid a visit." Marilyn shakes her head. "You want to talk about two people who are completely under my husband's sway? It's the Vickerses. Todd saved them from ruin just after their son was born. They allowed dozens of phony real estate deals to be run through their office. But officially, Paulette and Douglas worked for Russ and Russ alone."

Marilyn pauses. "They could have turned Todd in. I wish they had. But they were too afraid."

"Afraid of what?"

"Being killed," Marilyn says.

Killed, Irene thinks. For turning in Todd, which is what Marilyn is going to do. Irene has no idea how Marilyn is remaining so composed, though Irene admits that she's comforted by it. Marilyn reminds Irene a little of herself. She might not always have been strong, but she's strong now.

"They're both serving time instead," Marilyn says.

Irene recalls her initial meeting with Paulette Vickers, which was during her very first hour on this island. Paulette had seemed flighty and completely insensitive to Irene's emotional state, which was numb shock. She had prattled on about the hiking trails, about the landscapers. She had displayed nothing but calm acceptance that her employer was dead.

What else had Paulette told her?

"The villa was in Russ's name," Irene says.

"Everything is in Russ's name," Marilyn says. "That's what I'm telling you."

"Because of me," Irene says. "He allowed himself to be black-mailed *because of me.* Because he didn't want me to find out about Rosie and Maia."

"I can't speak for Russ," Marilyn says, "but I think some men get a thrill out of leading a double life. I'm sure Russ was sick with guilt most of the time. But there was also probably a rush or a high from... pulling it off. I think it made him feel superhuman."

Irene presses her fingers into her temples. "This is what I can't reconcile," she says. "At home, he was... the same. We had more money, yes, and we both changed because of that. We bought the Church Street house, we bought new cars, we ate out all the time, we donated to local causes, we set the boys up to succeed. But as people, we stayed the same. I worked at a magazine and oversaw the house renovation. Russ... he was *exactly* the same. Corny. Goofy. He could be insufferable with his earnest enthusiasm. The money didn't make him sophisticated... or smug... or self-congratulatory. But neither did he seem like a man who was racked with guilt. He did make the occasional grandiose gesture—he hired a plane to fly a happy-birthday banner when I turned fifty; he would send me lavish bouquets. But I thought he was doing these things because he could. Because he loved me. He felt bad about being away so much, and he apologized about this the normal amount, but he never overplayed his hand. He never seemed *tortured*. So what can I think but that he was a complete *sociopath?*"

Marilyn says, "I met Russ a handful of times in my capacity as office manager. He was always so... guileless, so genuine. Every time I talked to him, I felt sorry for him. He didn't belong in business with my husband. He was a sheep running with wolves."

"You'll forgive me for saying this, but Russ was neither guileless nor genuine. You knew he had a second family. There was no reason to feel sorry for him."

Marilyn stares at Irene. "Of course you're right. I just wanted you to know that he was... different from the other two. He was a nice person."

"Nice," Irene says. "But a wolf just the same."

"Maybe deep down I knew he wouldn't survive this," Marilyn says. "Todd is ruthless. He's greedy, and I'm not talking about money. He wants control, he wants power, he wants...*domination*. That's what led us here. Russ, I think, was more than happy to let Todd pull the puppet strings. But Stephen wasn't. Stephen realized that Todd was taking more than his share of the profits, and Stephen feared he wasn't as protected as he needed to be. The danger in any entity with three principals is that when one side of the triangle weakens, another is reinforced. Stephen did the predictable thing and cozied up to Russ. Russ was already having a crisis of conscience about the despicable people whose money they were laundering. They were working with a Russian company who moved assault rifles—big, big money—but there was that rash of school shootings in the States, as I'm sure you'll remember, and in several cases, the illegal guns could be traced back to our client. It was a tense time, and there were some uncomfortable inquiries into that client. Nothing came of it, but Russ and Stephen took advantage of the scare to say they wanted out. Before they talked to Todd, they both came to see me. Russ was first. He visited my office in Miami in early September."

September, Irene thinks. End of summer, beginning of fall, students returning to the university, football games on Saturdays, *Go, Hawks!*

"He told me he was ready to retire; he wanted to go home to Iowa and be with you. The house you'd been renovating for years was finally finished and he wanted to enjoy it—throw parties, host holidays. He wanted to spend time with his mother, who was quite elderly. He wanted to travel to Denver to help his younger son manage the outdoor-supply stores. He wanted to fly to Houston to see his grandson. He'd had a wonderful run in the

Virgin Islands, he said, and he was grateful for all Ascension had given him, but it was time for him to return home."

Irene can't believe it but her immediate thoughts are *What about Rosie? What about Maia? Was he just going to leave them behind?*

"I told him that wasn't possible. I told him he was too deeply vested in the company to just walk away. I told him the smartest thing to do was not to breathe a word of what he'd shared with me to Todd. I told him to protect his assets and protect you."

September was when Russ made his new will, changing the executor from Todd Croft to Irene. *Irene is the only person I trust to do the right thing,* he'd said.

"Russ listened to my advice but Stephen did not. He went to Todd and turned it into a test of wills. He said both he and Russ wanted out. He said there was nothing Todd could do to stop them. Todd was...furious. He pointed out that both Russ's and Stephen's fingerprints were all over incriminating deals, and if they left, Todd would go to the authorities. To his credit, Stephen called Todd's bluff. He didn't think Todd would sacrifice the company. He wrote up sophisticated NDAs and presented them to Todd, and, at that point, Todd changed his tack and said, 'Fine, you sign the NDAs, you can walk away.'"

Irene's breathing is shallow. She knows what's coming. She knows this is the end. She should stop Marilyn now; she doesn't need to hear any more. Marilyn can tell it all to the FBI, that's fine, but Irene doesn't want to hear the truth spoken. "Marilyn."

"Do you want me to stop?" Marilyn says. "Now?"

"Is there any way...I'm just afraid..." She's thinking of Baker and Cash. And Floyd. Ayers and the baby. She can't put them in danger just because she wants to hear how the story ends. Furthermore, she already knows how it ends.

However, to stop Marilyn now is to destroy, in some sense, the integrity of her intentions. "If you continue," Irene says, "will my family or I be in any danger?"

"When I leave here," Marilyn says, "I'm going directly to the FBI. Todd is still in custody. His boat captain was released and, I heard, fled the country. Todd's business was so sensitive that we weren't able to hire a lot of support staff. It was Russ, Stephen, the Vickerses...and Oscar. You're safe. Or you will be, I promise."

Irene takes a deep breath. Half of her wants to ask Marilyn to leave—but that might be even more dangerous. "Go ahead."

"Todd used Paulette Vickers to bug the villa and compromise Stephen's phone, Russ's phone, and even Rosie's phone. Todd discovered that Stephen and Russ planned to meet with British authorities on January second on Tortola. They were traveling in Stephen's private helicopter—he was an accomplished pilot. To make it seem like a holiday trip, Russ invited Rosie to Anegada. Stephen would fly them over, they would stay at the beachfront cottage owned by one of their shell companies, and then, the following morning, Russ would claim he had a work emergency. The three of them would fly to Tortola, Russ would put Rosie on the ferry back to St. John, and Russ and Stephen would go to their meeting. Todd knew all this. He asked Oscar Cobb to put explosives on Stephen's helicopter."

"Oscar?" Irene whispers.

"Oscar refused to do it. He knew what Todd was up to, knew that he was planning on killing Stephen, Russ, and Rosie. Oscar had been drinking, it was late on New Year's Eve, they had a fight, Oscar told Todd to find some other fool to do his dirty work because Oscar was out and Oscar was going to put a bounty on Todd's head with his friends over in St. Thomas. Todd told Oscar that he understood Oscar was angry, it had probably come time for them to split ways, new year and all that. He told Oscar he should come see me in the office the next morning, that I would give him his severance pay."

Finally, Marilyn shows some emotion. Her eyes glass over. "Oscar and I had a nice relationship. He did a lot of bad things, I knew this, but I could see glimmers of goodness in him, and I think I might have been the only one. He trusted me, he called me 'Mama.' He got to my villa on Water Island before Todd, woke me up with his pounding on the door. He told me what Todd was planning to do and begged me to stop it. He said..." Here Marilyn's voice cracks. "He said he'd called Rosie—he still had her number after so many years—to warn her not to go, but the call had gone straight to her voicemail. He begged me to call Russ." Tears are fully rolling down Marilyn's cheeks. Irene wants to offer the woman a tissue, but she's afraid to move. "So, if I were a better person, this would be where I would tell you that yes, I did call Russ and that through my connections, I saved them, and that they are still alive on an island so remote it doesn't even have a name."

Still alive, Irene thinks. Despite everything, her heart yearns for this—not only Russ, but Rosie, too. Still. Alive. Baker and Cash would have their dad back, Floyd his grandpa. Huck would have his daughter back. And Maia. What Irene wishes for *most of all* is for Maia to have her mother back.

Now that Irene knows what she knows, might it even be possible that she and Rosie could have been friends? Or was that just a hopeless fantasy?

"I've had dreams," Irene says, "vivid dreams, where Russ is alive."

"I was not a better person," Marilyn says. "I was the same pathetic, dutiful coward I've been since the day I married Todd.

I kept Oscar in the office, comforting him, when I should have been telling him to run for his life. Todd showed up with a gun and took Oscar to *Bluebeard*. I knew I would never see Oscar again, and I had an idea that I would never see my husband again. There was no way he could stay in the Virgin Islands after he killed Oscar. Oscar knew too many dangerous people." Marilyn wipes a finger under each eye. "Todd filled *Bluebeard* with documents incriminating Russ and Stephen. Then, with the captain's help, he tied Oscar up, shot him, and tossed him overboard as soon as they were on the open sea, and he took off for Venezuela." Marilyn takes a breath. "Todd has a girlfriend in Venezuela, girlfriends everywhere, but the most important thing is that Venezuela has no extradition laws. I think he dreamed of a life on Margarita Island with Gloriana—and he almost made it. I think part of him *enjoyed* the chase, to be honest. But it was the chase that got him arrested. Todd called me to let me know he'd been taken into custody and that I was to destroy all the incriminating documents in the safe on Water Island—Todd's offshore account information, payouts from the sensitive deals, correspondence from Todd to these clients. That had been our contingency plan for years."

"But you didn't do it?"

"I did the opposite," Marilyn says. "I made copies of everything."

"Why?" Irene says.

Finally, Marilyn looks like someone describing an epiphany. "I guess I realized I could go down with Todd or I could watch him go down alone." She shakes her head. "Wasn't that hard of a choice. He killed four people."

"And he has no idea what you've done?"

"None," Marilyn says. She gives Irene a rueful smile. "You

might think he would be more wary of the only person who knows everything."

"Yes."

"But Todd doesn't even see me," Marilyn says. "He stopped seeing me the second my father handed over the seed money. To Todd, I'm invisible."

Irene makes a noise of recognition. What had Lydia said during their New Year's Day dinner at the Pullman Diner? *The CIA should hire women in their fifties. We're invisible.*

"Of course, tomorrow that will change." She places her hands on her thighs and pushes herself to standing. "I should go. I need to get ready to meet Agent Vasco."

Agent Vasco, Irene thinks. She has completely forgotten about Agent Vasco.

Irene leads Marilyn Monroe to the front door; she wants to hug the woman. "You are...so brave. How can I thank you?"

"No thanks necessary," Marilyn says. "I was a coward for a long time, Irene. I had a chance every single day to come clean and I didn't, and now four people are dead. Their blood is on my hands."

Irene says, "Do you still love him? Todd?"

Marilyn's eyebrows shoot up; the question has clearly surprised her. "Do you still love Russ?" she asks, but she slips out the door without waiting for an answer.

Because, Irene realizes, there is no answer. Irene watches Marilyn climb into her Jeep. In the movies, this would be where Marilyn's car explodes into a ball of fire. Irene releases a breath as Marilyn backs out of the driveway and pulls away.

Irene lingers in the parking lot across from Mongoose Junction until she sees the *Mississippi* pulling up to the National Park

Service dock. Huck does the complicated choreography of pulling in and, at the same time, tying up.

He needs a mate, Irene thinks.

The family aboard hop off, a couple and two little kids, one of whom is screaming bloody murder. There are no fish to be filleted, so they must have struck out, even inshore. Irene watches the father tip Huck as the mother carries the kids off.

Irene smiles at her as she passes, but the mother doesn't see her.

Huck doesn't see her either. He's checking around the boat, making sure the family hasn't forgotten anything. He goes to lift the rope off the bollard, but Irene beats him to it.

He looks up. He's wearing his wraparound sunglasses so it's impossible to tell how her surprise is being received.

"Permission to board?" Irene says.

Any given moment can hold an infinite number of thoughts, Irene realizes. She wonders if he'll tell her to buzz off, that he's found someone new, Agent Vasco, that Irene has been replaced, sorry. She wonders if she'll have to cajole her way onto the boat by telling Huck she has finally learned the whole story from none other than Marilyn Monroe. Marilyn Monroe was the woman in the black Jeep with the tinted windows. How will he feel hearing it confirmed that Todd murdered Rosie and Russ? How will it feel to know that Oscar Cobb, of all people, *had tried to save Rosie's life?*

Irene travels back in her mind to the first time she ever saw Huck, which was nearly in this exact same spot. She didn't know him, he didn't know her, but somehow, *somehow,* she'd broken down his defenses or piqued his curiosity, and they became friends. More than friends. *It was a long shot,* Irene thinks, *maybe even a miracle.* Out of this whole ugly tale of deceit and betrayal, something pure and true was born.

As unlikely as it might be, the friendship is genuine.

Slowly, maybe even hesitantly, Huck spreads his arms. "Permission granted, AC."

The rope; her shoes. When one boards a boat, there is a protocol. But in the moment, Irene doesn't care. She jumps—and Captain Sam "Huck" Powers catches her.

ST. JOHN

April turns to May, and our high season officially ends. Rates at the hotels and villas drop, restaurants close one night a week to give their staff a much-needed rest, there are finally parking spots at both Trunk Bay *and* Oppenheimer—and it's hot, hot, hot.

We also get to see one another more frequently. Did you *hear?*

Douglas and Paulette Vickers are going to prison for money laundering and fraud. Douglas will serve three years; Paulette, five. Their son, Windsor, is living with Douglas's sister, Wilma, on St. Croix. He cried every night for a month, Wilma tells her friend Sadie on St. John, and then one day the crying stopped and now he's the same sunny child he was before. He's doing well in school, making new friends, asking for second helpings of dessert (which Wilma always gives him, poor, sweet child).

Ayers Wilson is showing a subtle baby bump. She has been to two prenatal appointments at Schneider Hospital and has had all the testing. She and Baker have decided not to find out the gender of the baby; all they care about is that the baby is healthy. Ayers is due September 23. She has opted to stay in her cottage,

Pure Joy, until the baby is born. She and Baker are now dating, but they haven't quite reached "boyfriend and girlfriend" status. Maybe soon, Ayers thinks.

Ayers's parents, Phil Wilson and Sunny Ray, are the proud owners of a two-bedroom time-share at the Westin; they're banking their weeks for when the baby comes. They arrive back from a seven-stop jaunt through the Caribbean—Bequia was their favorite, no surprise there—and immediately start planning a summer trip to Croatia. (Everyone raves about the city of Split.) Sunny decides that, instead of pretending to write a travel blog, she *will* write a travel blog. She calls it *Love, Mimi.* The blog takes an epistolary form; the entries are descriptive, evocative travel letters from grandmother to grandchild. As soon as Sunny's Caribbean letters are posted, she receives sponsorship from the AARP and Road Scholar.

Things are happening over on Lovango Cay (which was named for a region of Africa, *not* because a brothel there in the days of piracy had been so popular that the island was dubbed "Love and Go"). The cay has been approved for fifty bungalows, fifteen glamping tents, fourteen private homes, a restaurant, and a beach club with a swimming pool that will offer daily, weekly, and season passes.

Swan Seeley has been hired to handle the resort's marketing strategy, but when she saw the architect's plans, she feared she'd be fired. They don't need Swan to sell this place; it will sell itself. The design is ingenious—the eco-friendly resort will be the hottest spot in the Caribbean! Swan feels incredibly blessed to be part of it. She'd thought her life was over with the divorce, but she was wrong. The curtain is rising on her second act.

Swan is collaborating closely with both Tilda Payne, who works at La Tapa, and the guy who bought the island, Duncan

Huntley. Duncan and Tilda are a couple; they walk around all googly-eyed, holding hands. He calls her mate (he calls everyone mate); she calls him Stallion, which is almost more than Swan can handle. They treat Duncan's dog, Olive, a harlequin Great Dane that is the size of a show pony, like their child. They speak to Olive in baby talk; they constantly fret over whether Olive is hungry, thirsty, or tired, even though Olive is as chill as an ice sculpture.

One morning, Swan and Duncan are alone in the air-conditioned work trailer at the slanted drafting table reviewing Swan's marketing plan. Swan worked hard on the plan; she included ideas for Lovango resort merchandise that they could sell at the gift shop. She went so far as to sketch cute logos for the T-shirts—every woman Swan knows would pay good money for a flattering T-shirt or tank to wear over her Lululemons—and she created a list of local artisans whose work they can feature. She's hoping to impress Duncan. When she Googled him, she found out that he'd started two companies—a sex app and an edible marijuana concern—that he'd then sold, the first for eight figures, the second for nine. In addition to a whole bunch of money, he has a very appealing Australian accent.

Duncan glances at the T-shirt designs and then shuffles them aside.

Swan says, "Merch might be more important than you think because it serves as a source of revenue *and* a form of advertising. Have you ever heard of the Black Dog on Martha's Vineyard?"

Dunk blinks at her and brings his vape pen to his mouth. His eyelids seem a little heavy and she wonders if he has marijuana pods in his vape pen.

"No," he says.

"It's a restaurant," Swan says. "They have clam chowder and other New England specialties, but their T-shirts are what's making them millions. Millions! It's just a silk screen of a black dog, but that's part of the mystique. If you know, you know." She lifts her favorite design, a logo with the words LOVE AND GO. REPEAT. "This has potential, I think? I mean, if you don't mind propagating the myth of how Lovango got its name?"

"Propagating?" Duncan says. A smile oozes across his face. He's definitely high. Or maybe just creepy; Swan can't tell. Either way, he's one of her bosses. He owns the island. "Are you *smart,* Swan?"

Swan flinches. He's joking, right? And if she acts offended, he'll think she's rigid and humorless. "I am," she says pleasantly. "Which is why you hired me."

Duncan leans in so that the side of his body presses into the side of Swan's body. "I hired you because you're a hot little bird," he says. "A dime." His hand snakes up her back. He's touching her back. Swan holds her breath and thinks, *What do I do?* He hired her because she's *hot?* She isn't an underwear model!

She straightens up so that Dunk's hand slides off her back. "Smart *and* hot," she says. She points to the next page of her plan. "I made a list of influencers that we should invite to the property. Market research shows that influencers are worth more bang for our buck than regular print advertising—"

"Bang for our buck," Dunk says. "Now you're talking." He stands behind Swan and starts to massage her shoulders. His groin grazes her backside.

Nope, sorry, this is *not* okay. Swan twists away, gathers up her papers, and storms out of the trailer, stumbling into the searing-hot sunshine. There's a picnic table in the shade of the rocky path where the workers eat their lunch. Swan sits on the table with her feet on the bench seat and tries to steady her breathing. Did she overreact? Is she being too sensitive? No, she decides. That was classic #MeToo stuff back there. Swan shouldn't have agreed to meet with Duncan alone. But why is she blaming herself? She should be able to meet with whomever she wants under whatever circumstances without being touched inappropriately and told that she was hired because she was hot.

Her eyes sting with tears. She had been *so* happy to land this job, but she knows she can't stay on. She has a degree from Florida State, a business degree.

She doesn't want to cry. She put a lot of effort into her makeup today, not to lure Duncan or anyone else but because she wanted to look professional.

"Hey," a voice says. "You okay?"

It's Tilda, walking off the dock with Olive at her side.

Before Swan can think it through, she says, "I was just in the trailer showing Duncan my marketing ideas. He told me he hired me because I was hot, a dime, and then he touched me inappropriately."

Tilda's eyebrows shoot up above her sunglasses. She places a hand on Olive's back, and Olive stands still as a statue. When Tilda opens her mouth, no sound comes out.

Swan drops her head into her hands. On top of everything else, she has to be the one to let Tilda know that her boyfriend is a predator.

"Oh, Swan," Tilda says. "Do you think maybe you misunderstood? Dunk can be a little familiar, that's his personality, that's how he was raised back in Australia, I think, but I'm sure he didn't mean anything by it."

This is so *textbook!* Nobody *ever* believes the woman! "Listen to me, Tilda. He leaned against me in a suggestive way and put his hand on my back, and when I moved away, he started to massage my shoulders. He...grazed my behind."

"Swan," Tilda says. She's shaking her head when she should be either hugging Swan or storming into the trailer to kick Dunk in the nuts.

"Tilda," Swan says. She understands denial. Swan willfully ignored her husband's gambling problem for fourteen years. But how about some *solidarity* here?

"I'll ask Keith to run you back to Cruz Bay," Tilda says. "Thanks for coming over."

Irene Steele and Captain Huck Powers are living together, and Irene is back working as the first mate on the *Mississippi*. Irene is logging her days on the water, and as soon as she has three hundred and sixty, she'll take her captain's test. Huck thinks it's a great idea. He even goes to St. Thomas to look at the boat Irene inquired about.

The boat is in good condition and the seller is motivated; he's leaving the Virgin Islands altogether at the beginning of June. Huck advises Irene to make an offer of forty thousand.

"I don't have forty to spend," she says.

"How about we split it?" Huck says. "Add it to the fleet. It needs work, which I can do myself. And then once you get your captain's license, we can run two boats, the *Mississippi* and the *Angler Cupcake*. God knows we have enough business."

More than enough, Irene thinks, with a growing number of women-only charters. All it took was a few complimentary trips. The first of these was for Baker's school-mom friends Swan, Bonny, and Paula. The three of them took pictures with the fish they caught and posted them on Facebook and Instagram. Next, Huck and Irene invited Joanie's mom, Julie Judge, and her three sisters out on the boat, and *they* all posted pictures. And finally, they had a paying charter for a young woman named Gretchen Gingerman who came with her mother. It turned out that Gretchen had met Cash on her previous visit to St. John, a trip that had gone badly, and it was only because of Cash that Gretchen gave the island another try, with a different travel partner.

Gretchen's post brought in a flurry of business, including a bachelorette party. Six beautiful young women, five in matching pink T-shirts and one in a white T-shirt and a short white veil, all in great spirits thanks to a thermos filled with cosmo punch and a playlist of Lizzo and Billie Eilish. They caught a couple of small wahoo, which elicited high-pitched shrieks, and they took fifty million pictures, including one with Irene. All of the girls loved Irene, she was "such a beast," and when they were older they were going to do something "sick" like move to the Virgin Islands to work on a fishing boat.

The bachelorette party tipped extremely well but when the women got off the boat, Huck turned to Irene and said, "I can't wait for you to get your captain's license so I never have to do that again."

It all sounds rosy on the Huck-and-Irene front—until the story that united them rears its ugly head. Todd Croft is brought up on four charges of first-degree murder thanks to the evidence that Marilyn Monroe presented. (In addition to the three murders we all suspected he was behind, we learned Todd had also killed Oscar Cobb. Sure enough, once Marilyn Monroe had voiced her suspicions, traces of Oscar's blood were found all over the stern of *Bluebeard*.) Somehow Todd's lawyer cuts a deal. Todd pleads guilty to one charge of second-degree murder and three charges of manslaughter and pays fines of nearly four hundred million dollars. He's sentenced to twenty-two years in federal prison. With good behavior, he could be out in eighteen.

Both Huck and Irene are aghast. Four lives violently snatched away, and the guy gets only twenty-two years? It's the money, Irene thinks. The territory wanted Todd's money. Either that or he agreed to talk to the Feds about some of his clients—which may end up getting him killed.

"I'll tell you who will be waiting for him the day he gets out," Huck says. "Me."

Irene squeezes Huck's hand. The estates can sue for reparations in a civil case. Natalie Key is asking for two million dollars on behalf of Russ and ten million on behalf of Rosie. Stephen Thompson has a brother who lives in London, but the brother won't sue because he wants "nothing to do with the whole sordid mess."

Huck and Irene have decided not to even think about the possibility of that money. Instead, they focus on their daily blessings. Irene receives boxes filled with her clothes—most of which she'd forgotten she owned—as well as her books and kitchen implements. When she pulls her food processor out of the box, she says, "The cooking in this house is about to improve."

"How can you improve on perfectly grilled fish?" Huck asks. "How can you improve on Candi's barbecue?"

Another blessing: Agent Vasco's job on St. John is finished. She goes back to Puerto Rico.

Adios, Irene thinks.

Swan Seeley tells Baker what happened between her and Duncan Huntley, and Baker nearly drives out to the East End to give the guy the thrashing he deserves. When Baker tells Ayers the story, she mentions that Dunk routinely waits for Tilda across the street from La Tapa after service. Baker can jump out of the shadows and scare him to death.

But then fate intervenes and Baker bumps into Dunk at Pine Peace Market. Duncan is buying vape pods and Baker is buying pizza-flavored Pringles for Floyd and Ben and Jerry's Red Velvet Cake ice cream for himself. When Dunk sees Baker, he gives him a little bro-nod but it's clear he can't really place him. He's not important enough for Duncan to remember, Baker supposes. He stands behind Dunk in line, glaring at the back of his neck. Duncan seems shorter than he did when Baker met him on the plane, and he's downright scrawny. What does Tilda see in this guy? Is it just the money?

Dunk leaves the store and Baker sets his chips and ice cream down and says to Nestor, the cashier, "I'll be right back." He follows Dunk out and catches him as he pulls open the driver's-side door of a forest-green G-wagon.

"Hey," Baker says. "Duncan? Dunk?"

Dunk turns. "G'day."

"It's Baker. Baker Steele? My little boy and I met you on the flight from Houston. You gave me a ride over here on your boat?"

"Ah, yeah?" Dunk says, though it's not clear he remembers who Baker is. "How ya doin', mate?"

Baker reaches out his hand, and when Dunk takes it, Baker squeezes as hard as he can and holds on a little longer than he should. "I'm good. Real good. Except for a couple of things."

"Sorry, mate, wish I could shoot the shit but I'm in kind of a hurry."

Dunk makes a move to get into his car but Baker reaches over Dunk's head and slams the driver's-side door shut, then leans against the car, arms folded across his chest. He has six inches and at least sixty pounds on Dunk. Baker hasn't been in a fight since high school, and even then, he mostly scrapped with Cash.

He's thirty-one years old, the father of one with another one on the way. He never thought he'd find himself trying to physically intimidate someone. But that's exactly what he's going to do right now.

"First off," Baker says, "you moved in on Tilda when she was dating my brother, Cash."

"Cash is your *brother?*" Dunk says. He laughs nervously. "I didn't make the connection, mate, I'm sorry."

"But you did know Cash and Tilda were together," Baker says. "When you and Tilda went away, you knew she had a boyfriend. You had *dinner* with him."

"Right, but I wasn't sure how serious it was," Dunk says. "She told me they'd known each other only a few weeks. And she said that Cash moved in with her because he had nowhere else to go." Dunk fiddles with the packet of vape pods in his hands. He's trying to pop one out. "Your father was part of that whole Ascension thing? That's some nefarious shit, mate."

Baker snatches the pods out of Dunk's hands and tosses them beyond the truck. He whips the vape pen out of Duncan's shirt pocket and tosses that too.

"*Nefarious?*" Baker says. "Are you *smart,* Dunk? No, not terribly. Because the next thing you did that pissed me off was you insulted my friend Swan Seeley, told her you hired her only because she was hot—"

"It was a *compliment,*" Dunk says. "Show me a bird who doesn't like hearing she's hot, come on."

"It was *inappropriate,*" Baker says. "And then you touched her. You leaned into her, you put your hand on her back, you gave her a massage, and you rubbed up against her from behind."

"Her word against mine, mate," Dunk says.

Baker grabs the front of Dunk's shirt and pulls him in.

Will Baker hit him? He wants to. He would love to pop Duncan Huntley in the face and watch him bleed. "I'm *not* your mate."

Nestor pokes his head out of the market. "You okay?" he asks Baker. "Need any help?"

"*I* need help!" Dunk says. "He's attacking me!"

Nestor goes back inside.

"Here's what you're going to do," Baker says. "You're going to apologize to Swan in an e-mail. You're going to offer her her job back. Do you understand me?"

"Yes," Dunk says. His eyes keep sweeping to the other side of the truck. He's worried about his vape pen, Baker realizes. Baker is never going to let Floyd start vaping.

Baker lets Dunk go, and in a few quick strides, Duncan retrieves the pen and pods from the ground.

Baker leans back against the driver's-side door. "One more thing," Baker says. "There's nothing I can do for Cash—all's fair in love and war, and Tilda chose you, a decision I'm sure she'll come to regret. It was dirty pool. I know it; you know it. I now work with Jacqui at the Westin time-share office, and what you might not know about Jacqui is that she is *very* well connected. We wouldn't want her spreading any rumors about you. People on this island already think you're sketchy—the sex app, the weed-edibles company, the jeans-and-Sambas thing, the fasting—but what if they hear that you're an untrustworthy snake, a two-timer, a Me Too menace?"

"What do you want?" Dunk says.

"I'd like full use of your villa for one week this summer," Baker says. "I donated a week at my father's villa at an auction to benefit my son's school, but now my father's villa is gone so I'm left in a bit of a pickle. The high bidders paid fifty thousand dollars, so in addition to the villa, I'll need at least one vehicle and staff, if you have any."

"A housekeeper," Dunk says. "And a landscaper. Any week in July works. I spend the month skiing in Tazzie."

"Great, thank you," Baker says. "I have your card. I'll call you to confirm. Don't forget the e-mail to Swan."

"Granger will call her," Dunk says. "He wanted to hire her back anyway."

"*You* reach out to her," Baker says. "With a sincere apology." He moves toward Dunk and Dunk stutter-steps back.

"Okay, mate, I will."

"You'd better," Baker says. "Jacqui's a talker…"

"I will," Dunk says.

"Good," Baker says. "Now, if you'll excuse me, my ice cream is melting."

Everyone knows that Huck tries to stay away from Jake's at the Lumberyard because he had a brief fling with Teresa, the breakfast waitress, after LeeAnn died.

It's therefore unfortunate that when Huck asks Irene what she wants to do to celebrate her fifty-eighth birthday, which is in the middle of July, she says, "I want the whole gang to go to breakfast at Jake's."

"Jake's?" Huck says. He has to head this off at the pass. It's not that things between him and Teresa ended badly, but they do their best to steer clear of each other. Huck doesn't ever go up Margaret Hill Road, where she lives; he doesn't drink at the Quiet Mon Pub, where she likes to hang out; and he no longer goes for breakfast at Jake's, where she (famously) works seven mornings a week. "Why don't you pick another place? How about a nice dinner for everyone at Morgan's Mango? Or the Terrace?"

"I don't want anything fancy or over the top," Irene says. She gives him a stern look and he recalls that her husband hired an airplane to pull a banner on her fiftieth birthday. "And I want the kids to come. What I'd like is a long, leisurely breakfast with mimosas and Bloody Marys at Jake's."

"Or," Huck says, "we could all go to the Concordia in Coral Bay. They do a terrific breakfast and it overlooks Ram Head."

"Listen to me, Huck," Irene says. "The morning after my first night at your house, Maia offered me a piece of toast slathered with papaya jam from Jake's. It was the first thing on my new mental Pinterest board."

"Your new mental what?" Huck says.

Irene shakes her head. "I want to celebrate my birthday at Jake's. Besides, it's an island institution and I've never been."

"It's always crowded," Huck says. "And it gets hot up there."

"It's open-air," Irene says. "And we'll have nine people."

"Nine?"

"I want Ayers to come, obviously," Irene says. "And her parents, Phil and Sunny. Let's make it ten people—I'll see if Cash wants to bring a friend." She puts her hands on the sides of Huck's face and brings him in for a kiss. "They take reservations for parties over six. Do I have to call to arrange my own birthday party, or will you do it?"

"I'll do it," Huck says.

The day of Irene's birthday, July 21, is hot but not beastly hot—a stroke of luck—and the sky is a deep blue. The members of the Steele party (Huck made the reservation under Irene's name) climb the stairs to the legendary open-air breakfast-and-lunch spot, Jake's, which is decorated with fun tropical kitsch. The faux vintage sign that greets them says DRINK COFFEE: DO STUPID THINGS FASTER, WITH MORE ENERGY! The place is packed, as Huck predicted. Brian and Michelle Zehring, who own the sleek new Midnight Express charter boat *New Moon,* are there with their daughters. Candi from Candi's Delights is there with her husband, who some of us jokingly call Mr. Candi. Bridgett and Jimmy from Palm Tree Charters are having cocktails with their favorite clients, DeeDee and Michael Napp. A trio of National Park rangers are drinking coffee at the bar; James, the captain of *Treasure Island,* is having pancakes with his wife and daughter; Slim Man, who owns the parking lot in town, is there with his new bride. Skip, the bartender from La Tapa, is sitting next to Jacqui from the Westin time-share office at the bar counter in the front of the restaurant, which has magnificent views over Cruz Bay. (Skip and Jacqui were seated next to each other randomly, and Jacqui is worried people are going to think this is a morning-after date.)

Off to the left side is a table set for ten (though Cash did *not* end up bringing a friend). The Steele party has so much cross-over with people already in the restaurant that when they walk in, the decibel level rises considerably. Cash and Ayers talk to James; Maia talks to Candi and Mr. Candi; Baker talks to Jacqui; and Phil and Sunny talk to Skip. Huck stops to talk to the Napps, who own a racetrack in New Jersey. As he's hearing about life in the fast lane, he scans the restaurant for Teresa but sees only Diane, the other waitress. Is it possible that Huck has hit the jackpot and Teresa isn't working today? Did she maybe take a summer vacation to visit her sons in...Idaho?

Eventually the members of the Steele party settle; Irene sits between Huck and Floyd.

Huck feels a hand land on his shoulder, a subtle squeeze.

"How are we all doing?" Teresa says. "I hear we have a birthday!"

Mimosas: Irene and Sunny.

Bloody Marys: Phil, Baker, Cash.

Fresh pineapple juice: Ayers and Maia.

Fresh OJ: Floyd.

Coffee and a Bloody Mary and a michelada while you're at it: Huck.

"Looks like someone's *celebrating*." Another hand lands on Huck's shoulder. It's Rupert.

Rupert? In Cruz Bay? What's happening here? Well, it turns out that Josephine is providing the live entertainment at Jake's this morning. Rupert takes the tenth seat at their table, and when the drinks arrive, they all raise their glasses and toast Irene.

"To Mom," Cash says. "May this year be better than last year."

"I'll second that," Baker says.

"To Irene," Sunny says. "My sister-grandmother."

"To Grammy," Floyd says, holding up his juice glass. "My...grammy."

"To the Angler Cupcake," Huck begins. He waits a beat; he has to swallow the lump in his throat. "The most remarkable woman I know. Happy, happy birthday."

Josephine sings "Ain't No Sunshine." Cash checks his phone and answers a text under the table. Teresa asks Diane to help her run the food—biscuits and gravy, south-of-the-border omelets, a breakfast burrito with extra home fries, banana-walnut pancakes, sweet bread French toast, a "regular" (eggs, bacon, home fries, toast) with a side of chocolate pancakes (this is for Ayers, who is eating for two), and…an order of gingerbread pancakes with a side of sausage for the birthday girl, with two jars of papaya jam to go. Teresa sticks a candle in the pancakes. She cues Josephine and the whole restaurant sings "Happy Birthday."

More mimosas. More Bloody Marys. Coffee for Baker, who is falling asleep at the table. Ayers elbows him in the ribs. "You think you're tired now, wait until the baby comes."

Josephine sings Leonard Cohen's "Hallelujah," which has long been one of Teresa's favorite songs. It's a hymn, an anthem, and it only adds to the cinematic quality of the scene, the restaurant perched high above the streets of Cruz Bay on a summer Sunday morning.

I've heard there was a secret chord…

Churches across the island will be letting out about now, so the restaurant will get a little busier, but not much. Teresa always jokes that, for Jake's clientele, pancakes are their religion. (As is strong coffee. And vodka.)

Teresa takes a minute to gaze out at the water—the ferry coming in from Red Hook, the *Singing Dog* heading out for a sail, maybe with a stop at Carval Rock for a snorkel. When Teresa gets in the weeds at the restaurant, she always imagines herself afloat, her mask submerged in the clear turquoise water, taking in the teeming life of the coral reef. Other people like the fish, the rays, the turtles, but Teresa is fascinated by the coral itself: the intricacies of the brain coral, the grooves of which look like a maze; the staghorn; the boulder star; the elkhorn (Teresa's favorite); the layers of lettuce coral; the ivory bush; the clubbed finger. It's a city down there, a world, a universe that manages to be productive but very, very quiet.

That David played, and it pleased the Lord.

Teresa doesn't remember every detail of the night she first hooked up with Captain Huck Powers, but certain things stand out. She'd met her coworker Diane at High Tide, then they'd cruised down to the Beach Bar with a stop at Joe's Rum Hut. There was a band at the Beach Bar, and Teresa danced with a charter captain named Pat; he was a full head shorter than Teresa and a little handsy. She escaped to the bar, and that's where she found Huck.

"Why the long face?" Teresa asked. As soon as the words were out, she realized her mistake. She had heard that LeeAnn Powers, Huck's wife, had died a couple of months earlier. She didn't know Huck well, though he would, on occasion, come into Jake's for a cup of coffee and the breakfast sandwich to go, or he'd bring his granddaughter in for the chocolate pancakes. (That was back when the girl was small, five or six years old; Teresa can't believe how grown-up she looks now, and how much like her mother.)

To cheer Huck up, Teresa asked Mick to hand over the dice to roll, but the dice did nothing but take Teresa's fiver, so then she asked for the Connect Four. It was a kids' game but everyone at the Beach Bar was so far gone that it was just about all they could handle.

Huck and Teresa split the first two games and then Huck won the third, which cheered him a bit. They headed over to Drink for a shot—a prairie fire, which was whiskey with tabasco—and then, feeling no pain, they went to 420 to Center. Pat was there. He bummed a cigarette off Teresa and tried to engage her in conversation, and Huck took over then, wheeling Teresa out of the bar, saying, "Let's get you home."

He spent that night with her and was up and out at five thirty, which was when she left for work. He didn't ask for her number and she didn't offer it—but the next week, she was drinking up at the Quiet Mon and Huck took the stool next to hers. That was how he found her the third time as well, only the third time he suggested stopping by the side door at Castaways to get a couple of orders of the blackened mahi tacos and, why not, the disco fries. They ate on Teresa's tiny deck and they talked. Teresa told him about her kids, Jasper and Graeden, both working as bartenders in Sun Valley, Idaho, and their dad, Teresa's ex, a former member of the U.S. ski team who'd become a sales rep for Salomon and who lived it up, bouncing from one ski resort to the next, good for him. Huck didn't talk about LeeAnn but he did talk about Rosie and Maia and how he knew Rosie probably wanted to move out and get her own place now that her mother was gone but that he hoped to God she didn't.

Although I'd like her to meet someone, he said. *A good man.*

After that third time, Teresa thought maybe their relationship would continue; maybe she would be a rebound for a while or maybe it would become something more. She wanted that, naturally, because Captain Huck Powers was—excuse the pun— a catch in anyone's book.

But Huck must have gotten scared about sharing as much as he had, by their talking and breaking bread (stuffing cheese-and-bacon fries into their mouths) in addition to sleeping together. Teresa never heard from him again. There were a couple of times she felt someone take the seat next to her at the Quiet Mon and thought it was him, but it was just Pat—at which point, she got up and made the lonely walk home.

She didn't think much about Huck after that—not until Rosie was killed on New Year's Day. Teresa was serving up breakfast to a very hungover clientele when Clover, the hostess at La Tapa, came in with the news, and even though it was eighty degrees, a polar-cap wind blew through Jake's. Teresa remembered what Huck had said about wanting Rosie to find a good man, and she damn near cried.

How does it feel for Teresa to see Huck with his granddaughter and Ayers and the Invisible Man's widow and two sons? (Because we all know who they are by now; they aren't quite locals—that will take *years*—but neither are they strictly tourists.) Well, Teresa isn't hurt or jealous. What passed between Huck and Teresa was half a dozen years ago. If Teresa had to pick a word, she would say that she's *surprised*—not just by Huck and Irene cozied up together but by the whole situation. The people at the table are talking and laughing and singing along to Josephine and sucking down drinks and debating whether or not to start ordering food from the lunch menu now that they've finished breakfast.

They look happy, Teresa thinks. *They look like a real live happy family.*

ELLEN

Has anyone out there tried to plan a weeklong vacation for four women who are all single mothers of young children? That's what Ellen, the ringleader of Baker's Houston school wives, is trying to do. Simply finding a mutually agreeable week requires both a flowchart and a deep reserve of patience. Becky has full custody of her girls all summer while her ex-husband fishes for salmon in Alaska. She calls on her mother to stay with the girls, but her mother decides she wants to go to Branson during the week they've tentatively picked. Three of Debbie's four kids are with her ex all summer, but her son Teddy is with her because he has sports camps in Houston, though he can maybe stay with his buddy Campbell for the week. (Ellen knows Campbell's mother, Tish—stick up her ass. Poor Teddy.) Wendy's ex-husband, Ian, will take the kids "as a favor" (can parenting your own children ever be called a "favor"?), but he has to work such long hours and travel so often that she has to find a sitter anyway. Ellen has recently hired a full-time au pair from Thailand named Za; she is still learning English and still learning to drive, so this week will give new meaning to the phrase *trial by fire*. But Ellen's bar is low—"Just keep him alive" is her parenting motto. She promised herself when she became a single mother by choice at the age of forty that she would not act like a typical older parent. She would neither coddle Walter nor shield him, and she wouldn't insist on organic milk and produce. Ellen grew up on frozen waffles, Cheetos, and ice cream sandwiches—Walter can too.

Ellen has known her school-mom friends for over five years, ever since she had Walter, but in planning the trip, she discovers new things about them. Becky prefers to roll without a set plan while she's on vacation because her usual life is so regimented. (Ellen gets this, in principle, but she must have a plan at all times. If she went on vacation without a plan, she might miss something!) Debbie is a tough negotiator and enjoys herself more when she thinks she's getting a bargain. (Ellen just pays the asking price for things, like an idiot.) Wendy is very concerned about exercise. (Ellen is concerned with breakfast, lunch, happy hour— preferably with snacks—and dinner.)

Ellen learns something new about herself as well: she loves to take credit for everything.

They end up picking August 29 to September 5, Thursday to Thursday, because the one thing they all agree on is that there's no experience more soul-destroying than traveling on the weekend.

They fly United. Ellen would like to upgrade to first class but Debbie feels the best value is in premium economy. Then Wendy announces that her ex, Ian, has donated his miles so they can all fly first class. They immediately forgive Ian for his "as a favor" comment.

Ellen has booked two beachfront suites at Caneel Bay—one room for herself and Debbie, one for Becky and Wendy. She rents a four-door Jeep Wrangler hardtop, though Baker has warned her against ever taking the top off. It rains every day for fifteen minutes in the summer.

Baker! They will finally be reunited with their school husband, Baker. They will get to experience St. John, the island he now calls home.

"More important," Debbie says, "we'll get to meet the girl."

"She has no idea what she's in for with us," Becky says.

"We have to be nice," Wendy says. "She's pregnant."

Ellen obviously wants to meet the mysterious Ayers Wilson but she also wants them to have at least one night with Baker alone so they can find out what's really going on.

Not to toot her own horn, but Ellen's planning pays off. The trip down is smooth, their luggage is the first off the carousel, they get into a shared taxi that delivers them to Red Hook with just enough time for one rum punch before the ferry. When they disembark in Cruz Bay, they can't stop talking about the color of the water. It's pure Crayola turquoise, clear to the white sandy bottom. It's the most beautiful water any of them have ever seen. (They're used to the chocolate-milk-hued water of Galveston, and Debbie, the only East Coast transplant, grew up going to the Jersey Shore, which looked nothing like this.)

Caneel Bay is the epitome of old-school gracious hospitality. It's elegant. It smells like coconut lotion, frangipani, and money.

Their rooms are side by side in a one-story row that sits on a pure white crescent of sand. Each room has two mahogany queen beds sheathed in crisp white linens, marble bathrooms with soaking tubs, ice waiting in a silver bucket, rattan ceiling fans. The rooms have deep front porches with wicker furniture for lounging around with coffee or a cocktail. Beckoning out front are four chaises wrapped in rose-and-white-striped terry cloth. A server stands in the shade of the nearest palm, ready with cocktail and lunch menus.

Next door, Ellen can hear Wendy gushing: "I love it here. I need this. So badly."

They *all* need it so badly. Time away—from the swampy heat and humidity of Houston, from the Astros frenzy, from the Texans hype, from the incessant demands of small children. Ellen feels light and free, like she's lost forty-nine pounds, which is what Walter weighs. No one is asking her for juice, a snack, the bathroom, one more time down the slide, one more time watching *Wreck-It Ralph,* another story before bed, "Just sit here while I fall asleep, please, Mommy." *Mommy, Mommy, Mommy.*

They're free for an entire week!

"Does it feel like we're the only people here?" Debbie asks as she settles into a chaise.

The beach is deserted.

When Woodrow, their server, brings the menus, Ellen says, "Where is everyone else?"

"You're the only guests on this stretch," Woodrow says. "We're at low occupancy because of hurricane season."

Hurricane season, Ellen thinks. Yes, that's why these beach-front suites were so affordable. The hotel is due to close for two months the Sunday after they leave. They made it in just under the wire. Ellen lounges in her chaise, and not to toot her own horn again, but she feels like a wizard. They'll reap the benefits of hurricane season—low prices, the place to themselves—but there isn't a cloud in the sky.

Because of Ellen's impeccable planning, their first three days are packed with highlights: Trunk Bay, smoked brisket and live country music at the Barefoot Cowboy, happy hours at High Tide and Woody's, hiking to Ram Head and taking a mud bath in Salt Pond, dancing at the Beach Bar, a Kenny Chesney sighting inside the Parrot Club (although when Wendy runs in to check, she sees it's just a guy who *looks* like Kenny).

And then, finally, the day they've been waiting for—their charter to the BVIs aboard *Treasure Island.* This trip has all four ladies dialed up for a couple of reasons. One is that Baker is coming with them. (They've seen Baker only once in their first three days; he stopped by the afternoon they arrived to make sure they'd made it safely, but he had Floyd with him, so no actual news was exchanged. Their second evening, he sent two chilled bottles of Veuve Clicquot to their rooms, probably because he felt guilty about not spending more time with them. But they get it: They're on vacation; he's not.) The other is that Ayers Wilson, Baker's girlfriend, the mother of his child, is a crew member aboard *Treasure Island,* and so is Baker's brother, Cash. They're just as excited to meet Cash as they are to meet Ayers. They've seen Cash's picture, but he's never once visited Houston.

They're supposed to be at the dock across from Mongoose Junction at seven a.m., but Wendy is late getting back from her run, Becky is on the phone with her girls, and Debbie is taking forever to get ready even though all she needs is a bathing suit, a cover-up, and sunscreen.

"Let's go, ladies!" Ellen yells from the path behind their suites. Woodrow is waiting in the golf cart.

One by one, her friends appear. Not to toot her own horn yet again, Ellen thinks, but if it weren't for her keeping them to a schedule, they would miss their chance to meet Ayers, which—as far as Ellen is concerned—is one of the main reasons for coming.

Ayers Wilson is a goddess. She's one of those annoying women who glow during pregnancy and who don't gain weight anywhere except their baby bumps.

"Look at those legs," Debbie says. "I hate her. We all hate her, right?"

Except they can't hate her because she is as lovely as she is beautiful. She greets them all with warm hugs—not a trace of snark or jealousy. "Such an honor to meet you, Baker talks all the time about how much he misses his Houston school wives." Ayers lowers her voice. "He likes you better than his St. John school wives."

"You have St. John school wives?" Ellen says to Baker.

"I'll explain later," Baker says.

Not only is Ayers lovely, she's a badass. She's the one who explains how the trip will unfold—Virgin Gorda Baths, snorkeling,

Jost Van Dyke—and provides the safety regulations and a brief history of the island. There are only ten people on the boat—their party of five and a single father and his four teenagers. The father, Gary Dane, is cute in a rugged-ranch-hand kind of way; it turns out he's in real estate in Tulsa, which means he's best suited for Ellen, but Ellen passes him on to Debbie because she has too much urgent business to attend to at the moment. Debbie engages Gary Dane in conversation while Becky and Wendy chat up Cash. Cash is adorable, though he looks nothing like Baker; he's a whole different species. He's shorter than Baker, very blond, muscular. Does he work out? He's perfect for Wendy!

Ellen busies herself watching Baker watch Ayers. He's enchanted, that much is apparent; his eyes follow Ayers wherever she goes. She's wearing little white shorts and a green polo that is probably a men's medium to accommodate her belly. When they get to the Baths, Ayers explains that they're all going to swim from the boat to the shore.

"It's a little rough today," Ayers says. "The weather in early September is always unsettled." Ayers slips off her shorts and shirt to reveal a green tank suit that hugs her curves. She's a movie star, a superhero. Although she's eight months pregnant, she lowers herself down the ladder (thank goodness; Ellen worried for a second that she might dive in) and executes an elegant freestyle all the way to the beach. She takes the front as they tour the Baths—a series of granite boulders that have formed tunnels and chambers holding shallow baths. Some of the passageways are tight squeezes and there are steep stairs, but Ayers just glides along as though she's carved from butter.

Ellen brings up the rear with Baker. "She's remarkable. When I was pregnant with Walter, I gained fifty-two pounds and sat in my house eating cherry pie filling from the can."

"She's been craving steamed artichokes," Baker says. "Thank goodness her mother knows how to prepare them because I don't have a clue."

Steamed artichokes? Ellen decides not to comment. "How are things between the two of you? Is she still living alone in Mick's old place?"

"She is," Baker says. "Things are good. I see her almost every night. I've helped her fix the place up so that it's ready for when the baby comes. She's due in three weeks."

"She's going to stay in her own place after the baby is born? I thought she was moving in with you."

"She wants to wait until we organically reach the moving-in stage of our relationship," Baker says. "She's keeping our relationship on a different timeline from the pregnancy."

"What stage are you in?" Ellen asks. Up ahead, Wendy jumps down from a rock ledge, and Cash catches her. Becky is taking pictures with her phone, which Ellen hopes is waterproof. Debbie is asking the oldest of Gary Dane's kids what colleges she's looking at.

"Boyfriend and girlfriend," Baker says. "I'm madly in love with her. I tell her this all the time, and in response, she laughs and kisses me."

"She doesn't say it back?"

"Not yet. But she will."

He sounds pretty confident, Ellen thinks. "She better."

The bar on the boat doesn't open until after they finish snorkeling. "That's by design," Cash says as he pours painkillers for everyone. "To keep you alive."

*   *   *

When they anchor in White Bay on Jost Van Dyke, Ellen feels let down. The sand is like powdered sugar, the water a spectral blue, there's reggae music, and the smell of grilled meat wafts over from the Soggy Dollar, but there are only two other boats anchored there. Ellen had been anticipating something like an MTV beach party; this is decidedly more civilized.

The silver lining is that Ellen finds herself taking a seat next to Ayers in one of the Adirondack chairs placed in the shade of a small grove of coconut trees. The others are all up at the bar— Debbie is with Gary Dane, Wendy is with Cash, and Becky is talking to the bartender, who, Ellen can see, is falling in love with Becky (all men fall in love with Becky). Gary Dane's daughters are lying out on the chaises, and the boys are playing catch in the shallows. If Gary Dane and Debbie get married, Ellen thinks, they'll have eight kids—four girls and four boys. The Brady Bunch plus two.

"I don't know how you do it," Ellen says to Ayers. "Aren't you tired? Don't you want to sit in front of *Real Housewives* and eat Doritos?"

"My first trimester was like that," Ayers says. "But every week since then, I've felt healthier and stronger."

"Baker says you're staying in your place after the baby is born."

"I am," Ayers says. "Baker will be nearby. My parents too. But yeah, I want to live on my own for a while longer." She leans in. "You had a baby by yourself, didn't you?"

"*All* by myself," Ellen says. "Sperm donor."

"It wasn't Baker, was it?" Ayers asks.

Ellen hoots. "No! Ahhh, that would have made this a very awkward conversation."

"He's a good father," Ayers says.

"He's a good person," Ellen says. As she squints at the surreal view of the water and the green islands beyond, her vision blurs. Sunscreen in her eyes, maybe. "That's why we all came down here. I mean, yeah, we wanted a Caribbean vacation away from our kids"—she laughs—"but we came to see Baker. He was our best friend at home. He was always helping us out, and not in a douchey, mansplaining way; in a genuine, caring way. He would clean our gutters, change the oil in our cars, bring us homemade lasagnas when we were having a tough week. He went with us to the Houston Ballet every year to see *The Nutcracker.* He took our kids to the park when the four of us wanted to go to yoga together; he gave us solid investment advice; he came to pick us up when we were out on a bad blind date; he gossiped with us, sent us songs he thought we would like, asked us for advice when he was having trouble in his own marriage. He listened. He was there. All together, the four of us have dated—and married—a lot of guys, and we've all agreed that each of us is looking for her own Baker Steele. He's the gold standard." She swallows. "Diamond. Platinum. What I'm trying to get at is, you have a treasure. And what I'm also trying to say is, please don't hurt him." Ellen closes her mouth before she can add, *Or we'll come back down here and haunt you.*

Ayers puts her hand on top of Ellen's. "I won't," she says. "And thank you for telling me all that, but I assure you, I know what I have. I know how lucky I am."

Ellen studies Ayers for a second. *Do I believe her?*

Yes.

"Good," Ellen says. "Now, please dish on the St. John school wives."

*   *   *

When *Treasure Island* pulls into Cruz Bay at the end of the day, Ellen is happy, satisfied, and drunk. She's so drunk that when they get back to Caneel Bay, it takes her a minute to make sense of the paper that has been slipped under her door. The words are blurry. Maybe it's not the rum; maybe she needs reading glasses.

"What does this say?" Ellen asks, handing the paper to Debbie.

"They're evacuating the hotel tomorrow," Debbie says. "There's a hurricane coming."

TILDA

La Tapa closes at the end of August, which seems like a natural time for Tilda to give her notice. Her future is on Lovango.

She thinks maybe the staff will plan a party or an outing for drinks on her last night—this is what normally happens when someone moves on—but when Tilda finishes her last shift, no celebration is mentioned, so she hands in her uniform, hugs Chef, and leaves.

It's not that the staff members don't like *her;* it's that they don't like Dunk. He's developed the (admittedly, obnoxious) habit of waiting for Tilda across the street by the Tap and Still, vaping and glaring at the restaurant in a menacing way. Clover, the hostess, said she felt threatened; Skip wanted to punch his lights out. Ayers seemed indifferent, though Tilda knows that Ayers dislikes Dunk on principle because of Cash. Chef invited Dunk in for dinner but Dunk turned her down because Dunk doesn't eat. He has espresso in the morning, fruit juice at lunch, and either vegetable juice or broth at dinner. He drinks wine and Maker's Mark. Tilda isn't sure how he's still alive. There isn't an ounce of fat on his body; he's as lean and supple as a lizard.

If Tilda were being honest with herself, she would admit that Dunk's fasting bothers her. First of all, it's embarrassing that he can't socialize over meals the way other people do. No wonder he's essentially without friends and living like a hermit in the East End. Second, he makes Tilda feel bad when she eats. He stares at her with thinly veiled disgust when she bites into the Uncle Peep turkey sandwich from Sam and Jack's or when she asks him to stop at Scoops so she can get a cup of their salted peanut butter ice cream. Tilda is naturally slender, so she can eat whatever she wants and not gain an ounce, but Dunk makes her feel gluttonous and weak.

Tilda thinks back on her brief time with Cash, remembering how excellent it was to have someone to eat with. She and Cash planned every meal like it was their last whether they were cooking at home or eating out. It was sensual, Tilda thinks. Sexy.

Dunk's fasting isn't the only thing that's chafing at Tilda. There are also the accusations from Swan Seeley. Swan claims Dunk insulted her and touched her inappropriately during their marketing meeting, a meeting Tilda was supposed to attend until Dunk announced that he'd forgotten Olive's lunch at home, which was all the way back in Hansen Bay. Unlike Dunk, Olive ate like royalty—prime rib, lamb chops, chicken Kiev. It was twisted. Dunk asked Tilda if she would take the skiff back to Cruz Bay and buy two pounds of ground beef at Starfish Market for Olive. Tilda agreed even though by all rights it should have been Tilda meeting with Swan while Dunk ran the stupid errand. This was Tilda's resort—well, okay, her parents' resort. Dunk owned the land, and he and Granger and Lauren had come to some kind of agreement about a partnership, but Tilda didn't think that meant Dunk's presence was more important than her own at a marketing meeting. Still, she went to the market because she had a difficult time saying no to Dunk. And that's when the thing with Swan either happened or didn't. According to Swan, Dunk had said he'd hired her because she was "hot," "a dime" (Tilda abhors both of these terms), and then he'd touched Swan's back, massaged her shoulders, and brushed up against her behind.

Tilda had shocked herself by coming to Dunk's defense even though she knew that massaging a woman's shoulders and brushing up against her behind were two of Dunk's signature moves. He'd used both of these moves on Tilda! Tilda is a firm believer in the #MeToo movement; she always, *always* believes the woman—except, apparently, when the perpetrator is her own boyfriend. She was stunned by Swan's accusations—and hurt, too, of course. Why would Dunk go after Swan when he had Tilda? After Swan was safely on the skiff heading back to Cruz Bay, Tilda marched into the trailer and said, "What just happened with Swan, Dunk?"

Dunk had been poring over the designs for the T-shirts. He didn't even look up. "I was giving her a pat on the back, a good-on-ya, and she spit the dummy."

"Spit the dummy" was something Dunk said all the time; it had something to do with a baby losing his pacifier. "So you weren't inappropriate?" Tilda said.

Dunk inhaled on his vape pen—that thing drove Tilda crazy—and on the exhale said, "I was trying to give the woman a bloody *compliment*." Then he held his arms open. "Come here, mate." And like a fool, she went.

Swan e-mailed Granger and Lauren to tell them she didn't

feel comfortable working with Duncan or Tilda. She wanted to be paid for the time she'd spent on it so far, and thanks for the opportunity, but she was leaving the project. Tilda's parents had called from their business trip in Cape Town to ask for a full explanation, and when Tilda told them what had purportedly happened, they were livid. Especially Lauren. She said, "I'm calling Swan now to get her back. Your father will have a chat with Dunk. Is he trying to get us hit with a lawsuit?"

Lauren did persuade Swan to come back, but Swan said she would report to Lauren only. Not Dunk. And not Tilda.

Where do things stand with the Lovango resort? Well, that's the good news: Everything is moving swiftly and smoothly along with an anticipated opening date of April 1, right before Easter. The desalinization plant is nearly finished; the pool has been dug; the foundations of the cottages are in; the beach has been cleared. All the permitting is in place, and Granger and Lauren are in the process of buying boats that will transport guests from both Red Hook in St. Thomas and Cruz Bay in St. John to the resort. The restaurant is framed out, and only the week before, the granite was delivered for the bar. Lauren and Tilda FaceTime every day to discuss the design details—light fixtures, fabrics, paint colors. They both loved Swan's ideas for merchandise.

The Lovango Resort and Beach Club. It's going to be real. Tilda almost can't believe it.

After Tilda quits her job at La Tapa, she's on Lovango all the time. There's a tiny cottage perched just above the beach that came with the sale of the island. It's bare bones but livable, and Tilda spends a couple nights a week there so she doesn't waste precious time in the mornings commuting from Peter Bay.

She stays alone. Dunk prefers to sleep in his own bed, and so does Olive—fine, whatever. Tilda's feelings toward Dunk have cooled considerably; she's beginning to suspect that, behind the sexy accent and all the money, there's just a little man, like the Wizard of Oz. For dinner, Tilda runs the skiff over to the Pizza Pi boat or grabs sushi from the bar at Caneel, and then she sits in the cottage with the air-conditioning cranked and stuffs her face without anyone judging her.

One day, she sees *Treasure Island* heading out of the harbor in the wrong direction—toward St. Thomas—and realizes the boat is probably going for its yearly maintenance. They don't run charters in the autumn. Tilda wonders what Cash is doing over the break. She'd love to invite him to work on the resort. That had been the plan. Everyone is keen to have a robust water-sports program and a series of hikes across the island both as workouts and nature walks, and this was supposed to be Cash's department—but Tilda blew that chance. She hasn't even told her parents the truth. They know that Cash broke up with Tilda but they don't know that Tilda and Dunk hooked up on St. Lucia right after their couples massage, which was *before* she talked to Cash, so, technically, she cheated. And Cash could tell, she knew he could, so the breakup was her fault. Tilda generally discusses everything with her mother, but her behavior was so shameful and so unlike her that she can't share it with Lauren.

Tilda has just woken up in the Lovango cottage when her phone rings. Granger, calling from Dubai, where her parents are attending a conference this week.

"Inga is going to be a problem," Granger says.

Tilda must still be asleep because she has no idea who Inga

is. Maybe it's the woman at the Health Department over in St. Thomas? "Why?" Tilda says.

"She's picking up speed and strength, and right now she's on a direct course toward St. Thomas, St. John, Tortola, Jost, Virgin Gorda, and, although they didn't mention it by name, Lovango."

"Dad," Tilda says. "What are you talking about?"

"Inga," Granger says. "The hurricane."

Like a newborn with indecisive parents, a hurricane first forms without a name, as a collection of thunderstorms—so says Tilda's favorite weatherman, Dougie Clarence of the *CBS Evening News.* Tilda is watching Dougie on her phone in bed—the cottage has no TV, and even if it did, there's no cable—as he explains that Hurricane Inga started a few days earlier, August 27, as a Cape Verde hurricane, forming off the African continent and organizing near the Cape Verde Islands with a big push from the westerly trade winds, a term originating from the beneficial wind direction for early colonial traders. (Dougie always throws interesting factoids into his forecasts, which Tilda loves.) Inga has had a thousand miles of warm tropical waters to nourish her. In the past forty-eight hours, Dougie says, Inga's maximum winds have increased from forty miles per hour to one hundred and fifteen.

"It will bear down on Barbuda, the sister island to Antigua, in the next twenty-four hours," Dougie says. "It might disassemble a bit with landfall, but if it doesn't, it will hit the Virgin Islands with its full strength."

"Um...okay?" Tilda says.

She calls Dunk, gets his voicemail. She checks the time; he must be meditating. He'll meditate until eight thirty, then he'll drink four espressos while he prepares Olive's daily meals. Then they'll drive to town and he'll call Tilda to pick them up in the skiff right around nine thirty. Can she just wait until then?

The chyron on the screen beneath Dougie says HURRICANE INGA ON DIRECT PATH FOR VIRGIN ISLANDS.

She calls Dunk again. Voicemail.

Texts him: Call me! Urgent!

Calls him again, even though she realizes it's pointless. He's unreachable while he's meditating.

She calls him at 8:31 sharp.

"What?" He sounds pissed for some reason, maybe because she called during his sacred time. She doesn't care.

"There's a hurricane, category four, Inga, bearing down on Barbuda. And then, maybe, us."

"I've been tracking it all night," Dunk says.

Good, Tilda thinks. She doesn't want Dunk to accuse her of manufacturing drama, hurricane as monster under the bed. "Is it something we need to worry about?"

"Hell yes," Dunk says. "I have blokes coming to shutter this place up and I talked to Topher. He's coming to scoop up Olive and me tomorrow morning."

Wait…what? "You and Olive? Scoop you up to go where?"

"Back to Houston first, then probably on to Vegas. You know Topher."

Tilda does *not* know Topher; she only knows *of* Topher. He's Dunk's friend and bandmate in Wasps of Good Fortune (he's the bass player), and he's even wealthier than Dunk. He has his own plane, a G5.

"So you're leaving the island?" Tilda says. "You're just… leaving?"

"There's a hurricane coming, mate. A ballbuster. Maybe a cat five."

"What about... this place? Lovango? The construction, the work trailer, my cottage, the de-sal plant, the pool? We can't just leave it."

"If I were you," Dunk says, "I'd have Keith and the crew secure what they can over there and then you and your parents should have the caretaker shutter up Peter Bay and hunker down on the bottom floor."

"My parents," Tilda says, "are in Dubai."

"You must have the caretaker's number? Call him yourself. Be an adult."

"I *am* being an adult," Tilda says. "I'm not worried about my parents' house. It's made of stone."

"Even so, mate. It needs to be shuttered."

"I'm worried about here. Lovango. The resort we're building." She laughs. "I can't believe you're leaving with Topher. For Vegas. Do you not care about the resort?"

"I own the land," Dunk says. "Nothing is going to happen to the land."

"So now you care only about the *land?*" Tilda says. "What about the hundreds of thousands of dollars my parents have poured into building this place? That doesn't interest you, I guess. Unless it gives you a chance to meet one-on-one with a hot woman, then you're front and center." She understands in that moment that Dunk "forgot" Olive's lunch that day on purpose so he could meet alone with Swan.

"You're acting like a possessive child. If you're so worried about what you and your parents are building, then protect it, mate. I'm protecting what's mine, then I'm getting out of Dodge."

"I'm not going with you, Dunk. I'm staying on Lovango."

"I didn't invite you," Dunk says. "Did I?"

Did he? No, he didn't. Tilda can't believe how much she *hates* him in this moment. She isn't sure how to respond but she wants to pour gasoline on his heart and set it on fire with her words.

But she isn't quick enough. Dunk hangs up.

"I'm *not* your mate!" she says.

Tilda calls her parents and the three of them make a plan. Granger will get their caretaker to shutter the Peter Bay house. Tilda will meet with Keith and they'll secure Lovango the best they can. There are tens of thousands of dollars of building materials to protect. Tilda will shutter the cottage herself. There are three generators on the island; Tilda will get gas for all of them and stock up on provisions. She needs to go soon; the markets on St. John will be complete pandemonium. Or maybe not. Maybe she's overreacting.

"You'll stay at Peter Bay," Granger says.

"No," Tilda says. "I'm staying over here."

"Tilda," Lauren says.

"The cottage is sturdy, Mom," Tilda says. "It faces northwest and the storm is coming from the east-southeast. I'll be fine."

"I don't want you staying by yourself," Lauren says. "Call a friend. Or ask Keith to stay with you."

"Keith has a family, Mom. Little kids."

"Where's Dunk?" Granger asks. "Will he be there with you?"

"He's going to Vegas," Tilda says.

"Vegas!" Lauren cries.

"I don't know why you started seeing him," Granger says. "That had disaster written all over it."

You were the one who sent us away together, Tilda thinks. *What did you expect would happen?* Though there she goes again, acting like a child, not taking responsibility for her own decisions.

She entered the relationship with Dunk of her own free will—and yes, it was a disaster.

"What about Cash?" Lauren says. "Cash is so sweet."

Cash *is* sweet. And cool. And superior to Dunk in every way, starting with the fact that Cash would never abandon Tilda on Lovango with a hurricane coming and go to Vegas with his filthy-rich degenerate buddy. But Cash is also very, very angry with Tilda. And can she blame him? A couple months earlier, Tilda reached out to him via text just to see how he was doing, and he'd shut her down, saying, Fine, thanks for asking. Tilda deserved no more than this; she'd been awful to him, so awful that, frankly, she doesn't like to think about it. She ditched him for Duncan Huntley because...why? Dunk is rich, Dunk has a beautiful boat and an enormous villa with staff and a G-wagon and a lovely dog. Dunk has built and sold companies. Listening to Dunk's accent gave her a buzz. When they were on vacation together, he wowed her with how generously he tipped and how much he knew about the islands; he seemed like an evolved person who cared about the actual *place* and the actual *people,* and he made Tilda want to be more than just a resort tourist. All of Dunk's weird rituals made Tilda think he was *enlightened* and *interesting.* He knew a lot about old punk rock, which wasn't too surprising because he was in a band, but then one morning at breakfast on St. Lucia, he had identified Brahms, then Mozart, then Schubert coming from the piano player, and Tilda had been gobsmacked by his *range.*

Fine, he has range, but he's a jerk—and by *jerk,* Tilda means a lot of other things she's too polite to say.

She closes her eyes and does her own meditating. It was a mistake to date Dunk. Everyone could see that but her. But she's young, and Tilda is at least self-aware enough to admit failure, pick herself up, and dust herself off. She needs to apologize, big-time, to Swan Seeley. She will do that—but right now, there's a hurricane bearing down.

There's another person to whom she owes an apology, and this one can't wait.

She calls Cash.

HUCK

A hurricane watch is issued for the U.S. Virgin Islands. The clock starts ticking; they have forty-eight hours.

Cash calls Huck. "I need a favor."

Huck closes his eyes and summons every bit of patience he has as Cash talks. Cash would like a ride over to Lovango Cay because he's going to wait out the hurricane in a cottage on a cliff overlooking Congo Cay and Jost Van Dyke with...Tilda Payne, the girl who left him for the guy who bought Lovango.

"I have no other way to get over there," Cash says.

Huck and Irene swing down to the Happy Hibiscus so Huck can pick up Cash and drop off Irene. They find Cash and Baker talking in Baker's driveway. Cash throws his duffel in the back of Huck's truck.

"Are you sure about this?" Huck says. "I can take you there, but once I do, that's it. I won't be able to get you until after the storm passes."

"It's a terrible idea, bro," Baker says. "We should all stay here at the Hibiscus. Together. Besides, Tilda screwed you over, and the second she crooks her finger, you run back to her? Seems a little weak."

Huck's glad Baker is the one who said this.

"She's all by herself," Cash says. "Dunk left her. He's flying to Vegas with one of the guys in his so-called band."

What a douche-canoe, Huck thinks.

"She made her bed," Baker says. "You should *not* get back together with her. And besides, I thought you liked Wendy."

"She lives in Houston," Cash says.

"What about Bonny, then?"

Huck can see Cash's neck growing flushed. "Bonny's fine. I went on one date with her, she's nice, but it wasn't a love connection. Tilda means something to me."

"She let you stay with her for weeks," Irene says. "Do you feel like you have to repay the favor?"

"I want to be there for her," Cash says. "She can't stay over there alone." He appeals again to Huck. "Can we go?"

"We can go," Huck says.

First they stop at St. John Market, which has both registers open and ten people in each line, including—Huck gathers from eavesdropping—two couples who have only just arrived for a week's vacation at the Westin and who are provisioning with things like Doritos and mango-flavored Cruzan rum. Huck wants to tell these people that their time would be better spent trying to book a flight back to where they came from. For years, there've been false alarms—cat 1 or 2 hurricanes that fell apart and made landfall as nothing more than forty-mile-per-hour winds and two inches of rain—but this storm is picking up power like a snowball rolling down a mountain. This isn't going to be a "Let's get drunk, play gin rummy, and listen to that Scorpion song on repeat" kind of hurricane.

Cash buys two cases of water, two loaves of bread, peanut butter, jelly, crackers, Cheez Whiz, pickles, a bag of apples, a carton of pineapple juice, and two bottles of Cruzan aged rum. He wants beer as well but Huck steers him toward toilet paper, candles, batteries, bug spray.

From their spot way back in line, Huck texts Irene. Fill the gas cans first, then get to the store. This place is packed already.

Huck drops Cash off at the Lovango dock; Tilda is waiting at the end in a John Deere Gator. The construction site seems to have been secured but there's a trailer sitting on concrete blocks and all Huck can imagine is this bitch Inga picking it up like a toddler with a toy and tossing it into the sea.

"That's not where you're staying, is it?" Huck asks Tilda.

"No," Tilda says. "There's a cottage on the other side." She and Cash load the provisions into the Gator. "Thank you for bringing him."

"You two be smart," Huck says. "Charge your phones. Do you have a generator?"

"Yes," Tilda says. "And plenty of gas."

"Your place is shuttered?"

"It is," Tilda says.

Huck doesn't like leaving Cash and Tilda all alone on an island, not one bit, but he realizes he doesn't have any say in the situation and he needs to get out of there.

"Be safe," Huck says.

*　　*　　*

Huck is taking his boat to Hurricane Hole, where he will secure it with three anchors, strip it of all valuable electronics, then hope for the best. When he pulls into the Hole, he sees Captains Stephen and Kelly of the *Singing Dog* heading out.

Where are they going? he wonders.

He sees a few boats prepping in the Hole but not nearly as many as he thought he would. He putters over to *What a Catch!* "Where is everyone?" he asks Captain Chris.

"Hurricane watch just turned to warning," Chris says. "And they're advising everyone to pull their boats. This storm is going to be a monster, worse than anything we've seen. Sustained winds of one fifty or higher."

Huck swears under his breath. The *Mississippi* can't handle winds like that. "Where's the *Singing Dog* going?"

"They said the boat will be a goner on land or on sea," Chris says. "So they're going to try to outrun it."

"For the love of Pete," Huck says. "What are you doing, staying here or trailering up?"

"I was tempted to chance it here," Chris says. "But now I'm having second thoughts."

Yes, so is Huck—and the decision needs to be made immediately. He waves to Chris, spins his boat around, and heads back to Cruz Bay.

He calls Irene. "I need to trailer the boat," he says. "Then I have to shutter my house." Or should he shutter first, then deal with the boat? No, he can shutter in the dark if need be.

"What can I do to help?" Irene says.

"You and Baker are shuttering Hibiscus?"

"Yes," Irene says. "I'm making clam chowder, white chicken chili, a Mississippi roast, and your favorite cookies. Ayers is here, and so is Floyd. Phil and Sunny are on their way. Maia is at the school."

That's right; Maia begged to be allowed to go to the Gifft Hill gymnasium to assemble and distribute hurricane survival kits, which include gallon jugs of water, flashlights, extra batteries, granola bars, and fudge that some of the mothers made (because who doesn't need fudge in a hurricane?). All of Maia's friends are doing it, she said. Plus, she wants to *help*.

"Can you pick up Maia?" Huck asks.

"Already planning on it," Irene says. "Curfew is at eight. I figure I'll get her around seven thirty."

Huck breathes out a "Thank you" and marvels at how much better his life is with Irene Steele in it.

Huck hitches up his trailer and drives down to Chocolate Hole, where the boat is waiting. Getting the boat onto the trailer by himself isn't something he would do under any but the most dire of circumstances. He should have called Rupert for help but Rupert is all the way out in Coral Bay and Huck doesn't have time to waste. He has other friends but they all have their own boats to worry about. He considers driving back to Fish Bay to enlist Baker's help, but again, there's the issue of time.

There isn't a dinghy for Huck to borrow so he wades into the water up to his chest in order to climb aboard. The air is as hot and heavy as a blanket; the water feels wonderful. The sky glows an ominous green color. It seems to portend danger. Destruction.

Or maybe that's all in Huck's head.

* * *

He gets the boat trailered. That ends up being the easy part. The hard part is driving the trailer up Jacob's Ladder. He has to take it slowly, begging the chipmunks in his truck engine not to die on him yet. Right before he faces the final hill, the steepest, his neighbor Helen comes out of her house holding a covered plate. Helen was LeeAnn's best friend, a friend since childhood, though Huck has noticed she's kept her distance since Irene moved in.

"Chicken, beans, rice," she says. "Make sure you eat."

"Thank you," Huck says. "I will."

But there's no time just then. He gets the boat to the house, unhitches the trailer, secures the boat, and hopes like hell it doesn't go flying and end up through the roof of his house. It's getting dark. He's shuttering the house when his phone rings. Irene.

"I ate," he says. "Helen fed me." This is a lie—the plate is on the counter, untouched—but he assumes Irene is calling to check on him.

"Huck," she says. Her voice is an urgent whisper.

"What is it?" He *cannot* go back to Lovango to pick up Cash. Cash is stuck over there, sorry, unless he wants to swim.

Irene says something in such a low voice, Huck can't hear it. "I'm sorry, AC, what?" He realizes he sounds a little impatient. It's all fine for her to be making her white chicken chili and Mississippi roast, whatever the hell *that* is, but Huck has serious tasks to complete and he's racing against the clock.

There's a pause, then a noise—a door closing—and she says, "Ayers is in labor."

Well, she's going to have to wait, he thinks. "What kind of labor are we talking about?"

"Her water broke," Irene says. "The contractions are coming

every three to four minutes. It's pretty clear she's not going to make it over to Schneider. We called up to Myrah Keating, which is in full-on hurricane mode and has only emergency doctors on staff for the next twenty-four to forty-eight hours."

"The emergency docs can deliver a baby," Huck says. "Go now." It's almost seven thirty and there's an island-wide curfew that starts at eight. "Wait, where's Maia?"

"She's still at the school," Irene says. "I was about to go pick her up."

"I'll get Maia," Huck says. Goddamn it, he doesn't have *time* for this! He still has all the kitchen windows to shutter. "Why don't you take Cash's truck and get Maia, and Baker can take Ayers in his Jeep. Or Phil and Sunny can take her in their Jeep, it's bigger. Are Phil and Sunny there?"

"Oh yes, they're here," Irene says. "That's the issue. Sunny doesn't think Ayers should go to the health center."

"For crying out loud, why not?"

"I should rephrase that. Ayers claims she's in too much pain to move, and Phil and Sunny have assured her she doesn't have to go anywhere. They're telling her she can just have the baby *here in the house.*"

"Is anyone there a *doctor?*" Huck says. "If the answer is no, then get that girl to the health center. Have Baker step in if you need to. That baby is his as well."

"I've told them all that," Irene says. "What if there are complications? But Ayers said she had a checkup at the beginning of the week, and the baby is in place, apparently. Sunny keeps saying that women all across the globe have babies at home and there's no reason Ayers can't as well. She says it might actually be safer."

Huck can't believe this. "I can't believe this," he says.

"Apparently it's the low pressure that brings the babies," Irene says. "I should go get Maia now. Everyone else is with Ayers. Can you please come home?"

And do what? Huck thinks. He's not a doctor, and although he has sixty-plus years of wide and varied life experience, he has never delivered a baby. Then he gets an idea.

"I'm going to make a call," he says. "Long shot, but it's all we've got. You bring Maia home safely, please, and I'll be there as soon as I can." Huck hangs up and calls Rupert.

"This best be an emergency," Rupert says when he answers. "Not sure if you heard, but there's a storm coming."

Rupert's lady friend Sadie lives in Coral Bay on Upper Carolina. She's waiting at the bottom of her steep driveway, thank God, wearing blue scrubs and a silk scarf over her hair and holding a small duffel. Sadie is a nurse practitioner up at Myrah Keating; her mother, Blythe, was a midwife, the best in the Virgin Islands. When Huck called and told her about Ayers, she said, "If you come get me, I'll help out. I have my bag of tricks right here ready to go."

As soon as Sadie climbs in, Huck swings the car around and heads back down the Centerline Road like a bat out of hell.

"It's one thing asking you to deliver a baby at home and another thing asking you to deliver a baby at home with a category five hurricane on the way."

"Low pressure brings the babies," Sadie says. "I remember my mama delivering two or three babies during Marilyn in '95."

"I'm not sure how I'll ever thank you," Huck says.

"I'll tell you how you can thank me," Sadie says. "Convince your old friend Rupert to stop seeing Josephine."

Oh, boy, Huck thinks.

"And Dora."

It's a small island, Rupert, Huck thinks. He takes the curve above the Reef Bay Trail at breakneck speed. The wind is picking up; trees aren't swaying, they're *bending*.

"And anyone else he's got on a string," Sadie says. She slaps Huck's arm. "You hear me?"

"I hear you," Huck says.

MAIA

That was sick," Maia tells Irene as she climbs into Cash's truck. She puts down the window. "Bye, Shane! Stay safe! Text me!"

"Buckle up, please," Irene says. "And put up your window. It's starting to blow."

"We gave out six hundred and twenty-two emergency kits," Maia says. "Each one with two jugs of water, flashlights with batteries, bug spray, energy bars, and matches. The volunteers got to take home the extra fudge." Maia pulls a piece of fudge wrapped in wax paper out of her pocket. "Do you want some? It's fudge with Oreos."

"No, thank you, honey," Irene says. "Seat belt?"

"It's on," Maia says. "Is everyone at the house?" Maia knows this hurricane is going to be very destructive, but she can't help feeling something like excitement anyway. Shane and Bright and Colton and Joanie were all at the volunteer effort, and Bright said that every news station in the States is focused on the Virgin Islands. They keep calling it "America's paradise." Maia is happy people are paying attention; normally, the USVI are overlooked because they're a territory and not a proper state.

"Cash is on Lovango with Tilda," Irene says.

"Ahh," Maia says. She has been waiting for those two to get back together. Maia had caught Cash texting Tilda under the table during Irene's birthday breakfast at Jake's, and when Maia asked if they were starting back up, Cash said, *She's dating some-one else.* And when Maia kept staring at him, he said, *It's one text, Maia, relax.*

"Your grandfather will hopefully be back by the time we get home," Irene says. "And Maia..."

Maia has just popped fudge in her mouth. "Mmm-hmm?"

"Ayers is in labor."

"What does that mean?"

"She's having the baby."

"Tonight?"

"Tonight most likely, yes. Or first thing tomorrow. Her water broke." Irene sighs. "Her contractions were close when I left the house to get you. And she doesn't want to go to the health center..."

Maia asks, "Why not?"

"She thinks that because of the storm, it will be better to have the baby at home."

"Like in the olden days, when there were no hospitals?" Maia says.

"Yes," Irene says, shaking her head. She hits the gas.

When they get to the Happy Hibiscus, it's chaos. The front door is the only thing left unshuttered for now because people are still going in and out. Phil is on the front lawn on the phone with a doctor friend from Reykjavík, who is giving him advice. Sunny is guarding the bedroom where Ayers is. Nobody's allowed in, not even Baker.

"Is Huck here?" Irene asks.

"Not yet," Baker says. "Floyd fell asleep, thank God, *The Dirty Cowboy* does it every time. Someday I'm going to learn how that book ends. We filled both bathtubs and every pot we could find with water." He looks at Irene. "You made a lot of food."

"We have a lot of mouths to feed," Irene says. "How's she doing?"

"She's working through the contractions on her own for now," Baker says. "That's what she wants, and who am I to argue?"

"Huck told me help is on the way," Irene says.

Maia hears Ayers groaning in the bedroom.

Sunny says, "Make a knot and hang on, Freddy!"

"What should I do?" Maia asks.

"There's nothing any of us can do but wait," Irene says.

Phil comes inside as he finishes his call. "Anders says she needs to work with each contraction until it's time to bear down."

"That's not helpful!" Ayers shouts.

"Does she want some fudge?" Maia says.

"No, sweetie, thank you," Sunny says. "She already lost her dinner."

"Is that Maia?" Ayers says.

"Yes," Maia and Sunny say.

"Send her in," Ayers says.

The room is dark but there's an outline of light around the bathroom door. Ayers is sitting on the bed crying.

"Nut," she says. "It hurts. They tell you it's going to hurt but that doesn't prepare you for how white-hot, teeth-crushingly painful it is." She stand up, paces the room, then sits down again. "Here it comes, Nut. Hold my hand."

Okay, okay. Maia sits next to Ayers on the bed and Ayers grips Maia's hand so hard that Maia wants to cry out. Ayers is making a wheezing sound that turns to a whimper that turns to rapid breathing.

Finally, she relaxes. "Oh God," she says. She turns to Maia. "Hi."

"Hi. Is it over?"

"For now," Ayers says. "I can't recommend this. Promise me you'll never have children."

"Are you sure you don't want to go to the health center?"

"No," Ayers says. "No way. There's a storm coming, Nut."

"There is?" Maia says, and they both laugh.

"I don't want to be in a hospital filled with strangers when the power goes out. There are going to be emergencies that need to be addressed. And it sits up on that hill…I just don't think it's safe. Plus I can't ask all of you to come up there with me. I just…don't want to go."

"But what about the good drugs?" Maia says. Any time the topic of Ayers's delivery has come up in the past few weeks, all Ayers talked about were the good drugs. "Don't you want the good drugs?"

"I do," Ayers says. "I really do. Here comes another one, give me your hand."

Reluctantly, Maia surrenders her hand, and Ayers squeezes even harder than before, with nails, and Maia squeals but Ayers doesn't notice, thank goodness. Maia doesn't want to be asked to leave. She's honored that Ayers wants Maia—and apparently only Maia—in the room.

"You know who I miss right now?" Ayers says. "More than anyone else, do you know who I need here?"

"Mama?" Maia says.

"Rosie," Ayers says, and she starts crying again. "I need Rosie Small right here, right now! You know what she would be doing?"

The door to the bedroom swings open and a West Indian woman in scrubs walks in and says, "Rosie Small would be pouring two shots of tequila, one for you and one for her, we both know that." The woman puts her hand on Ayers's head. "How we doing, Mama? I'm Sadie. I'm here to deliver your baby." She glances at Maia. "You're the spitting image of your mother, sweetheart. If we hit a lull in here, I'm going to tell you some stories about your ancestors. Can you help me with a couple things?"

"Okay," Maia says. She will do literally anything to avoid holding Ayers's hand through another contraction.

"Clean towels," Sadie says. "Ice chips. And see if anyone has a Coca-Cola for me." She eases Ayers back onto the bed, spreads her knees, and says, "Let me check and see where we're at, doll. Whoa! Whoa, whoa, whoa! We got a baby crowning."

Ayers screams through the next contraction. Maia grabs a stack of towels from the bathroom and puts them on the bed.

"Ice chips," Sadie says. "And send the father in here, please. This baby is on its way."

When Maia leaves the room, she nearly collides with Phil and Sunny, who are stationed outside the door. "It's time to send the father in, she said."

"That would be me," Phil says.

"Why Phil and not me?" Sunny says. "That makes no sense."

"I think she means the baby's father," Maia says. "Baker, bro, it's time."

Baker leaps off the sofa and slides between Phil and Sunny and into the bedroom.

Maia fetches a bowl of ice chips and a Coke but she can't get back into the room because Phil and Sunny are blocking the way. Ayers is screaming. Maia gets tears in her eyes and thinks, *I am never, ever having a baby.* It's incredible that each and every person in this world had a mother who'd endured some version of this.

Rosie went through it with Maia; LeeAnn and Huck were there. Maia hands Sunny the ice chips and the Coke to pass into the room and then she goes out to the front yard and stands with Huck while he has a cigarette. Maia isn't supposed to hang around Huck while he smokes but there's a new life entering the world and a hurricane coming, so the usual rules don't apply.

"Do you remember when I was born?" Maia asks.

Huck exhales, then gives a dry laugh. "Do I *remember?* Maia Rosalie Small, that was the happiest day of my life."

Ayers screams again. They hear her, even outside.

"Must be getting close," Huck says.

Close but not yet, not yet. When Maia goes back inside, she hears Sadie saying, "Push, doll, push for me," and Ayers screaming, "I can't!" And Sunny calling out, "Push, Freddy, push!" Phil gently leads Sunny away from the bedroom door and back to the living room. He says, "I think I'm going to try some of that chili. Do you want some, my love?"

Sunny says, "How can you think about eating when our grandson is about to arrive?"

"Or granddaughter," Irene says, and Maia smiles. She knows that Sunny visited a medium on her trip to Croatia and the medium told Sunny the baby was going to be a boy. Sunny fully believes this and she has bought ten outfits for the baby in blue.

Ayers screams.

"There we go," Sadie says. "One more push, doll!"

Maia puts her hands over her ears so she doesn't have to listen to Ayers. A second later, Irene jumps off the sofa. Maia drops her hands.

"It's a girl!" Sadie calls out. "A beautiful baby girl."

A split second later, there's a noise unlike anything Maia has ever heard—it's a cry. A baby's first cry. Maia shivers. It's a girl. Her niece.

Maia stays up late because sleeping arrangements in the Hibiscus are a little crazy. Baker, Ayers, and the baby will sleep in one bedroom; Irene will sleep with Floyd; Huck and Maia are taking the sofas; and Phil and Sunny are sleeping in the laundry room on an air mattress. The wind has picked up but there's no rain yet; the storm is due to make landfall the following day between noon and two.

Once Sadie has finished checking Ayers and the baby— Ayers and Baker haven't given her a name yet because they want to get it just right—and helped Ayers latch the baby onto her breast and taught Ayers and Baker all about newborn care, Huck says that despite the curfew, he's going to run Sadie back to Coral Bay.

Maia approaches Sadie as she's scrubbing her hands and her equipment at the kitchen sink. "We didn't have a lull," Maia says, "so I didn't get to hear the stories about my ancestors. Did you...*know* my ancestors?"

"Well," Sadie says, "my mother, Blythe, was a midwife here on the island, and believe it or not, she delivered your mother."

"She did?" Maia says.

"When I was fourteen, my mother started bringing me with her to the births," Sadie says. "I'm fifty now. So...thirty-six years ago, the very first baby I saw being born was your mom."

For a second, Maia is left breathless. Here's someone who wants to talk not about Rosie dying but about Rosie being born. "What..." Maia isn't sure what to ask. "What do you remember?"

"Your grandmother was the most elegant woman ever to grace this island," Sadie says. "She was a model for a while, you know, in Paris and Milan."

"I know."

"She left all that and came back to St. John to marry Levi Small."

"Did you know my grandfather?" Maia asks. She checks around the house. Their voices are low, but this topic—Rosie's father, Levi Small—is so forbidden that Maia doesn't want any-one overhearing. It also feels wrong to refer to anyone but Huck as her grandfather.

"Course I did," Sadie says. She dries her hands finger by finger on a paper towel and lowers her voice to a whisper. "He was singing to LeeAnn the whole time she was in labor, mostly old Motown tunes—'My Girl' and 'You Can't Hurry Love.' Your grandfather had a magnificent voice."

"He did?" Maia says. She has never heard anyone say one kind thing about Levi Small.

"He used to sing in the church choir," Sadie says. "He was a soloist. I remember that from when I was younger than you are now."

"Do you know what happened to him?" Maia asks.

Sadie shrugs. "He left when your mama was little. Two or three years old. Some people say he ran off with another woman;

some say your grandmother kicked him out and told him never to come back. Nobody knows for sure what happened and nobody knows where he went."

"So he might still be alive?" Maia says.

"Man I dated before Rupert told me he saw Levi Small playing the piano at a fancy restaurant in Miami, Florida. But don't get your hopes up, honey. The man I dated is *very* untrustworthy."

Still, it's exciting for Maia to think that she might have one relative on her mother's side left. She imagines being older, in college or in her twenties, walking into a fancy restaurant in Miami, and coming face to face with her grandfather.

Sadie bends down and gives Maia a hug goodbye. "I bet you didn't know your family had so many secrets, did you?"

Huck calls from the living room, "Sadie, you ready?"

Sadie disappears with a blown kiss and a wave, leaving Maia in the empty kitchen.

Secrets? Maia thinks. *My family? Never!*

MARGARET QUINN

In the four years since Margaret Quinn retired as the anchor of the *CBS Evening News,* she hasn't felt a single pang of regret or experienced one moment of FOMO. She has been quite content to get her news like everyone else—online. Gracing her inbox every morning are the *New York Times,* the *Wall Street Journal,* the Skimm, the BBC, the *Hollywood Reporter,* and Refinery 29. She follows *New York* magazine and *People* on Instagram. She still has *Time* and *Vogue* delivered to the house. She watches the six o'clock news on CBS, but not every night—because she's busy!

Her daughter, Ava, and Ava's husband, Potter, and their twins, Maggie and Homer, live in the city, but Ava keeps threatening to move to New Canaan (the lawns! the schools!), so Margaret wants to spend as much time as she can with them while they're still just across the park. Margaret and her husband, Dr. Drake Carroll, travel to Boston to see Margaret's son Patrick, his wife, Jennifer, and their three teenage boys, and then often they take the ferry over to Nantucket to visit Margaret's son Kevin, his wife, Isabelle, and their children, Genevieve, Kelley, and baby Arnaud.

Just this past year, Drake has cut back his surgery schedule at the hospital in anticipation of full-on retirement, so he and Margaret have been able to travel. They took a Viking River cruise down the Rhine and the Rhône; they trekked Milford Sound in New Zealand. It's been a long time since Margaret has been able to travel for pleasure. While she was working, the network sent her places like Kosovo, Tel Aviv, Fallujah, Medellín, Lagos, Haiti, and, once—a happy lark—to London to cover William and Kate's wedding.

Margaret sits on the boards of three charities—one hospital, one museum, one homeless shelter. She emcees each of these organization's major benefits; she plays in celebrity softball games; she has been approached by *Dancing with the Stars* (she said no); and she's been toying with teaching at the Columbia School of Journalism.

She's been asked to write her memoirs but she's nowhere near ready for that—too much living yet to do.

She'd like to write a book describing the magic of being a grandmother, but Leslie Stahl beat her to it.

*   *   *

When Margaret's phone rings on the third of September and she sees it's her former boss Lee Kramer, head of the studio, she thinks he's calling to make an elaborate excuse for why he and his wife, Ginny (editor in chief of *Vogue*), can't attend the hospital benefit three weeks hence. *That's fine,* Margaret thinks. There are so many worthy causes in this city and you can't go to everything, though Margaret plans to hit Lee up for fifty thousand at least.

"Don't say no."

This isn't the greeting Margaret was expecting. "Good morning, Lee. How are you?"

"Please just hear me out."

"How are Ginny and the kids? How does Evie like Cornell?"

"I'd like you to come back for one assignment."

"Thanks for calling," Margaret says. "Bye."

"You don't even know what it is."

"No, but I know how this works. I say yes to one assignment, then another assignment comes along, then *Sixty Minutes* offers me a ten-segment deal, then you offer me my own half-hour show aimed at baby boomers, and the next thing you know, my grandchildren are seeing me more on TV than they are in person."

"This is one assignment and it's your favorite kind of story..."

Margaret's favorite kind of story is military moms and dads who come back and surprise their children at school. Margaret cries every time. But she knows Lee wouldn't ask her back for that reason. "What is it, Lee?"

"The weather."

Ahhh, right. Margaret does love a good weather story.

"Hurricane Inga, down in the Caribbean, is shaping up to be an event. It's aimed at Antigua and Barbuda right now and will likely hit the Virgin Islands after that. St. Thomas, St. John, Tortola, Virgin Gorda. This is a hundred-year storm, Margaret."

"Like Katrina?"

"Like Katrina, yes."

Margaret experiences a surge of excitement so powerful, it's almost sexual. "What about Dougie? He already fancies himself the next Jim Cantore, and I don't want to steal his thunder…so to speak. Send Dougie."

"Dougie won't go," Lee says. "His wife is due to have their first baby *tomorrow.* So he's going to man the anchor desk on this coverage, and when I asked him who he thought I should send down in his place…"

"He said me?"

"He said you."

"Even though I retired four years ago."

"He said you."

Margaret inhales, exhales, looks at herself in the mirror. They're sending her into a war zone, essentially, so there won't be any hair or makeup, which means the entire country will become acutely aware that Margaret is rapidly closing in on sixty-five. It's flattering; hell, it's an *honor*—not only for Margaret but for every woman of a certain age—to be chosen to cover this. Just being asked makes Margaret realize she does miss it.

"When do I leave?" she asks.

"When can you be ready?"

Margaret calls Drake at the hospital from her car service to Teterboro. CBS is sparing no expense—she has her driver, Raoul, back, and she's flying down on the CBS jet because commercial flights have been canceled.

Drake isn't happy. "I thought this part of our lives was over."

"So did I," Margaret says. She realizes she sounds giddy.

"Please be safe, Margaret," Drake says. "I need you."

Four hours later, Margaret lands at the Cyril E. King Airport in St. Thomas. The weather is surprisingly clear and sunny, and the island pops with all the bright colors that one expects from the tropics—emerald green, turquoise, coral, and near-blinding white. Margaret didn't tell Lee or Drake this but she has been to the Virgin Islands before. She and her first husband, Kelley Quinn, came for a week's vacation back when Patrick was three years old and Kevin just a baby. They stayed at the Maho Bay campground in a "cabin" with a canvas roof. Kelley filled a dark rubber bladder with water from the pump and left it in the sun to warm up for a "sun shower." It had been rustic, funky, unbearably hot, even more unbearably buggy—Kevin's pale, chubby baby body had been an all-you-can-eat buffet for the mosquitoes— but Margaret had loved every minute of it. Even when they found a scorpion in Kelley's shoe. Even when they got lost on a hike to Ram Head in the scorching heat with Kevin strapped to Margaret's chest. They spent luxurious afternoons lying under a cluster of palm trees on Trunk Bay, where Kelley rented one mask and snorkel and the two of them took turns marveling at the manta rays and the schools of brilliant fish.

When Margaret's marriage to Kelley hit the skids, she'd suggested a getaway to revive the romance. She went so far as to book a week at Caneel Bay—but they never made it.

Margaret has always wanted to come back. Now, here she is.

*　　*　　*

The crew from the CBS affiliate picks Margaret up, and although they've reserved her a room at the Ritz-Carlton on St. Thomas, the storm is predicted to be so fierce that the Ritz is no longer deemed safe. Plan B is an emergency shelter in the basement of the CBS studio building. It has cinder-block walls, a buffet "catering spread" that includes Kind bars and packages of ramen noodles. They have a generator. There's a men's room and a ladies' room on the first floor but no shower. Margaret is shown a cot. She thinks longingly of the Ritz-Carlton. She thinks even more longingly of the king bed in her apartment on the Upper West Side overlooking Central Park, where the leaves are just hinting at fall.

"We should get our outdoor shots now," the producer, Rhonda, says. "We'll take footage on Sapphire Beach first—"

"And then we'll go over to St. John?" Margaret asks.

"Yes, we'll shoot from the dock in Cruz Bay," Rhonda says. "Then we'll come back here and hunker down."

Good afternoon, Dougie. I'm reporting from the Sapphire Beach Resort in St. Thomas, where, right now, the water looks pretty inviting. However, by this time tomorrow, the scene will be quite different...

Good evening, Dougie. I'm reporting from Cruz Bay on the island of St. John, where both locals and visitors are preparing for what will very likely be a direct hit from Hurricane Inga...

*   *   *

Rhonda hurries Margaret into the boat. The waves are much choppier on the way back to St. Thomas; the wind has picked up and there's a line of gray clouds on the horizon. Is that the hurricane? No, not yet, Rhonda says. Tomorrow afternoon. If the weather is clement tomorrow morning, they might do one more live report from St. Thomas.

"Let's get you a proper dinner," Rhonda says. "How do you feel about goat?"

Maybe she's kidding. Maybe she's trying to see how tough Margaret is. Well, Margaret drank cow's blood in Nigeria; she ate rattlesnake in China. She's tough.

"Love it!" Margaret says.

That night from her cot, Margaret tracks the storm. It's now 215 miles to the east and has sustained winds of 155 knots. This is going to be devastating. Maybe Margaret isn't so tough after all. She's sixty-four years old and the grandmother of eight. What is she *doing* here? Has she lost her mind?

Both Rhonda and the camerawoman, Linda, are sleeping in the studio basement with her. Margaret bids them good night, and from her little corner, she calls Drake, then she calls her kids in order of age. Patrick is spending the weekend taking his oldest, Barrett, up to look at Colgate, Hamilton, and Skidmore; he doesn't seem to know there's a hurricane coming and Margaret decides not to mention where she is. He's bringing Barrett to the city the following weekend to look at NYU and Columbia. Margaret says, "Can't wait to see you!" then hangs up, hoping she makes it home in one piece—hoping she makes it home, period. Kevin is consumed with the closing weekend of Quinn's Surfside Beach Shack. He sounds harried; Arnaud is teething and Genevieve is starting kindergarten. *I can't believe she's going to school already,* Kevin says. *It feels like she was just born.* Yes, Margaret knows the feeling only too well. Kevin was once that chubby baby who was such a delicacy for the island's mosquitoes. The years—where do they go?

Finally, Margaret calls Ava, who says, "I stopped by your apartment today, and Drake told me you're in the Virgin Islands covering that monster hurricane. What were you *thinking,* Mom?"

The next day dawns calm and still. Rhonda makes a big pot of coffee and produces a beautiful tropical-fruit platter and a bakery box filled with muffins and bagels.

"The café down the street saw you on TV last night," Rhonda says, "and insisted on sending these."

They head out to do one more live spot for Dougie back in New York. The wind is picking up. The outer wall of the hurricane will be arriving in a matter of hours.

"Stay safe," Dougie says. "We'll see you on the other side."

Margaret, Rhonda, and Linda go back down to the studio basement.

Margaret traces the storm on her laptop. It's coming. She hears the wind screaming like a woman in labor (it must be the situation with Dougie's wife that puts this image in her mind). Then the lights flicker, and the power goes out; the studio's generator comes on, but the lights in the basement are low and there's no longer any air-conditioning. Things outside the studio crash, smash, shatter. Margaret can't see what's making the noise because the windows are shuttered. *Dear Lord,* she thinks, *please don't let the windows break. Don't let the roof blow off. Don't let the place flood. Please don't let anyone die.* But as the minutes pass and then the hours, as the wind gets so loud that Margaret can't hear her own voice praying, as her cell signal cuts out, as she lies on her back unable to even read the book she brought, she marvels at how profound the weather is, how mighty, how inexplicable and unpredictable.

Life on these islands is changing right now, right this second, she thinks. Maybe forever.

ST. JOHN

After Inga left us—as definitively as someone leaving a room and slamming the door behind her—we picked up our heads and looked around.

Let's start with Cruz Bay, our "downtown." It was...*ruined.* Wharfside Village lost its roof; the Beach Bar's dance floor was buried under two-foot drifts of sand; the palm trees along Frank Bay were snapped in half, reminding us of gruesomely broken bones. Someone's boat, *Nell,* landed upside down on the deck of High Tide, where so many of us had enjoyed rum punches during happy hour. The Lumberyard building—home to the Barefoot Cowboy, Driftwood Dave's, the barbershop, and Jake's—looked like the proverbial cake that someone had left out in the rain; the building simply caved in on itself. Homes were violently torn apart, their contents thrown out into the yard, the street. Who could tell what had been a ceiling or a wall or a bathroom door? There was plaster, glass, metal in heaps and piles everywhere. It looked like a bomb had detonated; the damage was...atomic, nuclear.

Word started rolling in from the North Shore Road, Chocolate Hole, Gifft Hill. One family of six survived by hiding in their laundry room. One man crouched behind a table on its side for three hours as the sliding glass door across the room bowed in and out as though it were breathing. Multiple witnesses saw telephone poles flying through the air like missiles. Cars were flipped. A couch ended up in the neighbor's front yard; a refrigerator ended up in the bedroom; a hot-tub cover was caught in the high branches of a tree.

What about beyond the stone gates at Caneel Bay? This was, perhaps, what most took us by surprise. The genteel, elegant resort had been ravaged—roofs ripped off, trees uprooted, buildings flooded and filled with sand, the entire place simply annihilated.

The Centerline Road was impassable due to downed trees. The hillside between Maho and Leicester Bays looked like a winter landscape; all of the trees were stripped bare, broken, left a burned-looking brown.

Eventually, we heard from our friends on the "other side of the world," in Coral Bay. Shipwreck Landing, one of our favorite places to order coconut shrimp and listen to live music, had been decimated. Concordia, which had such delicious breakfasts, was blown away. Boats were dashed against the rocks, or they capsized and sank. The carnage in Hurricane Hole turned our stomachs.

Few of us realized that tornadoes are a common phenomenon when a hurricane hits land. The friction between open ocean and hills can cause spin, especially when the feeder bands roll through. The spot on St. John that saw the most tornado activity was the East End because it has elevation and because it's so exposed. There were thirteen tornadoes recorded on the East End alone. Unlike a hurricane, a tornado's path is unpredictable. One villa remains untouched while the villa next door is turned into kindling.

The compound belonging to Duncan Huntley was pulverized. When his closest neighbor saw the damage, he said, "It seemed like Inga had a personal vendetta against the place." A cast-iron planter that must have weighed seventy pounds had smashed through the roof of Dunk's garage and crushed Dunk's G-wagon. Every building lost its roof; the 140-inch screen from the home theater ended up in the swimming pool. Nothing was salvageable. The neighbor said that even if Dunk lost his shirt in Vegas, he was still a lucky man. "If he'd stayed in the villa," the neighbor said, "he'd surely be dead."

Imagine our relief when, the morning after the hurricane ended, the *Singing Dog* came sailing into the harbor. Captains Stephen and Kelly had successfully outrun the storm—and not only that, they had a working satellite radio that allowed many of us to contact our relatives back in the States to let them know we were still alive.

At first, that's all we could claim: We were upright and breathing.

The satellite radio also brought news that help was coming; the National Guard and the U.S. Navy were on their way.

There was no power, no water. Never mind rebuilding it; just cleaning it all up would require a Herculean effort.

Someone discovered that if you stood on the third-floor balcony of the Dolphin Market building downtown, you could get a very weak cell signal. Hey, it was better than nothing, and before we knew it, that balcony was as crowded as the bar at Skinny Legs after the Eight Tuff Miles race. A line started to form because someone wisely pointed out that the balcony would hold only so much weight and the last thing we wanted was for someone who'd survived the hurricane to plunge to his or her death trying to call Cousin Randy in Baltimore.

The balcony and the line to get to the balcony became the place where we connected not only with the outside world but also with each other. Nestor from Pine Peace Market let everyone know that he would open the store. The owners of the Longboard would cook a community dinner, everyone welcome. There would be stir-fry and Chinese noodles over at 420 to Center.

Someone declared that what he really wanted was Candi's barbecue—but, alas, Candi's didn't survive.

Those who had generators and gas offered assistance to those who didn't. Other items we needed included chain saws, bottled water, shovels, and insect repellent—because the heavy, still, hot weather that arrived in Inga's wake brought all the familiar bugs as well as larger, flashier, meaner bugs that looked like they'd escaped from some exotic tropical zoo. Because money had no immediate value, people bartered. Overall, there was a spirit of gratitude and compassion for our fellow islanders, even those we had previously disliked. The hurricane had happened to all of us—West Indian, white, Latinx, Catholic, Episcopalian, evangelical, Cruz Bay, Coral Bay.

Had anyone seen the wild donkeys? Where, oh where, did the donkeys take cover in the storm?

*   *   *

No sooner does the storm clear than someone sees Margaret Quinn herself in a pair of Hunter rain boots and a bright green anorak broadcasting from the Cruz Bay ferry dock. Margaret Quinn! Candice from the St. John Business Center and several others saw Margaret's broadcast from the night before Inga hit, but the rest of us, of course, were too busy preparing for the storm to casually watch TV. After Margaret Quinn finishes her spiel on the dock—what can she say but that St. John sustained monumental damage that will take a long time to recover from?—she insists on walking over to the Dolphin Market building so she can talk to real people. We see her producer and even the camerawoman trying to dissuade her but Margaret Quinn strides ahead. That's why we love her, after all; she's a strong, independent woman who will do what it takes to get to the beating heart of a story.

Margaret sees a couple about her age waiting at the end of the line. The woman—nice-looking with a neat chestnut braid—is handing out what appear to be cookies to the people ahead of her in line.

"Lemongrass sugar cookies," Margaret overhears her saying. "Homemade."

This will be her first interview, Margaret decides. A woman who brought homemade cookies to share while she stands in line to maybe get a cell phone signal is someone Margaret would like to meet. "Excuse me," Margaret says, touching the woman's elbow.

The couple turn and the woman's eyes widen. "Why!"

The man says, "Holy smokes. Margaret Quinn!"

The woman holds out the platter. "Would you like one? They're lemongrass sugar cookies. Homemade."

"I'd love one," Margaret says.

Their names are Captain Huck Powers and Irene Steele. Margaret had pegged them for a long-married couple but she's apparently mistaken. This must be one of these magic relationships—not unlike Margaret and Drake—where people of a certain age find love later in life.

Huck reveals that he's a charter fishing captain who has lived on St. John for over twenty years. His boat is called the *Mississippi.* Irene is from Iowa City; she moved to the island in February because she needed a life change.

Huck wraps his arm around Irene's shoulder and pulls her in close. "She sure changed *my* life."

Who are Huck and Irene waiting to call? Family back in Iowa?

"Most of my family is here," Irene says. "My son Baker and his girlfriend, Ayers, had a baby last night at home."

Margaret thinks she must have misunderstood. "They had a crying baby last night at home?"

"They *had* a baby last night," Irene says. "Ayers gave birth in the bedroom with a nurse practitioner who happens to be a friend of the family. So I have a brand-new granddaughter."

Margaret can't help herself. "Will she be named Inga?"

"Oh," Irene says. "I hope not."

"No," Huck says. "They haven't settled on a name yet, but rest assured, it will not be Inga."

Irene says, "And that's not all. My other son, Cash"—here, Irene pivots and casts a concerned glance behind them, at the water—"is over on Lovango Cay with his friend Tilda. Her family is building an eco-resort on Lovango, and, if I'm not mistaken, Cash and Tilda are the only two people on the entire island. I'm going to try to call Cash to make sure they made it through okay."

This is such a good local story that Margaret feels like she hit the jackpot on the first try. She asks Huck and Irene to repeat all of this—including the shtick about the name Inga— with the cameras rolling. She has Linda get a close-up of the cookies and then she asks Linda to pan across the water toward Lovango Cay.

When they finish filming, Irene says, "I'm not one to play the name game but I think you know my cousin."

Margaret smiles. She loves this woman, this couple; they're authentic and charming, and even if Margaret has no idea who Irene's cousin is, she might pretend she does. "Who's your cousin?"

"Mitzi Quinn," Irene says.

Ha! Margaret thinks. *Ha-ha-ha!* "Mitzi? Mitzi is your *cousin?*"

Irene nods shyly. Huck looks lost. "Who's Mitzi?"

"Mitzi was married to my ex-husband for many years," Margaret says. "Mitzi's son, Bart, is my children's half brother." She beams. "We're practically *related!*" She pulls out a business card and hands it to Irene. "Please, let's keep in touch. If you ever need anything..."

"Thank you," Irene says.

Margaret tilts her head. "Before I move on, I have to ask one more question. How did the two of you meet?"

Irene and Huck smile at each other and Margaret can see something pass between them that seems to indicate it's a story too complicated for a sound bite. *Of course,* Margaret thinks. *All the best stories are.*

"We could tell you," Huck says. "But you'd never believe it."

IRENE

Cash and Tilda are okay. The cell phone reception when she's talking to Cash goes in and out but the gist is that they're going to stay on Lovango for a few days to try to clean up before they take the skiff back over to St. John.

"It was scary," Cash admits. "The cottage shook so bad, we felt like dice in a cup. During the worst of it, I looped my belt through the handle of the front door and pulled, and Tilda sat behind me, bracing me. We knew if we lost the door, the roof would be next."

Irene gets a chill. *You should have stayed with us,* she almost says. The Happy Hibiscus didn't sustain any damage because it's made of stone, because it's sheltered from the water, because the yard has only bismarckia trees, no palms. The wind was loud, the windows rattled, they could hear the branches of the trees coming down, but that was the worst of it. The baby cried a little, which was a sound everyone loved, and Winnie whimpered, which was a sound nobody loved but everyone tolerated. "Isn't it lonely being the only two people on that whole island?" Irene asks.

"Actually," Cash says, "it's kind of romantic."

Well, Irene thinks, *looks like Tilda is back in the picture.* "We have a surprise for you when you get home," Irene says.

"A what?" Cash says.

"A surprise!" Irene says. There's no answer. "A surprise!" She turns to Huck. "I think I lost him."

Suddenly she hears Cash say, "Thanks, Mom. Hug Winnie for me."

When Huck and Irene leave town, Irene says, "Shall we go to your house?"

"Our house?" he says. He sighs. "Can't put it off forever, I guess."

They've avoided it until now because the most important thing was making sure everyone was safe, including Cash and Tilda. The fate of Huck's house and the boat is secondary.

Sort of.

If the house is destroyed, where will they live? If the boat is destroyed, *how* will they live?

Slowly, they begin the climb up Jacob's Ladder. Irene is surprised when her phone pings with a text.

It's from Lydia. We saw you on Channel 2 with Margaret Quinn! it says. Congrats on your new granddaughter! Brandon was so happy his cookies made it on TV!

There are branches down on the road up to Huck's house that Huck has to clear. One of their neighbors lost his entire roof; it's like someone pried the lid off a jar. Where is it? Somewhere down the hill? The destruction is everywhere and it is epic. There's a truck on its side with the doors ripped off. Entire homes have been reduced to rubble—insulation and beams and crumbling bricks. The Ladder looks far, far worse than Fish Bay.

When they're still fifty yards away, they can see the *Mississippi.*

Huck exhales. It's a little crooked on the trailer but otherwise fine. It must have been shielded by the house. Huck jumps out to look at the boat more closely while Irene heads up the front stairs.

They still have a roof, and the deck is intact, although the railings are all broken. She has to wait for Huck to retrieve his drill from the truck so he can take the shutter off the front door. Together, they step inside.

Something is wrong—the windows in the kitchen have blown out. There's glass everywhere and the living room looks like it's been ransacked; lamps have been knocked over, cushions from the sofa are all over the room, everything is wet. There's at least three inches of water in the kitchen, the chairs are all smashed; the sugar bowl, the toaster, Irene's food processor are all sitting broken in the shallow pond of their kitchen. There's a palm rat feasting on what looks to be an overturned plate of chicken and rice.

Irene gags. Huck comes up behind her. "I'll get him out in a second," he says. "Let's check the rest."

Huck and Irene head down the hall to the bedrooms, the bathrooms. They're hot, stuffy, unbearable—but fine. Except...

"Uh-oh," Huck says. He emerges from Maia's room with the portrait of Milly. The glass has one long crack down the front. "I think the actual photograph is okay, though."

Irene takes the frame from him. Yes, it looks like the picture is okay. What this picture has survived in the past year. "Why...the kitchen?" Irene says.

"I didn't shutter the windows," Huck says. "I was about to when you called and then I got on the phone with Rupert and I had to track down Sadie and then I thought I'd come back and do it later." He turns to Irene with tears in his eyes. "I got so caught up in the baby coming that I completely forgot about those three windows. I forgot until just this moment."

"It's nothing we can't clean up," Irene says. The rat has disappeared, though no doubt he's lurking around here somewhere. "I kind of wanted to remodel the kitchen anyway."

They remove the shutters from the slider and Huck checks to make sure the deck boards are secure before they step outside. All the railings are broken; one whole side has disappeared. Irene is sure Huck is craving a cigarette but he busies himself with stacking the broken pieces of the railing in a pile. The whole thing will have to be torn down and rebuilt.

Irene remembers when she used to wake up believing that Russ was still alive. One nightmare in particular returns to her now: Russ staggering down the beach, his shirt soaking wet, his pants ragged. He wanted to tell her something. *The storm is coming. It will be a bad storm. Destructive.*

When Huck turns around, his breathing is shallow. Irene takes his left hand, the one with only half a pinkie, and presses it between both of hers.

"Look at this place," he says, pointing down the hill at the wreckage, which extends all the way to the water. "St. John is destroyed."

"Damaged," Irene says. "Not destroyed." *Like me,* she thinks.

This island—and this man—have taught Irene some things about resilience, about patience, and, most of all, about hope. Bad things can happen, terrible things. You can lose the people you love the most; you can lose homes, cars, antiques, hand-knotted silk rugs that cost five figures; you can discover that the very life you're living is a terrific lie. And despite this, *despite all this,* the sun will continue to rise. Tomorrow morning, over the bruised and broken body of St. John USVI, the sun will rise again.

Irene Steele knows this better than anyone.

EPILOGUE

Millicent Maia Steele
September 6, 2019
6 pounds, 14 ounces, 21 inches

I can't believe you named her after me," Maia says.

"We did," Ayers says. "Because, you know what, Nut? I want Milly to grow up and be smart and strong and fun, just like you."

"And precocious?" Maia says.

Ayers laughs. "And precocious."

Maia leans over into the bassinet to look more closely at her niece. She's asleep, and her little bow of a mouth is making a sucking motion. Maia reaches out her pinkie, and baby Milly's impossibly tiny hand grasps it.

"Just watch me," Maia whispers. "I'll show you how it's done."

ACKNOWLEDGMENTS

I want to start by thanking my brother, Douglas Hilderbrand, who is a meteorologist with the National Weather Service and who provided all the weather details in the last section of this book based on his research of Hurricane Irma. He is also the inspiration for the character Dougie Clarence, the CBS weatherman who appears here and in my novel *Winter Storms*.

There is a real-life version of the Lovango Resort and Beach Club being built as I write this, and no one like Duncan Huntley has any part in it. The owners are my dear friends Mark and Gwenn Snider, who own the Nantucket Hotel and Resort and the Winnetu on Martha's Vineyard. I've held my bucket-list weekends at both of their properties and we all hope that at some point in the near future, we can host a St. John bucket-list weekend on Lovango!

I have taken ten trips to St. John. Eight of these were my usual five-week writing-retreat visits, one was at Christmas, and my most recent trip there, in March of 2020, coincided with the outbreak of COVID-19. I ended up staying on St. John for seven weeks and "sheltered in paradise." Over the course of these visits, I have made friends and acquaintances. I always say that the places we love are about people, and that is certainly true in the U.S. Virgin Islands.

Thank you to Julie, Matt, and Shane Lasota; Beth and Jim Heskett of St. John Guest Suites; Bridgett and Jimmy Key of Palm Tree Charters; Captains Stephen Sloan and Kelly Quinn (no relation to "our" Kelley Quinn!) of Singing Dog Sailing Charters; Brian and Michelle Zehring of New Moon; Alex Ewald of La Tapa; Ryan Costanzo of Extra Virgin Bistro and 1864; Allison Gould of Sam and Jack's; Hank and Karen Slodden; Sarah Swan; John Dickson from the Papaya Café and Bookstore; Dana Neil of Cruz Bay Watersports; Richard Baranowski of Lime Inn/Lime Out (who saved my son Maxx's life, but that's a story for another day); Karen Coffelt, head of school Liz Morrison, and all of the amazing teachers and staff at the Antilles School; Jorie Roberts; Meredith DeBusk from St. John Provisions; Sarah Bigelow, Peter Bettinger, Mattie Atkinson, Rhonda McCay, and Linda Beer (I told you I'd get you in!); and Heather Hearn Samelson of Pizza Pi VI. If I have forgotten any of you, it's because I'm old, not because I don't love and appreciate you.

A huge and special thank-you to Judy Clain, my new editor at Little, Brown, who took me in as an orphan and made me feel like her favorite child. She is brilliant, and this book owes her an enormous debt.

To my kids, Maxwell, Dawson, and Shelby: Everything, always, is for you.

For me, St. John is, above and beyond all else, about Timothy Field. The man has been setting up my towels, pouring my cocktails, and keeping the water from washing me (and my notebooks) away for years. I love you in Love City, HB. XOX